Dear Reader,

After a long hiatus, I'm pleased to be writing again, and even more pleased to bring my stories to new readers through Tor's paranormal romance line.

Oracles have been around for a long time, and the tarot may be just as ancient. Some believe the tarot was used as a divination tool in ancient Egypt, when priests and pharaohs consulted powerful oracles to see what the future held for the Land of the Nile.

The greatest oracle of all time, the Oracle of Avaris, is said to have used a special deck of tarot cards known today as The Forbidden Tarot. The cards were covered in gold leaf and symbols on one side, and inscribed with fantastic pictures of gods and monsters on the other.

In the ensuing millennia, however, all records of this tarot have been lost. All that remains are the tales of people who have set eyes upon the cards and suffered the consequences—raising gods or monsters who either exalted them or destroyed them.

Come with me now, to the dark side of the Land of the Nile . . .

*The Forbidden Tarot:*

# The Dark Lord

## Patricia Simpson

**tor romance**

A TOM DOHERTY ASSOCIATES BOOK
NEW YORK

This is a work of fiction. All the characters and events portrayed in this book are either products of the author's imagination or are used fictitiously.

THE DARK LORD

Copyright © 2003 by Patricia Simpson

A Tor Book
Published by Tom Doherty Associates, LLC
175 Fifth Avenue
New York, NY 10010

www.tor.com

Tor® is a registered trademark of Tom Doherty Associates, LLC.

ISBN 0-765-34861-6
EAN 978-0765-34861-6

First edition: January 2005

Printed in the United States of America

0  9  8  7  6  5  4  3  2  1

———

*To my husband, Garry,
who has opened the world to me in many ways.
and to my daughter, Camille.*

———

In all chaos there is a cosmos,
in all disorder a secret order.

—*Carl Jung (1875–1961)*

# Chapter 1

*Luxor, Egypt*

"Hurry, ladies!" the guide exclaimed, pointing toward the distant horizon. "The *khamsin*! The *khamsin*!"

Twenty-eight-year-old Rae Lambers followed the line of the guide's finger and saw a wall of darkness rising on the southwestern horizon of the Sahara Desert. Her younger sister Angie ran up beside her as the guide dashed away toward the temple. "What's he mean?" Angie asked. "What's a kom-seen?"

"A desert windstorm." Rae narrowed her eyes. She felt a strange chill pass through her even though the Egyptian desert was a furnace that day, with the temperature at least a hundred and fifteen degrees. The Luxor area had been suffering from an extended drought, and their entire vacation had been an endurance test. Even the oasis they had traveled to that morning had dried up—for the first time in centuries, according to their guide. A windstorm would only make the place more unbearable, and could very well endanger their lives if they didn't take shelter. For Rae, who loved both Egypt and the relief it had brought to her physical condition, the weather was something to appreciate. But for her sister Angie, the oppressive heat was a constant source of complaint and another reason she never wanted to set foot in the land of the Nile again.

"Come on, Angie, we'd better run for it!"

Gusts of wind buffeted their khakis as they hurried toward the tour bus. Though the quick pace sent spikes of pain through her knees and hips, Rae said nothing, and pressed on, trying not to hobble or grimace. She could see the two guides gathering up the others who had drifted off to view the old temple and the ruins of a sphinx. At another time, they would have had to run in a circular path, following the ring of palms bordering the water of the oasis. But since the water hole had dried completely, they could cut straight across the bottom of the lake. Angie followed Rae, puffing and complaining, struggling to run in her sandals. Her footwear was meant for show, not for the uneven terrain of a desert lake bottom, and she had never been much of an athlete, even as a young girl.

"Wait up, Rae!" she wailed, the wind whipping away her words.

Rae looked over her shoulder at the same time the toe of her left boot struck something hard. The impact spun her off balance. She toppled forward, throwing her hands out to cushion her fall, and landed with a thump on the cracked mud squares of the lake bottom. As Rae rose to her feet and brushed the gray powder off her cargo pants, Angie wheezed to a stop beside her.

"God, Rae," her sister exclaimed. "You should watch where you're going!"

"There was something there."

"You could have broken a wrist." Angie glanced anxiously ahead of them, checking to see if anyone had witnessed Rae's tumble. Rae flushed, aware that her medical condition had always been somewhat of an embarrassment to her sibling, even though Rae strove to hide all outward signs of distress.

She'd experienced a great deal of pain in her life, beginning the moment she was born. When the doctor had spanked her, he had lost his grip on her slick ankles, and she had dropped to the floor. That tumble seemed to have set her up for a life of bad luck.

Before the age of ten, she had broken both an arm and a leg. She had contracted every childhood illness. And then there had been the dark years after her mother had married

Albert—the years she had put far behind her. Later, at fifteen, a demon had come to life within her, making her body do battle with itself, swelling her joints, burning her with fever, and dragging her down with fatigue. She often wondered if the darkness she had taken in during her early adolescence was still trapped inside her, sometimes lying dormant, sometimes raging out of control.

Though Rae didn't consider herself accident-prone, she had trained herself to refrain from making sudden movements, which slowed down her reaction time. And what a healthy person might laugh off as a silly trip on an unseen step, Rae would experience as a burst of shooting pain in her spine and days of relentless discomfort in her neck. There were times she could not conceal the agony she endured when a big man crushed her fingers in an exuberant handshake, or a preoccupied person suddenly let a door swing shut on her outstretched arm. Often her joints could not withstand such jarring shocks, especially when she was in the midst of one of her spells.

According to the doctors, there was nothing to be done, except for physical therapy and medication. She would simply have to live with her condition. She could have told the experts that, even as an adolescent. Some things in life, especially the unspeakable things, had no cure.

Angie, on the other hand, sailed through life without a care. She was the consummate beauty, a natural blonde with a tall, svelte frame, uncommon grace, and startling large blue eyes. She was the type of woman who could look disarmingly feminine just taking out the garbage, and during high school she had garnered every title that had anything to do with beauty. She'd been homecoming queen, varsity cheerleader, Miss Marina Days, Miss Alameda, and winner of the Junior Miss pageant.

Through all their twenty-something years together, Angie had been the sister everyone noticed while Rae was rarely remarked upon. Rae knew she might have been as beautiful as her sister, had it not been for her arthritis. But dealing with pain had faded her looks and doused her fire.

Presenting a normal façade to the world sapped all her energy, leaving no reserves with which to play the coquette as her sister did. Rae's hair was not quite as blond as Angie's, not quite as shiny or thick; her frame was much more frail than Angie's; her skin stretched a little too tightly over her cheekbones; and the celebrated Lambers eyes had been muted to an opaque navy blue by the wisdom that came with suffering.

As a child, Rae had not resented her sister's good looks, because her illness had always set her apart from the rest of her peers, and she had grown up never expecting to participate as fully as the others. Now that Rae was an adult, she didn't envy Angie at all, as she had come to realize the world of a beauty queen was not all roses and tiaras. There was a flip side to Angie's golden life—the unhealthy dieting, the unending maintenance of hair and nails, and the need to be loved and admired by men.

Rae kept her life unencumbered and uncomplicated. Men were strictly outside the range of possibility.

THANKFUL THAT SHE hadn't hurt herself in the fall, Rae brushed the dirt from her palms. As she stood on the old lake bottom, a strong gust of wind blew up, swirling the dust of the lake bed into a small funnel cloud. Something glittered near Rae's boot, catching her attention. What could be shining in the silt of a dried oasis? She *had* tripped on something, just as she had thought.

"Wait, Angie, I *did* trip over something!" In a fluid motion, Rae bent down and brushed away the dirt near her toe. The corner of small golden box poked out of the silt. Curious, Rae lowered to her knees, grabbed a nearby rock, and started to scrape away the dried mud in which the box was submerged, forgetting about her tender hands in her frenzy to see what she had found.

"Rae! Come on!" Angie grabbed her right arm. "It's just trash, like everything else in this godforsaken place!"

"No, I think it's something valuable!" Rae shook her off

and continued to dig hastily. Bits of stinging sand struck the left side of her face, a harbinger of the gale to come.

"The storm is getting closer! Come on!"

"Go ahead. I'll catch up."

Angie heaved a big sigh and then took off at a run, her ankles twisting in her fashionable footwear and her designer scarf blowing out behind her like a flag.

Frantically, Rae scraped away the silt, until she could get a good grip on the box, which was not quite as large as a small paperback. Sweat trickled down her neck and over her rib cage as she struggled to pull the small box out of the dried muck. At last it broke free, and she held it up, amazed to find the smooth metal box perfectly intact, even down to the thick rust-colored material that sealed its edges.

Figuring that it was probably an old cigar holder or something equally modern, since it bore no telltale hieroglyphs or decoration of any kind, Rae stood up, slipped the box into the side pocket of her cargo pants for later, and sprinted toward the tour bus, fear of the storm outweighing her pain. Though she was a good runner when in remission, the loose sand impeded her progress considerably. By the time she got to the bus, she could hardly make out basic shapes through the swirling sand—when she could open her eyes at all— and she had to breathe through the sleeve of her shirt at the crook of her arm, which she held pressed against her nose.

"Miss!" The guide grabbed her and pulled her up the stairs into the bus. "You are making us all dangerous!"

"Sorry!" Rae's eyes burned from the grains of sand swimming beneath her eyelids, and tears streamed down her face as she stumbled toward her seat. The bus lurched forward, and Rae plunged toward her sister, nearly falling into Angie's lap. The other tourists stared at her dusty hair and clothes, and one small Japanese woman tittered behind her hand.

"Rae, just sit down," Angie hissed, pulling her into her seat. "You're a sight! A mess!"

"But I got it!"

"So? You nearly got us killed." Angie rolled her eyes and leaned back in the cracked leather seat. "God, I can't wait to have a nice cool bath."

And a drink, Rae wanted to add. She knew her sister probably wanted a drink even more than she wanted a bath, but if everything went as Rae planned, the unhealthy wants and needs would be replaced by a decent job and plenty of exercise. Once she got Angie far away from the influence of her friends—especially Brent—the drinking and the drugs would stop. Rae was sure of it.

This trip to Egypt was Rae's way of showing Angie that she could exist—and happily—without her domineering boyfriend, Brent. Once Angie realized how Brent stifled her, perhaps she would agree to leave him and move out west. Rae had always protected little Angie, and Brent was just another page in Angie's tattered history of bad relationships.

Rae decided to get her thoughts off her sister's problems and onto a more constructive subject. She patted the box concealed in her pocket. "I don't think it's that old, though,"

"What's not old?"

"The box. It's not ornate enough to be an artifact."

"Rae, just once I'd like to hear you talk about hair conditioners or the state of your cuticles."

"I don't find cuticles all that fascinating."

"But they're something people can relate to. Cuticles are part of real life, Rae. Egyptian artifacts are not." Angie closed her eyes and sighed again. "I tell you, I'm glad we're leaving tomorrow. I really am. This place has done a number on my skin."

As her sister fell silent, Rae leaned back in her seat and ignored the hum of discomfort in her hands and feet. She listened to the *khamsin* as it howled around the lumbering bus, plunging their world into darkness, as dark as midnight.

"Listen to that wind," Rae whispered. "It sounds like someone crying."

Angie nodded without speaking or opening her eyes, and Rae returned her gaze to the darkness beyond the window of the bus. They'd never outrun the storm. Soon, they would have to pull over and wait it out. She could feel the box pressing against her thigh. She would have to wait to investigate it as well.

BY THE TIME they got back to the hotel, it was late afternoon. Angie collapsed onto the bed and called room service, ordering a gin and tonic for herself and an iced tea for Rae. As she put the phone down, she glanced at Rae, having felt her sister's dark regard.

"It's only one, Rae."

"But you promised."

"My nerves are shot, that's all." She rose and walked toward the bathroom, moving like a movie star in an old forties film. "It's not like I'm going to go on a binge or anything. Relax!"

Rae frowned and dropped the subject, knowing that nagging her sister would not have any positive results.

"We'll get cleaned up and then go find some dinner," Angie continued, conveniently changing the subject. "How about that?"

"Fine." Rae slipped her hand into her pocket and drew out the box. As she heard Angie start a bath, she carefully inspected the sticky seal, wondering if she held something valuable in her hands or just a discarded piece of junk someone had tossed into the lake. She knew enough about Egyptian artifacts and had enough respect for the cultures of ancient peoples not to blindly destroy an object just to satisfy her curiosity. But as she had told Angie, this box looked far too modern to be of much value.

In the distance she was aware of Angie's voice as she droned on about all the things she was going to do when they got back to the States and all the things she was going to eat, but Rae didn't listen to her sister's constant chatter. Instead, she reached for the letter opener at the writing desk and carefully slipped it under the seal. Painstakingly, she ran the knife around the edge of the box, until the gummy paste came off in one long strip, which Rae gently placed on the desk blotter. Her heart pounded as she placed her hands on either side of the box to slowly pull the two pieces apart. They didn't budge. She tugged a little harder and felt the metal pieces slide apart.

The smell of cardamom drifted up as she lifted the lid from its bottom half, revealing the contents of the box. There in her right hand sat a bundle wrapped in parchment and bound with copper wire, amazingly free of verdigris, knotted and sealed with more brown paste. The sheepskin was covered in lines of writing, and upon closer inspection, Rae recognized the script as a form of Aramaic, an ancient language from the time of the Dead Sea Scrolls.

A chill washed over her. What had she found?

"Rae?" Angie appeared in the doorway of the bathroom, wrapped in a huge white towel, with her blond hair piled on top of her head and wet tendrils stuck to her long white neck. "Hello?"

"Sorry. What did you ask?" Rae set the box on the desk and stood up.

"I said, what do you feel like eating tonight?"

"I don't know. Anything. "

Angie drifted closer, gazing at the desk behind Rae. "You opened the box?"

"Kind of."

"What do you mean?"

"Well, there's something in it that's all wrapped up. I'm not sure I should go any further."

"Why not?"

"The writing looks pretty old. I think I should have someone look at it. It could be valuable."

Angie gazed down at the box. "It does look kind of old. Do you think it might be worth something? Some real money?"

"Probably not money so much as knowledge of another time," Rae mused, looking down at the box as well. "And that's priceless."

"Right." Angie dragged the towel from her head and shook her long mane of blond hair. "But it won't buy a house."

Rae thought of the condo she lived in near the Berkeley campus, and how she longed to move into a real house, a place where she and Angie could build a new life. But living in the Bay Area was unbelievably expensive, and a decent piece of property was impossible to buy on her salary as an assistant professor compromised by medical bills and a large student loan payment. As far as she could see, she would have to win a lottery to ever achieve her dream of buying a real home.

A knock on the door interrupted her thoughts.

"That would be our drinks," Angie called gaily, ducking back into the bathroom.

Rae reached for some coins in her pocket and walked to the door to get their refreshments. Then she took a quick shower while Angie labored at the mirror, applying her makeup and sipping her gin.

IN A MUCH better mood after her bath and drink, Angie cheerfully led the way through the hotel and out to the busy street, chatting constantly about what they should have as their last meal in Luxor. Should they go to the Moroccan restaurant they liked the best or try something new? Rae only half-listened as she searched the shop fronts for the antiques store she remembered seeing the day before.

"There it is!" she exclaimed, nodding at the place across the street.

"What?"

"That antiques place. The one with that statue of Amenhotep that you liked."

"I don't want to go there now. I'm starving."

"Just for a minute. Before it closes. I want someone to have a look at the box."

"Don't you ever give up?" Angie shook her head, but allowed herself to be dragged through the evening traffic. Rae watched anxiously as the middle-aged shopkeeper came out of his door and reached for the metal grate he intended to pull out to protect his glass storefront during the evening hours.

"Sir!" she called. "Please wait!"

The man paused and looked over his shoulder. He wore a dark red fez, a baggy Western-cut pin-striped suit, and a slight frown at the sudden appearance of two customers at closing time.

"It is closing time," he said.

"I know, but could you spare just a moment, please?"

"Is there something you wish to buy?"

"Perhaps your time? We're looking for someone who can read Aramaic."

"Pardon me?"

"We are trying to find someone who can read Aramaic. Do you know of anyone? Can you read it, by any chance?"

"Maybe." He released his hold on the grate and turned to face them. His glance slid up and down Angie's white silk sheath. Twice.

"Would you look at something for me?"

"Miss, I don't even know you."

Angie reached into her purse. "Do you know Benjamin Franklin?" She held out a fifty-dollar bill.

"Ah!" The shopkeeper's eyebrows shot up and he grinned. "This is an American for whom I have the deepest respect!"

"I thought so," Angie purred as she gave the money to him.

"Come." He swept them forward with an expansive gesture, and Rae followed her sister into the shop. Leave it to Angie to know how to get results from a man. They walked through a narrow aisle flanked by stacks of plaster statues, wooden furniture, and tall, brightly painted urns. The shopkeeper bustled behind his counter and placed both palms flat on the worn wooden surface. "Now, what is it you have that needs to be read?"

"This." Rae fished the box from her purse and carefully opened it, setting the bottom of the box and its contents on the counter while she held the lid in her hand. The shopkeeper leaned forward, squinting at the lines of tiny writing on the parchment. Rae stared at him anxiously as he studied the parchment, and waited without taking a breath for him to speak, but he remained maddeningly silent. Would he ask for more money?

The shopkeeper reached for a magnifying glass and pulled a lamp closer.

"I have never seen anything like this," he remarked.

Rae leaned forward. "Can you read it?"

"I am trying! This is a strange form of Aramaic." The shopkeeper frowned, concentrating. "Water," he murmured, following the line with his finger, but not touching the parchment. "Soul. Dark. Lord. Otherworld? I am not certain of this word."

He looked up.

"Where did you find this?"

"Near the temple of Nut, at the oasis there."

He studied the writing again. "Typhon, the Devil, the Dark Lord," he whispered, and then he pushed the box toward Rae. "No!" he exclaimed. "I will read no more of this!"

"What?" Angie protested. "What's wrong?"

"I read no more!"

"But I paid you fifty American dollars!"

"I give it back to you!" He slapped the money on the counter. "Leave, please, at once!"

"But what does it say?" Rae asked, reaching for the bottom of the box. "What is it?"

"These are the Forbidden Tarot."

"What the heck are they?" Angie asked.

He ignored her question. "Throw them into the Nile, miss. Do not open them. Do not look at them. Throw them into the river! They are cursed!"

"Oh, come on!" Angie protested. "What do you take us for?"

"Angie!"

The shopkeeper backed away as if to distance himself from the box upon his counter. "Discard them, I tell you. Do not look upon them. One look and you open your soul to darkness. The parchment bears a warning. I am serious when I tell you this!" He backed against the wall, put his palms together and pressed his fingertips to his lips. "Allah be praised. Allah be merciful."

Rae believed him. The look of utter terror on his face was enough to convince her that he was telling the truth. To see a man driven to desperate prayer like this alarmed her. She put the lid on the box and pushed it closed.

"Thank you," she said, leaving the money on the counter. "Come on, Angie."

"Get rid of the cards!" he called after them. "In water!"

They hurried out onto the street, where the dying summer light startled them back to reality.

"Can you believe that guy?" Angie exclaimed.

"I think he was genuinely frightened."

"What did he say was in the box? The Forbidden Tarot?"

"Yes."

"Tarot. You mean, like fortune-telling cards?"

"I think so."

"What are you going to do with them?"

"I don't know. I can't see throwing them into the Nile. They seem far too valuable for that."

"How about getting a second opinion?"

"Maybe. But what if there is something evil about them? That man was really frightened, Ange." Rae put the box back in her purse. "I've never seen anyone actually pray like that in real life. Only in movies."

"People around here are very superstitious, though, aren't they? There's probably nothing to be afraid of. Not really."

"As long as we don't open the packet." Rae walked beside her sister, lost in thought. "Surely there will be an expert in San Francisco who will be able to read the script for us."

"And find a buyer for us. We could make a fortune, Rae! Think of the things you could do if you had some money!"

"I'm not sure we'll get the box past customs, though."

"I didn't think of that."

"Maybe I should just toss them like he told us to. Leave well enough alone."

Angie stared at her. "Are you kidding?"

"And there's another thing. I'm not sure of the legal ramifications of taking something like this out of the country. We could be thrown in jail."

"You worry about the weirdest things." Angie rolled her eyes again, a gesture Rae had come to resent more than anything, as if her opinion and reasoning counted for nothing. "Come on, let's get dinner and then decide what to do."

# *Chapter 2*

That evening as Angie packed her toiletries and numerous pairs of shoes, Rae sat at the writing desk resealing the box with the old paste she had kept. Angie looked up from her suitcase.

"Why are you doing that?" she inquired.

"I'm going to leave this box the way I found it."

"You're not taking it back with you?"

"No. As far as I figure, the risk is too great."

Angie stared at her in disgust, one hand on her slender hip. "You're really something, Rae."

"What?" Finished with her task, Rae stood up and faced her sister.

"You come to Egypt, the land of your dreams, and you find something really interesting. Do you take a memento of a lifetime back with you to treasure and show that Dr. Gregory of yours? No. You believe the lame story some religious freak tells you, and you leave it all behind."

"It's my choice, Angie."

"And that's been the story of your life, too, hasn't it, Rae? Always playing it safe. Never taking one adventurous step."

"I've learned not to take chances. Especially ones like this."

"That's half the fun in life!" Angie threw a wad of bras and panties into her suitcase. "Learn to live a little!"

Rae fell silent and trudged to her own much smaller suitcase. She *had* always played it safe. But that was her way. Through diligence and hard work, she had slowly but surely pulled herself up from a sordid childhood in a shabby house to a blossoming career at a prestigious university. Granted, she had never experienced a single love affair in her twenty-eight years, but what she had seen of love affairs—especially those of her sister—made her conclude that romance was highly overrated.

However, that was not to say she was content with her life. During the last few months she had become increasingly aware of something integral missing in her life, that something important was passing her by as she went about her daily routine. Yet she was too busy with her job and her writing to spend any time worrying about it.

"You think you know everything." Angie slammed her suitcase shut. "Always reading. Getting a Ph.D. Landing that teaching job. You think I'm an empty-headed party animal, don't you?"

"I never said that."

"But you can't learn everything from books. There's a lot you don't learn in school."

"Such as?"

"Learning to take what you want." She reached for the box on the writing desk.

"No!" Rae held up her hands. "Wait a minute, Ange—"

"Learning how to see through the bullshit," Angie continued, easily pulling apart the two sections of the box.

"Angie, don't!"

"Not being afraid of a bunch of wire and goop and some stupid writing!" She yanked at the copper wire, which broke apart with a ping. Rae stared in horror as her sister tore the parchment away and triumphantly held up a deck of cards. "Here is your Forbidden Tarot, Rae. Here's your Egyptian hocus-pocus! All it is, is a deck of cards!"

She threw them on the floor at Rae's feet, and the cards spewed out around her sandals like glossy leaves. Rae just stood there, stunned as much by Angie's tirade as she was by the violation of the box. She looked down, her ears burning, her mouth dry, so angry at her sister that she couldn't think of anything to say.

"I don't see any lightning bolt coming down to strike

me," Angie taunted. "I don't see a huge black crack in the earth coming to swallow me up. Do you?"

"I can't believe you just did that!"

"Sometimes with a person like you, Rae, you have to be dragged kicking and screaming into the world of the living. You can't always stand in the background, watching everything, thinking everything over!"

Rae stared at her sister as Angie stepped closer. She didn't know whether to laugh out of sheer relief that no cataclysm had occurred or whether to chastise her sibling for ruining what might very well have been a valuable Egyptian curio.

Angie bent down, picked up a card, and held it in front of Rae's nose before she could think to look away. "See? Scary, huh? Some naked crocodile with wings and a big dick. Ooh. Typhon, the Devil. I'm frightened."

Rae gaped at the card, compelled to look at the images she saw there—the green, bat-winged beast; two people with the heads of rams, their hair in flames, chains binding them together; broken columns; a serpent wriggling from the beast's navel; and the creature's large erect penis.

She looked away, flooded by a dark wave of emotion that had nothing to do with the card in front of her. After all these years, she still could not sort out her emotional reaction to the naked male or even name it, as fear, hatred, revulsion, and shame boiled inside her—like bubbling tar she could never wash away. Sometimes she thought she could even smell the oozing blackness inside her.

"See?" Angie continued, unaware of her older sister's inner turmoil. "Nothing to be afraid of."

How innocent Angie was. Rae shook off her memories and glanced down at the cards scattered upon the floor. A feeling of doom settled over her. She was certain she and her sister had seriously trespassed into a territory far beyond their imaginations. But Angie, with her focus on the surface of things in her simple, uncomplicated world, would not understand such a sensation.

"Help me pick up the cards," Rae said, carefully dropping to one knee.

THAT NIGHT, RAE had a hard time sleeping. She kept waking up, worrying about the flight to come, worrying about the cards sitting on the writing desk, thinking she saw shapes moving along the wall. The bones in her hands and feet throbbed. She longed to wake up her sister so she wouldn't have to spend the endless hours alone, but knew Angie would deride her for having an overactive imagination.

When morning came, Rae rose, exhausted. But during the ensuing hours, no evil transpired. No one questioned them at customs. The plane left the terminal exactly on time. They didn't crash at takeoff. No bombs exploded in Paris when they changed planes, no cloaked men followed them in the shadows. And when they parted ways in New York, Rae had forgotten all about the Forbidden Tarot.

On board her final flight, Rae settled into her seat near the wing, ready for the last leg of her journey westward which she would make alone. She would miss her sister, but she also looked forward to the quiet time on the plane, and would use it as a chance to recover from the excitement of the last few days.

But as she tightened the seat belt around her, she felt the pressure of someone staring at her, a strong sixth sense she had always possessed. Curious, Rae glanced up.

A SLENDER MAN with ash brown hair and an expertly tailored gray suit stood in the aisle looking down at her, his head slightly tipped to the left, one hand in the pocket of his trousers. Rae stared back, momentarily mesmerized by the unusual light gleaming through the slits of his silvery eyes. His expression was completely unreadable, and she could not begin to guess what he was thinking, only that he regarded her with a frank, measuring interest. Rae knew that most men looked at women's eyes, at their breasts, or at their legs. This man seemed to be looking straight through her eyes to something lying hidden deep within her. What was he looking at? Rae's mouth suddenly went dry, and she swallowed, unnerved that he might see through the well-honed façade she usually presented to the world.

Before she could break from his stare on her own, she saw his silvery regard glitter down to the sweater she had tossed on the middle seat.

"Shall I stow your garment before I sit?" he asked. His voice was brusque, laced with an accent that hovered between German and French.

"No, thank you." She reached for the black sweater and pulled it into her lap. "It's for later. I always get cold on planes."

"I see." He glanced at her again. His sharp features and narrow, Flemish nose hinted at a northern European descent, and she guessed he might be Belgian or Dutch. Then he moved into the row and lowered his lean frame into the aisle seat. Rae realized he had asked her about the sweater, not because he wanted to sit in the middle seat, but out of sheer politeness. She was surprised to find thoughtfulness paired with such attractive features, having grown accustomed to the shallow self-absorption of beautiful people like her sister.

He fastened his seat belt and looked at the side of her face. "It appears you've been somewhere hot, judging by that healthy tan you've acquired."

Surely he was joking. No one had ever used the word "healthy" in reference to her appearance.

"I was in Egypt." Rae fussed with folding her sweater, hoping he would take the hint that she was too busy to chat. She planned to rest and recuperate on the flight, not waste her energy talking to a complete stranger whom she would never see again.

"Ah, Egypt." He smiled. "I have not been there for many years. Was it your first trip?"

"Yes." She placed the sweater upon her knees and reached

for the airline magazine. How monosyllabic would she have to be until he realized she didn't wish to talk?

"Did you enjoy it?"

"I did." She opened the magazine and flipped through the pages, not really seeing any of the pictures.

He pressed onward. "And where did you go?"

"Luxor mostly. My sister won a vacation in a contest." She sent him a quick glance, wondering why he was so interested in her vacation.

He nodded. "Excellent choice. Karnak, the Valley of the Kings, the tomb of Senneferi—"

"You've been there?"

"Many times. I am particularly fond of the Land of the Black Earth." He placed his right palm upon the armrest, and she noticed he wore a bloodred carnelian surrounded by a dragon setting upon his smallest finger. "The people there have been very good to me at times."

Most tourists would have referred to Egypt as the Land of the Nile. Not many people knew the country's real and ancient name. How odd that a fellow lover of Egypt should sit down beside her on a plane. Rae forgot all about the magazine in her hands and turned to glance at her companion.

Though it was early in the day, his beard already shadowed his jaw, making him appear slightly unkempt and entirely masculine. His hair was longer than the conventional style, combed backward from his high forehead with plenty of pomade, and casually tucked behind his ears, at odds with the crisp edges of his sideburns and the elegant lines of his spotless suit. He seemed untamed and cultured at the same time, like a gunfighter posing as the CEO of a prosperous corporation—a provocative combination that intrigued her.

"Do you go to Egypt on business?" she asked.

"Of course." He smiled again, and she noticed his teeth were small and well ordered in his sensual mouth. He seemed to have a lot of teeth. Or maybe it was just the way he smiled, a little bit off center and to the right. "But I always mix a bit of pleasure with business, just to make it more interesting."

Then he winked at her, and a sudden, unfamiliar torrent of sexual awareness swept through Rae, so strong she felt pinned to her seat with it. Behind the metal clasp of her seat belt, she felt as if a comet had struck her, sending streams of pleasure through her belly and down her legs. She had never experienced such a strong reaction from a man. Stunned, she fumbled to close the magazine and stuff it back in the seat pocket, hoping if she kept her hands busy she could dispel the disturbing sensation coursing through her. What was wrong with her that made such lascivious thoughts creep into her mind?

"Does flying make you a little nervous?" he asked, his voice softened by a knowing smile.

"Yes," she lied, still not looking at him. The only thing making her nervous was the all-too-close proximity of his long lean thigh and the corner of his broad shoulder. "Yes, it does."

"I have some medication you could take to ease your discomfort, if you wish."

Nothing but a bucket of ice water would help her right now.

"Thank you," she answered, "but I'll be fine once we're in the air." She looked back at him and tried to smile, but his knowing gaze—as if he knew what effect he was having—only made her more upset.

"Maybe, as they say, we will get lucky?"

"Excuse me?" She couldn't believe what she had just heard. Was he referring to the Mile High Club? Surely not with her.

He chuckled. "I mean that maybe no one will sit in the middle. Yes?"

"Of course." Rae felt relief mingling with a strange sense of letdown. "More room for us."

"Exactly."

She glanced at the empty seat between them and could think of nothing she would have liked more than to have it filled with a nun or somebody's grandmother, anything to neutralize this man's disturbing presence. In the meantime, she would divert her attention by working on the second draft of her book, which she had stuffed in her carry-on bag. She bent down to retrieve the notebook containing her project, and for the rest of the flight immersed herself in work, the only thing in the world that made her feel whole and unafflicted.

Unfortunately, the seat remained empty, and though Rae tried to work, part of her mind was aware of the man to her left. His expensive watch glinted, distracting her, as he casually turned the pages of the *Wall Street Journal*, and all of the flight attendants made it a practice to chat with him whenever they passed down the aisle.

When lunch was served, he took Rae's meal from the attendant and handed it to her.

"Your feast," he commented wryly.

"The usual, hmm?"

He nodded at the notebook on the spare seat. "Are you a writer?"

"In my spare time."

"What do you write?"

"Nonfiction. I'm working on a book."

"And what is the subject, if you don't mind my asking?"

"It's kind of specific—it's about the undercurrent of mathematics and how it affected ancient cultures. Egypt in particular."

"Really?"

"Mathematics is not just a bunch of numbers, but another language. Much more universal than spoken languages. And in a way, much more powerful." She was probably boring him, but she couldn't tell by his expression. He seemed truly interested. "That's what I'm trying to convey in my book."

"Do you think such a manuscript will sell?"

Rae shrugged. "I'm not sure. It won't hit the charts like a pop psychology number, that's for sure." She gave him a wry smile.

"Why do you not write such a book instead?"

"And ruin my career?" She turned to face him. "Young math professors do not write pop psychology. Not if they want to get tenure."

"You are a math professor?"

"Yes." She opened the dressing packet for her crushed salad and was relieved to discover the joints of her fingers didn't complain. "At UC Berkeley."

"How intriguing." He sliced his chicken breast with a deft stroke. "I know a professor there. He's in the history department, or was. He is retired now."

"One of my favorite people is a professor emeritus from that department. He inspired me to visit Egypt, as a matter of fact."

Rae smiled, thinking back on her strange relationship with Thomas Gregory, a man old enough to be her grandfather. For the past eight years she had kept in touch with Professor Gregory, but only by mail. She had invited him for coffee and for lunch many times, but he always turned her down, giving one excuse or another. His reluctance to meet face-to-face didn't bother Rae, however. In fact nonthreatening Thomas Gregory was the only male she had allowed in her life. She'd heard rumors that Dr. Gregory was possibly suffering bouts of dementia or might be afflicted by an undiagnosed phobia. But she didn't give much credence to gossip. He always sounded quite lucid and well balanced in his notes.

The man next to her finished his chicken. "The professor I know was quite an explorer in his day."

"So was Dr. Gregory."

"Did you say Gregory?" Her companion laughed and his silvery eyes glittered and sparked. "I speak of Thomas Gregory as well!"

"Really?"

"Yes." He leveled his glance at her, and she felt the same warm glow enveloping her. "Isn't that peculiar?"

"It's a small world."

He held out his hand. "Simeon Avare."

Rae reached across the empty chair and allowed his

smooth hand to gently press hers. His touch caused her no pain whatsoever.

"Fay Rae Lambers."

"Fay Ray?" His level brows pulled together slightly. "As in the old movie?"

She rolled her eyes. "*King Kong.* Yes. My mother was a big movie fan. Unfortunately, she wasn't much of a speller." She slipped her hand from his. "She spelled it R-A-E on my birth certificate. I was stuck with it."

"Why don't you go by the name of Fay?"

"When I was a kid, I thought Fay sounded like an old woman's name."

"Not at all. Fay is a wonderful name." Simeon pushed his tray aside. Rae noticed he'd only eaten the meat. Maybe that was how he stayed so lean. "Do you know what it means?"

"Not really."

"It means touched in a special way." His glance slipped down her body, and she sensed that he was evaluating her again. "Gifted with a special power. Usually magical."

"Well, that's certainly not me!" She opened her cookie wrapper, and realized she was enjoying Simeon's company more than she would have believed. He made her feel good, seriously good.

"But it suits you." His voice was like a soft caress along her arm.

She glanced at him, and their eyes held for a long moment, until she blinked and broke off the gaze. Suddenly the cookie had no appeal. She lowered it to the tray while a red-headed flight attendant leaned over to take their trash.

Afterward, Rae resumed her work and Simeon read a magazine he had brought with him. She tried to concentrate but found it difficult, and not just because of the man sitting next to her. The more research she did for her book, the more she found herself drawn from the mathematics angle toward the history of Egypt—to the inbred families who had ruled for centuries, to the temples they had erected, and to the glorious panoply of their gods. She constantly had to force herself back to the theme of her book, and was finding it increasingly difficult to write.

Given a choice, she would have jumped into a historical treatise of Egypt instead of the math-based book she was working on. But she was not a history teacher. She was a calculus professor, and she had a career to forge. Her only success in life had come from her skill with numbers, and she was not about to switch gears now that her career was taking off and she was just beginning to pay her bills. Egypt and all its mysteries would have to remain a hobby. An interest. Nothing more.

She and her seat companion did not speak again until the plane touched down and they had disembarked. At the gate, Simeon turned to her and extended his hand.

"I am pleased to have met you," he said, shaking her hand again.

"And I you."

"I have come to San Francisco to see Dr. Gregory, actually. Perhaps I can arrange a luncheon with the three of us while I am in the area."

"That would be nice, Mr. Avare," she replied, although she didn't hold out much hope for such an event, as she was well aware of Gregory's reluctance to appear in public.

"Until then." He winked and smiled and, with a small wave, disappeared into the crowd of passengers heading down the corridor.

Rae watched him go, while the soothing cloud of warmth he had brought into her world quickly cooled, leaving her feeling more alone than she'd ever been in her life. She frowned at the strange sensation. Loneliness was something she had ceased to recognize. If she ever made reference to the quality of her quiet, single life, she preferred to call it solitude. And she liked her solitude.

Perturbed by the odd emotional roller-coaster ride she had just taken on the plane, Rae adjusted the strap of her purse and stepped forward, expecting fatigue to drag her down. But as she walked toward baggage, she didn't feel tired at all. In fact, she didn't have any joint pain either.

Maybe her trip to Egypt and the hot weather had sent her disease into remission for a while. How blessed that would be.

## UC Berkeley Campus

ON MONDAY, TWO days later, Rae walked toward her office after giving her first lecture of the day, picked up her mail, and was shuffling through the envelopes when the departmental secretary glanced up.

"Why, Dr. Lambers, it's you!"

"Hi, Connie."

"Wow!" Connie rolled back in her chair to get a better view. "You look great!"

"I do?"

"Yeah." Connie bobbed her head, bubbling with enthusiasm, an attribute Rae had admired the moment they had met nine months ago at the beginning of fall quarter when Connie had been hired. The moment had been a real milestone in Rae's life. Rae had come from a poor family in a small town, and had gone on to earn a doctorate, teach at a prestigious university, and have her very own office and the assistance of a secretary, albeit one she had to share with the rest of her group. Not bad for a girl who had been born on the wrong side of the tracks, literally. "Egypt must have suited you."

"It did. I loved it."

"Did you go to a spa or something? You look so relaxed!"

Rae glanced over the stack of letters at the twenty-year-old assistant, wondering why Connie was going on about her appearance. "It must be the tan."

"No, there's something else. You look really different."

Rae touched her gaunt cheek. She hadn't noticed an outward change in her appearance, but she had noticed a spring in her step that had never been there before, and a general feeling of well-being. Perhaps that was the difference Connie saw in her.

"Do you have pictures of your trip? Slides to show?" Connie continued.

"If you really want to see them."

"I love slide shows. I know that's weird . . . "

"Not at all." Rae smiled at Connie. "I'll bring them in when I get them developed." She turned for the door of her private office.

"Oh, and Dr. Lambers?"

Rae paused and turned back around.

"Did you hear the terrible news?"

"What news?"

"About Dr. Gregory—that old professor with the weird handwriting who wrote to you?"

"What about him?"

"He died over the weekend."

"What?" Rae felt her tan vanish and her sense of well-being dissipate, as the news sent her entire body into shock. She lost her grip on the envelopes in her hand, and they plummeted to the ground.

"He died." Connie hurried to help her retrieve the mail, and Rae absently thanked her, overwhelmed by the shocking news.

"How did it happen?"

"They think it was natural causes. Wasn't he ninety or something?" Connie handed her the last envelope. "He collapsed at his desk. The cleaning lady found him this morning."

"My God." Rae looked at the wall behind Connie and her vision blurred. She had planned to call him that morning, to ask if he wanted to see the strange box she had found in Luxor. "Thomas—"

JUST BEFORE HER last class of the day that afternoon, as Rae caught up with her numerous e-mails, she was interrupted by Connie's pert rap on the door.

Rae turned from her computer screen. "Yes?"

"There's someone here to see you." Connie smiled knowingly and wiggled her eyebrows, as if she were excited about the visitor in some way. "A Mr. Avare?"

"Simeon Avare?" Rae caught herself flushing. "Show him in."

She took off her glasses and set them aside as Connie ushered in the man Rae had met on the plane. He was dressed in a similar fashion as he had been while traveling, in a well-tailored suit and tie, although this time he wore dark green, which appeared nearly black in the filtered light of her office. Connie stood behind him and gave Rae two thumbs-up and a huge grin, an antic which made Rae smile. She fought down the expression and struggled to retain a professional composure.

"Mr. Avare," Rae greeted, rising from her chair and extending her hand. "What a surprise!"

"Fay Rae." He winked and shook her hand. Once again, his personal magnetism coursed through her like heat therapy. "It took most of the afternoon to find you, but I finally tracked you down."

"I'm amazed you found me in this building. It's a rabbit warren."

"That it is."

"Please." She swept the air between them. "Have a seat."

"Thank you." He sank to the blocky university-issue chair facing her. His designer suit and expensive loafers looked out of place against the worn upholstery.

"Would you like coffee?" Rae asked. "Tea?"

"Oh, no thank you. I do not wish to take too much of your time. You are probably busy?"

"I have a class in five minutes."

"Then I will be brief." He leaned forward. "I assume you heard about Thomas Gregory?"

"Yes. Only this morning."

"Unfortunate news. Unfortunate."

"I know. I will miss him. A lot."

Simeon nodded and glanced out the window, his face troubled.

"Did you have a chance to see him?" Rae asked.

"We were to meet today."

"I'm sorry."

He turned back to face her. "He told me he had something that belonged to me. That he would give it to me when we met."

"Do you know what it was?"

"I have an idea what it might have been. But I have no way to get into the house now, especially with all the police about." He sighed and his glittering eyes met hers. "You don't have access to his house, do you?"

"I'm afraid not."

He sighed again and a frown of frustration creased the corners of his well-formed mouth. "Well, perhaps he will mention me in his will. Or his heirs will allow me to look through his possessions."

"I doubt it."

"Why is that?"

Rae shook her head, thinking about the despair Thomas had suffered regarding his son, from whom he had been estranged for more than fifteen years.

"I doubt Dr. Gregory's son will indulge anyone who has the slightest interest in his father's things."

"And why is that?"

"Michael Gregory despised his father's interest in Egypt."

"You know this Michael Gregory?"

"We went to high school together. But he was a jock."

"Jock?" Avare asked, seemingly confused as to the meaning of the word.

"An athlete. Our paths did not cross very often." Their paths had crossed at one time, but that was before the dark days with Albert began, before her world had spiraled down into fear and shame, and before she had shut off her feelings. It had been the only way to survive. "I was a nerdy little bookworm."

Avare shot her a small smile, and his glance flitted over her again as if to reassure himself that she was no longer a nerdy little bookworm.

"Do you think you could talk to this Michael for me?"

"I haven't seen him for ten years."

"I see." Simeon's expression hardened with disappointment, and Rae watched him as he slowly rose to his feet.

"I'll see what I can do, though," Rae put in.

"I would appreciate it." He reached into the breast pocket of his suit coat and retrieved a white card. "Here is where I am staying. Would you please let me know where the funeral service will be? I would like to attend."

"Yes. Of course."

She took the card. He was staying at the Hyatt in San Francisco, which was an appropriate choice for someone who loved Egypt. The architecture of the Hyatt, with its multitude of sloped causeways, had always reminded her of an Egyptian temple.

She walked around her desk to show him out. "I'm sorry you came all this way for nothing."

"Oh, it was not all for nothing." He looked down at her and smiled in his warm fashion. "Especially if you will have dinner with me some evening. Perhaps Friday?"

"That would be nice." Rae flushed with pleasure as her heart did a little flip-flop in her chest. Her body wanted to jump into this man's arms, but her head told her to run far, far away. Men were dangerous. They wanted things from females that she had no intention of giving. And having this particular man—with his worldly charm and good looks—take an interest in her did not make sense.

She held up the card he'd given her, putting an object between them. Even as she did it, she realized she was using the card as a typical and very lame self-defense mechanism. She should be ashamed of herself. "I'll call you when I find out about the funeral."

"Thank you. I shall leave you to your students now."

She watched him walk past Connie, tell her good-bye, and then close the door quietly behind him. As soon as he had left, Connie jumped to her feet.

"Who was that?" she exclaimed, her eyes wide.

"Someone I met on my trip. Simeon Avare."

"What a hottie!"

Rae looked at the doorway through which Simeon just passed, and could almost see a residual glow hanging in the air, the fallout from his electric presence. She looked down at the card, knowing she would call him.

"Connie," she said, slipping the card into her pocket. "Find out where the service for Dr. Gregory will be, would you?"

"Aye, aye, Captain!" Connie replied.

## Chapter 3

That same afternoon a registered package arrived for Rae. She glanced at the return address, which listed the name of an attorney in San Francisco, but she did not recognize the firm. Curious, she pulled the tab to open the padded envelope and emptied a CD, a key, and a letter onto her desk.

She opened the letter first.

*Dear Dr. Lambers,*

*This compact disk is being sent to you upon the occasion of the death of Thomas Gregory. As executors of his estate, we were instructed to impress upon you the importance of the message contained in the CD. Please do not show the contents of this package to anyone until you have viewed the CD.*

*In addition, Dr. Gregory requested your presence at the reading of his will, which will take place Friday, July 29, at 3 P.M. in our office—*

Rae slowly lowered the letter in her hand. What a strange turn of events. What kind of message could Thomas Gregory need to give her from beyond the grave?

Still, she would take him seriously. Rae shut her office door for extra privacy, even though Connie worked diligently at her desk outside. Then she picked up the CD and opened the plastic case. Sitting back down in her chair, she slipped the CD into her computer and waited until the drive whirred into action. Only one file showed on the disk. She double-clicked it, and an image of Thomas Gregory filled her monitor screen.

"Good day, Miss Lambers," he greeted, standing by his desk in what she guessed was his library. He always called her Miss Lambers, even in e-mails. Many times she had asked that he call her Rae or Fay Rae, but he never dropped the formality. Perhaps it was his way of keeping his distance. Rae respected that. She was a person of boundaries herself.

Rae stared at the vision of Thomas Gregory. She hadn't seen him since her undergraduate days and was appalled by his appearance. He had wasted away to skin and bones. Though he had once been as tall as his basketball-playing son, he had shrunk to what looked like Rae's height of five and a half feet, with no more than 130 pounds of weight on his spare frame. His face was a road map of wrinkles, permanently darkened by many years spent working as an amateur archeologist on digs in Egypt and the Middle East. His hair, still as thick as a young man's, had turned completely white.

"If you are viewing this, my dear, you must know that I am dead."

He raised a glass of water from his desk and toasted her.

"And if I haven't contacted you any other way than this crude movie—then so much for life after death." He grinned, but his expression was hollow. Without drinking any of the water, he replaced the glass upon the desk blotter, and slowly took a seat. She could tell that his bones creaked with the effort and felt a wave of empathy for the old man.

"You might be wondering why I've sent you this—"

Rae leaned closer, finding it difficult to hear the audio track. A trickling sound muffled his voice. She scanned the video and noticed a little fountain on the far corner of his desk. The poor old guy must not have realized how much noise the small water feature would make.

"—but you are the one person in the world who might not think I am crazy for what I am about to say."

Rae fussed with the volume setting while Thomas

Gregory took a sip of the water and toasted her with the glass again. Though she turned up the volume, the audio track was still muffled by the sound of running water. Thomas continued.

"Many people think I had a nervous breakdown years ago, and that is why I closed myself up in this house. But it isn't true, Miss Lambers. I stay in this house to protect what I brought home from Egypt, especially during my last visit there. I cannot tell you what I protect, specifically, and I cannot tell you why, because I cannot take the chance of this video being viewed by the wrong person. The only thing I can tell you is this: there are those in the world who, should they come into possession of a particular object held inside this house, could possibly cause complete havoc on earth."

Thomas Gregory laced his bony fingers around the glass and pulled it toward him. "Do not take me lightly, Miss Lambers. It is imperative you use the key delivered in the packet you just received to gain entrance to my house in Alameda. You must remain in the house. You have a good heart, a pure heart, and it is such a heart as yours that can protect the world from an ancient evil. Do not leave the house unless it remains in the hands of someone you know well and trust implicitly. Do not leave the house empty."

He toasted her again and took a sip of the water. "If you are viewing this video, then I must not have completed my research. I must not have discovered what will render the object powerless.

"I implore you, Miss Lambers, to think back on our recent telephone conversation, about the Rosicrucians. In that conversation are clues to what I am referring. I uncovered something in Egypt that was never meant to be unearthed. And I have paid the price for interfering. I beg of you, Miss Lambers, to do your best to keep the world from the evil I have unearthed."

Then he took a pen from his desk drawer and dropped it in the water glass.

He looked up at the camera and bowed his head slightly. Then, in a totally uncharacteristic manner of speaking, he delivered an Elvis impersonation. *"Tank you, tank you very much."*

Immediately afterward, the video went black. Rae sat back in her chair, shocked, alarmed, and perplexed. What a strange video! She knew now why some people whispered that Dr. Gregory wasn't in complete control of his faculties. What had he been doing for the last twelve years, sequestered in his old house?

She leaned forward and ran the movie again.

ALL THROUGH RAE'S last class of the day, she could not keep her mind off the strange video Thomas Gregory had sent her. She constantly lost her train of thought during her lecture, and barely remembered to inform her students of the change in the finals schedule for the coming week.

Instead of lingering for questions as she usually did, Rae unhooked her laptop, picked up her notes, and hurried out of the lecture hall. She had the most compelling urge to drive to the Gregory house, so strong in fact that she didn't stop to chat with Connie as she grabbed her purse, shut her office, and hurried out to her car. If she made good time, she'd have an hour to look at the house before she had to leave for her volunteer job in Oakland.

Fifteen minutes later, Rae drove her Jetta through the underwater tube that connected the mainland with the island of Alameda. She came up from the darkness of the tunnel to the familiar rise in the road and burst of sunlight, and made the curve toward the center of the island, her old hometown, a place she hadn't visited in ten years.

Rae watched the sights of her youth pass by her car window like a newsreel from the forties—the old Alameda High School, home of the Alameda Hornets, with its Greek Revival architecture, Washington Park with the line of palms bordering the main street, Pagano's Hardware—an old-fashioned family-owned store that stocked everything from car repair items to supplies a person might want on an Antarctic expedition—and Z's, the little tavern nearby where her mother and Albert had spent most of their Friday and Saturday nights. Traffic was light on the island, with lots of people riding bikes and walking their dogs along avenues lined with massive sycamore trees whose branches met high above, shrouding the streets in dappled shadows.

Any other person might have viewed the island as a peaceful backwater, a place to retire or raise a family. But Rae had lived through the inverted version of Alameda, and the closer she got to the old neighborhood, the tighter she clenched her jaw. She wouldn't drive to the rundown part of town, the shabby houses by the now defunct packing plant where she had lived during her childhood. She had no desire to revisit bad memories.

But she had a great desire to visit the good ones, especially the Gregory house, and especially after viewing Thomas's curious video.

Within minutes, she came to the intersection that marked the perimeter of the Gold Coast, the portion of the island that boasted blocks of graceful Victorian mansions, neatly-painted Italianate stuccos, and squat Craftsman bungalows. The area had once been the summer retreat of wealthy San Franciscans but was now an enclave of newer money, fueled by the high-tech industry of nearby Silicon Valley. The Gold Coast had always represented the good life to Rae, a place of solid families where she envisioned people gathered around huge kitchens filled with wonderful grandmothers and aunts and uncles laughing and joking, with fresh-baked cookies stacked on plates and well-mannered dogs sitting upon window seats, fresh flowers in the living room and clean towels put out every day.

The Gold Coast world was totally dissimilar to the life she'd known as a child, where she would often struggle to get to sleep at night while couples fought, either her own mother and stepfather, or the people next door.

Frowning, Rae headed toward Chisholm Avenue, driving the route she had walked after school so many times in her young life when she had dawdled in the library or in the park, anything that would keep her from going home. She didn't mind the punishments for being late, as long as she could avoid Albert, who worked the night shift and was usually home in the afternoon.

Shaking off her memories, Rae drove to the Gregory house and parked her sedan. For a moment, she sat in the car and looked up at the mansion, wishing someone had left lights on in the house, for it looked unusually dark and forbidding in the late afternoon, especially when compared to the rest of the gaily painted houses on the block.

She was surprised at how wild the landscaping had grown during the years she'd been away from the island. Two immense pines dwarfed the front tower, unpruned camellias and jasmine blocked the sun from the lower windows, and mounds of bougainvillea smothered the rails of the large wraparound porch.

Rae slipped through the half-open iron gate, walked up the old narrow sidewalk and climbed the front steps, pausing for a moment at the top to allow the discomfort in her hips to pass as she took out the key Dr. Gregory had mailed to her. She couldn't help but notice the wood of the front door was weathered, badly in need of refinishing, and the cream-colored paint on the nearest windowsills was cracked and curled. Whatever Thomas had been doing for the last twelve years, he certainly hadn't spent any time on home maintenance.

The state of the house alarmed her. What strange passion had kept Thomas Gregory from tending to his valuable piece of property and induced him to swear off human relationships? Had Thomas gone completely mad?

Still, this was the Gregory house, a place of wonder for her as a child, a gingerbread mystery, a house and a way of life that had inspired her. And now she—Fay Rae Lambers—was about to pass over the threshold of the Gregory house, just as she had dreamed of doing since she was six years old.

The slight pain in her hip forgotten, Rae slipped the key in the lock and slowly opened the door of the house. For a moment, she could see nothing of the foyer in front of her, because the closed draperies and the directional placement of the house plunged the front rooms in shadow, even on a summer afternoon such as this. She closed the door behind her while her eyes adjusted to the gloom, and then glanced around, only to suck in a sudden breath.

"Oh, my God!" she murmured, horrified.

The Gregory house had been vandalized.

Every room she could see from her stance in the foyer was a jumble of overturned furniture, toppled sculpture, spilled books, dishes, and papers. Even the huge staircase directly in front of her was a cascade of boxes, crates, paintings, and clothing. It looked as if a tornado had passed through the interior of the house.

Then she heard a thump in the dining room on her right and saw a flash of light. The vandals must be still in the house! Rae whirled to reach for the knob of the front door, but before she could pull the door open, someone grabbed her elbow and yanked her backward.

Yelping in pain and fright, Rae lost her balance, but her attacker kept her on her feet by clutching her upper arm in a firm grip that sent shards of agony spiking into her shoulder. He held her at such a height her feet barely touched the floor.

"Not so fast!" a deep voice barked, pointing the huge beam of a flashlight into her face. The light blinded her and she blinked as her eyes teared up.

"Let go!" she exclaimed, jerking at her arm and trying to kick his shins. "Let me go!"

"What are you doing here?"

"Let me go! You're hurting me!"

"And you're trespassing!"

"I am not!"

His grip loosened somewhat, but he did not release her arm.

"Let me go!" Rae's initial fear was quickly turning to anger at being manhandled. This man was obviously not the vandal, and she was obviously not a threat to him. There was no reason for him to be holding her against her will like this. Not since Albert had she allowed a person to violate her personal space. A cold sweat passed over her as her rage mounted. She threw a hand up, shielding her eyes from the strong light in her face, trying to see her assailant. "And get that flashlight out of my eyes, dammit!"

The man averted the beam, and she pulled out of his grip. She stumbled backward, rubbing her arm where he had grabbed her. She glanced at the man who now stood between her and the front door. As her eyes readjusted, she made out the tall, lean frame of a dark-haired man dressed in jeans and a dark blue shirt. He was much taller than she was, almost as tall as the door behind him. She raised her eyes to his face. Black hair, nearly black eyes, straight, grim mouth, and high pronounced cheekbones. There was no mistaking the identity of the man before her: Michael Gregory.

Rae was struck by the way the sharp planes of Michael's once oversized adolescent features and great beak of a nose had matured into a stark, well-balanced countenance. She had always considered him an attractive guy, but his mere good looks in high school had taken on a fierce, hard cast, as if an artist had taken a rough bronze of very fine lines and polished it to a glossy sheen.

"Rae?" he gasped. "Rae Lambers?"

"Yeah." She was surprised that he actually remembered her name. She brushed away imaginary wrinkles from her light sweater.

"What are you doing here?" He snapped off the flashlight and took a step forward.

"I came to see—" She paused, realizing it would be difficult to explain her presence without appearing like a common snoop. "I was a friend of your father's."

Michael's dark, dark eyes narrowed, and she saw his gaze flick over her.

"Friend?" he asked.

"And former student."

"At Berkeley?"

"Yes."

His questioning gaze swept across her again, as if evaluating whether a friend of his insane father might be insane as well. But there was something more in his gaze, the opacity of resentment that she was certain she had contributed to.

The hardness of his regard made her uncomfortable. "Your father asked me to look after the house, so I thought I'd come by."

"How'd you get in?"

"He gave me a key."

"Did he?" Michael swept the air behind him. "Then do you know anything about this? How it might have happened?"

"No." She swallowed and glanced around at the debris. "This is the first time I've been in the house."

"Since he died?"

"No. Ever." She looked back up at Michael to find him staring intently at her again. The only thing about him that hadn't changed in ten years was his eyes. She could still picture him in algebra class, staring at her until she looked over at him, wanting to know what she got on her test, and then teasing her good-naturedly if she missed more points than he did. Of all the students in the class, they were far and away the brightest and enjoyed an ongoing friendly competition.

But the older they became, the less frequently Michael got to tease her, because Rae nearly always achieved a perfect score. In fact, sometimes he would even call her at home to ask what she'd got for an answer on a difficult extra-credit question in their homework. But that had been before Albert arrived in her life, before she'd had to erect boundaries around herself because she was afraid someone might look at her too closely and realize something was wrong. It was before the infamous Day of the Dark Blue Dress with Michael.

After the Day of the Dark Blue Dress, the phone stopped ringing, and Michael left her to her silence while he joked around with the other boys. Sometimes she would look up to find him gazing at her, and she knew he was trying to figure out what had broken down between them. But she hadn't been able to tell him the reason why she'd changed, and had lashed out at him.

After that, Michael went on to become a basketball star and she took ever-accelerated math classes. For the remaining years of high school, they rarely spoke to each other, and never with any of the old spark. Like most important things in life that die over time, her friendship with Michael dwindled imperceptibly to nothingness—to a cold nod in the hallway, to a distant wave from a car, and then years later for Rae, to an occasional sigh of deep regret in the wee hours of the night when differential equations could no longer make her forget her staggering loneliness.

"And you have no idea who did this?" The rasp of Michael's voice pulled her out of her memories and brought the barriers back up with a hard clang. "Any enemies he might have had?"

"No." She adjusted the purse strap on her shoulder. "None that I know of."

Michael gave her another dark, darting glance. "Well, I shouldn't be standing here gabbing. Not with all this garbage to clean up."

"You're not going to throw things away, are you?"

"Are you kidding?" He crossed his arms over his broad chest. "Of course I am! The place is a rat's nest."

"His papers are valuable. They represent years of research."

"They're the ramblings of a crackpot."

"No they're not." She looked over at the littered parlor. "And what about all the furnishings? The sculptures—"

"Cheap souvenirs. Copies, I'll bet."

"How do you know? Are you an expert?"

"No, and I don't care to be. All this junk will be crated up and disposed of."

"Please! Not until I look at it!"

"Why bother? It's none of your concern."

"He was my friend!"

"Well, he isn't now, is he?" Michael's reply was sharp with bitterness. Was he referring to his father or to himself? "Listen, this house is nothing but a stone around my neck. It's a money pit. And if there's one thing I don't need right now, it's another money pit. I'm going to clean this place out, slap on some paint, and put it on the market."

"No!"

"Yes." He opened the door and motioned toward the porch beyond it. "Not to give you the bum's rush, but—"

Rae stared at him. She couldn't believe it. She hadn't so much as got past the front room of the Gregory house, and now she was being asked to turn around and leave. What of Thomas's warning?

But what could she say to Michael Gregory to change his mind and let her stay, to allow her to at least catalog Thomas's belongings? She could see that his son was adamant that she leave the premises, and he was, after all, the legal owner.

Rae heaved a sigh, raised her chin, and walked past his outstretched arm and onto the front porch. She didn't bother to say good-bye. They were both too intelligent to stoop to meaningless civility. Anger, frustration, and a good deal of regret roiled inside her as she strode down the steps and out to her car. She got in and pulled away from the curb with more speed than necessary, determined to find a way to carry out Thomas's request without having to go through his son.

By the time Rae got to the community center in Oakland where she helped teenage mothers deal with financial problems, she had made herself stop thinking about Michael and the alarming effect he had upon her. She got out of the car, slipped a quarter in the meter, and hurried into the old building where she had volunteered for the past two years. As she climbed the stairs, she made a conscious effort to banish the stress from her body by breathing deeply and relaxing her facial muscles. It was essential she not bring her emotional turmoil into this building. There were enough troubles here already.

As Rae climbed upward, she felt herself rising from her cloud of personal conflict. Maybe this was what heaven was like: climbing a staircase to complete and utter peace, leaving all darkness behind.

* * *

THURSDAY, THE DAY of Thomas Gregory's funeral, Rae parked her car at the graveyard and sat back, allowing the pain in her knee to subside before she made a move to get out of the car. As the week had rolled on after she had returned from Egypt, her rheumatism had gradually crept back into her joints. Even though the sun shone in a cloudless sky on the July afternoon, it wasn't the hot baking sun of the Sahara Desert, and Rae received no relief from the weather.

After a moment, Rae got out and brushed the wrinkles from her black dress. Then she grabbed her purse, locked the car, and straightened, just as a sleek black limousine pulled up behind her. She wasn't surprised to see Simeon Avare, as elegant as ever, climb out of the rear seat.

He padded closer, his black suit setting off the silvery tones of his ash-brown hair, and his long narrow feet barely leaving a mark in the plush lawn behind him.

"Good afternoon," he said, his usual charm muted for the occasion.

"Hello." She glanced at his newly shaved face. "How are you?"

"As well as can be expected, thank you." He gave her a fleeting smile. "Shall we go?"

She nodded and allowed him to take her elbow to gently guide her toward the small crowd standing near a green awning set up for the service. The moment he touched her, she forgot about the swelling in her left knee and the stiffness in her neck. She found herself walking with ease down the path toward the somber cluster of friends, colleagues and relatives of Thomas Gregory.

For the first time in her life, Rae approached a gathering with a man by her side. She had never attended a prom or gone on a date, and hadn't realized until this moment with Simeon how comfortable it felt to be part of a pair and not a single entity as she had always been.

While she waited to be seated, she again felt the strong sensation of someone looking at her. She glanced in the direction of the stare and met the stormy gaze of a man standing with the priest. There was no mistaking Michael Gregory's height and black hair. He towered over the white-haired clergyman beside him.

For a few seconds their stares held, and Rae was surprised at the anger and hardness she saw in his face. Surely he couldn't still be upset with her for entering the Gregory house. Perhaps the hardness covered his grief.

AS SHE AND Simeon took their places near the back row of chairs, she noticed many curious eyes turning to look at them. Did the others not know who she was? Had Thomas Gregory been as private about his relationship with her as he had been about the rest of his personal life? Certainly they stared at Simeon Avare simply because of his presence—his faultless posture, the proud tilt of his chin, and the ever-calculating, ever-evaluating silver eyes. Even in the shade of the awning, his eyes glinted as if lit by a fire of their own.

But Rae soon forgot about staring onlookers and the man beside her as she recalled her old friend Thomas Gregory. He had brought history alive for her in college and had been a mentor for the rest of her academic career. She owed her position at Berkeley for the strings he had pulled for her.

Even as a child she had been influenced by Thomas Gregory. She had walked by the Gregory house every day after school, intrigued by the shadowy Egyptian sculptures she could see through the rippled glass of his Victorian mansion. Then, when she was still in junior high, the drapes had been pulled closed and the blinds drawn, never to be opened again.

When she and Thomas had first begun to correspond, she had politely asked him why he had become a recluse, but he had never answered her, and she had let the subject drop. Now she would never know for sure.

She gazed at his casket, covered with bouquets, and a lump burgeoned in her throat, making it difficult to swallow. She would miss him, more than anyone she had ever known.

Rae felt Simeon's arm slip around her shoulders as she fought to hide the tears welling up in her eyes.

He bent near to her ear. "Death is not the end, Fay Rae." His smooth voice soothed her. "It is but a door through which most must pass."

Mutely, she nodded, and he gave her shoulders a gentle squeeze of comfort.

At the time, his words didn't seem all that strange.

## Chapter 4

On Friday afternoon, Rae pushed open the large brass door of a century-old office building in San Francisco and ignored the slight twinge of pain in her elbow. She rushed toward the bank of elevators just ahead, her low-heeled pumps clicking on the marble floor in a quick staccato. Due to a traffic accident on the Bay Bridge she was late for the reading of the will, and she abhorred being late.

The elevator dragged up to the seventeenth floor while Rae checked the letter for the office number of the attorneys she had come to see, and then looked at her watch. She was only ten minutes late. With hope, they hadn't started without her.

She found the office suite, and walked up to the reception desk to introduce herself. A moment later, a young woman appeared to show her into a conference room. Rae stepped into the large room paneled in dark wood with a huge wooden table and substantial chairs upholstered in brown leather. The only two people in the room were an overweight man in an ill-fitting dark blue suit who rose to his feet as she crossed the threshold, and Michael Gregory who stood at the far end of the room drinking a cup of coffee. His expression darkened as he watched her advance. Once again, he seemed displeased to see her.

"Sorry to be late," she explained. "Traffic was horrible on the bridge."

"Miss Lambers, I presume?" the overweight man asked.

"Yes."

He held out his hand and introduced himself as Kirk Dickers, attorney of the late Dr. Gregory.

"And I take it you know Michael Gregory?" he asked, gesturing toward the tall man behind him. Michael slid a cool glance at her and then immediately looked away.

"Yes. We are acquainted."

"Very good." He indicated the chair to his left. "Then let's get started, shall we?" When Michael did not join them at the table, the attorney turned around in his chair. "Mr. Gregory?"

"I prefer to stand." Michael's voice was dry and flat.

Rae settled into the chair and put her purse on the floor beside her. She wondered why she had been asked to attend the reading of the will, and wondered even more that no one else from the university was there. At the very least she expected Thomas to fund a scholarship for needy history students. Perhaps setting up a scholarship in his name was to be her task and the reason for her presence.

The attorney put on a pair of reading glasses and droned on in the circuitous language of the law while Rae only half-listened, overly conscious of Michael's imposing figure looming in the periphery of her vision. She could feel his dark regard, as if a huge bird of prey were watching her.

" . . . and as for the Alameda house at 506 Chisholm Avenue," Mr. Dickers droned on, "the property shall be bequeathed to my son, Michael Robert Gregory, and to my long-standing friend and colleague, Fay Rae Lambers, in equal shares, with the provision that one may buy out the other if both parties so desire."

"What?" Michael exclaimed, stepping out of the shadows at the end of the room.

"—if both parties so desire," the lawyer repeated.

"No, before that!" Michael snatched the paper out of Dickers's hands and pored over it.

Rae watched him read through the will, her heart in her throat. Thomas had made her co-owner of the Gregory house? Unbelievable!

Apparently Michael didn't believe it either. "My father left the house to *her*?"

"Half of it."

"Christ!" Michael tossed the paper on the table. "Fucking hell!"

"Mr. Gregory, please!"

"What kind of inheritance is that?"

"It was your father's last wish."

"What kind of father bequeaths half a house to his only son and half to a mere acquaintance?"

"I'm not here to discuss family issues, Mr. Gregory," Dickers replied, his tone chilled by Michael's high-handed behavior and foul language. "I'm merely here to read the will. Now if you will allow me to continue—"

"I can contest this," Michael put in, ignoring the attorney. "And I intend to!"

"Only if you can prove your father was not in his right mind when he drew up the will."

"Of course he wasn't. Everyone knows that."

"He seemed lucid to me." The lawyer gave him a watery but nonplussed stare.

Michael scowled and glanced at Rae, who slowly stood up. She couldn't blame Michael for his outrage at having been disinherited, but at the same time she couldn't forgive him for turning his back on his father. Such long-term disloyalty did not deserve full inheritance.

"So being half owner . . ." Rae crossed her arms over her chest. "That means I can come and go on the premises?"

The lawyer looked over the tops of his glasses at her. "Of course."

"And it means I am owner of half the contents of the house as well?"

"The furnishings and the like. Yes."

She looked up at Michael, whose eyes were opaque with anger.

"That means Michael can't dispose of the contents of the house without my permission?"

"One would assume, yes."

Michael's brows drew together. "I can dispose of half of it," he growled.

"But what half?" she asked.

He crossed his own arms. "Any half I damn well please."

The lawyer sighed, exasperated. "Do you two need a mediator?"

Rae answered yes at the exact time as Michael answered no. They both frowned at each other.

"I can have someone advise you—"

"Later." Michael looked at his watch. "I don't have time for this now. I have an appointment."

"But there are documents to sign—" Dickers put in.

"Send them to the house." Michael put down his coffee cup and turned to leave. "I'm booked solid today." He looked over his shoulder at the attorney. "And while you're at it, draw up papers for a buyout of Miss Lambers and send them to the house as well." Then he brushed past her and left the room without closing the door behind him.

Rae watched him go, astounded by his rudeness and the assumption that she would relinquish her rights to the Gregory house. His boorish behavior of the last few minutes only made her want to hold on to the property more. She'd be damned before she signed any buyout papers.

RAE WAS STILL upset when Simeon Avare arrived to take her to dinner early that evening. She was glad to have company to take her mind off her brief but maddening encounter with Michael, and was looking forward to spending a few hours with a man who had no connection whatsoever to her past and no chip on his shoulder as far as she could discern.

She opened the door to find him standing on her doorstep holding a bouquet of purple iris and wearing a navy suit and light yellow shirt, open at the throat. As usual, he looked as if he had stepped out of a male fashion magazine. Rae was glad she had put on her black silk dress—the only decent dress she owned—and a pair of pumps. Her feet would kill her tomorrow, but at least she would look her best for her charming companion tonight.

"You look beautiful," Simeon commented as she showed him in.

"Thank you." She remembered looking at her reflection in the mirror as she put on her makeup earlier that evening. She had to admit her Egyptian tan did make her appear more healthy than usual. In fact, she had thought her image in the mirror had seemed altered, just as Connie had mentioned. She seemed to have a radiance about her that she had never been able to achieve even with the expensive cosmetics she had tried over the years that promised a "radiant glow."

"These are for you," Simeon continued, holding out the flowers.

"Thank you." She took the bouquet. "Irises are my absolute favorite. How did you know?"

"Just a lucky guess."

"I'll say." She smiled at him. "Let me put them in water. I'll just be a moment." She motioned toward her kitchen, which lay behind them to the right.

"I like your taste," he commented, trailing after her.

Rae glanced at the vanilla-colored furniture of her living room clustered around the maroon carpet she had purchased in a Luxor market, with a copy of David Roberts's watercolor *The Temple of Philae* hanging above her sofa. She had surrounded herself with a few objects that pleased her, never considering how another human being might view her house, as she rarely entertained visitors.

"Your home is simple and understated." Simeon slipped a hand in his pocket and surveyed the ironwood table and chairs of her dining room, and the translucent alabaster bowl placed in the center of the table. "It suits you."

Rae glanced at the back of his head as she arranged the irises in a tall narrow vase. She had never invited a single male guest into her home. And yet, she felt as if Simeon Avare belonged among her things, as if he saw her possessions for what they truly were, and understood they sprang from her love of Egypt and her appreciation for a few exquisite objects over a jumble of meaningless knickknacks.

She almost suggested that he pull out the drawer in her coffee table and look at the strange deck of cards she'd brought home from Egypt, but something made her think twice about it. She closed her mouth before the words formed on her lips.

"It's peaceful," he added.

"But a condo isn't a home. It's like living in an apartment. I'd like a real home someday." She swept into the dining room and replaced the alabaster bowl with the huge bouquet of irises. She stepped back. "My, aren't those magnificent?"

Simeon nodded but then caught her hand before she had time to step away.

"What is wrong, Fay Rae?"

"Nothing. Why?" She shot a quick look at him, knowing her reply had been too quick and too breezy to be believed.

"I sense that something is wrong." His eyes leveled on her lips, and he gently brushed the left corner of her mouth with the back of a fingertip. "I see it there. You are upset."

Rae looked down, knowing it would be best to draw away from this man and his uncanny perception of her, but she could not bring herself to slip from his light grasp. His slightest touch soothed her, melted the pain from her joints, and set her at ease. She wanted to feel such ease for as long as possible, even if it meant enduring the touch of a man. Yet with Simeon there was no suffering involved, and no threat.

But he was right about the fact that something bothered her. She was still upset over the incident in the lawyer's office.

"Do you have a glass of wine we could share?" he asked. "While you tell me what is troubling you."

"Don't we have to go?" She looked up at his kind face. "I mean, didn't you make reservations for a certain time?"

"The Lapis will wait for us, believe me."

"We're going to the Lapis restaurant?" She knew of the classy waterfront restaurant with its stylish logo but had never dined there.

"I was intrigued by the name, lapis lazuli being from Egypt as you are most certainly aware."

"I've always wanted to go to Lapis."

"But first, I wish to know what is troubling you."

She studied his silvery eyes and his fine, sensuous mouth,

knowing she wanted to tell everything to this wonderfully warm man.

"All right." She took a step toward the kitchen, backing toward it and feeling very much out of her element. "Do you like zinfandel? I think I have a bottle of it in my pantry. Someone gave it to me last Christmas—"

He chuckled and cocked his head, as if to tell her he found her engaging. "I love zinfandel."

"Zinfandel it is then." She escaped from his regard into the kitchen while he ambled toward the living room.

She brought them each a glass, although she rarely drank alcohol, and then sat beside him on the couch and told him about the run-in with Michael Gregory. Simeon listened quietly, his legs crossed casually, sipping his wine and nodding every once in a while. When she was finished telling her tale, he set his glass upon the coffee table near his expensive leather shoes.

"May I suggest that you establish your rights immediately," he said. "I would advise you to go there this very evening. Stay the weekend. Take the chance to get Thomas's things in order."

"But I have grading to do and some last-minute changes to make on a final exam. It's the end of the quarter."

"Well then, at least stay at the house over the weekend and make it your own."

"I suppose I could."

"And if you need help, I would be glad to offer my assistance."

She glanced up at his relaxed face. "That's very nice of you."

"In fact, I would be most happy to accompany you to the house tonight to meet this Michael Gregory face-to-face."

"He might not even be there." Rae rose to her feet and Simeon immediately stood up as well. "But if he is, I could use the moral support if you wouldn't mind."

"Not at all. Why don't you pack what you need for the weekend, and then we shall go to the house after we have dinner. I will call a cab from there to take me back to the city."

"Really? I hate to put you out."

"Put me out?" He smiled. "You make me sound like a pet cat."

"It's just an expression." She picked up his empty wine goblet. "It means to impose on a person, take up their time."

"I will make the time," he answered, his voice soft and warm. "Especially for you."


BY THE TIME they got to the Lapis restaurant on the waterfront of San Francisco, they had missed their reservation by nearly an hour. They took a seat in the bar to wait for a table to become available. Rae settled into her chair and looked at the sparkling aquarium that separated the bar from the restaurant.

"What a beautiful idea," she commented.

"What?"

"Having an aquarium like this!"

"Yes," He picked up the advertisement for the drink specialties of the house, "Yes, it is." But his voice was absent of interest, belying his words.

Rae glanced at him. "You're not crazy about aquariums?"

"Not particularly."

"But this one is stunning. I've never seen such fish before. Look at that blue one!" She pointed to a bottle-nosed fish she could not identify. It looked like a cross between a surgeonfish and a trumpetfish. "What do you suppose that is? Do you think it might be a fish from the Mediterranean?"

Simeon cast a bored glance at the tank. "I don't quite see it," he replied.

"There." Rae pointed again as the fish darted out of a clump of coral and swam along the front of the tank.

"Sorry. I'll still don't see it."

"You don't?" Rae looked at Simeon, surprised to see his gaze fixed on the spot the fish had initially appeared. Hadn't he noticed the path the fish had just taken? Couldn't he see the blue creature hovering just beneath the surface of the water? Was he just bored or playing games with her? She decided to play a game right back.

"You can't see the bright blue fish?" she asked, pointing to the middle of the aquarium where no fish swam at all. "Right here?"

"Oh, *that* one," he replied. Then he looked back down at the drink flyer and replaced it next to the wall. "Sorry, Fay Rae, I can't help you. I am no fish expert."

Slowly Rae lowered her hand and turned to face Simeon. Why was he being so strange, pretending not to see what she had pointed out, and then pretending to see something that wasn't even there? Was he that disinterested?

Just as she leaned closer to question him about his odd behavior, the waiter came up to take their order, and the subject of conversation shifted.

BY TEN O'CLOCK that evening, Rae was back at the Gold Coast, parking in front of the Gregory house. She got out and grabbed her overnight bag from the back seat of the Jetta and then led Simeon Avare up the walk toward the mansion. Lights glowed from the second-story corner room at the front of the house, opposite the shrouded tower. Michael must be upstairs or had left lights on. The porch light wasn't lit, nor were there any lights on downstairs. The absence of light sent a message loud and clear: no visitors desired. Keep out.

She turned the key in the lock and opened the door, stepping into the foyer while she brushed her hand along the wall, searching for a light switch. She found it, an old-fashioned switch comprised of two separate buttons. She pressed one and nothing happened. She pressed the other. Still the lights did not come on.

"Is there something wrong with the electrical system?" Simeon asked, coming up behind her. She could feel his breath on the back of her neck.

"Apparently."

So there *was* a physical reason for Michael's inhospitable behavior. But even if the lights *had* been working on the first floor, she wondered if he would have left the porch light on, as all the neighbors did, making the block cheerful and welcoming except for the dark overgrown Gregory property.

Before they had ventured any farther than the main hall, Rae spotted a shadowy figure at the top of the stairs. A flashlight beam passed over her.

"Who's down there?" Michael's voice boomed.

"It's Rae Lambers."

She heard him mutter *shit* under his breath but refused to let his displeasure at seeing her bother her. She watched him descend to the landing and aim the beam at her companion.

"Who else?"

"A friend of mine. He'd like to use the phone."

She glanced at Simeon, who had a hand up in front of his face to ward off the glare of the light.

Michael walked down the rest of the stairs and lowered the beam of the flashlight to guide his descent. The staircase was clear of debris. Michael must have been hard at work cleaning the house for most of the evening. When he came closer, she saw that he was dressed in an old T-shirt, a pair of faded jeans that hung on his lean hips, and a pair of tan boat shoes with the laces trailing on the floor.

"Do you have any idea what time it is?" he asked, his voice cold.

"Around ten."

"Did we wake you, sir?" Simeon asked.

Michael swept a black glare over him. "No, but I was just about ready to get in the shower."

"What's wrong with the lights?" Rae asked.

"A fuse must have blown."

"And you can't fix it?"

"If you wish to look for the fuse box out in that jungle in the middle of the night, be my guest."

"Sir!" Simeon took a step forward. "There is no need to take such a tone with Miss Lambers."

Michael glanced at Simeon, as if seeing him for the first time.

"This is Simeon Avare," Rae put in, motioning toward her companion, who seemed short in comparison to Michael's towering height. "He was a friend of your father's."

"I was sorry to hear of his death." Simeon extended his

hand. Michael switched the flashlight to his left hand and shook Simeon's right one.

"Thanks." Michael's every word seemed begrudging, as if it pained him to speak in a civil fashion. Rae shook her head, wondering how Michael survived in the world with such a bad attitude. She'd heard he'd married well and owned a home in the Marina District in San Francisco, one of the priciest areas of town. Maybe rudeness paid off. Or maybe he wasn't short-tempered with anyone but her and his soon-to-be-ex-wife.

"Phone's in the study back there." Michael pointed the flashlight in the direction of the hallway leading toward the back of the house.

"Are there any more flashlights?" Rae asked. "Or candles?"

"There's probably a million candles in this garbage heap." He nodded to the left. "If you can find them."

"Well, then could Simeon and I use the flashlight for a moment?"

"I'll take you." Michael frowned. "This way."

He padded toward the study, and they followed him, careful to avoid stepping on the litter on the floor. He showed them into a small interior room that had no windows and was lined with shelves of books that had been left untouched.

"This was where he was found," Rae murmured. "Wasn't it?"

"At his desk." Michael's voice was laced more with acid than emotion. "Facedown."

Rae glanced around in the gloom, looking for the little fountain that had been so noisy in the video he had made for her. But she couldn't locate it. Perhaps Thomas had realized how distracting the sound of running water could be, and had disposed of the desktop water feature.

The study wasn't half as disturbed as the rest of the house. The drawers of the desk had been pulled out and emptied, and a file cabinet against the wall had been tipped over. But the top of the desk was clear.

Rae surveyed the surface of the desk as Simeon dialed the number of the cab company, the same company he had used to get to her condo in Berkeley. She noticed Thomas's Rolodex was open, displaying a black business card, which caught her eye because of its unusual color. She bent closer and could just make out the metallic silver script at the top of the card. The name Maren Lake and only a phone number were listed on the card. An odd name. An odd card. She wondered if the card referred to a person or a place.

Simeon put down the receiver of the phone and turned to her. "They can pick me up in about a half hour."

"Good. Would you like a cup of tea or coffee while you wait? I'm sure Thomas had some tea in his kitchen. He liked tea."

"Fuses," Michael reminded her.

"You do not have to bother on my account." Simeon motioned toward the door. "Instead, you may wish to use the time to get a room in order so that you can sleep."

"Sleep?" Michael trained the flashlight on her face. "Wait a minute. You aren't intending to stay—"

She reached out and averted the bright beam of light. "As a matter of fact, I am."

"But the place is a mess!"

"I am aware of that." She moved toward the door. "As I am also aware that I have just as much right to stay here as you do."

Simeon directed a slow and knowing smile toward Michael.

"Jesus!" Michael ran a hand through his hair. "Can't you respect a person's grief?"

"Do you grieve, Michael?" she countered. "It doesn't seem like it."

"How would you know!"

Michael stormed out of the study, taking the light with him. Rae made a move to follow him, but Simeon lightly grasped her hand. "Let the man be," he said. "He is more distraught than he reveals to you."

Rae paused, looking at the blackness of Michael's wake

and wondering that she could still feel so responsible for part of his dark mood. She would have thought their old friendship was long forgotten, a barely remembered slice of time. But perhaps, like she, Michael had never forgotten those days, and perhaps he had yet to forgive her as well. "A more boorish man I have not met," Simeon commented, "in quite some time."

"Right." Rae slipped from his grasp. "My eyes are adjusted now. Let's go upstairs and see if we can find a decent bedroom."

"As you wish."

THE NEXT MORNING, Rae awoke from a deep sleep and sat up in bed. For a minute, she had no idea where she was. And then the dim light filtering down through the old lace curtains reminded her that she had awakened in the Gregory house, that it was Saturday, and she had spent the night in a room in the tower that Simeon had helped clear out to reveal a perfectly decent guest bedroom.

Yawning, she got out of the queen-sized bed, scratching both sides of her head. Her hair, which she never tied back for the night, hung in limp blond strands down her back. She had fallen asleep in the clothes she had changed into last evening after her dinner with Simeon—a pair of flannel pajama pants and a light blue T-shirt.

Still half-asleep, she padded to the bathroom, and then went downstairs to make her mandatory pot of coffee, taking the bag of ground Starbucks that she had brought with her in her overnight bag. When she flipped the switch on the coffeemaker, however, no corresponding light flicked on, and she remembered the blown fuse.

"Damn!" she muttered, squinting at the toggle switch.

She tried again, not believing the kitchen wiring could be connected to that of the entryway and living room. Apparently she was wrong. Or two fuses had blown. And come to think of it, what had blown the fuses anyway? Had Michael been using too many appliances at once during his cleaning frenzy Friday evening?

Normally Rae was even-tempered and good-natured, but not in the morning before she'd had at least one cup of strong coffee to jump-start her sense of humor, and certainly not around Michael Gregory. She had to have her java, especially with him in the house. She squinted at her watch. Nine-thirty. She hoped he would sleep until noon and not bother her.

Rae saw no alternative but to go around to the back of the house and look at the fuse box. In her worn, once-blue slippers, she scuffed her way through the pantry, across the back porch, and down the rickety stairs, squinting in the bright summer morning light.

As Rae walked down the steps, she glanced at the back yard of the Gregory house, which was surprisingly large for a lot in Alameda. An intimate brick patio graced one corner of the yard next to an old fountain. A heaving brick path led off through high shrubbery and a pair of oak trees to a small garden shed. Huge black locusts lined the driveway, their roots crawling over the yard, their thorny branches hanging low. Vines grew everywhere—honeysuckle, morning glory, and jasmine—over the fence, over the patio chairs, and around the fountain, which reflected black water choked with milfoil. The morning sun did its best to infiltrate the dense foliage, but most of the yard remained in shadow, oddly soundless. She had never seen the Gregory back yard and realized that here, too, was a lot of work to be done. But she would wait to tackle the shrubs back here until she'd seen to the front ones.

Suddenly, the thought of all the work ahead, and the responsibility of ownership, seemed overly daunting. How would she and Michael handle maintenance expenses? Would he refuse to go along with anything she wanted to do with the house? If she wanted the trees cut back, would she have to pay for it herself? Would he paint the interior of the house in outlandish shades of blue and green that she didn't like? She suspected Michael would be difficult to deal with, and that the past few days of conflict might be just a mild harbinger of the storm to come.

There had to be a way to deal with the Day of the Dark Blue Dress without revealing everything, and she had to find it. Until she cleared the air with Michael, there would be no way of living with the man.

With the morning sun dappling her back, Rae scuffed her way to the side of the house and located the fuse box, where the yard narrowed to a walkway and the line of locusts which bordered the alley leading to the garage. Just as she spotted the fuse box, she heard the downshifting of a sports car and looked over her shoulder to see a shiny black Audi TT roll up the slight slope of the driveway, looking every inch like a black panther corning home to its lair. Michael Gregory had not been oversleeping after all.

"Out playing," Rae muttered to herself, turning back to her task. She pulled at the metal loop of the fuse box. The door didn't budge. She pulled again. She heard the engine of the car shut off and a car door open and close.

"Dammit!" she swore. Severe caffeine deficiency frazzled her nerves. She reached up and tried again. What in the hell was wrong with the stupid box? She shoved her always slipping glasses back up to the bridge of her nose and planted her hands on her hips, exasperated.

"Turn the little handle and then pull," Michael said behind her.

"I knew that." She was suddenly very conscious of the way she was dressed. Her hair was limp and scraggly, she hadn't removed her makeup the night before. She hadn't even brushed her teeth. The outfit she wore was an unmatched ensemble of disreputable bagginess, she hadn't put on a bra, and she'd thrown on a pair of glasses she wore only when no one was around.

She reached up, turned the handle and pulled. At first the door didn't budge, so she yanked on it, struggling to hide the flare of pain the movement caused in her shoulder. The door gave way suddenly and popped open, its rusty hinges squeaking in protest.

"Let me do that," Michael demanded, stepping up behind her.

"I can manage."

"Know what you're looking for?"

"Of course," she lied. She wanted more than anything for him to leave her alone. She didn't want to talk to him in her present condition, let alone turn around and face him. She was highly aware of the light cologne he wore, which was subtle and expensive. It swirled around her, a distracting cloud. Forcing herself to concentrate, she unscrewed one of the fuses and looked at it. Nothing seemed cracked or discolored.

"You're not tall enough to see if the fuses are blown." He inched closer, almost touching her. "Let me do it."

"I said I could manage." She glared over her shoulder at him, willing him to leave her in peace, but he just stood there, seemingly nonplussed by her disarray. He was dressed in jeans, loafers, and a crisp white cotton shirt, not a wrinkle in sight, not a lock of his black hair out of place or even thinning—handsome and well groomed, just as he'd been in high school. "I'm perfectly capable."

"But I'm taller than you."

Of course he was. He'd been a basketball star. She wasn't a short person, but she came nowhere near his six-foot-three-inch height.

She ignored his comment and turned back to her task.

Where had Michael been so early this morning? She guessed he'd just got back from a late-night conquest. Last night she had assumed he had showered and gone to bed in a huff. But maybe he'd showered and gone out. As to that, where was his socialite wife?

While she mulled over Michael's night life, she scanned the rest of the fuses for a melted midsection. He stood on the path behind her, as if waiting for her to finish her task. Didn't he have better things to do at nine o'clock in the morning than to witness her lack of handyman skills and take stock of her on the worst bad hair day of her life?

Then she found two blackened fuses in the row nearest the bottom of the box. She unscrewed them.

"There," she announced triumphantly, turning to face

him, proud that she had accomplished the task by herself. "Now all I have to do is get some replacements."

He held up a small brown paper bag.

Rae flushed. Michael had been a step ahead of her all along. He hadn't been out carousing. He'd been to Pagano's Hardware and back before she'd gotten out of bed.

Suddenly, Rae's thoughts turned back to her attire. Could Michael see her breasts under her thin T-shirt? She hoped not. But she couldn't take the chance to look down at herself. Instead, she crossed her arms over her chest.

His gaze flitted over her and settled on her face, which was probably smeared with smudged mascara. "Interesting look you have going there, Rae."

"Thanks," she replied, refusing to admit to her embarrassment. "I call it Clown at Nine A.M." She saw the flicker of a smile in his eyes, and in that instant she recognized the Michael of her youth. An old pain tugged at her. She blinked, struggling to bring up her well-honed barriers, but not before her heart made a strange and unfamiliar protest, a pitiful little flip like a half-dead fish hurling itself one last time toward the sea.

Rae immediately snatched the paper bag from Michael's hand, determined to deflect his gaze before he noticed how the smile in his eyes had affected her.

"Are you sure they're the right fuses?" she asked.

"Fifteen amps. I checked." The flicker of recognition had died. "Screw two of them in. Leave the extras in the fuse box. The lights should work."

He left her at the side of the house, standing with the bag in her hand and a second, more heated flush creeping over her face. She shouldn't care what Michael Gregory thought of her, and she shouldn't care about the light of recognition in his eyes. But that look had flipped a switch inside her, a circuit breaker long turned off. Now a current was running through her, and the vibration was alien to her, disquieting.

"Get a grip," she muttered to herself. Her hands shook as she finished replacing the fuses. Taking a deep breath, she finally mastered her runaway physical reaction and closed the metal door with a clang.

As she walked up the back steps, she could smell the heavenly fragrance of brewing coffee. She would take the high road and offer some to Michael. She had to end whatever immaturity remained between them. To achieve anything as co-owners of the Gregory house, they would have to learn to get along as adults.

## Chapter 5

Rae found Michael in the dining room, bagging up broken dishes and throwing papers into a pile. He heard her step at the threshold and looked up.

"So what did you do," he asked without greeting her first, "to coerce my father?"

"What do you mean?" She stopped abruptly, holding the two mugs of steaming coffee in her hands. She had planned to initiate the conversation, and was surprised at Michael's sharp question.

"To give you half the house."

"I didn't do anything."

"Bullshit." Michael clenched his jaw, and she saw a muscle in his cheek tense and flare. How could he have gone from half-laughing at her one moment to this brusqueness the next? Was he struggling with his own barriers and demons as much as she was?

"Maybe your father wanted something of me in return," she retorted. "Have you ever thought of that?"

"Yeah? Like what?"

She opened her mouth to tell him the real reason she was at the house was to serve as a protector of sorts. Protecting what, she didn't quite know and from whom she didn't know either. But she had to take Thomas's video seriously until she found a reason not to. Yet he had warned her not to share the video with anyone, and to leave the house in the hands of a person with a good heart. That eliminated Michael.

"I'm not certain yet." She put down one of the mugs of coffee on a stack of papers on the table. "Surely you don't think I'm here for the fun of it."

"No, I think you're here for the money."

"What money?"

"The money this house represents. I remember your family. The Lambers. Eagle Avenue, right?"

"You know nothing of my family!" she retorted hotly. At least she hoped and prayed he didn't know anything.

"Oh, yes I do. Your folks didn't have a dime. Your mother worked at Ed's Pancake House on Park. Then at the laundromat on Oak Street. Didn't she?" When Rae made no reply, he continued. "You probably worked my father for years, knowing he was here all alone, and you somehow managed to get on his good side."

"We were colleagues. We shared an interest in Egypt."

"Right."

"I just returned from there as a matter of fact."

"So?" Michael threw a broken china plate into the bag he held. "That doesn't prove anything."

"As if I have to prove anything to you!" She glared at his wide shoulders as he leaned over to pick up a broken vase. "Good God!"

He stood up, and she glowered at him, more angry at Michael than she had ever been at another human being. The last thing in the world she would ever become was a gold digger.

She had been prepared to suggest a truce, to try to explain that day long ago. But why should she bother? Michael would probably throw it back in her face anyway.

Then his glance angled down to the steaming mug on the table, and she touched the handle of the coffee cup. "I brought you some coffee, but I can see you're too busy insulting me to take a break."

Before he could make a reply, someone rapped on the front door behind her, and an instant later the door opened. Rae spun around, startled when a small redheaded woman breezed into the foyer without waiting to be let in. She wore a lime-green shell and crisp white slacks. Her hair was cut in a short sleek style that feathered around her ivory face. Her large green eyes tilted upward slightly at the corners, giving her a feline appearance. She was slick and gorgeous and trim, and she didn't seem to notice Rae standing at the side of the dining room table.

"Michael!" the woman called out, opening her arms as she minced forward in her backless sandals. A tiny white purse dangled from a perfectly toned arm. Rae noticed she wore an expensive watch as well as a huge diamond and a wedding band.

He made no move to embrace her, and she stopped short in front of him, pouting prettily. "I came the moment I heard."

"Really?" His voice was as chilled when speaking to this woman as when speaking to Rae. Maybe he treated everyone with equal frostiness. The woman's arms slowly lowered to her sides.

"I'm so sorry about your father, Michael. So, so sorry!"

"I don't know why you should be." Michael dropped the broken vase into the garbage bag. It clinked as it shattered other items in the bag. "You never met the man."

She ignored the comment by glancing around the dining room, still not noticing Rae standing behind her near the wall. "God, what happened to the place?"

"Someone broke in."

"Did they damage the house?"

"No, just tore it up."

"Why?"

"I'm not sure."

"What did the police say?"

"Teenage gang."

Rae wondered how the police had come to the conclusion that a bunch of kids was responsible for the mess at the Gregory house. Had the teenagers been looking for money? She didn't think a gang of adolescents would so thoroughly ransack a house. Maybe someone else had been here—the someone Thomas had warned her about. She took a sip of coffee.

The movement of Rae's hand caught the other woman's eye.

"Oh," the stranger said, her beguiling expression souring

to a forced smile. "I didn't know you had company, Michael." She kept staring at Rae, expecting to be introduced, as her eyes slowly narrowed with suspicion. "Not a new girlfriend, surely?"

"Off the mark as usual, Vee." Michael shook his head. "Way off."

Rae straightened her shoulders, knowing she had been insulted again, but not sure why this woman felt it necessary to be catty. Michael nodded toward Rae.

"Meet the new co-owner of the house."

Vee's green eyes flashed at her, and took her measure in a quick and calculating downward sweep, checking for designer labels and evidence of a recent pedicure, Rae was sure. Rae suffered the sharp perusal with aplomb, uncaring at this point that her hair was unwashed and that she wore mismatched baggy clothes. She even hoped Vee noticed her lack of a bra.

"Co-owner, did you say?" Vee repeated, turning away.

"My old man bequeathed half the house to her."

"Sorry to be so dense." Vivian stepped around an overturned chair while bracing herself on the shoulder of a toppled statue of Seti I, unaware of the disrespect she showed the valuable piece of art. "But I'm not quite getting all of this."

"I knew Dr. Gregory," Rae explained, holding out a hand. "And he apparently wanted to reward me. I'm Rae Lambers."

"Vivian Rogers." The redhead shook her hand.

"My dear, soon-to-be-ex, wife"—Michael picked up the still-steaming coffee—"who has come all the way from the Amalfi coast to tender her sympathies regarding my loss." He gave her a mock salute with the mug. "But more importantly to check out what she believes is a new asset to add to the long list of things I should share with her upon our divorce."

"Michael!" she admonished. "I would never—!"

"Sometimes the truth hurts, doesn't it, Vee?" He swallowed a gulp of coffee. "Like the news you were getting the Marina house."

"You never liked the Marina house."

"Not after you had that designer paint the entire first floor purple."

"Aubergine." Vivian rolled her eyes. The color of the first floor was obviously a much-visited source of contention between them. "It's aubergine!"

"Whatever. You might have asked me if I liked the color first."

"I didn't think you cared."

"I sure don't. Not any more."

Rae glanced from Michael to his wife and back again, wondering whether they would fight all day if someone didn't intervene. Their harsh words made her feel uncomfortable and invisible at the same time. She decided to interrupt them.

"Vivian, would you care for a cup of coffee?"

"No thank you," Michael answered for her. "She was just leaving. Weren't you, Vee?"

"Go ahead," Vivian sneered. "Treat me like shit. You'll pay when we meet in court, Michael Gregory."

"I'll deal with that when the time comes."

"I only meant to be civil."

"Do me a favor. Spare me your civility."

"I hoped we might end our marriage as friends at least." She raised her chin. "But I see you haven't changed."

"That was always the problem, Vee." Michael lowered the coffee cup. "You were always expecting me to change."

Vivian glanced at Rae as if to seek sympathy from a fellow female, but Rae only sipped her drink and looked away. She bore no sympathy for someone who had used Thomas Gregory's valuable statuary as a handrail. Frustrated, Vivian minced to the door and opened it. Before she left, however, she glanced over her petite shoulder.

"I meant it about your father," she said.

"Sure. Thanks." Michael reached down for the garbage bag.

Rae showed Vivian out while she wondered how a man like Michael—once a happy-go-lucky basketball star with a home on the Gold Coast—had apparently fallen into such an unhappy life.

* * *

A FEW SECONDS later, Rae returned to the dining room and picked up Michael's cup. "Want any more coffee?" she asked, holding up the mug.

"No, thanks."

Rae watched him continue to work for a moment. The air had cleared since Vivian's departure, and Rae felt a definite shift in Michael's demeanor. He seemed much more calm, even unaware of another person's presence in the room. "May I make a request?" she asked.

He straightened and looked at her. "What?"

"Would you put the papers and books in a pile? I'll take care of them."

"Even though they're a bunch of crap?"

"They're not crap to me."

His gaze hovered on her for a moment.

"I'll do the living room," she added. "And clean up the kitchen. Just do me a favor and don't throw away anything your father has written."

"Whatever."

"In return, I'm here to do my fair share. I just wanted to make sure you knew that."

"Aren't you afraid you'll break a nail?"

Rae placed a hand on one hip and did a mocking sweep of her disheveled outfit with the other. "Do I look like a person who cares about nails?"

Her self-effacing remark made a begrudging half-smile pull at the corner of his grim mouth. He picked up a shard of glass from the table. "I've never met a woman who didn't worry about her cuticles and all that shit."

"Well, I'm not like other women." She turned for the kitchen. She would never be like other women, certainly not the women Michael had known, if his wife was any indication.

But before she left Michael to his work, she had to ask him another question, a question that had been niggling at her since the moment she'd met him in the attorney's office.

"Just answer me one thing," she said. "What happened between you and your father?"

"What do you mean?"

"That made you bitter, so closed off?"

"I'm not bitter." Michael crushed a wad of paper in his fist.

"You could have fooled me."

He glanced at her, and she had the feeling that he was thinking of something to say to satisfy her enough to leave him alone. "If you want the truth, I don't consider the bastard my father."

"Why?"

"He chose this house over my mother for starters."

"I believe he felt staying here was of vital importance."

"And seeing his wife and son wasn't?" Michael threw the wad of paper into the garbage sack. "Maybe going to a few of my games? Did you ever see old man Gregory at any of my games?"

"No—"

"Never a card, never a letter, or God forbid, a personal visit!"

Rae stared at him, truly surprised that Thomas Gregory had severed all contact with his only child. "Your father didn't seem like that kind of man."

"Well, he was!" Michael leaned forward to grab a broken bowl. "And I spent a lot of years training myself not to think about him. It just made me mad. So don't go bringing him up. And don't go trying to convince me he was anything but a bastard—because I couldn't care less!"

Rae begged to differ but said nothing. Michael's old hurt lay just beneath the surface of his skin, still painful enough to create an outburst such as this one. His baggage was obviously heavier than hers, or he hadn't developed the skill it took to successfully bury the dark part of his life. Or maybe it was a matter of self-control, which Michael seemed not to possess in any great quantity. He could lose his temper more quickly than most men she'd seen.

In the father department, they shared their only commonality. They both had suffered the effects of an absent parent. Yet while Michael had known his father and had grown to hate him, Rae had no idea who her father was, and had never even seen a picture of the man. Her mother had refused to talk about him, and had even slapped Rae once when she pressed for information long ago.

Unlike the rest of her life, Rae was safe from questions regarding her father. No one ever asked about him. He was like an amputated limb. No one looked at the missing part, and no one ever asked what had happened. But the silence hadn't made her bitter. It had just made her sad.

LATE THAT EVENING, Michael palmed some ice cubes in a tumbler, poured himself a hefty portion of Laphroaig, and added a dash of water to the glass. Ordinarily he didn't drink his best scotch on an everyday occasion, but tonight he needed a boost. It was difficult being here in the house where he had been born, a house he had been dragged from by his mother, and a house he had shunned for so many years. There were too many ghosts here for his peace of mind, too many images of his mother and father's sharp words and the long weeks of icy silence afterward.

Being here put him on edge and made him more short-tempered than he usually was. But staying at the Marina District house was not an option.

Michael turned away from his memories and took an appreciative sip of the single-malt whisky. He could hear Rae Lambers taking a shower down the hall, washing off the sweat and dust from the long day spent cleaning the house. He had to give the woman credit. She had worked as hard as he had, had matched him hour for hour without complaint. She had gone the entire day without eating or mentioning a break. He almost felt guilty for having pushed her so hard.

But she was an adult. She could have said something. She could have stopped and ordered a pizza or Chinese food. Instead, she'd ended the day with a simple peanut butter sandwich and a glass of milk. She'd even offered to make him one. Of course, he'd refused. He wanted nothing from her, or any female for that matter, even something as insignificant as a peanut butter sandwich.

Michael scowled and paced across his bedroom floor. Seeing Rae Lambers standing in the foyer of his father's house had brought the past roaring back like a bad dream, a dream that he hadn't been able to block from his mind since. The whole day he'd run the stereo full blast as he'd cleaned the parlor, the study, and the sunroom, trying to blot out his thoughts, but even a good dose of classic Led Zeppelin hadn't kept the goblins at bay.

He brought the whisky glass closer to his nose and breathed in the sweet smoky fragrance laden with overtones of peat. Each time he smelled the fine single malt, he thought of his high school days, and how he had turned the anger he felt at his father's withdrawal from his life into a weapon. He used the anger to make him hard, to win games, to jump higher, to shoot longer and more accurately, as if to say to his father, "Too bad you won't see this, you bastard!"

Sometimes he even visualized Rae watching him playing, awed by his ability and speed, just as he was awed by her academic achievements. He had never stopped competing with her, even though she had abandoned the game long ago. And whenever he saw her name in the school paper or someone mentioned her in passing, he felt the pang of loss, as if a valuable teammate had deserted his squad.

Every game he played, Michael would look for Rae's face in the crowd, knowing he would never see her, but always hoping one day she would come forward and tell him she'd been wrong about everything, that their friendship meant everything to her. But she had never come crawling back, and he had been too proud to approach her. And so their high school days had ended.

Then there had been his mother. His mother never lost the chance to criticize her ex-husband, which only fueled Michael's anger. There had been no presents, no letters, and no phone calls from his father. By the time he graduated from high school, he had become closed off and silent, wholly focused on getting out of town. He accepted a full scholarship to a university in North Carolina and never looked back. But it was in college that his dreams began to fray.

As a junior, he'd had to face the painful realization that he would never be tall enough for an NBA career. What could he do? Basketball had been his entire focus all his life. On a lark, he enrolled in an architecture class and discovered he had a natural aptitude for seeing forms in space and translating them onto paper. The last two years of college, he had turned his powerful concentration on becoming the best architecture student in the department. And he had succeeded. Upon graduating from college, he was hired by one of the premier architectural firms in San Francisco, and had traveled all over the world designing huge glass office buildings and hotels.

But nothing gave him a feeling of success these days. He had come to believe that if he could accomplish a task, then it must not have been that difficult. Only an NBA career would have made him truly happy. And that was a happiness he would never know.

Now, almost divorced from his wife, not really a star in his chosen field, and back in Alameda forced to share digs with an old classmate who had spurned him, he felt as if he were being forced to start over, repeat the play, try a little bit harder. And he just wasn't accustomed to failure.

Scowling, Michael set the tumbler on his desk and looked down at the nearby drawing table where plans for the new development lay. Idly, he flipped through the layers, scanning the drawings for flaws, for problems. There were sure to be some, if his work were to run parallel to his life as of late. But he wasn't really mentally engaged with this project, not as much as he should be.

Unable to concentrate, he rubbed the back of his neck and ambled over to the computer in his makeshift office. He'd had such a beautiful office in the town home he owned in the Marina District of San Francisco. Correction—*had owned*. Vivian had probably already painted the second floor in that god-awful purple color. Correction—*aubergine*. She'd wanted kids, but he'd been too concerned about their swift courtship and shaky marriage to take a chance on extending their family. No wonder she'd called it quits. But in a way, he felt a sense of relief, for his life with Vivian had never felt right. Then again, when *had* his life felt right? Maybe a guy like him wasn't supposed to be married.

Michael moved the computer mouse to activate the screen and sat down to work for a few hours, at least until he was so tired he would fall asleep immediately, giving him less time to brood. Since the separation a year ago, during which time he'd lived in a cramped, lonely apartment, he'd had plenty of time to think—far too much time in fact.

But as he worked, he kept seeing Rae Lambers's face as she declared his father's writings to be valuable. She was one of the smartest people he'd ever met. Why had she allowed an old madman to bamboozle her with his far-fetched theories?

THE NEXT MORNING the phone rang and a female voice asked for Rae. Michael carried the phone to the study, where Rae sat hunched over a stack of papers.

"Phone," he said, holding up the handset.

"Thanks." She reached for the desk phone, and Michael noticed she flinched when she picked up the receiver. The cleaning frenzy yesterday must have left her with aching muscles. He had a few himself in his lower back.

"Hello?" Rae asked, her voice husky. "Oh, hi, Angie."

Satisfied that Rae's anal retentive friend from Friday night—that Simeon character—wasn't on the line, Michael turned from the study doorway and ambled to the kitchen to put the phone back in its cradle. The last thing he wanted was a visitor in the house. He planned to have a low-key day, put the final touches on his presentation for tomorrow morning, and turn in early.

He and Rae had made such great strides yesterday, setting to rights all the rooms on the first floor, that he decided to waste an hour reading the Sunday *San Francisco Chronicle* and have a second cup of coffee in the sunroom. He took an appreciative sip. He had to admit that whatever Rae did when she made coffee, she certainly had a knack for brewing a smooth pot of java. He clicked on the television set, found some golf to watch in the background, and picked up the business section.

Not more than fifteen minutes had elapsed before Rae appeared in the doorway of the sunroom. Michael sighed and lowered the magazine section. It was just like a woman to find a way to barge in on a man's private time.

"Yes?" he asked tersely.

Her gaze was directed not at him but at the television. "Turn it up," she ordered. "Turn up the TV."

He reached for the remote and obeyed her command, too surprised at the insistence in her voice to argue with her.

He glanced at the set. A fifty-something woman with silver hair and a black tunic was being interviewed, and she was holding up a card, a fortune-teller's card, if he wasn't mistaken.

" . . . something has begun," declared the woman being interviewed. "And it has something to do with the death of Thomas Gregory."

"Then you do not believe Dr. Gregory died of natural causes?"

"I am sure that he didn't."

"But you have no proof, other than the card you hold in your hand."

"It's all the proof I need." The silver-haired woman did not smile and her gaze was intense and full of intelligence. Still, Michael discounted everything about her because of the card she held in her hand. He had never put any stock in astrological signs, forecasts, or any of that other hocus-pocus crap. He gave a disdainful snort.

"I implore the authorities to exhume Dr. Gregory's body and perform an autopsy."

"When hell freezes over," Michael retorted to the television.

"And how do you propose the doctor died?" the reporter asked.

"I would venture to say his death involved an energy exchange."

"Energy exchange?" The camera switched to the reporter, a young black woman in a red suit and brightly printed scarf. "What do you mean by that?"

"Some kind of electrical zap, like being shocked."

"And why would you think that?"

"As I said," the gray-haired woman replied. "The card has indicated such a death."

The camera returned to the interviewer, who pivoted slightly in her upholstered chair. She smiled for the camera, and tilted her head. "It's all in the cards. And those are our latest findings in the unusual case of Dr. Thomas Gregory, the mysterious recluse of Alameda, California. This is Callie Cameron, reporting live from Rockridge for KSFB News."

"Mysterious recluse, my ass!" Michael shut off the TV with a forceful click of the remote. He jumped to his feet, angry that he couldn't spend a single hour without being reminded of his father.

"So the Typhon card isn't just in The Forbidden Tarot deck!" Rae exclaimed.

"What?" Michael wasn't following her train of thought.

"And that was Maren Lake!" Rae exclaimed, pointing at the greenish-black screen. "She's a person, not a place!"

"Maren Lake?" Michael glanced at her, still not getting a thing she was saying.

"The name in your father's Rolodex in the study. It was open to the name Maren Lake."

"You noticed that?"

"Yeah. It was such a weird card that it caught my eye. It was black. Do you think he tried to call her?"

"Who knows and who cares?"

"Don't you wonder what happened to your dad?"

"He's dead." Michael put the remote on the end table near the arm of the small sofa. "That's all I need to know."

"Don't you wonder what he was doing all these years in this house?"

"I *know* what he was doing—avoiding my mother."

"Michael, this isn't a joke!"

Amazed at her vehemence, Michael took a step backward. Did Rae actually care about his father and what had happened to him? And if she did, why?

"I didn't say it was a joke," he replied.

Rae let out a frustrated breath and glared at the television, as if she were thinking over something important and thinking about it hard. Then she took a deep breath and turned back to Michael.

"I think Maren Lake is right."

"What do you mean?"

"I think you should have your father's body autopsied."

"Why? So we can find out he is really, really dead? No chance. No way."

"Michael, think about it for a minute. What caused the fuses to blow in the house?"

Michael shrugged. "I don't know."

"Were you here when they blew?"

"No."

"When did you first come to the house?"

"Right before you did, on Friday."

"And the lights were out then."

"Yeah." Michael ran a hand over his hair as a cool shiver coursed through him. He tried to ignore the inexplicable prickle of unease and focused his mind on the search for a logical explanation instead. "Maybe the lights had been out for a while. Maybe the old man lived without power on the first floor. Eccentrics are like that."

"Not if his study was unusable. He was a scholar, Michael. He was involved in constant research. He would have needed light to read, to run his computer, to search the Web."

"So what are you saying?"

She crossed her arms over her chest. "Maybe something happened to him, just like that Maren Lake woman said."

"Bullshit, Rae. That was the biggest load of crap I've ever heard." He picked up the loose sections of the paper and threw them into a stack. "There is no way I'm going to dig up my father's grave because some wacko tells me he was electrocuted. Next thing you know, she'll be on the news claiming alien intervention."

When Rae didn't respond to his outburst, he glanced over his shoulder at her to find her looking toward the window, with the morning light outlining her sharp nose and chin as she stood there deep in thought. He'd never met a woman who stopped and thought like this one. What lay so heavily upon her mind?

"What?" he asked, knowing she wasn't done talking even though he was finished with the subject and more than ready to begin the day's work.

She bit her lip and glanced at him. He felt the disdain of her regard, as if she had just judged him and found him lacking. Lacking in what? What *was* it about him that she found so disgusting? He straightened, stung at being brushed off, especially by Rae. She had spurned him for the second time, and it hurt just as much as the day long ago. She looked back at the window.

"It's just that I've seen that card before."

"That fortune-teller card?"

"Yes. That exact same one. Typhon, the Devil."

"So what? A million people must see that card every day in carnival tents all over the world." His voice cut through the air between them. "Typhon the Devil. A dark evil man will come into your life. Woo-ooo." He wiggled his fingers in the air.

Rae whirled and glared at him, her arms stiff and her hands balled into fists at her sides. "Is everything a joke with you now?"

"Only the goofy stuff."

"Goofy? Can't you open your mind, just this once?"

"I don't see the point."

"You wouldn't!" She stormed toward the door to the hallway. "You don't care one iota about your father, do you? It's all about the house. No, it's all about you!"

He stared at her, unable to refute the truth.

"And by the way," she continued, her blue eyes blazing.

"My sister Angie needs a place to stay for a few weeks, and I told her she could come here."

"What?"

"It's one place her boyfriend would never think to look."

"And I care because?"

"She thinks he's out to kill her."

"Oh, great. More excitement. Just what I need."

"She'll be here tomorrow."

"The Lambers sisters. Both of them. Here with me." He mocked her. "How can a man get so lucky?"

She scowled at him, and for a fleeting moment he felt like a jerk. Then she turned her back on him and was gone, making herself scarce for the rest of the morning.

Michael felt the sting of her absence, but had no intention of making an apology. Rae had allowed herself to be deluded by the television program, and it was only a matter of time before she realized how preposterous it was to think his father may have been murdered. For crying out loud, the old man had been eighty-three years old. Maybe electricity had been involved. But the only electrical problem had been the failure of his father's heart to keep pumping.

Maybe the arrival of Rae's younger sister wouldn't be so bad. Angie might be able to convince Rae that she was wrong about his father. He could talk some sense into Angie, make her see the advantage of selling Rae's share of the house, thus making his life less complicated. Besides, if he recalled correctly, he remembered Angie as a great-looking girl, carefree and fun—the exact opposite of Rae. He could use some fun in his life about now.

# Chapter 6

On Monday afternoon Rae sat in the lecture hall, idly watching her Calculus I class as the students toiled over the final exam. As she watched them, her mind jumped from one dark corner to another. She mentally replayed the strange video made by Thomas Gregory, then dwelled on the news brief with Maren Lake, and then wandered through images of what Angie might have gone through with Brent that made her desperate enough to move to Alameda.

Apparently Brent hadn't forgiven Angie for taking the trip to Egypt and leaving him all alone. Angie had told her on the phone that Brent had even accused her of going on the trip with another man. Rae had volunteered to talk to Brent to tell him what had truly gone on, but Angie assured Rae it wouldn't make any difference. She had to get away from her boyfriend once and for all.

Rae scribbled a list of things she had to do that afternoon—get clean clothes from her condo, pick up Angie at the airport in San Francisco that evening, buy groceries, and purchase new bedding for Angie for the bedroom she'd cleaned out on Sunday afternoon. The day would be a long one.

After she made her list, she sat quietly, pen poised above her small notebook while she considered the idea of calling Maren Lake. The older woman obviously knew something about the tarot. Maybe she would know something about the Forbidden Tarot as well. Rae mulled over the pros and cons of coming forward. She wouldn't have to mention Thomas Gregory. And maybe, just by talking to Maren Lake and getting a feel for her character, she could find out if any connection existed between the psychic and Michael's father.

* * *

NOT UNTIL TEN o'clock that night did Rae and Angie arrive from the airport. Angie lugged her huge suitcase up to the door while Rae grabbed the three plastic bags full of groceries. The day had been busy, and she hoped Angie wouldn't want to stay up and talk.

As they swept into the house, Rae half-expected to be accosted by Michael and accused of more crimes against his family, but he was nowhere in sight. A lamp glowed in the living room and a light was on in the kitchen and main hall, but other than those small signs of humanity, all was quiet on the first floor. Maybe Michael was upstairs or out for the evening. Rae felt a sense of relief at his absence.

"The place doesn't look so bad," Angie commented, turning around in the foyer.

"That's because Michael Gregory and I worked our butts off this weekend."

Angie nodded and peeked into the shadowy dining room. "Lots of space," she said.

"It's a huge house. There's also a third floor and a basement. But I haven't been in them yet."

"No tours for me to the basement, thank you." Angie held up her right hand. "I hate old cellars."

Rae pushed the front door shut with her upper arm and propelled herself toward the back of the house.

"Hungry?" she called over her shoulder.

"No, but I could use something to calm my nerves. Got anything?"

"I bought some chamomile tea."

"I was thinking of something a little less herbal." Angie ambled across the black-and-white tile of the large kitchen and ducked down to look into the bowels of the built-in wine rack. It was empty.

"Shit," she said.

"What about a soda?" Rae put in.

Angie pulled open kitchen cupboards, looking for bottles,

and then drifted out to the dining room. She returned, rolling her eyes. "There's no alcohol in this house?"

"None that I know of." Rae kept her voice level. "You could take a look in the cellar, though."

"Oh, funny!" Angie pulled open the fridge. "Like I *would*." She pulled out a cola and twisted off the lid, and then proceeded to drink most of the contents in an extended swig.

Rae watched her. She was worried that her sister had been tipsy coming off the plane, even though Angie had sobered up considerably during the trip home. But the worry for her sister now mingled with a sudden glow of happiness that Angie had come to Alameda. No matter how rash and thoughtless Angie could be, she was still far better company than Michael Gregory. Maybe with Angie in the house serving as a buffer, she and Michael wouldn't go for each other's throats quite as much. Then again, maybe anger and bitterness were the man's constant companions and nothing could help the situation.

She was also glad to be able to offer a haven to her sister. So many times during her childhood she had wished for such a place to go—somewhere to run to for help and understanding. That's why she volunteered in Oakland—to give a hand to young women who were in the same predicament she'd been in.

Then the thought struck her that she could make the Gregory house not just a home for Angie and herself, but for troubled young women like those she helped once a week. She could offer them space for classes, for clinics, for study, and in a building that was beautiful and inspiring—a true escape from their tattered lives. Such a haven could have a powerful impact on a young girl. It could inspire her to want more, to seek the tools to change her life, and then achieve her dream.

Rae heard Angie burp.

"Want one?" Angie asked, holding up the glass bottle.

"No thanks." Rae stuffed the bread into a drawer and stacked tins of tuna in the cupboard above. Angie lived on tuna and salad. She watched her younger sister drink the rest of her pop. Though Angie might laugh and smile, she could not hide the lines of care and disappointment that hovered around her pretty mouth.

"So what about Brent?" Rae began, slowly ambling toward Angie. "Does he have any idea where you've gone?"

"I don't think so. I told him I was going to see my friend Julia in Connecticut."

"That's good."

"He knows you live in Berkeley, but that's it."

"Do you think he will try to come after you?"

"Not really." Angie threw the pop bottle in the trash. "That would require spending time and effort on his part. And money. Get real!"

Rae thought back to the succession of husbands their mother had taken on throughout her difficult life. Every one of the men had been just like Brent—smooth-talking, easy going, and not overly interested in keeping a job. Why hadn't Angie learned from their mother's mistakes and their traumatic childhood?

Yet, on second thought, Rae realized Angie's experience had been quite different from hers. She had been the golden child, the kid everybody liked, the girl kept safe from her stepfather by another's sacrifice. Yes, Rae had known a far, far different world than Angie. Her adolescence had solidified her opinion of men and marriage forever. She would never indulge in either one. Only fools set themselves up for heartache and financial disaster.

Rae snapped out of her thoughts. "What about your things?" she asked. "Did you just leave everything at your apartment?"

"For the time being. I didn't want to raise Brent's suspicions. If I decide to move out here permanently, I'll just get new stuff. All I had was pretty much junk anyway."

Rae thought of her condo and the few belongings she had collected. She would never leave her household goods behind. Her few hard-won possessions meant a lot to her. In the kind of environment with which she surrounded herself, she was again unlike her sister. She knew she was overly careful, as Angie had reminded her in Egypt. Maybe she was even stuck in a rut. But she would never be a risk taker like Angie. Such a life would drive her crazy.

Rae looked up from her musings to find Angie gazing at her, the corners of her mouth curved into a small smile. "And don't worry, sis. I won't mooch off you. I already have a lead regarding a job in San Francisco."

"You do?"

"At Nordstrom. Remember my old roommate Suzanne? She works there."

"That's great, Ange."

"So there." Angie tossed her hair over the shoulder. "I'm not as helpless as you think I am."

Not until she found a new loser, Rae thought. But she turned away before her sister could notice her expression.

"Let me show you your room upstairs. Then I have to correct a few papers before I go to bed."

"Okay." Angie followed her out to the main hall.

"Is there cable in my room?" Angie inquired as she lugged her heavy suitcase up the wide stairs.

"No. Sorry." Rae did a quick mental assessment of the house. "In fact, I don't think there's a TV except the one in the sun room."

"Are you kidding me?"

"I could bring mine from the condo."

"No cable!" Angie wailed as Rae opened the door to the room across the hall from hers. "I'll go through withdrawal!"

"Sorry, Angie. There are lots of books to read, if you need something to do."

"I'm not *that* desperate." Angie drifted past her, into the bedroom, and looked up at the ceiling and then all around. "Rae, this bedroom is humongous!"

"Isn't it?"

"And that wallpaper. Wild!"

While Angie dropped her suitcase onto the bed, Rae walked to the center of the bedroom. A green and lavender floral print covered all four walls and was trimmed by the dark original woodwork of the 1880s. Like most of the house, the bedroom hadn't been updated for decades. She wouldn't even try to guess the age of the Persian carpet on the floor, but recognized the high quality of the weave and the expert craftsmanship. The only change Rae had made to the room was to dress the bed in green and put new lavender towels in the adjoining bathroom, which Angie was now exploring.

"Oh, look!" Angie squealed, pointing at the bathtub. "An old-fashioned claw-foot tub!"

"I thought you might like this room." Rae smiled at her sister's obvious delight. "I think this might have been the master bedroom."

"I'm going to take a nice long bath and read my magazine."

"Okay. See you in the morning then?"

"What time do you get up?"

"Six-thirty."

"God, I'm not getting up then!" Angie walked back to her suitcase. "When do you get home from work?"

"Around five, I hope. It's finals week, which is always a bit unpredictable."

"I'll see you at five then. Maybe we can go out to dinner."

"Great." Rae headed for the door.

"And what about Michael Gregory?"

She stopped in her tracks. "What about him?"

Angie pulled a robe out of her suitcase. "Didn't you say he's been living here, too?"

"I thought he was. He was here all weekend."

"Didn't you ask him if he was going to live here or not?"

"No, I didn't." Rae put her hand on the doorknob. "It's difficult to have a normal conversation with the guy."

"Why?"

"Because he's turned into a real—pardon my French—asshole."

Rae saw Angie's expression shift into a mischievous smile and her gaze raise to an object beyond Rae. It was then

Rae felt a presence behind her and caught the light scent of a man's aftershave. Michael had slipped up behind her as she was talking about him. She was mortified.

Rae stood frozen, her back to the door, resenting his sneaky tactic and the way he had allowed her to rattle on.

In the ensuing awkward silence, Michael stepped around her and passed through the doorway. "You must be referring to me," he quipped.

"I was." Rae was too angry to apologize or make excuses for her opinion of his character.

"I've been called worse," Michael retorted, holding out his hand to Angie. "Hi, there. Michael Gregory."

"I remember you, Mike. I'm Angie." She shook his hand and did her trademark little sway toward him that never failed to pique a man's interest. Michael's gaze ran over her tall, shapely body and long legs.

"You haven't changed a bit." He lifted Angie's hand and gave her a slow twirl and an equally slow perusal.

"Why, thank you!" Angie's eyes flashed at him, and Rae felt the old invisibility descending upon her again. She could slip out of the room, walk downstairs and no one would notice her absence, she was certain of it.

"I'll leave you two to get reacquainted," Rae announced, pivoting on her heel.

"Night, sis."

"Good night, Angie."

Michael didn't say anything. Rae counted herself fortunate.

RAE CROSSED THE hall to the room she had claimed for herself in the front tower. She'd always wanted to live in a tower, and though this chamber was shrouded by the tall pine trees outside, she liked the privacy they afforded. She felt as if she were living in a tree house, surrounded almost entirely by the wide arc of windows made of curved glass too expensive to be used in modern construction. She could look out the windows to the street below, fairly certain that no one could see her if they looked up at the house. She especially enjoyed the way the morning sun filtered through the windows on one side of the tower and the afternoon sun streamed through on the other side at the end of the day.

Rae exchanged her shoes for slippers and then scuffed her way over to the secretary by the fireplace and turned on the lamp. She could hear the faint laughter of Michael and Angie across the hall, so she closed her door and slowly returned to the desk. Unlike the feminine master bedroom with the flowered wallpaper, this room was done in a more somber hue of maroon with a subtle taffeta pattern stamped into the paper. Her hearth was not made of pale green marble like the one in Angie's room, but was tiled in garnet-colored ceramic tiles fired to a high gloss and topped by a walnut mantel. Rae's favorite features of the room were the two hand-carved griffins whose wings supported each end of the mantel. The detail of their fierce faces was amazing.

Never in her life had she slept in such a grand room, and she decided at that moment, standing there at the century-old desk, that she would live here the entire summer if she could come to an agreement with Michael. And if she could somehow raise enough money to buy him out, she would transform this house into a haven for troubled young women.

But that was a conversation for tomorrow. Tonight she had a stack of tests to correct.

AFTER STAYING UP working until two in the morning, Rae dragged herself to her office the next day, where she greeted Connie with a wan smile.

Connie looked up from her computer. "Tough night?" she asked.

"Long tests," Rae replied. "Long, disappointing tests. It's like my students forgot everything from the beginning of the quarter."

Sympathetic, Connie nodded. Then she pointed to a covered paper cup sitting at the corner of her desk. "I got you a latte."

"You did? You're a saint!"

"I thought you might need one."

"Remind me to get you a merit raise." Rae opened her office door and put her briefcase on her desk. She sat down at her computer to check her mail, and remembered she'd left Dr. Gregory's CD in her computer drive. She shouldn't have taken such a chance, leaving it lying around for anyone to see. But before she tucked it safely into her purse, she decided to watch the video again, to see if she noticed anything new, now that she had learned Thomas might have been killed in his study and not just succumbed to natural causes.

Sipping her latte, Rae turned down the volume so Connie wouldn't be able to hear the video and played the clip again. The part that struck her after watching it a third time was Thomas's reference to their conversation about the Rosicrucians.

Rae frowned as she ejected the CD and snapped it into its case. Their chat about the Rosicrucians had been the last conversation they'd had, after she'd found a mathematical link between the beliefs of the Rosicrucians and those of the Egyptians. She had called Thomas about it, hoping he could recommend additional resources for her book research, and they spent nearly two hours talking on the phone. He had made the CD quite recently, no more than two months ago.

The Rosicrucians were a secret sect started somewhere in Europe in the seventeenth century. What was Thomas trying to tell her in his reference to them? She slipped the CD jacket into an inner section of her bag and turned back to her computer to search the Web for information about the sect, in hopes she might find something that would link it to whatever Thomas had discovered in Egypt.

She found plenty of facts, such as that the mysterious society was known as "the Brothers of the Rosy Cross" and was severely attacked by the Roman Church and others. Apparently early followers traveled the world incognito, healing the sick and spreading their esoteric knowledge to those deemed worthy enough to receive it. In an online encyclopedia, she found a description of the Rosicrucians as a society devoted to the subject of alchemy. But an entry on the Web page of a supposed member of the society warned against assuming all Rosicrucian alchemy was performed on physical matter and claimed the Rosicrucians focused most of their attention on mental or spiritual alchemy. There were even texts that mentioned rites where initiates underwent tests, including being put to death and revived again, through the power of alchemy.

Rae shivered, wondering how many initiates had "mysteriously" disappeared over the centuries when things went wrong during the alchemic revivals. But as she pondered the literal translation of the word *Rosicrucian*—red cross—she sat back and mentally scanned through her many conversations with Thomas Gregory.

For years, Thomas had been researching various societies which were based on ancient and mostly non-Christian tenets, and which were almost entirely derived from the Egyptians and the Chaldeans, and passed on by the schools of Pythagoras and other ancient Greeks. All of the organizations which embraced this ancient knowledge were persecuted by the Catholic Church, their members often tortured and executed as grisly examples of what would happen to those involved in heresy, forcing many of the societies to go underground and swear their initiates to secrecy.

He had told her of the Freemasons, the Illuminati, the Rosicrucians, and the Followers of the Temple of Set, all of whom closely guarded their beliefs and swore their acolytes to secrecy. She remembered well how Thomas became so frustrated with trying to find material on these ancient societies because their rituals and lore were forbidden in written form for fear the information would fall into the hands of nonbelievers and those would hunt them down and kill them. Thus, not much more than their history, always tied to the religion and politics of the day, could be found.

On the night Rae had called Thomas about the Rosicrucians, he had talked heatedly about the Holy Grail and a new theory he had come up with about a centuries-old search. He had followed up their chat with an e-mail, which was still on her computer's hard drive.

Rae bent to her keyboard and typed *Holy Grail* in the find box of her e-mail program. She took a gulp of her latte while she waited for the results to show up in the window.

Quickly she scanned through the beginning pleasantries to the meat of the e-mail.

. . . and I have come to the conclusion that man is on a quest, Miss Lambers, but now I'm not so sure the quest is allegorical—and by that I mean simply a quest for knowledge. Perhaps the quest is something more, a search for a physically tangible object.

Do you remember the knights of old who searched for the Holy Grail? Are you aware that even today, experts aren't certain what the Holy Grail was? Was it a chalice that held the blood of Christ? Was it the bloodline of Christ? Or was the Holy Grail a mere figure of speech, symbolizing the search for faith, something man found within himself only after experiencing a harrowing journey that taught him the real meaning of life? Was the quest for the Holy Grail an inward or an outward journey?

I propose, Miss Lambers, that there existed in medieval Europe, and still exists today, an opposite to those brave knights, an opposite force we have been told nothing about, a force whose existence has been covered up and the knowledge of which has been withheld from the common man. Think about it. In our world there is always an opposite to everything. It's the first law of physics. For every action there is an opposite and equal reaction. There is right and left. Sun and moon. Day and night. Up and down.

What if these ancient sects, so set upon by the Christian Church, were also searching for something—but opposite in every way to the Holy Grail? But if they did not search for the Holy Grail, if not for Christian faith, then what? The opposite of these things? What is the opposite of faith? And I don't mean the absence of faith. I mean the opposite of faith. And suppose for a moment they searched not for a red cross but a red sword? What would that sword represent? And why red? Is it for letting the blood of Christ? The hacking to death of Osiris? Could the sword represent a search for an Antichrist?

Though I may shock you with this concept, my dear Miss Lambers, let me ask you to consider something else. Perhaps the Antichrist sought by this opposite force is not as evil or as heinous as we have been led to believe.

We have been lambs for centuries, we Westerners. Most of us have been led to slaughter for so many years that we have ceased to question anything we are told. But wouldn't you agree that some leaders of the church have made a practice of deluding the common man, of withholding knowledge and bending the Gospel to serve a temporal kingdom, to conquer enemies, to steal property and wealth from indigenous peoples in the name of the Almighty? What if all we have been told is just one side of the story?

*Chapter 7*

Rae reached for her coffee cup without breaking her gaze from the computer screen. Thomas may not have known it, but this e-mail contained the major epiphany of the old man's life, a culmination of countless hours of research and the sacrifice of his family. She continued to read, drawn in even more now that he was dead, and searching for clues as to what might have happened to him.

. . . Suppose for a moment the red sword was found before the Holy Grail. Would the world as we know it be thrown into chaos? Would violence and war dominate the earth? What if the sword fell into the wrong hands? What if it fell into the right hands? What is its power? How would a person discover its power when there is nothing to be found on the subject? Or would it come to pass as in the legend of Arthur Pendragon that the rightful owner of the sword will pull the weapon from the stone and wield it for the good of humanity?

But who is the Arthur of our time, Miss Lambers? What path does he take? Does he follow the sun or the moon? How do we define a good person, a moral person, in this tumultuous age of ours? And how can we judge in fairness if we suspect the church has withheld information all along and suppressed a truth they did not want man to discover, leaving us with only half the evidence from which to make a decision?

Rae sat back in her chair, deep in thought. When she had read this e-mail the first time, she had assumed Thomas was asking rhetorical questions. But now that he was dead and she had seen the video he'd made, she wasn't so sure. Thomas obviously had believed he was protecting something all those years, and he was so worried about it that he refused to leave his home. The poor old man! Had he found something in Egypt, something he felt he could not show another living being because he didn't know whom to trust? Had he found the red cross of the Rosicrucians and the Knights Templar?

Her mind buzzing with possibilities, and not recalling the rest of the e-mail, she turned her attention to the final paragraph.

It is because of the brilliant text which you allowed me to read that I write this to you, Miss Lambers. I believe you understand the skill and mental acuity it would take to make a discerning decision about such a discovery, since prior knowledge of ancient objects and religions may be too skewed to be of service regarding this matter. In your manuscript you wrote of three ways of seeing the world: through faith of the heart, through logic of the brain, and through that special sight of the spirit, which you defined as soul vision.

Rae nodded to herself. She'd done months of her own research on the subject, which paralleled much of the investigation Thomas had conducted and involved the teachings of many different cultures. She had given him the part of the manuscript that would never be allowed in her mathematical treatise, the part that had begun to fascinate her, to lure her attention from its proper focus. She had given the section to him to read, anxious for his review, and fully aware that his eyes would be the only ones to ever read it.

In the separate nonmathematical manuscript section, she had focused on soul vision, the voice within every human being that tells them what is right for them and only them and has nothing to do with facts and figures, morals, religious tenets, or common sense. It simply is. Where it springs from cannot be proved. How to measure it is unknown. But if a person is truthful with herself and confident of facing the consequences, she can hear the soul vision speaking. It cannot be taught, and can only be fully developed through experience and self-knowledge.

Rae purported in her text that those who knew themselves thoroughly and possessed the courage to live their lives augmenting faith and logic with the power of soul vision became the greatest sages on earth.

But as soul vision could not be measured or proved or even taught, Rae could never include the section in her book. She only half-believed the theory herself. But Thomas had been convinced she was on the right track. The last line of his e-mail confirmed her research as nothing else could.

I believe, Miss Lambers, that a long-time practitioner of soul vision is the only person who will be able to recognize the truth and to decide how to go forth.

The night she had called Thomas, he had never divulged the fact that he had discovered an actual object. And at the time, she had not been as certain as she was now that Thomas had hidden something within his mansion in the Gold Coast, something for which someone had completely ransacked his house and perhaps killed him. But in the aftermath of such violence, had the murderer found what he was looking for?

Rae shivered, knowing she should get rid of the e-mail. For the first time since coming back from Egypt, she wondered if she could be in danger as well, for knowing too much about Thomas's obviously delicate subject.

She clenched her jaw and pressed the delete button.

For a long moment she sat in her chair, her vision blurring out of focus as she considered her next step. She realized she was now in the same predicament Thomas had been in, having found something in Egypt that she knew nothing about but at the same time was afraid to ask anyone about.

She switched programs back to her browser and used a

search engine to look for the words *Forbidden Tarot*. The search results came up with nothing. She tried another search engine and then another. Nothing.

BY THE TIME Rae left the university for the day, she was still so upset from reading the old e-mail that she couldn't keep her mind on her driving and almost pulled out in front of a package delivery truck on the way home.

"Get a grip!" she mumbled under breath. As she drove through the Posey Tube, headed for the island, she realized she was in no mood to talk to anyone, especially her chatty sister, whose entire conversational repertoire was comprised of the latest movies, the list of actors and actress involved in marital upheavals, and any personal problem she had at the moment. Rae expected they would spend most of dinner discussing Brent. And if she knew her sister, she could predict that by the time dinner ended, Angie would be defending the creep.

Rae glanced at her watch. It was four forty-five. She had time for a brisk walk to clear her head. And even if she was a few minutes late getting home, Angie would be none the wiser. She was likely watching television anyway.

Rae looked up, and saw there were plenty of places to park near Alameda High School, her old alma mater. She guided her Jetta into a parking space, locked her car, and headed out for the old familiar streets of her youth.

The late afternoon was balmy and a mockingbird sang high in a tree, and Rae tried to concentrate on the peaceful street ahead of her where gardeners were busy trimming the hedges and mowing the lawn of a huge Dutch Colonial. But Rae could not clear her mind. She walked for blocks and blocks, knowing she would probably regret the joint pain in the morning. Finally, when she knew she had gone far past the twenty minutes she'd allowed for her respite, she headed back to the school, this time around the rear of the complex on Oak Street.

It was a path she'd rarely taken as a kid, as numerous sport courts bordered the sidewalk, and she never liked passing by boys who might throw taunts at her. As an adult she had no such worry and strode forward. As she walked the tree-lined street, she could hear a group playing basketball—the muffled grunts, the rattle of the backboard, an occasional sharp cry of victory, and the tight thud of the ball as it was dribbled back and forth. A deep voice rumbled under the higher calls of the boys, and she guessed that a coach or a father was watching the play and giving advice.

As she passed the huge oak tree near the chain-link fence, she caught sight of a tall, black-haired man standing behind a slight boy of fourteen or so. She watched him adjust the kid's stance and angle of his shoulders in regard to the basket. Then he pointed at the net and said something to the boy, who giggled, which sent ripples of movement down his spare frame, as if his bones were loose. But when the boy tossed the ball into the air, he sent the orange globe sailing high and true, and it plunked through the net without touching the rim. The kid whooped and jumped into the air, and gave the black-haired man a high five. The man turned, and it was then Rae caught a glimpse of his face.

She was astonished to see the coach was Michael Gregory. And she was even more astonished to see him laughing. The last thing she would have imagined him doing was wasting his time playing with a group of kids, and even more so taking the time to teach them the fine art of shooting a basketball. As she stood there at the fence watching him trot back and forth along the court, she suddenly felt like a trespasser, witnessing something private that belonged only to him. Hoping he hadn't seen her, she stepped back and briskly walked to her car around the corner.

Seeing Michael as a teacher instead of an asshole was enough to alter her mood. Rae drove to the house, ready to face a few hours with her sister. She decided one defense against the underbelly of American cinema would be to talk to Angie about establishing a resource center for girls. Maybe she could get Angie interested in a good cause and off the negative aspects of life.

* * *

WHEN RAE RETURNED to the house, she was surprised to find a huge bouquet of purple irises waiting for her on the coffee table in the living room. Angie showed them to her and urged her to open the little envelope held aloft by the prongs of a plastic stake.

"Have you ever got flowers like this before?" she asked. "I haven't! There must be a hundred of them!"

Secretly pleased and guessing who had sent them, Rae reached down and plucked the envelope from the holder. She opened it and read the message out loud.

"'My dear Fay Rae,'" it began. "'Pardon my silence of the last few days. I have been busy finding a suitable place to live. I would love to show it to you. Would you join me for dinner Wednesday night? I will pick you up at seven. Eternally yours, S.'"

Simeon had found a place to live? Did that mean he intended to stay in the Bay Area for a while? Why?

Angie craned her neck to see around Rae's shoulder and get a glimpse of the small back-slanted handwriting on the card. "S?" she teased with a grin. "Eternally yours?" She tilted her head. "Why, Rae, what have you been keeping from me?"

"Nothing." Rae felt a flush of heat in her cheeks. She stuffed the note into the pocket of her slacks. She wished Angie had not seen the flowers, not seen the note.

"Nothing?" Angie stepped closer. "A man sends you a thousand flowers and you don't even tell your own sister about him?"

"I didn't have a chance, with all that trouble about Brent."

"So who is he?"

"A guy I met on the plane from New York."

"Really?" Angie tried to hide her scathing glance of disbelief, but she wasn't quick enough to fool Rae.

"He knew Michael's father. We kind of hit it off."

"He's not a nerd, is he?" Angie glanced at the flowers. "He doesn't seem like one, but—"

"He's as far from a nerd as they come."

"Well!" Angie gave a little laugh. "I'm glad for you, Rae. I really am."

"Thanks." Rae bent to the flowers and inhaled deeply of the soft powdery scent. These were not the hothouse Japanese variety of iris, but the real thing—luscious velvety bearded iris. She plucked one out of the bunch to take with her upstairs, and slowly turned toward her sister.

"Angie," she began. "This one time, just this once I'm asking you, don't move in on this guy."

Angie's pretty features screwed into an expression of disbelief. "What?"

"You know what I mean." Rae hated the fact that she always stood in the shadow of her more beautiful sister, hated the inevitable moment when Angie appeared and every man forgot Rae existed. She hated even giving voice to the fact, knowing that to recognize the trend was to admit to her own lack of female allure. "Don't make a move on Simeon." She looked up at her sister, aware that her gaze was as grim as her intent. "He's mine."

"Fine!" Angie retorted, giving another little laugh. "Jesus, Rae! Like I'd try to steal him!"

"You know what I mean," Rae repeated, knowing it would be best to change the subject. "I'm going to put on some jeans. I'll be right back."

As she walked up the stairs to change, she realized the import of what had just transpired. She had claimed a man for herself. How unlike her! But Simeon Avare was unlike any man she had ever met and was certainly unlike any of the men her mother had brought into their lives. He had manners. He had money. He had drive. Maybe there was a chance that Simeon would be a positive influence on her life, not a negative one. He deserved to be given a chance. And she deserved some happiness.

Rae rushed to her room and closed the door, willing Angie to stay downstairs and leave her alone. She buried her nose in the fragrance of the iris again and walked to the bathroom, where she took a good hard look at herself in the mirror.

Her cheeks were still flushed, giving her more color than usual in her pale face. She ran the fingers of her left hand over the gaunt line of her cheek, wishing she had the soft supple skin of her sibling. How many men had kissed Angie's cheek, her lips, her neck? Rae touched all three points on her own skin and closed her eyes, trying to imagine what the warmth of a lover's mouth might feel like, and willing away the memories of the desperate pawings and threats she'd known at the hands of her stepfather. Even now, the effort it took to keep the old darkness at bay brought a sweat to her skin, making her feverish and chilled at the same time.

Then a second image burst in unbidden, that of Michael's young face drawing down to hers, his dark eyes intense and full of hunger, his hands clamped around her arms, the blue dress tangled between her legs.

"Not you!" she heard herself cry. "Not you!"

Rae jerked, dashed the memory from her mind, and desperately sought her reflection again to prove she was no longer a girl.

Rae nailed her gaze to the mirror and saw the serious stare of her reflection. Did she appear that worried and hard to other people? To Simeon? If so, why did he pursue her? Did he consider psychotic women a challenge?

And her hair. So lackluster. So thin. Rae gently placed the iris on the counter and looked back at the lank blond strands hanging to her shoulders. She pulled back the side portions of her hair, revealing the narrow bony oval of her face and the easily seen tendons of her long neck. Her jaw jutted out on both sides of her throat, like that of a wooden marionette. She grimaced at her reflection. She was an emaciated freak. No wonder Angie couldn't believe a man had sent her flowers.

She let her hair fall back around her face and let out a slow sigh of resignation. She was all hardness and angles, but there was nothing she could do about the way disease and pain had ravaged her body. She would never be like her sister. She would never be like other women, soft and luminous and beautiful. If Simeon were ever to come to care for her, he would have to love her the way she was.

\* \* \*

THAT EVENING AT dinner at a local Mexican restaurant, when Rae brought up her idea of turning the Gregory house into a safe house for teenagers, she was surprised at Angie's reaction.

"Rae, I don't think you should even consider it."

Shocked, Rae held a bite of chimichanga in front of her mouth. "Why not?"

"Mike says the house needs a lot of work."

"So?"

"He says it isn't worth the powder to blow it up." She frowned, seemingly confused, and leaned forward. "Do you think he meant pressed or loose powder?"

"He meant gunpowder, Angie."

"Oh." She took a sip of her diet Coke while Rae watched her, wondering just how much Michael had talked with her about the house and why. "I thought it was kind of weird, what he said . . ."

"Don't listen to him." Rae shook her head. "He's just trying to devalue the property."

"Why?"

"He wants me to sell my portion to him." She stabbed another bite of chimichanga. "And probably for far less than it's really worth—the bastard."

"Well, I don't see why you shouldn't sell to him, Rae. I mean, think of it. It's tough enough living with a guy and trying to get along with him when you think you're in love with him. It would be crazy to try to keep a share of the house and deal with Mike, especially when you think he's such an asshole."

"I don't *think* he's an asshole, I *know* he is." Rae lifted her own glass of soda while a vision of Michael playing basketball in the schoolyard came back unbidden, undermining what she'd just stated. But she didn't say anything. She took an agitated sip and shut off the image.

"He says the roof is bad, Rae, and the foundation is unsound."

"They can be repaired."

"But where would you get the money?"

Rae looked down at her meal, which was covered with a thick blanket of melted cheese. Her stomach turned, both at the sight of the heavy layer of cheese and the reality of her bank account. Where *would* she get the money to fix the house? Even more, where would she get the money to buy out Michael Gregory? The mansion had to be worth over a million dollars. She would need nearly three-quarters of a million to buy him out and fix the house, and that didn't include the hefty mortgage she'd have to pay. That kind of money did not come easily to an assistant professor.

Angie sighed. "I know you love the old house, Rae, but look at it this way. If you sell your half to Mike, you could walk away with enough money to buy a decent house of your own, just like you always wanted."

Rae nodded glumly, knowing Angie's words were logical and sensible. But she didn't want just any house. She wanted the one at 506 Chilsholm Avenue.

WHEN ANGIE AND Rae got back to the house after dinner, Angie announced she was going to watch television for a while. Rae left her to her own devices and climbed the stairs. When she got to the top, she noticed light streaming through the open doorway of Michael's bedroom. Rae paused, her feet and knees aching from her long walk around the Alameda High School neighborhood and her stomach feeling uncomfortably heavy with the meal she'd just eaten. All she felt like doing was taking a warm bath and falling into bed, but she had unfinished business with Michael Gregory.

Even though Rae had no idea where she would get money to fund a center for young women, she still had to talk to Michael about the house. Though arguing wasn't her idea of a pleasant way to end the day, she forced herself to turn her steps in the direction of his room.

Michael sat at a large table near the window, hunched over a piece of foam core board which he was busy cutting with an art knife and a metal ruler. She couldn't help but notice how long his fingers were, how slender his wrists, and how carefully he scored the paper. Before him on the table was a three-story model of a building, which he was constructing with the art board. It was obvious he was so enthralled with his task that he hadn't heard her in the hallway, and she didn't wish to startle him. Rae waited until he was done with his cut and then knocked on the woodwork.

He turned his head, still holding the tools in his long, slender hands, and the only greeting he made was to slightly arch his right eyebrow to question the interruption.

"May I talk to you for a minute?" Rae asked.

"I'm busy."

"You always are."

"I'm a busy man." He lowered the tools to the table.

"It's about the house."

"What about it?" Michael turned in his chair, never asking her into his room. Then he crossed his arms over his wide chest, and by the looks of his body language, Rae knew she was in for another confrontation. How could she have once considered Michael Gregory her best friend?

She rose to her full height, thinking that if she were a dog, she'd raise her hackles as well, to make her look more powerful. She hadn't thought of how she was going to approach Michael, but looking at his scowl, she knew she'd better get to the point quickly.

"I just wanted to let you know that I intend to stay here for the summer," she said. "In the house."

"Why? I thought you had a condo somewhere."

"Yes, but this place is quieter. More conducive to writing. I need to finish a book during summer break." She kept her gaze steady, refusing to be bullied by his increasingly stormy expression. "I also wanted to know what your plans were."

"My plans? To have you sign the buyout papers as soon as they get here."

"I'm not going to do that."

"Oh, yeah?" He rose, probably to try to intimidate her further. "Why not?"

"Because I don't want to. I don't want you to tear down this place. I want to preserve it."

"It's old, Rae. It needs a lot of work."

"But I love it. And I have plans for it."

"What do you mean, plans?"

"I want to turn it into a center for young women—at least on the bottom floor. A place where kids I know can come if they need help, or advice about family planning, or tutoring, or anything like that. I can retain living quarters on the second or third floor."

Michael rolled his eyes and looked up at the ceiling.

Rae refused to let him throw cold water on her dream. She stepped into the room. "The house is in such a perfect place. It's near the high school. It's near that old folks' home. I could have older people volunteer to help the kids—" She took a deep breath, hoping her words would convince him. "It would help both generations."

"Nice dream, Rae," Michael retorted. "But I can't afford to donate this place to the community."

"I'm not asking you to donate it."

"You are if I don't sell this place at a hefty profit. The divorce will wipe me out financially."

"What if I bought you out at a decent price?"

"You?" He swept a scathing glance over her. "Where would you get that kind of money?"

"I don't know yet."

"Well, let me tell you something, Rae. I'm in the property development business. And right now, it's pretty bleak out there, especially for a project like yours. You'd have to get a grant from the government, and you'd have so many hoops to jump through because of the nature of dealing with young kids that you'd be crazy to even think of starting a project like that."

"I don't care. It's what I want to do."

"Well, I can't stake my future on your dream, Rae. I've got retirement to think about, and probably a pretty stiff alimony settlement coming up, if I know Vee."

Rae clenched her jaw and sank her weight against the doorjamb. How would she and Michael ever settle this property situation? Thomas had been cruel to bequeath them half a house each. She looked at the floor, and the polished wood grain swam before her eyes as she caught herself tearing up in frustration. But she refused to let Michael Gregory see her cry. She willed herself out of the emotional lapse, which was a strange occurrence for her, and took another deep breath.

"Okay," she said, raising her glance to Michael, who stood in the center of the room, his arms still crossed, but his expression not quite as dark. She hoped he hadn't noticed her moment of weakness. "What about this? If you find a developer first, you get to buy out my half of the house. If I find the money, I get to buy yours."

"Rae, you don't know what you're getting yourself into."

She stood up straight again, resenting his condescending tone. "Do you agree or not, Michael?"

He stared at her, rubbed the back of his neck, and then heaved a sigh. "Okay. Why in the hell not? You're never going to get a grant. And if you do, it'll take months to find the money."

"You're awfully sure of yourself," she retorted, now the angry one.

"I know the development business."

"But I'm still staying here for the summer."

"Fine." He picked up his ruler. "You buy the groceries. I'll pay for the rest."

"You'll be living here, too?"

"What do you expect me to do, live in my car? Vee has the Marina District house until our divorce is final."

"When is that?"

"October first." He reached for the art knife. "By then we should also know which one of us will be the sole owner of this place."

He turned his back and Rae guessed she'd been dismissed. She frowned at his lack of manners, which he never wasted a chance to display.

"Good," Rae replied to his back. "I'll mark my calendar." She turned to leave.

"Good," he called after her, just to have the last word. "I'll throw you a going-away party."

Rae fumed as she retreated to her room across the hall.

# Chapter 8

Though Rae had no more scheduled classes for the quarter, she headed for the university earlier than usual in the morning so she could work all day and leave a little early to get ready for dinner with Simeon. On the way she picked up two coffees and some Krispy Kremes, knowing Connie had a weakness for doughnuts. When she arrived at her office, she found Connie just arriving.

"Hi, Dr. Lambers," Connie greeted, glancing down at the box in Rae's hand.

"Hi. I brought you a little reward for all your hard work," Rae said, holding out the carton.

"Oooh." Connie grinned. "Krispy Kremes!"

"All different kinds."

"Thanks!" She opened the box while Rae turned to unlock the door to her office. "Want one?"

"I might just have one." Rae peered into the box. "I like the plain ones, myself."

"I like the filled ones." Connie took a big bite and chewed happily as she reached for the coffee. "You know, I keep forgetting to tell you about a book I'm reading for that zoology course I'm taking—"

"Yes?"

"It says that scientists are studying the effects of bee stings and snake venom on people with autoimmune diseases. Have you ever tried venom to see if it would help your arthritis?"

"No." Rae took a sip of the piping hot coffee. "But I've heard of the treatment."

"Would you ever consider trying it?"

"It's too new for my taste, especially when no one knows what long-term side effects are involved."

"Yeah, and who wants to let a snake bite them?"

Rae had to smile. "I'm sure the venom is extracted first, Connie, and then administered through a syringe."

"Probably, but, ooh"—she shuddered—"just the thought of it gives me the creeps."

"Me too." Rae picked up her coffee cup. "Well, I should get to work. I have a huge pile of exams to correct, and I hope to get out of here early today."

"Anything exciting going on?"

"Well, as a matter of fact, that gentleman you met last week—Mr. Avare—has invited me to dinner at his new house."

"Really?" Connie wiggled her eyebrows and grinned. "Way to go, Dr. Lambers!"

Rae fought down a blush.

"What are you going to wear?" Connie replaced the lid on the box of doughnuts.

"I don't know. My wardrobe isn't exactly centered on dates with handsome men."

"There's that new mall in Emeryville. Maybe you could stop there on your way home and get something slinky and sexy."

"Good idea."

Rae slipped into her office and tried not to think about the night to come. She didn't have anything appropriate to wear, at least nothing besides her little black dress, and Simeon had already seen it. Yet on second thought, how sexy did she want to dress? Was she ready for an intimate dinner with a man? Tonight Simeon might try to go farther than she wished to venture. Was she ready to tell him no—to tell him yes? What would happen if he tried to kiss her? Would she be able to handle it? Or would she run off, frantic to get away? The familiar cold sweat broke out. Disturbed, Rae reached for the stack of Calculus II exams and pulled off the top one, her hand trembling and her stomach suddenly in a knot.

But as she stared at the exam in her hand, she realized just how silly she was acting. She was a grown woman, for heaven's sake. She could handle herself and Simeon Avare. He wasn't the type to force himself on a woman. If she said no, he'd back off. And she wouldn't say yes until it felt right to her, really right.

Rae refused to agonize over Simeon or her wardrobe. It was silly and a waste of time. Instead, she focused on the work at hand. Soon she forgot all about the upcoming evening, and spent the day at her desk, only getting up a couple of times to use the restroom, grab some lunch, and counsel two students who were worried about upcoming fall classes. By the end of the day, she'd corrected the entire stack of exams, and congratulated herself on making excellent progress. As she finished writing her comments and the score on the last exam, she glanced up at the clock on the wall, horrified to discover it was five-thirty.

"Oh, God," she gasped. She'd completely lost track of time. At this late hour, traffic would be horrendous on the freeway. She wouldn't have time to do much with her hair. She would be lucky to have enough time for a quick shower.

Connie stuck her head into her office. "Good night, Dr. Lambers. Have a nice time!"

"Thanks."

"Don't forget," Connie grinned. "Sexy and slinky!"

"Right." Rae saluted her with a red pen.

SEXY AND SLINKY. Sexy and slinky. Rae sped through the back roads from Berkeley to Emeryville, and parked her car in front of the new row of stores just opened a few weeks ago. She hurried into a store for young career women, told the clerk what she wanted the outfit for, got a backup slacks and shirt just in case, and then raced back out to her Jetta without trying anything on.

By the time she pulled up in front of the Gregory house, it was six-fifteen. She swore under her breath, grabbed her bags, and rushed up the front steps, her knees crying out in protest.

She met Michael coming down the stairs as she hurried upward, greeted him courteously, but didn't even look at his

face as she went by. Then she took a shower, closing her
eyes as the hot water soothed her aching joints and forcing
herself to calm down. She decided to take her time. If
Simeon arrived before she was ready, he could have a nice
glass of iced tea or something. Surely Michael would entertain him while he waited for her to come downstairs.

After her shower, she slipped into the parchment-colored
silk skirt and shell, elegantly simple but casual enough for a
summer evening. As she was brushing on some blush, she
heard a man's voice at the front door. Simeon was right on
time. Quickly, Rae dried her hair, pulled it up into a loose
ponytail, found the pounded brass bracelet and earrings
she'd purchased in Egypt, and slipped her bare feet into a
pair of tan sandals. She didn't even take time to check herself out in the mirror. Mirrors had never been her friend anyway. She hoped her shoulders didn't look too scrawny, but
didn't wish to see proof one way or the other.

MICHAEL HEARD RAE'S step in the living room doorway and glanced up, surprised to see her in a dress, and even
more surprised to see her wearing makeup. She looked
totally different from the waif who had slaved away the
entire weekend cleaning the house with him. The outfit she
wore, some whitish ankle-length flowing thing, and a little
pair of strappy sandals, made her look, well . . . feminine—
especially when coupled with her neat unpainted toenails.
And the look on her face, that little half-smile on her lips as
she gazed at Simeon Avare, was equally feminine and vulnerable. There wasn't a single calculating gleam in her eye.
Her throat and shoulders were the most delicate things he'd
ever seen, and he caught himself staring at her, thinking how
fresh and happy she looked, and how startling was the
change in her.

"Fay Rae!" Simeon exclaimed, rising to his feet and holding out a hand to her. "You look marvelous."

"Thank you."

Michael saw her flush with pleasure. Rae actually
flushed. Amazed, Michael shook his head and stepped back

to allow Avare to stride past him. He hadn't seen an honest reaction in a woman in years. The women he'd known had always been so sure of their beauty, they didn't need a man to say anything. But of course, they wanted to hear compliments anyway, just so they could brush them off. Rae had actually thanked Avare for the comment.

Michael watched Avare kiss Rae's hand. He called her Fay Rae? That was too much. The man was too much. And the flowers. Just a little overboard for Michael's taste. He thought back, trying to remember the last time he'd bought Vee flowers. It had to have been more than five years ago. She'd brushed them off too, as he recalled, as if a dozen red roses were too commonplace for words. He'd thought all women loved red roses.

He glanced at the huge bouquet of purple flowers Rae had received. Hell, he didn't even know what kind they were. But apparently they'd made a big impression on Angie and Rae. Not that he had any intention of ever buying flowers for Rae. She'd probably throw them in his face and follow them up with the vase.

Still, he didn't like Avare, even if the man did know the kind of flowers women liked. Michael didn't trust him. Never had and never would. There was something about the guy that warned him he would do something to douse the hope shining in Rae's eyes, and that would be a shame. Though Rae was a thorn in his side at the present and had caused one of the deeper wounds in his past, he didn't want her to get hurt. It was plain to see she didn't have much experience with men, and it was equally obvious that Simeon Avare had been around the block a few times.

"YOU HAVEN'T BEEN waiting long, have you?" Rae asked, glancing from Simeon to Michael.

"Not at all," Simeon assured her. "And Mr. Gregory graciously provided me with an excellent glass of chardonnay."

"Chardonnay?" Rae repeated, her good mood snapping.

"Want some?" Michael asked, turning at the sound of someone coming in the front door.

"Where did you get chardonnay?" Rae demanded.

Michael shrugged. "I thought you had bought it."

Just then, Angie appeared in the doorway of the living room, her cheeks flushed, her hair piled on her head, and dressed in a pair of running shorts and a tight-fitting top that showed a good portion of her trim midriff.

RAE WATCHED ANGIE pause in the center of the wide doorway, as if allowing both men to have time to take in the full impact of her brief but very sexy outfit.

"Have I missed the party?" she asked, smiling her bright white smile that lit up the room as well as her face.

"Not at all," Simeon answered, and Rae saw his glittering regard take in the sight of her tall, healthy, beautiful sister. She had asked Angie not to move in on her territory, and yet all Angie had to do was walk into a room and the men were hers. It wasn't her fault. It was just the way she was made, and the way men responded to her.

"I'll get you and your sister a glass of wine," Michael said, heading for the hallway.

Rae clamped her lips together, deciding not to bring up the issue of Angie's drinking in public.

"You must be Angela," Simeon began, making sure Rae knew he wished to be introduced.

"This is Simeon Avare, my friend from the plane," Rae said, motioning toward him. "And this is my sister, Angie. She's visiting from the East Coast."

"You're the flower guy!"

"Indeed."

Angie flowed forward, the smile still lighting her features. They shook hands, and she swayed one hip toward him in her provocative manner, breaking her promise to not flirt with him. In fact, she didn't release his hand right away, and held it between her own. "I hope you know Rae's been keeping you a secret, Simeon."

"Has she?"

"She never even mentioned you until those beautiful flowers showed up."

Rae pressed her lips together again, embarrassed to hear Angie spout such personal information and jealous that her sister was still touching Simeon. She put her hand on Simeon's forearm. "Maybe we should go," she suggested.

"Oh, don't be such a spoilsport, Rae!" Angie released his hand and pointed at the goblet of wine on the coffee table. "Simeon hasn't even finished his drink yet."

"But what about dinner?" Rae asked.

"Don't worry." Simeon patted the back of her hand. "We are not eating until later in the evening. Relax." He motioned toward the couch behind them, and Rae felt obligated to sit down so she wouldn't appear rude. A moment later, Michael breezed back into the living room with two more glasses of wine, one of which he gave to her. She set it down next to the irises.

Gracefully, Angie sank onto the wing chair, crossed her shapely legs, and took a sip of her white wine. "Rae tells me you have bought a place."

"Yes. In the Piedmont area."

"Really?" Michael remained standing near Rae's end of the couch. "That's a pricey part of town."

Simeon crossed his slender legs, as graceful and as elegant as Angie. He sat back, not overly quick to defend his choice of neighborhood and taking his time to reply, which defused Michael's tart remark. "It is quiet there. It suits my needs."

"I would have thought you'd buy a place in San Francisco."

Simeon shook his head. "I am not overly fond of bridges, Mr. Gregory."

"And the Piedmont area! I love the Piedmont area!" Angie exclaimed. "There are so many big old houses up there! Do you have a view?"

"Yes, I do. And it is especially charming at night." Simeon held his goblet in one hand and draped his slender fingers over his wrist. "In fact, if you would like to join us for dinner—both of you—I would be delighted to show you my new home."

"You are moved in already?"

"Of course."

Surprised, Rae turned to him. "Did you already have your belongings stored here in San Francisco?"

He smiled. "Some, but I have other homes as well."

"You're not staying in the house yet, I take it," Michael interjected.

"Of course I am. I have fully furnished it already."

"Since last week?" Rae asked, surprised even more.

"Of course." Simeon turned to her again and smiled warmly. "When you know what you like, it does not take much time to acquire it. It's all about knowing yourself, Fay Rae, and then choices can be made swiftly."

His gaze showered her with heat that permeated her bones. On the surface, he spoke of household furnishings, but was he not speaking metaphorically of much more? And he was still connecting with her on that inner level, even though Angie had joined them with her provocative clothing and her equally provocative smile. Rae glowed inwardly, realizing Simeon had not abandoned her.

Then he turned his engaging gaze back to the other two. "I repeat, I would be most gratified if you would join us for dinner."

"I would love to!" Angie said, jumping to her feet, even though Rae drilled her with a death stare. Angie totally ignored her.

"Excellent," Simeon purred.

"I'll throw on a pair of slacks and be right down." Not once did she glance at her older sister.

"What about you, Mr. Gregory?" Simeon asked.

Michael glanced at him and then at Rae, and seemed to pick up on Rae's agitation. He threw a dark glance at Angie, who was already halfway to the front staircase.

"Thanks, but I have to prepare for a meeting tomorrow."

"Perhaps some other time, then."

"Sure. Yeah." Michael took a drink and frowned. For a brief moment his gaze bored into Rae's, and for the first time since she'd returned to Alameda, she felt as if he were aware of what she was feeling, that she didn't want Angie going anywhere with them, that she didn't want her sister cutting in on her private time with Simeon. Rae looked away, somewhat taken aback. She hadn't expected Michael to notice or to care about her feelings anymore. This sudden view of him, coupled with seeing him play basketball with the kids, was enough to make her rethink her initial impression of him as hard and overbearing.

WHEN THE THREE of them finally left the Gregory house, they found a sleek black limo waiting for them at the curb. As soon as Angie realized the car belonged to Simeon, she turned to him. "Should I have dressed up?"

"You are perfectly fine," Simeon replied. "It is but a simple dinner we are having."

"But the limo—"

"Only because I do not drive."

"You don't drive?" Rae asked, as the chauffeur opened the door for her.

"I prefer not to. Driving puts me into a state of mind that I choose to avoid." He motioned the young women into the vehicle.

"Wow!" Angie ducked into the car and gracefully slid along the seat. Her long, slender limbs looked right at home in the luxurious car. Rae sat to one side and was glad when Simeon joined her, his knee touching hers. Instantly, she felt at ease. What was it about this man that had the power to soothe her physically as well as mentally? He made her feel like a partner and not the third wheel she had always been in her life.

The driver apparently knew which way to go, but as he drove up Grand Street, he turned right, and Rae looked around, perplexed.

"It would be faster to go through the Posey Tube at this hour," she commented, referring to the underwater tunnel to the mainland.

Simeon patted her thigh. "Perhaps, but I prefer to take the High Street bridge."

"I thought you didn't like bridges," Angie countered.

"I don't. But I like underwater tunnels even less."

"I'm with you." Angie gave a little laugh. "Think if there was an earthquake when you were in the tunnel! What would a person do?"

"Exactly."

THE LIMO GLIDED through traffic as the three of them talked idly about San Francisco earthquakes and the history of the area. Before Rae knew it, they were pulling into a driveway that formed a semicircle in front of a sage-colored Italianate house with a large round portico in the front. Gas lamps burned on columns at either side of the steps, and lights shone through all the front windows, casting a homey glow into the deepening indigo of the summer evening.

"Very nice," she murmured, as Simeon reached for her arm to guide her up the walk.

"Do you like it?"

"It's beautiful!"

"Wait until you see the view."

He led her and Angie through the front door and down a hallway that split the house into two equal parts. The hallway led to a set of French doors that opened onto a huge piazza.

"Oh, my God!" Angie exclaimed, flowing out the doors onto the slate of the piazza. "Oh, my God!"

While Simeon poured champagne, Rae sucked in a deep breath of wonder as she beheld the splendor of the sun going down behind the rooftops and hills of San Francisco. From the hillside on which she stood, she could see three bridges—the San Mateo Bridge, the Bay Bridge, and the Golden Gate—all twinkling with streams of white and red from the traffic moving across them. The sky glowed lilac and cerulean behind Telegraph Hill and Coit Tower, deepening to a teal color on the horizon. She had never seen anything so grand.

Simeon gave a glass of champagne to Angie and then one to Rae.

"It's lovely," Rae breathed, glancing up at Simeon, to find him looking down at her, drinking in her reaction.

"I thought you might like it," he replied, putting his arm around her shoulders in a gentle embrace. She let him pull her close. In fact, she allowed her head to tip ever so slightly into the small of his shoulder.

"Do you think you would ever get tired of a view like that?" Angie asked, turning around to face them, and leaning upon the balustrade.

"Never," Rae replied.

"There is always something new to find in the oldest of things," Simeon added. "Life is about appreciation, about truly seeing. And nothing remains the same if you really look. Nothing."

Rae glanced up at him. She had never met anyone like Simeon Avare. And the more she knew of him, the more she wanted to learn.

Angie crossed her left leg over her ankle. "So tell me," she began, gazing at him over the rim of her delicate goblet. "When you're not out on this patio, what do you do for a living?"

"I come from old money," he replied, his arm still draped around Rae's shoulders, "which I take care to invest wisely."

"Then what do you do for fun?" She winked at him. Rae wanted to wring her neck.

"Fun?" He gave a low laugh. "I collect things. I travel. And occasionally I do a good work."

"You mean charity work?"

He nodded and reached for the remaining wine glass which he had set upon a nearby table.

"Really? Because Rae and I had an idea about turning the Gregory house into—"

"Angie!" Rae broke from Simeon's embrace, embarrassed that Angie would bring up her money woes at a time like this, and upset that Angie had presented the project as partly her idea, when she had been dead set against it the night before.

"Let her finish." Simeon touched Rae's forearm. "What were you saying, Angela?"

"Rae and I thought it would be a good thing to turn the Gregory house into a place for young women to go—you know, like a crisis center."

"A resource center," Rae corrected.

"Where they could get help. You know for math and birth control, adult advice and stuff like that."

"That sounds like a wonderful plan."

"The only thing is, Rae doesn't have the money."

"Angie, this is not the time to discuss the center." Rae blushed. "Please pardon us, Simeon."

He smiled at her. "No apologies necessary, Fay Rae. I think it's a marvelous idea."

"Would you contribute?" Angie stepped closer, pressing him with a provocative smile.

"I would consider it, yes."

"That would be great!" Angie grinned and stooped down slightly to look into her sister's eyes. "See, you only get what you ask for, Rae."

"But we can't ask for his help. I'm sure Simeon has extended himself with the purchase of this house." She glanced up at him, providing him a graceful way out.

"I never overextend myself," he commented.

"But you do understand the scope of such a project?"

"How much would it cost?" he replied.

"Over a million, and that's just a guess. I haven't really crunched the numbers. It could be more."

"Then crunch the numbers and let me know." Simeon winked at her. "We can come to an arrangement."

"You could be a partner," Angie continued, eager now that he had agreed. "You could sit on the board!"

He nodded and lifted his goblet. "Then partners it may be."

"Are you serious?" Rae fell back so she could see his face. He seemed perfectly lucid and calm, as always. "You would help fund the center?"

"Of course, Fay Rae." He smiled warmly. "It would be a fitting memorial to the man we both admired. We could call it the Thomas Gregory House. How does that sound?"

Rae gazed at him, amazed at how wonderful this man

was, but still not entirely trusting him. He was too good to be true. Yet she wanted to believe in him, she wanted him to be as good as he appeared at that very moment. A warm wave of love and appreciation washed over her.

He held her glance for a brief moment and then looked toward the house. "But enough talk of charitable projects. Let us have an appetizer, and then I will show you the rest of my home."

AFTER HORS D'OEUVRES of duck liver and guava jelly on crisp rounds of toast, Simeon took them on a tour through the house, making sure Angie's champagne flute was never empty. Rae made a mental note to have a chat with Simeon about Angie's unhealthy penchant for alcohol. It would be better for all concerned if he were less generous with the bubbly. Rae rarely drank, and never when she was taking any pain medication. But since meeting Simeon, she hadn't taken a single pill, so she allowed herself a few sips of his excellent champagne while she strolled around on his arm.

Each room Simeon showed them was fully furnished, complete with artwork on the walls, and not just prints but original paintings, mostly landscapes done in oils. Rae was impressed by his taste, and wondered how much money the man possessed to be able to buy a house and furnish it so completely in such a short amount of time. He'd even mentioned owning more than one residence. The guy must be a billionaire.

Returning to the ground level, Simeon opened a door near the bottom of the stairs and paused.

"And this, ladies," he said, motioning them inside with a flourish, "is my pride and joy."

*Chapter 9*

R ae ambled into the room, the champagne flute forgotten in her hand, as she took in the display surrounding her. All four walls were covered with velvet-lined cases fronted with glass, containing Simeon's extensive weapons collection, from very early arrowheads of flint to the most delicate rapiers. In the center of the room he'd placed a bench upholstered in red velvet, which Rae assumed Simeon must sit upon when gazing at his prizes.

Barely aware of the other two people in the room, Rae slowly padded around the perimeter, looking at the weapons, and reading the little brass plates attached to the frames of the display cases. "Obsidian arrowtip, Washington State, USA." "Medieval iron spearhead, 11th Century, Germany." "Ceremonial Mayan knife, 10th Century, Mexico." Then she came to a wavy-bladed dagger, unlike anything she had ever seen before. "Kerambit, 14th Century, Malaysia," she read out loud. Then she turned to Simeon.

"What is this one?"

Simeon stepped close behind her. "It is a dagger from Indonesia, also known as a *lawi ayam*," he explained.

"What was a knife like that used for, with such a rippled blade?"

"It was a ripping weapon. Women often carried small versions of these upon their bodies or in their hair."

Angie wandered closer. "Better than mace then?" she asked.

"Much more deadly." Simeon answered, turning back to gaze at the weapon. "The making of such knives was full of ritual, as the Malaysians believed that every *keris* possessed a protective spirit. One must be respectful of such a weapon."

"Oh," Angie said, dutifully admonished.

Rae continued to inspect the collection as Angie drifted along the walls of the room as well. She was soon back to making jokes about several of the pieces, commenting that she would hate to meet a man in a dark alley with one of *those*. Or that club looks like something an Oakland Raider fan would love to add to his costume. Simeon did not react to her comments, and Rae wondered if the comic treatment of his treasured collection had offended him. She glanced over her shoulder and was startled to find Simeon staring at Angie, his gaze fastened upon her, not in anger but in intense concentration, an expression more hard than she had ever seen upon his face. As soon as he felt Rae's regard, however, he broke his gaze and gave a small laugh.

"I confess," he said, "to a certain helpless fascination for these ancient items. They consume me."

"They must be worth millions!" Angie interjected, although Rae was sure Simeon hadn't been addressing her.

"Oh, they are priceless," he replied, "especially to me."

"The thing you mentioned to me the other day"—Rae glanced at him, watching his eyes—"the item Dr. Gregory was going to give you before he died. Was it a weapon?"

Simeon's silver gaze flared, but only for a fraction of a second before he caught himself. "Weapons are what I collect."

"Do you know if it was a dagger? A spear?"

"Why? Have you found something at the house?"

"No." Rae shook her head. "But if I did, I would know to tell you."

"Perhaps I may help you in the search?"

"Sure." She smiled at him, but felt uneasy. If Thomas Gregory trusted no one, she should be wary of everyone as well, even Simeon Avare. "But I warn you, there are dozens of crates and boxes. It will be some task!"

"It would be a labor of love, Fay Rae. Truly."

"Well, then, when my schoolmarm duties are over and I have time to start cataloging, I'll let you know."

"Excellent." He glanced at his watch. "I see that it is nine o'clock. Shall we go in to dinner?"

He turned to take Rae's elbow, and she allowed him to guide her out to the hall. But all the way to the dining room she kept seeing that unsettling look in his eyes when he'd been staring at Angie. She must have mistaken the direction of his glance. Maybe he'd been looking at a weapon on the wall behind her and not at her sister. She wanted to think that—for his sake and for her own.

LATE THAT EVENING, the limo took the two young women back to Alameda, and most of the way home, Rae idly listened to Angie's jabbering about what they'd eaten, what they'd seen, what Simeon had been wearing or had said. Angie had been totally impressed with the man, but the more she carried on about him, the more angry Rae became.

"I thought you promised to keep away from him," Rae put in sourly.

"I did!"

"Oh, come off it, Ange," Rae glared out the window. "You were flirting with him the entire evening."

"Yeah, but look where it got you! He's going to help with the center!"

"That I will believe when he signs on the dotted line."

"Jesus!" Angie shifted in the seat. "What's with you, Rae? Don't you trust anyone?"

"No."

"Not even Simeon?"

"Not even Simeon."

"But he's different from other guys."

"Oh?" Rae leveled her gaze at her sister. "In what way?"

Angie shrugged. "Well, he has buckets of money for starters."

"Maybe."

"And he's so genteel!"

Rae turned her gaze toward the lonely streets of Oakland passing by the window of the limousine. "He is that."

"And he seems to like you, Rae. A lot."

And that's the part Rae didn't understand. Why would an independently wealthy world traveler with a beautiful body be interested in her? She wouldn't give voice to her doubts, especially in the presence of her sister, but she'd been thinking about that exact question the entire evening. She wanted very much for Simeon to genuinely care for her, but she must not delude herself. No man had ever looked at her twice. Except for Michael, and he hadn't really been a man then. Why would Simeon pursue her?

After a few minutes of silence, Angie leaned forward. "Are you mad at me, Rae?"

"Yes."

"For taking Simeon up on the dinner invitation?"

"What do you think?" Rae snapped back, especially grouchy now that the light effect of the champagne and the soothing company of their host were swiftly wearing off. "How many times do you think someone has asked me to dinner, Angie? I'm not like you. Men aren't breaking down any doors to get to me."

"But I thought—"

"You didn't think, Angie." Rae reached for the handle of the door as the limo eased up to the curb. "Why don't you try it for a change? Why don't you grow up?"

Without waiting for the driver to help them out of the car, Rae opened the door and walked quickly toward the house. The porch light was on, and the foyer glowed, welcoming them home. She tried the front door handle and was glad to find it unlocked so she wouldn't have to stand there with Angie waiting behind her. Without pausing to turn on any more of the lights in the house, Rae stormed up the shadowy staircase and hurried to her room.

Just as she opened the door to her bedroom, she saw a movement out of the corner of her eye and paused as Michael Gregory ambled halfway across the hallway and stopped.

"What's with you?" he asked, a half-smile on his lips.

"Nothing." She turned back toward the door.

"Turf war?" he added, stepping closer.

"You could call it that." She looked down at the floor, not wishing to encourage any more questions as her feelings about Simeon and Angie were still raw. She pushed her door open a crack, to show her intent to withdraw.

"So what's the score?"

Rae gave a wry smile at his dark sense of humor. She glanced at him over her shoulder. "Blondie, nine. Not-so-blondie—oh, probably four and a half."

"Ouch!" His black eyebrows rose.

Rae shook her head and sighed. "I'm used to it."

"Well, it's her loss and your gain." Michael stepped closer. "The guy's a creep, Rae."

"And you know because . . . ?" Her voice trailed off, as she waited for an answer.

"It's a vibe I get from him."

"A vibe. That's really scientific." Rae reached in and turned on her light. "Goodnight, Michael."

"Hey, wait a minute." He put his hand out, preventing her from closing the door. "There's something I need to show you."

She turned to face him. "Look, Michael, it's really late and I—"

"You'll want to see this." He indicated something back in his room.

Rae studied his expression, not trusting Michael any more than she trusted Simeon, but all traces of his former smile were gone from his face. He'd probably found a crack in the wall that made razing the house the only alternative.

"It will only take a moment," he added.

"Okay." She dropped her purse on the floor inside her bedroom door and followed his tall lean figure into his bedroom, where they had argued the night before. He walked to his worktable and turned.

"I was working here after you and Angie left earlier this evening, but all I kept hearing was a drip, drip, drip sound that started to drive me nuts."

Rae nodded, only half-interested, and feeling tired after the long day and the emotional strain of competing with her sister.

"So I go into the bathroom, and I see that not only is the faucet dripping but the basin is half-full of water."

Rae put a hand on her hip. "So far, this is pretty darn exciting."

"Wait. It gets better." He held up his hands to stop her from interrupting with her premature doubt. "So I find out the drain is clogged. I get a bucket and some tools, and I'm inside the cabinet trying to maneuver when I see something taped on the underside of the counter."

"What?"

"There was a plastic bag with something inside it taped under the counter." He reached behind him to his worktable and slid a large manila envelope into his left hand. "This."

Rae's fatigue vanished. "What is it?"

"See for yourself." He gave the envelope to her.

She opened it, and pulled out a small stack of eight-by-ten photographs. "What are these?"

"Looks like shots taken at a dig to me. See what you think."

Rae walked to the powerful lamp clamped to the far corner of Michael's worktable and bent over to hold the photos under the light. Slowly she inspected the first couple of shots as Michael hovered behind her, looking over her shoulder.

"It looks as if he discovered a tomb," Rae murmured.

"For an awfully small mummy," Michael put in. "Look at the size of the sarcophagus."

Rae studied the black-and-white photo of the barren room in which stood a box made of dark stone, and by the looks of the worker standing near it, the box was only about four feet long, as Michael had noticed.

"And look at the sarcophagus itself," Rae murmured. "I've never seen anything like it!"

"What do you mean?"

"You know what the Egyptians were like."

"Not really." Michael shifted behind her. "I couldn't tell King Tut from Cleopatra—and I'm keeping it that way."

Rae brushed off his remark and continued. "The Egyptians buried their pharaohs and noblemen in splendor. Everything they constructed was covered with paintings and designs, even the corridors leading to the chambers themselves. But look at this."

She indicated the bare dark walls.

"I see your point. It's plain."

"I can't tell what the sarcophagus is made of. Looks like some kind of stone." She flipped through various views of the sarcophagus, shown at different angles. Most of the photos were of very poor quality, grainy, and badly illuminated. Whoever had taken these shots, and she guessed it had been Thomas Gregory, was far from being a professional with a camera. Before she had looked through the entire stack, Michael interrupted her.

"But that's not what I wanted you to see." He reached for the photographs and she relinquished them to him. He shuffled through them, intent on the task of locating a particular image.

As Rae watched him, she experienced a startling wave of déjà vu. Suddenly she was back in algebra class, sitting next to Michael, and he was bent over his desk, scrawling madly on a paper, his left hand curled around in that awkward position most lefties write, his every thought focused on the problem he raced to solve.

She remembered that version of Michael fondly. She remembered the way his eyes would glow when he'd finished the hardest problem before she did, and then eagerly wait until she arrived at her own answer. And then they'd compare. They'd argue. They'd work out the best solution. There had been no egos involved, no hidden agendas, no sexual undertones. Just pure enjoyment of the moment.

They had shared a love of math, of quick thinking, of challenges, even of words—just as they were sharing this moment of discovery.

Rae felt a sharp shaft of love for that old Michael spear

through her, and the residual ache the loss of that love caused whenever she thought about him. She missed his friendship. She had missed it for twelve long years. And not until this moment, standing next to him, hearing his eager voice, and watching him race for an answer, had she realized just how much she had missed him. A lump burgeoned in her throat.

"Rae?" He nudged her arm, bringing her back to the present. "Have a look at this."

She couldn't speak. She couldn't look at him. Without saying anything, she took back the stack of photos while she wrestled with her self-control. The photo blurred before her eyes. He still even smelled the same: clean and fresh and slightly musky. If she could just close her eyes and go back to that day, she'd say everything differently, respond differently, and make sure he knew what he meant to her on every plane but that particular one.

How could she have been so frightened of Michael—the friend she had loved for years? Why hadn't she explained how betrayed she felt by the way he had so thoroughly violated their friendship? Yet she hadn't possessed the words or the sense to explain such a concept, not at sixteen years of age. She hadn't been able to grasp all the implications of it herself, not until she was an adult. But even more than that, far worse than his betrayal and her lack of communication skills, was the fact that she had been cruel to him. Wildly cruel. Undeservedly cruel.

"Rae? Hello? Are you on the planet?"

"What?" She brushed back her hair, struggling to keep from crying.

"Look at the photo. What do you see?"

Rae bent closer, squinting through her blurred vision. This photograph was not of the inside of the tomb, but the outside. At the base of a cluster of ragged palms, three men dressed in baggy khakis posed for the camera beside a dusty all-terrain vehicle. Rae recognized Thomas in the picture even though he was much younger than she'd ever seen him, simply because he bore such a strong resemblance to Michael.

"Wow," she murmured. "Your father must be thirty years old there."

"What would you say the year is?" Michael asked, crossing his arms.

"Oh, looking at the truck, the clothing, and your dad, I'd say sometime around World War Two. The forties?"

"That was my guess. Probably right after the war." Michael pointed toward the third man. "Now look at that guy. Take a good look."

Rae raised the photo closer to the end of her nose. She hadn't even noticed the third man, as she had been too distracted by the way Thomas had looked as a young man. Now, turning her gaze to the person on the end, a slight man of medium height wearing a scarf tied jauntily around her throat, she let out a small gasp.

"Look familiar?" Michael inquired.

"He looks like Simeon."

"That's what I thought." Michael stood back with a triumphant expression on his face.

"So what are you saying?" Rae glanced at the photograph again and then back at Michael.

"I'm saying there is something fishy about that Avare character."

"And a photo proves it?" She felt resentment rising in her and used it to flush away the painful memory she'd just experienced. She might allow herself her own secret concerns about Simeon, but she wasn't about to allow Michael to criticize him.

"Think about it, Rae. The guy's in a photograph from the nineteen forties, and he looks exactly the same today!"

"So you're saying he's a vampire? An immortal?"

"No!"

"What are you saying then, Michael?"

He rubbed the back of his neck and glared at her. "I'm not sure. I just don't want him around, that's all! I don't want him in the house."

"Why don't you just come out and admit it?" Rae lowered the photographs to waist height. "You're jealous of him!"

"Jealous, hell!" Michael's nearly black eyes flashed at her. "Why would I be jealous?"

"Because of me."

"You?" He raised his chin. "Why would I be jealous of you?"

"I don't know." She crossed her arms, knowing the time had come for them to confront their pasts. "Maybe because of what went on between us way back when."

"So because I couldn't have you, no one else should either?" He planted his hands on his hips. "Is that it?"

She shrugged one shoulder. "Maybe."

"God!" Michael gave a sharp guffaw. "That's a laugh!"

"Is it?" She had intended to soften her approach, but his reaction to her question hurt her feelings, and her response came out more caustic than she meant it to be. Would they always rub each other the wrong way as adults?

"You think I think about those days?"

"Maybe." She let her arms fall to her sides, willing to put her pride on the line this time. "Sometimes I do."

"Well, don't bother. We were kids. Just crazy kids."

"Crazy, maybe. I know I was." She sighed and glanced up at him. "Look, Michael, I've been meaning to tell you something—"

"Don't." He held up a hand and shook his head. "I didn't ask you to come here to rehash old news."

"But I've always—"

"Rae, listen." He lowered his head to stare straight into her eyes. "I don't make it a practice to revisit the past, I am not jealous of Avare, and I don't care what in the hell you think of me or what kind of crazy ass psychosis you're carrying around in that head of yours. All I'm saying is that man in the photograph is Simeon."

"Michael, get real!" She held the photo up to his face. "That can't be Simeon!"

"It is!"

"It's probably his father. Just like that man on the left is your father, but anyone would swear it was you!"

Michael stared at the photograph, his color high, his dark

eyes hard, and his teeth clenched tightly. Then he let out a sharp sigh and turned away. "Fine. Good explanation, Rae."

"You always jump to conclusions, Michael. Have you noticed that? About Simeon, about me, about your father—"

"Don't bring my father into this!"

"You never give people the benefit of the doubt!"

"I only know what I feel," he answered, patting his stomach. "In here. In my gut. And my gut says Avare is a creep."

"Well, I like him."

"Then like him somewhere other than in this house."

He glared at her, two patches of crimson glowing on the tight planes of his cheekbones. Rae stared back, aching to say what was on her mind, to repair the damage that had destroyed their friendship. But she knew now that Michael would never allow such a conversation. He had made up his mind about her, and that was that.

Frustrated, she shook her head, amazed at how a simple chat with Michael invariably turned into a heated argument. Without another word, she turned and headed for the door.

"I don't want him here!" Michael called after her. "I mean it, Rae!"

Rae was so upset, she stomped to her room, slammed the door, and threw the photographs on the desk, not caring that some of them fluttered to the floor. Still fuming, she undressed, hung up her new clothes, and took a long hot shower, trying in vain to wash away the frustration and doubt of the evening.

THE NEXT AFTERNOON when Rae returned home from the university, she climbed the stairs to change, more tired than usual. She had spent a sleepless night. Her joints throbbed and her head ached. All she wanted to do was take a little nap. But as she slipped out of her skirt and loafers to change into a shirt and jeans, she heard Angie call her name. Rae wandered out of the closet, zipping up her jeans, to find her sister standing in the doorway.

"Hi," Angie greeted her sheepishly.

"What's up?"

"I just wanted to apologize, Rae." Angie stepped into the room. "For last night."

Rae nodded, still not willing to forgive her sister.

"I don't like it when you're mad at me."

"I'm not mad now, Angie. I'm just disappointed."

"Well, listen." She leaned over and picked up the photographs still lying on the floor. "I promise to stay clear of Simeon. I really do."

"That would be a step in the right direction."

"And I wanted to tell you I went in for that interview at Nordstrom today."

"You did?" Rae buttoned the cuffs of her light blue blouse. "How did that go?"

"They said I could start on Friday!" She did a little happy dance, running in place until her hair bounced.

"That's great!" Rae's bad mood lightened considerably. To get Angie settled and working would be the best thing for her sister. "Good for you!"

"Yeah, I'm excited!" Angie smiled and glanced down at the photographs in her hands. "So is this what Simeon was looking for?"

Rae looked up from her task of buttoning the front of her shirt. "What do you mean?"

"This sword." Angie held up the photo. "Is this what you were talking about last night?"

"Let me see that!" Rae grabbed the photograph. She hadn't looked through the entire stack of pictures last night, and had missed this particular shot. It showed a sword with a fairly plain hilt, except for a ruby in the center surrounded by a gold disk. She leaned closer, and could just make out a flame pattern in the copper-colored metal. Thomas had placed a ruler next to the item to show how large it was, and Rae estimated the sword was just over three feet long. Then she realized she was looking at a color photograph, obviously much more recent than the black-and-white shots she had looked at with Michael. Why was the picture of the sword hidden with the other older photos? She stared at the weapon in the photo as a chill prickled her scalp and swept down her spine.

"Rae?" Angie stepped closer. "You okay?"

Rae couldn't answer. She was too struck by what she was looking at. Was this the rosy cross, the sword of the Rosicrucians, the thing that Thomas had never shown to another living being? Had he kept proof of the discovery, but was so wary that he had to hide the documentation in a place no one would ever think to look?

"Rae, you're as white as a ghost. Are you okay?"

"Yeah," she murmured. "Yeah." She swallowed and nodded, and then glanced up at her taller sister. She didn't want to lie to Angie, but she couldn't trust her to keep a secret. She'd known Angie to blurt out sensitive information, not because she couldn't keep a secret, but because she couldn't keep her head. Rae knew she had to concoct a story that would prevent this new evidence from being shared.

"Don't tell anyone about this, Angie."

"Why?"

"Because I'm thinking of giving the sword to Simeon. But as a surprise. A thank you. You know what I mean?"

She grinned. "He'll be ecstatic!"

"I think he will. But until I give him the sword, you have to keep it a secret!"

"Where is the sword anyway?"

"In the house." Rae turned, wanting to be as vague as possible. "Where he can't find it." And that was the truth, unless someone had stolen the weapon already.

"This will be fun!" Angie exclaimed. "You won't give it to him unless I'm there, will you?"

"No, I'll make sure you're part of the surprise."

Angie looked around, once again perfectly happy with her world. "So, what about dinner? Want to go get a salad somewhere? I'm buying!"

"Sounds like a plan." Rae picked up her purse and carefully slipped the photographs into a side pocket, concealing them from curious eyes until she had a chance to hide them again. She followed Angie down the hall and down the stairs, barely able to keep her mind on where she was going or what she was doing. Her mind raced, full of thoughts of the rosy cross. Where could it be? Had someone found it? If not, where had Thomas hidden it?

She knew now that she had to search the rest of the house, and that meant this weekend she would have to tackle the attic and the cellar, neither of which she had any desire to investigate.

# Chapter 10

Shortly after midnight, and long after Michael had finished the last drop of wine in his glass, he stood up from his worktable and stretched, deciding to turn in. He switched off the light at his table and let his eyes adjust to the dark, allowing his mind to disengage from the project he'd been working on for the last four nights. Tomorrow was Thursday. He had a big meeting in San Francisco with the concert pianist who wanted a house designed around four grand pianos. He didn't like working with rich eccentrics. They were the absolute worst. But as a special favor to his boss, he had taken on this unusual client. Besides, he was weary of designing high-rise office buildings. He could do it in his sleep.

Michael padded through the shadows of his room and stood unbuttoning his shirt without turning on the lights. He let his gaze wander across the garden below where he'd once had a rope swing. The oak tree was still there but the rope was long gone, as were all traces of the little boy who had once lived here. Michael scowled. He had told Rae he didn't dwell on the past. Who was he trying to kid?

Michael was down to the last button on his white shirt when a sudden flash of light outside caught his eye. He took a few steps closer to the window and focused his eyes on the moving object across the way. Someone was out there. The light moved to the right, piquing his interest further. Was fashion diva Rae Lambers outside again in her dowdy nightwear doing midnight repair work? Or was somebody trespassing? He'd heard a lot of the island kids had joined gangs these days and spent many nights in deadly turf wars. Maybe these were the kids the police suspected of vandalizing the property.

Michael reached for the baseball bat he always kept in the bedroom where he slept, slipped down the stairs, and crept through the kitchen and out the back door. Soundlessly he picked his way across the weed-infested patio. Though his ears strained for a scrap of sound coming from the side yard, he couldn't hear a single human voice. What were the kids doing? Had they heard something? Were they waiting for him? Had they fled?

He paused near the huge oak tree and waited in the shadows. He saw the light again, and this time realized it was the reflection of the moon on someone's clothing. Then the someone came closer, a blond-haired woman, one hand lifted in the air, as if making a blessing, like he'd seen the pope do in photographs. He recognized her tall, lithe figure and the cut of her hair.

"Angie?" he called softly. She didn't respond and he took a closer look, wondering what she was doing out in the yard in the middle of the night. She had to be cold, dressed as she was in a tiny little T-shirt, drawstring pants, and with nothing on her feet. What was she doing out here?

"Angie?" She didn't look his way. Maybe she hadn't heard him. He put aside the bat and stepped into her path.

"What are you doing out here?"

Still no response. She kept slowly walking down the brick path holding her hand up and murmuring to herself. And though her eyes were wide open, she didn't seem to see him.

Not wanting to startle her as he had startled her sister last week at the fuse box, he decided not to reach out and grab her, in case high-strung nerves ran in the family.

"Hey!" he called out as she went by.

No response.

He trotted around her and stood in her path. She seemed to look at him, but her gaze went through him, not at him.

"Where is it?" she asked, her voice slurred.

"What?"

"You know, the—the . . ." Her voice trailed off. Her arm lowered to her side. "The—"

She was sleepwalking. She was outside in her nightwear,

wandering through the garden in the middle of the night. Michael decided the best recourse was to play along with her instead of trying to wake her.

"I think I know where it is," he said.

"You do?"

"Here, let me show you. "

Gently he took her left hand. She allowed him to grasp it and slowly turn her around.

"But that's not—" she murmured, looking back at the way she had been headed. "The, the—"

"It's this way, Angie. You'll see."

"But—"

He urged her down the walk, taking it easy so she could follow in her dreamy amble. He felt like a parent leading an awestruck four-year-old through an amusement park. He left her at the bottom of the back stairs, and bounded up the stairs to check the door before she had time to wander off. The back door had locked securely behind him when he had left the house. Damn, they'd have to go around to the front.

By the time he hurried back down the stairs, he saw her turn around for the brick path.

"Angie," he called softly, not wishing to alert any of the neighbors. He reached for her hand again to interrupt her stroll through the back yard just as the automatic sprinkler system leaped into action with a loud *phssst*.

Instantly Angie cowered, staring wide-eyed in the direction of the sudden sound.

"Hey, it's just sprinklers," Michael cooed, reaching down for her.

"Sprinklers?" she repeated, her tongue thick in her mouth, making the word sound foreign. She'd almost sunk completely to the ground, as if she were afraid of the most commonplace occurrence at night in the state of California, that of automatic watering systems turning on.

"Sprinklers—"

Then he felt her body sag, and her eyes rolled back in her head.

"Great," he exclaimed, looking down at her. She had

collapsed in a dead weight at his feet and had fallen soundly asleep.

RAE WAS DREAMING of being in a factory, her sleeve caught in a conveyer belt, a huge machine ahead of her buzzing each time it stamped through a shiny metal plate. Bzzzt. Bzzzt. In seconds, she would be under that die cutter, stamped to death.

Bzzzt. Bzzzt.

Frantic and sweating, she yanked at her sleeve, but she was suddenly enveloped in a smothering roll of heavy fabric, like an old quilt. She couldn't move. She couldn't get away . . .

Bang, bang, bang.

Rae jerked awake, sitting up in bed, ramrod straight, her blond hair matted to her temples, damp with sweat. She tried to move her legs, but her bedclothes were twisted around her legs like the wrappings of a mummy. No wonder she'd been having a nightmare.

Bang, bang, bang.

What was that banging noise? That wasn't part of a dream. It sounded real, and it was coming from downstairs at the front of the house. Was someone at the door?

She squinted at the alarm clock beside her bed. Good Lord, it was one-thirty, the middle of the night. Who would be knocking on the door at this hour?

Rae scrambled out of bed and hurried down the hall, poking her head into Angie's room to wake her up for moral support. She was surprised to see Angie's bed vacant, the down comforter thrown back, and her sister nowhere in sight. Alarm washed over Rae as she trotted down the long hall to the stairs. When she made the turn at the landing, she could see two dark shapes through the frosted oval glass of the front door. Grabbing an afghan from the couch in the parlor, she threw it over her shoulders and clutched it at her neck, and for a moment stood unmoving in the foyer, wondering what to do. The house was too old to have a peephole on the door.

Bang, bang, bang.

"Rae?" a male voice called. "Are you in there?"

A small sense of relief swept through her. It was Michael.

She reached for the handle of the door and pulled it open, shocked to see her sister in the arms of Michael Gregory.

"What happened?" she gasped.

He ignored her question and stepped into foyer. "Where should I put her?"

"On the couch." Rae pointed at the living room to her left. "In there." She followed at his heels as he turned for the large room with the bay window.

Breathing heavily, he strode forward, obviously struggling from carrying her sister's limp body, and then gently deposited her on the old burgundy-colored velvet couch. Angie's body melted into the contours of the cushions, and her head lolled to the side. Rae could see no blood, no broken bones.

"What happened?" she repeated, rushing closer.

"I found her sleepwalking outside."

"What?" Rae bent over Angie, inspecting her sister for signs of trauma.

"Sleepwalking," Michael answered. "She's okay. She just fell dead asleep. I couldn't wake her up."

Rae straightened and slowly pulled the afghan from her shoulders. Michael had already seen what she slept in. There was no need to hide her disarray from him with the afghan. Any chance to dress to impress had been blown the moment he'd seen her at the fuse box the other morning. Besides, he'd made it clear he wasn't interested in her anyway. She draped the warm knitted throw over her sister's sleeping form. In the dim light, Angie's face looked uncommonly pale and touchingly childlike. She'd never seen that side of her sister.

"She used to do that when she was a teenager."

"Sleepwalk?"

"Yes. But she never left the house. Not as far as I know."

"She was out in the side yard, wandering around. I was going to bed and just happened to look out the window."

"Lucky for her, you were up late."

"Yeah."

She glanced over her shoulder at him, and he suddenly seemed to realize he was in a state of disarray himself, for he looked down and began to button his white shirt. Rae caught a full glimpse of the hard plane of his abdomen. Quickly, she averted her gaze.

"Hey, thanks," Rae said, concentrating on his hands instead of his naked torso.

"No problem." He shot a glance at Angie. "Think she'll be all right?"

"Sure. I'll get another blanket from upstairs and put something in front of the doors."

"That will stop her?"

"I hope so. She never walked twice in a night as far as I remember."

"Were you always the one to get up with her?" Michael asked. It was an innocent question, and anyone would have asked the same thing, but it brought back a flood of memories that Rae did not wish to review.

"Yeah. I was a light sleeper."

Someone had to be when your stepfather worked nights and your mother was a closet alcoholic who began drinking at five P.M.

FRIDAY WAS RAE'S last official day at the university, at least for the summer. She celebrated by stopping at the grocery store to get supplies for dinner, and then hurried back to the mansion. Rae guided her Jetta into the parking space in front of the house and turned off the engine. For a moment she sat in her car and looked up at the old mansion, backlit by the setting sun, with everything in silhouette but the spire on the top of the tower, glinting like a fiery sword. The house made her think of a fortress or religious bastion in a foreign land. Each time of day brought out a different character in the place, a changing display of its ever-shifting personality. She kept waiting to see the cheerful, welcoming version of the place, like that of a grandmother's house at

Christmas—but such a view might never occur until she got the pruning done and hacked a path through the shadows.

Rae got out, wedged the bag of groceries into the crook of her arm, and then strode up the walk to the front door. Soon she was in the kitchen, frying bacon and getting the pasta, cheese, and peas together for spaghetti carbonara, one of her favorite quick dishes. She heard Angie come into the front entry, and a moment later, her sister appeared in the kitchen doorway.

She was dressed in a lime-green pantsuit, with her hair swept up, and swirls of silver at her ears and around her throat. Her makeup looked as if she had just applied it, and her eyes sparkled, like a person who had enjoyed a perfect night's sleep. Rae wondered how she did it.

"How was your first day at work?" Rae asked, still stirring the minced bacon.

"Just like the Newark store. Same shit going on, as always."

"Nice coworkers?"

"A catty forty-something. I think she's jealous. I'll bet she wanted my position. And a guy just out of college." She licked her mouth and smiled, and her upper lip curled to reveal her eyeteeth, making her look like a cat. "I could have him tomorrow, if I wanted."

Rae turned her attention back to her bacon. Funny how a guy out of college held no appeal to her, especially a guy who was a buyer for a department store.

"Change and make a salad, Angie?" Rae asked.

"Sure. I'll be right down."

Angie hadn't been gone five minutes when Rae spotted Michael Gregory out in the yard near the oak tree. She took the skillet off the stove and held it over the sink, idly watching him as he picked up something by the tree and scratched his head. Then, before she could duck out of sight, he turned and glanced up at the house.

Rae blushed, and busied herself by pouring off most of the bacon grease into an old juice can. She hoped he hadn't caught her staring. There was a good chance he hadn't, since the oak tree was a good fifty feet from the kitchen window.

She was just mixing the mascarpone cheese with the egg when she heard him walk up the back stairs.

"Hi." It was the first real greeting Michael had ever used in her presence. He glanced at the stove. "You're cooking?"

"I do sometimes." She wiped her hands on a towel, wondering if he wanted to join them for dinner but not certain where she stood with him anymore, or if he would even remain in the same room with her.

"Smells good," he commented.

"There's plenty, if you want some."

He glanced at her and the light shifted in his eyes. "I might just try it."

"I'm overwhelmed by your enthusiasm."

He gave her a smirk and then looked past her, his gaze angling through the hallway behind her. "Is Angie home yet?"

Although Rae tried to hide her reaction, she felt his friendly interest in Angie and his belligerence toward her cut through her like a knife.

"Yes. She just went upstairs to change."

"I was wondering how she was this morning. If she remembered last night."

"Ask her yourself. She'll be down in a minute."

Michael walked across the kitchen and for the first time Rae noticed he carried a battered stick in his hand.

"What *is* that?" she asked, pointing at the stick, which looked like it had been buried by a dog and unearthed many years later.

"A bat." He held it up.

She grimaced in disgust as she stepped closer for a better look. The long wooden shaft was covered in green and black mold and chewed up at the end, as if a giant dog had gnawed at it.

"What's left of it, anyway," he added.

"From a hundred years ago?" Rae asked with a laugh.

"From last night, believe it or not."

"What do you mean?"

He told her how he had left the house with his bat as protection against what he had guessed might be teenage gang members, and how he had propped it against the tree and forgot it overnight.

"How can that be?" Rae inquired, staring at it. "Are you sure that's the same bat?"

"I'm positive."

"But what happened to it?"

"That's what I want to know. If it's somebody's idea of a joke, I'm not laughing. This bat was autographed by Reggie Jackson."

His tone was more grave than she would have imagined hearing from Michael. She glanced up at him.

"My father gave me this bat," he added.

Before she could say a word in sympathy, she heard a quick step behind her and a sharp intake of breath.

"Yuck!" Angie cried out. "That's the grossest thing I've ever seen!"

Michael gave her the same explanation that he had just given Rae.

"You mean I was outside last night?" Angie asked.

"You don't remember?" Rae said, turning to check the pasta.

"No." Angie strolled to the refrigerator. "But I wondered why I woke up on the sofa. I was almost late for work—and on my first day!"

"Do you remember what you were dreaming about last night?" Michael inquired.

"No." Angie pulled out romaine, carrots, and avocado for the salad. "I never remember my dreams. Do you?"

Michael shook his head.

Angie reached for a paring knife from a wooden block on the counter. "What was I doing out there?"

"Just wandering around, mumbling to yourself."

She smiled. "I hope I didn't say anything too embarrassing!"

"You were fine."

"That's a relief." She picked up a carrot. "Why don't you

set the table, Mike? We can eat together, like one big happy family. Right, Rae?"

Rae drained the steaming pasta water while she thought of sitting down with Michael Gregory, and wondered if she would be able to choke anything down. "Right," she mumbled.

LATE THE NEXT afternoon, as Rae came up out of the basement, she heard Angie answer the doorbell, and talk animatedly to someone in the foyer. She paused at the door to the cellar stairs to listen, and recognized the smooth tone of Simeon's voice.

"Great," Rae muttered to herself, wiping her dusty hands on the front of her equally dusty shirt. She had spent the morning in the attic and the afternoon in the basement, going through boxes and trunks, and affixing labels to them to catalog their contents for the future, but had found nothing out of the ordinary.

The only item of interest she had discovered was a box of old correspondence, which she had sifted through, hoping to find documents that might give her a clue as to what had gone on at the dig involving the unusual black tomb. But what she had found in the box of correspondence had nothing to do with the mysterious sword and tomb, and everything to do with Michael's relationship with his father. She had tucked the file folder under her arm and carried it upstairs, sure the contents would make Michael Gregory think twice about the harsh opinion he had formed of his father.

But showing the folder to Michael would have to come later. Her mission now was to endure the upcoming embarrassment of Simeon catching sight of her present state of filthiness. She was in no condition to greet company: her hair was pulled back into a messy knot, she was wearing a pair of old lounging pajama pants and T-shirt, and every inch of her clothes and skin was covered with sweat and grime.

In the distance Angie told Simeon that Rae was somewhere in the house but she wasn't quite sure where. Rae sighed. There was no way to avoid confronting Simeon in her disheveled state, as getting upstairs to change meant going through the hall that opened onto the foyer.

Taking a resigned breath, Rae brushed what dust she could from the planes of her face, and then strode forward. She was certain she looked worse than the morning Michael had surprised her out by the fuse box. As she rounded the corner to the main hall, she saw Simeon standing next to her sister at the doorway to the living room. He was dressed in khakis and a dark blue polo shirt that set off the frosty highlights of his light brown hair. As she approached, he turned and smiled.

"Fay Rae!" he greeted as his gaze flitted over her.

"Hi." She pushed back a strand of stray hair. "What brings you to the island?"

"I just dropped by to see what you were doing this evening."

"This evening?" She put a hand on her hip. Now that she had stopped working, she realized how stiff her lower back felt and how tired her arms were from moving heavy boxes. Her bones ached. If he asked her to go dancing or anything that involved physical activity, she would have to refuse. "I haven't really thought about it."

"You look like you've been busy."

"Just going through stuff. Preliminary work."

"Are you at a stopping place or am I interrupting?"

Rae rubbed the back of her neck. "No, I'm done for the day. In fact, I'm done in!"

"So unfortunate," he answered, his mouth tilting into a smile. "I was going to ask you to fly to Paris with me."

"Ha, ha." She had to smile at his teasing.

"Seriously, I was hoping you might like to go out for a light dinner, maybe watch a film—"

"I rented some videos," Angie put in. "Just a few minutes ago. Anybody interested in just hanging around here?"

Rae should have been upset that Angie was once again butting in on her private time with Simeon, but she was too tired to muster the energy to protest. In fact, taking a shower and then putting her feet up in the cozy sunroom at the back of the house sounded like a heavenly way to end the long, arduous day.

"Fay Rae?" Simeon asked, leaning closer to see her face better in the dim light. "It is your preference."

"Hanging out sounds okay to me," Rae answered. "But I've got to take a shower, the sooner the better."

"Why don't I order Chinese food and have it delivered," Simeon suggested, "while you run upstairs?"

"That sounds great." Rae put her hand on the newel post of the stairs, thankful that Simeon had been too much of a gentleman to give her appearance a single disparaging look.

He turned to Angie. "May I use your phone and phone-book, Angela?"

"Right this way." Angela motioned for him to follow her to the kitchen.

RAE TOOK A quick shower, slapped on the barest of makeup, dried her hair, and then slipped into jeans and the pink blouse she'd bought the other night. Her arms were so tired she could barely hold them up long enough to style her hair, and her back ached so much she wished she could crawl into bed and sleep. Fifteen minutes later, she headed back downstairs, grabbing her purse on the way so she could pay for dinner this time. As she hobbled down the stairs, struggling to mask the lines of pain she knew were etched in her face, she remembered the photographs still hidden in her purse. She would ask Simeon about his father's life and prove to Michael that he was wrong about her friend.

As she gained the bottom of the staircase, she heard Angie and Simeon chatting in the kitchen, so she headed in that direction, not certain if she would be able to keep up a care-free front. She had completely overtaxed herself and was paying for it in ever-increasing waves of pain.

Angie had opened a bottle of white wine, a glass of which Simeon handed to Rae upon her arrival in the kitchen. Where was Angie hiding the stuff? She hadn't seen anything in the fridge or in the cupboards.

"Mmm," he said, as she thanked him. "You smell good."

"Soap and shampoo," she answered. "When will dinner be here?"

Simeon rotated his wrist and glanced down at his watch. "In about fifteen more minutes."

Angie raised her goblet. "Here's to Saturday night with my sister and her friend, and no Brent!"

Simeon lifted his glass to hers. "Brent?"

"My ex-boyfriend. A real skank."

"Hear, hear." Rae clinked her glass against his. "I'm so glad you are leaving him, Angie. I'm proud of you."

"*A votre santé!*" Simeon put in, nodding at her.

Rae took a tiny sip, and lowered her drink, holding the stem in her fingers to keep her body heat from warming the wine. She intended to nurse a single drink for the entire evening. "So, Simeon." She turned to him. "Tell me, did your father share your love of history too?"

"My father?"

"Is that where you got your love of ancient weaponry— from your dad?"

He blinked and smiled, showing the line of his small even teeth, and she could see he was confused by the question. "Pardon me?"

"Your father. He knew Dr. Gregory, didn't he?"

"I'm not sure what you are talking about." He took a sip of his wine.

"I found an old photo of Dr. Gregory and someone who looks just like you."

"Really?" He lowered his goblet. "May I see it?"

"Sure. It's in my purse." Rae set her glass upon the tiled countertop and reached for her purse, casually shielding it with her body so Simeon could not see the other photos she had hidden in the side pocket. She pulled out the group shot and handed it to him.

"I just assumed the man on the right was your father."

Angie stepped up beside Simeon and looked around his shoulder to study the photograph as well. "That person does look a lot like you, Simeon."

Rae watched the puzzled expression on his face smooth into a smile. "Why, that must be my uncle Omar."

"Not your father, then?"

"No. My father looked nothing like me." He handed the photograph to Rae and gave a quiet laugh. "I had no idea my uncle knew Dr. Gregory! What a small world!"

"Was your uncle an archeologist?" Rae inquired, still holding the photo.

"Indeed, no! He was probably the driver of that vehicle."

"Then your family lives in Egypt?"

"Part of my family did at one time. Alas, I am the last of the line."

"Really? Darn!" Angie pursed her lips, pretending to pout. "I was hoping you had a cute younger brother."

Just then, Rae heard footsteps on the wooden boards of the front porch. She put the old photo on the counter and picked up her purse, surmising the delivery person had arrived. With Angie at her heels, she walked down the hall to pay for their dinner. But before she could reach for the doorknob, the door opened and Michael burst into the house.

# Chapter 11

"**H**appy to see me?" Michael asked, glancing from one to the other, as if he were equally surprised to find them at the door.

"We thought you were the Chinese food," Angie replied.

"I've been mistaken for a lot of things in my life" Michael took off his light jacket. "But never Chinese food."

"She meant the delivery guy." Rae saw Michael look past her and his eyes darken—which she had come to learn was a sign of his quick-to-escalate anger. Michael pointed at Simeon, who had come up to stand behind Rae.

"What's he doing here?"

Rae raised her chin. "He's having dinner with us."

"And watching a movie," Angie put in.

"Not in my house, he isn't!" Michael's glare burned across Rae. "I thought I made myself clear the other night."

"This is my house too!"

"Mr. Gregory." Simeon stepped around Rae to face the other man. "Have I offended you in some way?"

"I don't want you here," Michael growled. "I told Rae that specifically."

Rae glanced at Simeon, whose silvery eyes narrowed to slits and whose previously relaxed posture was stiff with affront.

"Then I shall leave."

"Good."

"Mike!" Angie protested.

"No, Simeon, wait." Rae turned to him. "There is no need for you to leave."

"I do not wish to cause disharmony in your household."

"Michael isn't the boss here."

"No one will enjoy their evening should I stay now, including myself."

"You got that right." Michael pointed to the front of the house. "The door is that way, Avare."

"I am aware of the floor plan." Simeon glared at him and then turned to Rae and Angie. "Good night, ladies. Perhaps another time."

"I'll see you out." Rae took his elbow and walked with him to the front door, her cheeks on fire. She didn't look at Michael as she brushed past him at the foot of the stairs. Out on the porch, she stopped Simeon with a slight squeeze of his forearm.

"Simeon, I'm so sorry. I don't know what to say."

"You don't have to say anything."

"But I am appalled by Michael's behavior."

"It is no reflection on you, Fay Rae."

"Still, would you like to go somewhere and eat?" she asked, even though she was so beat she couldn't bear the thought of spending a single moment in public.

"You've had a big day," he replied kindly. "I can see that you are very tired."

"But—"

"I will give you a call." He reached down and gently cupped her chin with his warm fingers, sending spirals of pleasure through her. Then he leaned over and softly kissed her lips. Rae shut her eyes as his firm mouth sank upon hers and slightly pressed her lips, almost opening them. She'd never been kissed, and she stood there, frozen, suspended in time while the touch of his mouth lingered long after he had raised up. His kiss had been dry and gentle and nothing like the hungry sensation she'd imagined a kiss would be. When she at last opened her eyes, she found him smiling down at her, his eyes glittering with amusement.

"Did you like that?" he asked.

She grinned, but before she could answer, she saw a small sedan pull up in front of the house, and the deliveryman climb out with two paper bags in his hand.

"Your dinner is here," Simeon announced, breaking away. "I'll bid you good night."

"Good night, Simeon. Call me. We can do something tomorrow if you wish."

"All right."

He hurried down the steps as the deliveryman came up the walk. While Rae paid the man, she watched Simeon wave and then duck into his limousine, which had been parked down the block, probably discreetly waiting there since he'd first arrived.

RAE CARRIED THE bags of fragrant food into the house, and hurried into the kitchen, where she found Michael and Angie having another glass of wine.

"Thanks a lot, asshole!" Rae tossed the bags upon the counter near the sink.

"Rae!" Angie gasped at her unusual profanity.

"Look." Michael crossed his arms. "I told you I didn't want him in the house."

"I never agreed to it."

"I don't care if you agreed or not." Michael scowled. "If you insist on seeing the guy, keep the romance out of my face."

"But why?" Angie asked.

"Because the guy gives me the creeps, that's why."

Rae grabbed the photograph she'd put on the counter while she turned to look at her sister. "Does he give you the creeps, Angie?"

"No. He's nice." Angie glared at Michael. "He's probably one of the nicest guys I ever met."

"He's too nice." Michael took a gulp of his wine. "Haven't either one of you noticed?"

"Oh, I've noticed all right." Rae turned on him. "Anyone would seem too nice in comparison to you!"

"I'm serious, Rae."

"So am I."

"All I'm saying is I don't want him here."

"Fine. Fine!" Rae slung her purse strap over her shoulder,

too disturbed to eat dinner. "But just so you know, Simeon has offered to donate money to help buy the house for the center I want to develop. So treat him with respect. Or we'll both be out a great deal of money."

"Not me. I'm not going to sell to that guy."

"Oh, yes you are. You agreed, remember? Whoever gets the money first gets to buy the other person out."

"Oh, no." Michael put his wine glass down on the counter with a loud clink. "Not to him."

"You made no such stipulation before."

"But I had no idea you'd already talked to him about it."

"Well, I did," Rae replied. "And he agreed to help."

"You're making a mistake." Michael glowered. "A big one."

Angie glanced from Rae to Michael, obviously concerned by their heated words, never having witnessed one of their discussions before.

"Jesus, you guys!" She stepped between them. "Argue later. I'm starving." She opened one of the bags of food and pulled out a small white carton. Michael watched her, distracted by the sudden turn in the conversation.

Rae took advantage of the lull to slip the photograph back into her purse. It was then she noticed a peculiar hole, like a cigarette burn, that had scorched through the figure of the man on the right, obliterating the image of his face. Not believing her eyes at first, Rae held the photo up to the light. Sure enough, she saw light streaming through the hole. She glanced at the counter, wondering if she had put the photo in something caustic that had eaten through the thick glossy paper. But the counter was clean.

"Are you two going to eat?" Angie asked, busy taking out all the cartons and opening their flaps. "Or just stand there?"

"I've lost my appetite," Rae replied, perplexed about the hole in the photograph, angry at Michael, and unbearably tired.

"What did you order?" Michael asked, stepping up to the counter beside Angie.

Rae glared at his back. He'd thrown Simeon out of the house and now planned to eat the food she had purchased, as casual as could be. He had some nerve.

But Michael remained oblivious to her stare, and Angie took no notice of how disturbed she was. Rae clenched her jaw and left the kitchen. She hoped Michael Gregory choked on a wonton.

RAE TRUDGED UPSTAIRS, flung herself on her bed, tried to recall what her first kiss had felt like, but fell asleep before Simeon's mouth had touched hers during the mental instant replay. She didn't wake up until deep into the night, when she was startled to consciousness by the sound of the back door banging shut.

Wide awake with alarm, Rae sat up in bed. Angie must be sleepwalking again. It would be best to catch her before she wandered down the street and caused a scene in her skimpy nightwear.

Rae had fallen asleep in her clothes, and her left hand was numb from having been slept on for hours. She shook life into her fingers as she scrambled out of bed, moaning out loud at the stiffness in her back, shoulders, and calves. She shoved her feet into her slippers, and then scuffed down the hall to the stairs and out of the house. At the back door, she turned to make sure it was unlocked, so she could get her sister back through the rear entry and would not be forced to go around to the front as Michael had.

Sure enough, she found Angie in the back yard, slowly walking down the weed-infested brick path, the loose pant legs of her pajamas billowing in the midnight breeze.

"Ange!" Rae hissed, trying to get her attention. Her sister ignored her. Then Angie slowly dropped to the ground and began to scratch the earth with her nails.

"Angie!" Rae trotted toward her, hampered by her thick-soled slippers made of pieces of foam.

Angie's blond hair fell around her face, concealing her features as she scrabbled at the dirt and weeds in front of her knees.

"Ange, wake up!" Rae stopped short of her by a couple of feet.

"Close now, *neb*," Angie mumbled. "Close now."

Rae bent down, trying to make sense of the words Angie had just uttered.

"Close?" Rae asked, urging her to talk while she dreamed.

"Very close."

"Close to what?" Rae knelt beside her, peering into the track Angie had made in the weeds and dirt but unable to see anything. "Close to what, Angie?"

"To what we saw."

"Where?"

"You know."

"I forget, Angie," Rae baited her. "Where?"

Angie ignored her once again and dug deeper into the black soil, ruining her manicure, which was something she would never have done in a conscious state.

"Where did we see it, Angie? Where?"

"You know—the card."

The card? Rae sat back on her heels, shocked by her sister's last words. She knew exactly what Angie was talking about now. The Forbidden Tarot. Angie was out in the garden in a subconscious state searching for something she had seen on the Forbidden Tarot card. But what?

"What are you looking for?" she asked once more. "I could help you find it."

Angie stopped digging and looked up at the sky, which was unusually opaque and heavy with low-hanging clouds. A cold wind buffeted her hair, but she seemed unaware of the chill. Rae watched her, wondering what Angie was seeing or hearing in her dream. Then Angie turned to her sister and blinked, and Rae could tell by the clearing in her eyes that she had come slowly awake. Angie glanced at Rae and then down at herself.

"What in the hell?" she gasped.

"You were sleepwalking."

Angie raised her hands up in front of her face. "What have I been doing?"

"Digging."

Angie grimaced and rotated her hands to look at her nails. Even in the dark she could see the damage she'd done to her costly manicure. "Jesus! I've ruined my nails!"

"You were intent on finding something."

"What?"

"Something you'd seen on the tarot card."

"The one in Egypt?"

"I assume so." Rae stood up and Angie quickly followed, shuddering.

"God, it's cold out here! Let's get inside!"

Rae followed her sister down the path and back to the rear door. Angie had no slippers on her feet. She must be freezing.

"Get cleaned up," Rae instructed as they scampered into the house. "I'll make you a hot cup of tea."

"Thanks."

AS THEY HUDDLED at the small kitchen table with their cold hands wrapped around hot mugs, Rae looked up at her sister's pale face.

"You don't remember anything about the dream?"

"No." Angie shook her head. Even her lips were colorless. "Nothing."

"You were talking to someone when I found you," Rae went on. "You called whoever it was *neb*."

"Neb?"

Rae nodded as she studied her sister's face. "Who do you think you were talking to?"

"Christ!" Angie retorted. "How should I know? And what kind of name is *neb*?"

Rae took a thoughtful sip of tea and savored the sensation of the warmth radiating throughout her chest. Then she looked over at her sister. "This has got to stop, Angie. We can't have you sleepwalking every night."

"I can't afford to wreck my nails every night!" Angie glared at her cup. Then she slowly looked up. "Maybe it's that tarot deck, Rae."

"What do you mean?"

"Maybe it *is* cursed."

"If it were, surely we'd have been dead by now. It's been weeks since we looked at it."

"Maybe it doesn't work that way. Maybe it takes longer."

Rae frowned. She might believe a lot of things, especially about the ancient Egyptians, based in part on the fact of their construction technique, which went far beyond normal capabilities of that bygone time. She believed the Egyptians had possessed knowledge that far exceeded the puny technical accomplishments of modern man, and that most of their ancient knowledge had been lost over the centuries. She would even entertain the notion that Thomas Gregory had found a sword in a strange tomb and that the sword might possess untold powers. But could a deck of tarot cards induce sleepwalking? She wasn't so sure.

Angie leaned forward and put a hand on Rae's forearm. "Maybe we should have someone look at the deck of cards. Someone who knows about them."

"And who would that be?"

"Someone at the university, maybe?"

Rae did a quick mental rundown of her colleagues and those of Dr. Gregory, and couldn't come up with a single person she would trust with her secret. Besides, she had her professional reputation to consider. If she showed too much interest in anything paranormal, she would lose all credibility in her department at Berkeley. It would be best to keep the goings-on at the Gregory house separate from the workplace. She slowly shook her head.

"There has to be someone." Angie lifted her mug.

"Well, I did see a person on television the other day—"

"And?"

"She had the exact same deck of tarot cards in her hand. She claimed that Michael's father hadn't died of natural causes, and that something had come to life, or something like that." Rae paused, thinking of the news program. "She held up the very same card we saw in Egypt, Angie. Typhon, the Devil."

"That's kind of weird!"

"It was."

Angie's brows drew together. "Why didn't you get a hold of her?"

"I couldn't decide if I should trust her."

"But how will you know if you can trust anyone?"

"That's just it." Glumly, Rae stared at the pine tabletop. "That's the problem. Who do we trust?"

For a moment, they sat together in silence. Then Angie sighed and stood up. "Well, I think we should find that woman. We don't have to tell her everything. Just see what she knows."

Rae gazed at Angie, surprised by this new and serious dimension of her sister. For once, she thought Angie was right. It was time to seek out some answers before the sleepwalking went any further.

"Where *is* that deck you found?" Angie asked.

"At my condo in Berkeley. I'll go get it first thing tomorrow."

"And make an appointment to see that woman?" Angie put her cup in the sink. "When I can go with you?"

"Yeah." Rae rose from her chair. "And don't tell anyone yet. Not even Simeon. And especially not Michael."

"Okay." Angie rubbed the backs of her bare arms. Her face was pinched with worry. "I have to admit I'm a little spooked, Rae."

"Don't worry." Rae gave her a gentle squeeze with her left arm and a reassuring smile that she did not feel inside. "I'll figure out what's going on."

"I know you will," Angie said. "You're my rock, Rae. You always have been." She pulled away and headed for the stairs. "Good night."

"Night, Ange." Rae watched her go, surprised by her sister's last words. She had never thought of herself as anyone's rock, and certainly not Angie's.

Just as Rae lowered her cup into the sink, she was startled by the sudden ring of the phone.

Rae reached for the receiver, wondering who could be calling at one o'clock in the morning.

"Hello?" Rae asked, keeping close to the cradle of the phone, expecting to hang up on a prank caller.

"Angie?"

"No, it's Rae." She looked toward the ceiling and frowned, recognizing Michael Gregory's voice.

"Oh." He paused.

"She just went back to bed, Michael."

"What do you mean, back?"

"I found her outside a few minutes ago, sleepwalking again."

"Great." He sighed, and she could tell he found it as difficult to talk to her on the phone as she found it difficult to stand there listening to him. "Listen, Rae—"

"Michael, it's one o'clock in the morning."

"I know. But I have to ask a favor." He paused again. "I didn't know who else to call."

"What's wrong?"

"I had a car accident."

"What?"

"I had a car accident. My Audi's pretty well smashed up."

She straightened, suddenly at full alert. "Are you okay?"

"Do you really care?"

"Of course I do."

"It's hard to tell sometimes with you."

"So *are* you okay?"

"I'll live. But my car is undrivable."

"Where are you?"

"Alameda Hospital. Emergency. The cops made me come here to be checked out. See if anything was broken."

"Do you want me to come and get you?"

"Yes, if you would."

"I'll be there in a few minutes."

"Thanks." He hung up.

Rae hurried up the stairs, put on a pair of tennis shoes and a sweater, and poked her head into Angie's room. Her sister was fast asleep with the down comforter pulled up to her chin. She hoped Angie would stay put until she got back.

Rae walked out to her car, turned on the engine and then

the heater, and headed for the hospital, which was only a few minutes away. She parked on the vacant street near the emergency entrance and went into the building to locate her roommate.

She found Michael sitting in a chair in the busy waiting room, and he rose when she came through the automatic doors. She felt a deep sense of relief upon seeing him standing there, no limbs broken, and no bandages in sight.

"Hey," he greeted.

Rae had a sudden urge to fling her arms around Michael, to tell him she was glad to see that he was okay. But she had no right to touch him, not after all that had transpired between them, and he had made it clear he wanted nothing from her in that regard.

"Car's outside," Rae replied, reverting back to her cooler self. She led him back to the Jetta and told him the passenger side was already unlocked. He sank into the seat as she got in behind the wheel.

"Thanks for coming, Rae," he began, turning toward her. The streetlight illuminated his profile, and she couldn't help but notice the strong line of his sharp nose and masculine chin. She wanted to touch that chin, draw her fingers down the side of his face, feel his heat and the life force that beat so strongly within him—so different from her own frailty. "I didn't know who else to call."

"So no broken bones?"

"No. Just bruises."

She started her car and pulled out onto the street. Then she glanced at him. He stared straight ahead, his mouth grim. "So what happened?" she asked.

"I couldn't sleep, so I drove to the gym out by the golf course."

"And?"

"I worked off some steam and was driving back over that bridge by Fernside—"

"And some drunk hit you?"

"No. It was the weirdest thing. A huge piece of black plastic came out of nowhere and *blam!*" He raised both hands and spread wide his fingers. "It stuck right onto my windshield. I couldn't see a thing."

"A piece of plastic?"

"Yeah. It was as big as the whole windshield of my car."

Rae made a left turn and continued down the deserted street. "What did you do?"

"I was in the curve at the end of the bridge when the plastic hit the car. I tried to judge where the curb would be when I slammed on the brakes, knowing I would skid. But I misjudged and plowed into a telephone pole."

"The wind must have kicked up the plastic."

"That's what I assumed too."

"Where'd you damage your car?"

"The right-hand side. It folded up like an accordion."

"You're lucky to be alive."

"I am." Michael nodded. "I'd have been dead if there'd been any traffic." He leaned back against the head rest and fell silent. Rae made another left onto Grand.

"The weird thing was," Michael added, his voice as dark as the night outside. "Seeing that piece of plastic coming at me. It was like a bird. Like a bat."

"Flapping."

"Yeah—what I saw of it in the split second before it hit, anyway. I thought it was a giant bird coming at me."

"Just an optical illusion," Rae put in. She glided to a stop in front of the house.

"Yeah." Michael opened the door and got out. He didn't say a word all the way up to the front door. His step was measured, his demeanor thoughtful—his mood unlike any of the previous ones she'd witnessed.

"Thanks again," he said and headed for the stairs.

"You're welcome." Rae watched him slowly ascend to the second story and wondered if he'd hit his head. He certainly wasn't behaving in his usual blustery manner. He'd been checked by the medical staff, but she knew only too well how rushed emergency doctors could be. They might have missed a slight concussion, and she knew a person with a head injury should not be left alone. She couldn't go to bed without making sure Michael was really all right.

She decided to make him a cup of tea and use it as an excuse to check in on him before she turned in for the rest of the night.

# Chapter 12

The grandfather clock in the main hall struck two by the time Rae carried the chamomile tea up the stairs. She could see a shaft of light shining out of Michael's bedroom doorway, and padded toward it, two mugs in her hands. When she got to the doorway, she saw Michael sitting at his worktable, leaning on his forearms and staring into space.

"I made you some tea," she announced.

At the sound of her voice, he glanced up and looked at her as if seeing her for the first time. Gone was the usual hardness in his eyes. He didn't respond.

"Do you want it?"

He snapped out of his thoughts. "Sure. Thanks."

Rae walked across the floor and placed the mug on the table in front of him. "It's herbal. It won't keep you up."

"I was just thinking of getting a whisky. To settle my nerves."

"Tea's better for you."

"So it is." He reached for the tea. "Thanks."

Rae took a small sip from her mug and let the steam bathe her skin as she inspected Michael's face. When she'd looked at the photograph of Thomas Gregory taken in the 1940s, she had been struck by how handsome the old man had once been. But Michael was even more attractive than his father as a young man, perhaps because he existed in her own time, wore modern clothes, and had a contemporary haircut. He wasn't classically handsome like Simeon, but was attractive on an entirely different scale. His beauty sprang from the intensity and intelligence of his dark, dark eyes and the fluid way his thoughts fired his expressions. She'd heard the phrase "wearing your heart on your sleeve." She would have to say that Michael wore his heart on his face. She doubted the man had ever lied and gotten away with it, as his face was such a looking glass of his emotions.

His guilelessness made her judge him less harshly for the way he'd treated Simeon earlier that evening. He didn't like Simeon, and he couldn't hide the fact. It wasn't in him to dissemble.

While Michael took a swig of his tea, Rae glanced at the model on the work table, grasping for a conversation starter. If she could get Michael talking and keep him talking long enough to be sure of his mental acuity, she would feel more confident about leaving him alone for the night.

MICHAEL SWALLOWED THE hot tea. He still would have preferred whisky, but he drank Rae's herbal concoction instead just to be nice. Rae had gone to a lot of trouble on his account this evening, and it was sweet of her to look in on him like this. He could feel her studying him, looking for clues that he was healthy enough for her to leave him by himself. Ordinarily, having someone fuss over him would annoy him. But for some reason, he didn't mind Rae's concern. It proved she cared about his well-being, at least on a general level.

"So what is this?" Rae asked, nodding at the model made of white foam core board.

Michael followed her glance. "Just something to keep me busy."

"I thought it was for your job."

"Not this one. It's a personal project."

Rae bent down to the level of the front entry. He watched her, gratified that she showed an interest in his work, if not him. "Is it an apartment complex?"

"Not exactly."

"Then what is it?"

"An integrated living center."

"What's an integrated living center?"

Michael stood up. "It's a concept I've been working on, for people who live in large cities. Oakland in particular."

"An atrium design?"

"Kind of." He pointed to the center of the model, which was a hole ringed by three levels, each stair-stepped outward. "This is a parklike space, where people can walk their dogs, where kids can play—"

Rae nodded and pointed at the stair-stepped portion. "And these are residences?"

"Yes, each with a balcony that allows every dwelling a usable portion of sunshine."

"And on the two sides?"

"Stores that people can walk to on one side. Services on the other."

"Where will people park?"

"Underground. Under the park."

Rae smiled, obviously approving of his design, and Michael felt a flush of pleasure. Vee had never been more than perfunctorily interested in his work, and never if it was speculative.

"But everything within walking distance?" she added.

"That's the idea. It's a little village within a huge metropolis." He set down his cup. "It's designed to be self-contained, just like it was for us growing up here in Alameda. We could walk anywhere."

"We could."

"Old people didn't have to drive."

"Neither did teenagers."

"It was a community."

"Yes," Rae agreed. "It was."

She glanced up and their eyes met. For an instant Michael forgot that she had once scorned him, shamed him, and broken his heart. For an instant he thought of bending down and drawing her into his arms, of telling her how much he had missed her and how amazing it was to be talking like this with her again.

"I like it," she said, breaking off the eye contact in her

matter-of-fact way and bursting the bubble he'd been in. "But isn't it a departure from what you usually do?"

"Yes, but I'm sick to death of building high-rises, Rae." He dashed the vision of holding her in his arms and switched back to being just another architect talking to a vaguely interested party. It was easier that way. And a whole lot safer. "High-rises are so sterile. So unfriendly. They even change weather patterns. Did you know that?"

"I've heard that, yes."

"How presumptuous is that?" He scowled. "The buildings my company is famous for cast the rest of the world in shadow, changing it forever. People don't need that. Especially people crammed together in places like Oakland."

"But I thought you liked designing high-rises. You've won a lot of awards, haven't you?"

"Yes." He sighed. "But the more of them I design, the more I feel like a whore."

She shot another glance at him. He must have surprised her with his choice of words.

"I became an architect," he continued, "because I wanted to make a difference, Rae. But all I've done so far is make money." He gave a bitter laugh. "And given it to Vee."

"Well, look at the bright side," Rae replied, sending him a wry smile. "That's soon to change."

"Right." He gazed at her, and had the weirdest sensation, as if all the years that had passed had fallen away, and they were still just sixteen years old with nothing to regret and everything to live for. He could still picture Rae back then, still the same old serious soul but much more alive— her blond hair shining, her dark blue eyes sparkling, and her skin tinged with a rosy glow. What had happened to douse the fire he'd once loved in her, to mute the wit he'd always appreciated, to change her *joie de vivre* to such reserve?

He had another compelling urge to reach out and touch her face, to smooth away the lines around her mouth and banish the crease between her fine brows. He wanted to pull her to his chest, hold her close, and tell her not to worry so much, that nothing in life was worth worrying about so much.

He raised his hand but checked the movement, knowing from experience that Rae would shrink from his touch. And the last thing he wanted was for her to run away again.

"We're not so dissimilar, you know," she remarked, innocent of what he was thinking. "In our basic goals. We both want to make a difference."

He took a big gulp of tea in an effort to calm himself down. "But not with this house, Rae. It's just not the right time."

"I beg to differ."

"I know you do." He sighed. "And that's what we have to agree upon. We have to agree to differ and leave it at that. Or one of us is going to rip out the other's throat."

"You have that right." She picked up her mug and held it aloft in a toast. "To differing opinions, then," she said, "and the right to hold them."

He raised his cup and arched a teasing brow, just as he used to do. "To your opinion, Rae, even if it's wrong."

"Michael!" She glared at him, but only in mock outrage.

Then a quick burst of laughter broke from his chest, laughter that had been bottled up for years—how many years, he'd lost count. But being here with Rae like this, talking just like they had in the old days—had made something hard break apart inside him, startling him with both the pain and pleasure the fracture caused.

Startled by the feeling, he clinked his mug against hers, and in that single instant felt a deep sense of camaraderie pass between their hands, up their arms, and into their eyes—joining them in the spiritual and intellectual communion he had experienced with no other person but Rae.

Stunned that she could affect him so strongly even after so many years, Michael lowered his mug and broke away from her regard. "I should let you get to bed," he said. "It's late."

"It is."

"So good night, Rae."

She looked at him, still standing there on the other side of the worktable, her expression unreadable but thoughtful. "Good night, Michael."

He watched her cross the floor and pull the door shut after her. Had she lingered a moment longer, he would have begged her to stay and made a complete ass of himself.

SUNDAY MORNING CAME far too quickly for Rae, who had fallen into bed so late the previous night. She showered and dressed, and went downstairs to find Michael just coming in from a run and carrying a thick Sunday-morning edition of the *San Francisco Chronicle* under his arm.

"You went jogging this morning?" she asked, amazed that he had recovered enough from the car accident to engage in strenuous exercise.

"Yeah." He followed her into the kitchen for a glass of ice water. "Exercise always makes me feel better than anything."

"So you're not too bruised up?" She reached for the coffeepot to start a fresh morning batch.

"Not too. Just this." Michael held out his left forearm, which had a deep purple splotch on it the size and shape of a banana. "And a big one like it on my thigh."

"Ouch!" Rae grimaced, imagining how sore his flesh must be.

"It's not that bad."

She filled the coffeemaker filter with scoops of rich brown espresso roast and flipped on the switch.

Michael glanced around. "Angie isn't up yet?"

"No. The sleepwalking must have worn her out."

He glanced at the coffee. "Well, I'm going to take a quick shower and then read the paper." He left the large roll of newspaper on the counter and headed back down the hallway for the stairs. While Rae waited for the coffee to brew, she fixed herself a small bowl of granola and stood eating it while she idly scanned the headlines of the front section of the paper. Just as she finished the last bite, she remembered the file folder that she wanted to show to Michael. He seemed to be in a halfway decent mood. It would be best to talk about his father when Michael was receptive to conversation.

Rae hurried back up the stairs, wondering if her sore muscles hurt her more than Michael's bruises hurt him. She could tell she would be stiff for days. When she was still in her room, she glimpsed Michael going back down, his black hair damp, and his skin still rosy from the hot water. She trailed down the stairs after him, and found him pouring a cup of the freshly brewed coffee.

"It's all right if I have some?" he asked.

"Sure. Help yourself."

He poured a second mug for her.

"Your coffee is the best I've ever had," he said, blowing the steam off the top of the cup.

"It's all about a clean pot and filter." She gave a wry smile. "It's the only thing my mother ever taught me."

Michael nodded and his wide mouth rose at the left corner in a small smile. "My mother taught me to take clothes to the dry cleaner."

"I remember your mother as always being perfectly groomed."

"She should have been. She spent enough time and money on it."

"I admired her. She wasn't like my mother, all frowsy and worn out."

"My mother never worked a day in her life, Rae." He raised the mug to his lips, and then paused. "You would have thought such a pampered woman would have lived forever."

"She's not alive?"

"No, she died of cancer five years ago."

"I'm sorry to hear that."

"She wasn't a happy person," Michael replied, sipping his coffee. "I always thought that had something to do with her illness."

"You are awfully hard on your folks."

"I've reason to be."

Rae held up the folder that she'd been holding at her side. "Maybe you might want to rethink that."

"What do you mean?"

"Sit down at the table for a minute and have a look at this."

He glanced at the manila folder. "What is it?"

"Something I found in the attic. Something that might surprise you."

Michael walked to the small table by the window and sat down as she pulled out a chair beside him. "More photos?"

"Letters."

He gave her a curious stare and then looked down at the table as she opened the folder to display the stack of carbon copies of letters Thomas had typed over the years.

"What are these?"

"I only read a few. But I gather they are duplicates of letters your father wrote to you."

Michael picked up one of the thin pieces of paper and quickly scanned it. "I never received this." He looked back up at the date. "I must have been sixteen when he wrote this."

"There are dozens of letters, going way back."

"I don't get it." Michael sifted through the papers. "He must not have sent them."

"Then why didn't he keep the originals instead of these carbon copies?"

"I don't know." Michael ran a hand through his wet hair. "I wouldn't even try to guess what motivated the old bastard to do what he did."

"Maybe he cared, Michael. Why would he write all these letters to you if he didn't?"

"Why didn't I ever get a single one of them?"

"Would there have been a reason you wouldn't have got mail addressed to you?"

"What are you insinuating?" Michael frowned. "That my

mother screened my mail? Christ, what kind of family do you think I had?"

"I'm not insinuating anything." After a long, intensely silent moment in which Michael studied more letters, Rae leaned forward. "Thomas never called you? Never sent you a birthday present?"

"No."

"Didn't you ever go back and visit him?"

"I wanted to when my parents were first divorced, but my mother wouldn't let me. She was sure the old man was crazy. And later"— Michael pushed back his chair and stood up—"I was too angry to bother."

"I think it's a shame."

"Well, it's over and done with, Rae. There's nothing anyone can do about it. The man's dead."

"Not entirely." She rose and closed the folder. "He's still alive inside you, Michael. Your resentment of him is very much alive."

"I'm used to it."

"But what if it's based on a lie?"

"Then I'm wrong." He shrugged. "End of story."

"But it has made you so bitter!"

Michael set his mug onto the counter and turned back to her, his expression black. "Don't go analyzing me. I'm warning you, Rae."

"I was just trying to help you see the Thomas Gregory I knew. He was a good person."

"You knew your version of the man, I knew mine." Michael turned for the doorway.

Rae picked up the folder. "Don't you want these?" she asked.

"Why would I?" Michael shot her a scathing look. "Can't you get it into your head that I am over my father? That he is best left in the past for me?"

"At least he cared enough to write!"

"Sure. Yeah."

"At least you had a father!"

Michael stopped in the doorway and paused as if he were going to make a reply, but he didn't. He grabbed the Sunday paper, and then plowed down the hall, leaving a black cloud of his usual anger smoldering in his wake.

Rae stood in the middle of the kitchen, holding the folder she had thought would change Michael forever. But she had misjudged the thickness of his emotional shell. It would take more than a stack of letters to convince him of Thomas's good character. And it would take a miracle for him to choose to investigate his father's death.

# Chapter 13

That same morning, on the way back from Berkeley where Rae had retrieved the deck of Egyptian tarot cards, she decided to pay a surprise visit to Simeon, just to let him know she didn't share Michael's poor opinion of him. Simeon's home in Piedmont was not far out of her way, and she guided her small sedan through the gracious tree-lined streets, climbing ever higher up the hill, until she recognized the large sage-green home with the circular drive. Rae parked on the narrow brick street, set her brake, and walked up to the front door.

She rang the buzzer and waited until Simeon's manservant opened the door.

"Miss Lambers." The manservant greeted her with a polite smile.

"Good morning." She couldn't remember the butler's name, and glanced around his short squat body for a sign of Simeon in the background. "Is Simeon home by any chance?"

"He is, but he does not receive visitors before four P.M."

"Four P.M.?"

The butler nodded. "Mr. Avare retires very late in comparison to most people, and rises late as well."

"Oh." Rae couldn't disguise her disappointment.

"Would you like me to tell Mr. Avare that you called upon him?"

"That's all right." Rae took a step backward toward the front steps. "I will telephone him later. Thank you."

The butler nodded and quietly closed the door. Rae returned to her car, wondering what kind of schedule Simeon kept. He must stay up half the night.

* * *

LATER THAT DAY, Rae and Angie headed back up to the same area to meet Maren Lake, who had seemed quite anxious to talk to them and had insisted that they meet her at her home in Rockridge to be assured of privacy.

"She sounds like a nut," Angie commented, hunching down in her seat to get a view of the Lake house, which was built on a ridge. Maren Lake's home was a modest Craftsman painted white and surrounded by grasses of all sizes, from the small Japanese ribbon variety to towering pampas grass. "Are you sure we should go in?"

"She didn't seem all that bad." Rae grabbed her small purse. "And she doesn't know what we have with us."

"Yeah. How could she?"

"Come on." Rae led the way up the walk and then introduced herself and her sister to the tall woman with silver hair who met them at the door.

"Come in. Come in." Maren swept them forward with a wave of her hand. She wore a loose-fitting black tunic and pants with a large moonstone hanging on a silver chain around her neck. Her feet were bare except for a pair of simple black thongs. She wore neither nail polish nor makeup, and yet she exuded a radiance ablaze with serenity and confidence.

The two young women were ushered into a living room decorated in the same simple taste as Maren Lake's clothing. All the furniture was made of dark wood with off-white upholstery. Bamboo mats covered the floor, and a black curio cabinet displayed simple but elegant Japanese teapots, most of which Rae guessed were very old. A painting of San Francisco dominated one wall, but it was done in the style of the Chinese masters of ink and brush, and did not show the overused Golden Gate Bridge, but concentrated instead on the Presidio area, a parklike section of the city covered with pines and eucalyptus.

"Let's go out to my garden." Her melodious voice was almost too deep for that of a female. "It's pleasant out there. A good place to talk."

"All right," Rae agreed.

They walked past the kitchen and another closed room, down a short hall, and out into a terraced back yard—an exquisitely tiny version of a Japanese tea garden complete with koi pond and bridge.

"How beautiful!" Rae exclaimed.

"This is my refuge from all that is stressful."

"I can see how it would bring a person peace."

"I strive for tranquility," Maren commented, motioning toward a seating area. "But even a student of simplicity such as myself sometimes finds it difficult to maintain a state of serenity in this frantic world of ours."

"Are those goldfish?" Angie pointed at the bright orange and white creatures swimming just inches from her feet as she walked toward the benches. "They're huge!"

"They're carp." She gestured toward one of the benches. "Please sit down."

Rae sat down and carefully placed her purse at her feet. She had brought the tarot deck with her, concealed in her bag, just in case she decided to show it to Maren Lake. And the more she saw of Maren, the more she believed the woman was far from being a nut. In fact, her calm outward appearance and her simple yet perfectly groomed home impressed Rae more than Simeon's much larger, more opulent house.

She glanced at the older woman's kind expression, studied the steady turquoise eyes, and wondered if Thomas Gregory had ever looked into this woman's face.

"So you are Fay Rae Lambers," Maren began.

"And my sister, Angela."

"Of course." Maren smiled in a motherly way at Angela, and Rae got the distinct impression that Angela had just been mentally dismissed. Rae had spent a lifetime receiving such looks from people who had been interested only in the charms of her more beautiful sister. It was a shock to experience the role reversal of being the center of attention for once.

Maren turned her intense eyes back upon Rae and crossed

one palm over the other, as Rae had seen in statues of the Buddha. "I didn't mean to alarm you, Miss Lambers, in my eagerness to see you—"

"I *was* kind of surprised."

"It's just that I was anxious to meet you." Maren's gaze swept over her, and Rae was certain the woman's eyes missed nothing—not the doubt Rae harbored, not her intensely private nature, and not her debilitating illness. She watched Maren's gaze soften momentarily, as if in sympathy for the pain she had discovered just beneath Rae's skin.

For the first time in her life, Rae felt laid bare for another human being to evaluate. She struggled to break from the woman's thorough perusal, but she could not hide herself from view. She didn't want anyone looking this close to the bone at her or feeling sorry for her either. But she couldn't move or say a single word as she sat skewered by the intensity of the woman's stare. Then all of a sudden the evaluation broke off, and Rae felt the hard probing lift, replaced by a waft of cool air.

"You see, Miss Lambers, I knew your father."

"My father?"

"Yes." She nodded.

"At least somebody did!" Angie put in, rolling her eyes.

Maren glanced at her, and then turned back to Rae, dismissing the younger sister again. "I've often wondered what happened to him."

Rae shrugged. "We have no idea. We never knew him."

"Didn't you?" Maren tilted her head in disbelief. "He was a most fascinating man. Very gifted. And then one day, without a word, he simply disappeared."

"The story we got from our mother"—Angie crossed her legs—"was that he ran out on us. Probably with another woman."

"I doubt that. I always imagined Robert had reached xeper."

Not understanding Maren's last word, Rae leaned forward. "Pardon me?"

"Xeper." Maren smiled as if contemplating a secret

thought that brought her much pleasure. "Or *kheffer*. It is an Egyptian word meaning to 'come into being.' The ultimate in self-enlightenment."

"Like nirvana?" Rae asked.

"In a way. But just the opposite of it."

"What do you mean?"

"Well, to put it simply, and I mean *very* simply—nirvana is the state one achieves by completely diffusing the concept of individuality. As I understand it, to reach nirvana, one becomes part of the universe. Xeper is the opposite of that. It is a coming into the complete self. Achieving the ultimate in independence of intellectual consciousness."

"That's a mouthful!" Angie exclaimed, giving her usual short laugh. "'Independence of intellectual consciousness.'"

Maren barely took notice of Angie's comment, and Rae suddenly wished she had not brought her sister along.

Rae drew her brows together, trying to make sense of what she'd just been told. "So if nirvana is a diffusing of self, then xeper is a focusing of self?"

"In a way, yes."

"What happens when a person reaches xeper?"

"Truthfully? I don't know." Maren sighed. "So few have attained the state. None that I know of, certainly. But I would imagine a person who reaches xeper may be able to alter his physical state. Or perhaps the physical state is no longer a necessary part of that person's reality."

"So our father may have literally disappeared?"

"To our consciousness, yes. We may not be able to perceive such a being, because we cling to conventional thought too much."

"Whatever." Angie gave a pert snort of disbelief. "Our dad is still MIA one way or another. He was never there for us, and that's what really bugs me."

Rae heard in Angie's voice the same bitterness she'd heard in Michael's. Funny, how she felt only sadness at the absence of a father, perhaps because she had led such a solitary life from very early in her childhood and didn't expect much from others, or perhaps because she didn't need much from others.

Maren smiled indulgently at Angie. "One does not need a father when one reaches maturity. When one is a true adult, there is no need to maintain the ties of dependency and guilt to another human being."

"Yeah, well maybe—" Angie mumbled, never one to participate with any enthusiasm in theoretical discussions.

"Consider for a moment how unfair it is to burden someone else with your life," Maren continued. "To expect them to take care of you. To criticize them for not hand-feeding everything in life to you, for expecting them to love you no matter what. And what do you give in return? Nothing. And the parent allows it. What weaklings most of us are raised to be!"

Angie glanced at Rae and rolled her eyes again, signaling that she thought Maren Lake was a wacko and the sooner they got out of the garden, the better. Rae, however, was fascinated and made no move to leave.

"It is not natural," Maren added. "There exists no parallel of this model of guilt and dependence in nature."

"But people have never fit in with the rest of the world," Angie replied. "That's what makes humans different."

"What makes us different is our minds, Angela. And if we could all learn to focus our minds on what's truly important, what a different world it would be!"

Rae gazed at the koi glinting vermilion and ivory in the dark water, and fell silent, struck by Maren's philosophy and sensing deep in her bones that what the woman was saying was a truth Rae had always known but had never given voice to.

"Miss Lambers?" Maren's soft voice intruded upon her thoughts. "Are you still with us?"

Rae forced herself to return to the present conversation but knew she would revisit in private the concepts Maren had just stirred to life within her. "Yes," she murmured. "But I am confused as to how you knew our father."

"He and I belonged to the same organization at one time."

"You mean you worked together?"

Maren shook her head slightly. "No, it was a spiritual type of organization."

"A church?" Angie asked.

"Of a kind. But that is not important." Maren tilted her head and gazed back at Rae. "You are so like your father, did you know that? I am amazed that you did not know him."

"I don't even remember what he looked like," Rae replied, glancing up the terraced hill behind the house, and casting her memory far away to when she was a little girl of three. Her father had run off just before her third birthday. That's all she could recall of the man—that he hadn't been there when she blew out the candles on her cake. She could still hear her mother saying tersely, "We are not waiting for your father, Fay. So blow the damn candles out. Now!"

Maren Lake interrupted her thoughts. "On the phone you mentioned the television program you saw me on—that you had a question for me about it."

Rae scooted forward on the bench. "Yes. I wanted to know what you meant by that tarot card you held up. What you meant about something coming alive."

"Because we've seen that card too," Angie blurted.

Rae shot her a glare, hoping to silence her from further outbursts of information.

"Oh?" Maren asked, her eyes darting from one to the other.

Rae held up her hand. "Let's get to that in a moment. First, could you explain what you meant when you held up that card?"

Maren nodded. "In conventional decks of tarot, the card I held up represents the devil, which most people think is a death card. But it isn't. It's a card that foretells great change—cataclysms that can be both mental and physical."

Rae took in Maren's every word, while Angie seemed caught up in an inspection of Maren's clothing.

"My deck is different. It is an Egyptian version, a very old version of the tarot. The devil is called Typhon in my deck. Essentially, however, the meaning is the same."

"But Typhon isn't the Egyptian version of the devil," Rae put in. She didn't know much of the tarot, but she certainly knew her Egyptian deities.

"You are right. He isn't. It wasn't until much later that Christians turned one of the Egyptian gods into Satan, and attributed to him all manner of evil, because he was the god of future things, of awakenings, of the chaos that occurs before new ways of thinking are adopted or great changes in the world are made—something established religions, based on security and the status quo, were very fearful of. And continue to be."

"What god was turned into Satan?" Rae asked, sorting through her knowledge of Egyptian history and coming up blank.

"Set." Marin waited for the concept to sink in. "The Greeks called him Typhon."

"So Satan is coming into our lives?" Angie gasped, her jaw falling open. She appeared to be genuinely afraid.

"Not Satan." Maren frowned for the first time. "You miss my point entirely."

Rae thought of Set, the serpent-dragon god of Egypt, ruler of thunder, lightning, and darkness, the mortal enemy of Ra. She could see why some people might have considered him evil. But in Egyptian mythology, every god had a purpose and played a necessary part in the ancient world, where chaos was accepted as part of the process of life, just as night followed day.

"The Typhon card means great change is coming," Rae corrected her sister. "Not the devil. Chaos and change."

"Exactly." Maren nodded. "And when I drew that card, I knew. I *knew*."

"Knew what?" Rae asked, her mouth dry.

"That something had occurred. Something huge. Like an axis shifting."

"You just knew it," Angie repeated, her tone scathing from being rebuked a moment ago.

"There are other portents." Maren rose to her feet. "Mount Etna has begun to erupt. Were you aware of that? In Greek mythology, Mount Etna is the mountain under which Typhon was trapped long ago."

Rae followed her with her gaze as Maren slowly paced the small gravel-covered area near the benches.

"And then there's the Hale-Bopp comet."

Rae straightened. "Didn't that already pass by?"

"Not completely. Not its tail. Some scientists believe that in a few years, somewhere in the tail of the comet, we will discover a tenth planet, a celestial body that actually belongs to our solar system. It will have a dramatic effect on the earth as it passes close to us. The tail of the Hale-Bopp might also bring noxious fallout to the earth. Do you remember your Bible stories—and the plagues of Egypt?"

"We never went to church," Angie answered sourly. "Our mother thought religion was a bunch of crap."

Rae didn't answer immediately, as she was too busy thinking back to the reading of her junior high school years. Even though she had attended very few church services, she had read the Bible as a young woman, as well as many other religious texts, simply to satisfy her curiosity. She couldn't remember any mention of the Hale-Bopp in the Bible, but she did remember her plagues. "When you say plagues, do you mean when the Nile turned red and the crops failed?"

"Yes." Maren turned and skewered Rae again with her vibrant blue regard. "There were seven plagues. And most of them could have been attributed to the effects of a comet, especially the red substance that turned the waters to blood. Such an effect was likely caused by particles of iron falling from the tail of the comet. Enough iron fallout would have sickened people, killed crops in the field, and fouled water supplies."

"Comets have iron dust flying around with them?" Angie asked.

"Iron, other minerals, ice, you name it, and gases. Plenty to make human beings ill. And guess who is the god of iron in Egyptian lore?"

"Set," Rae murmured. "Typhon."

"And guess who sat on the throne of Egypt in the days of the red rain?" Maren threw back her head, her face alight with triumph. "A pharaoh whose name paid homage to Set. Read your history."

Rae stared at her, struggling to take in all this new and

strangely connected information. Her mind leaped from Egypt to the heavens and back again to the little Japanese garden where the fish swam so innocently, so blithely unaware of the future. Were the koi at one with the universe? Rae's thoughts bounced wildly around, making her feel giddy and filled with a sense of doom all at the same time.

"That's it!" Angie jumped to her feet. "That's all I want to hear. It's just crazy!"

Maren glanced at her. "Is it?"

"What if it's all coincidence?"

"Do you think it's mere coincidence?"

Rae shook her head, clearing her thoughts, trying not to connect the dots because of the cataclysmic reality the new image predicted. She didn't want the world to suffer what Egypt had suffered for seven years. It would mean the complete breakdown of society as modern man knew it. Too much of the world was interconnected these days, too interdependent, a delicate balance that could easily overturn into absolute chaos.

Maren waited for Rae to look up at her, and then the silver-haired woman's gaze burned into hers, as if to tell Rae that everything she had just considered was a distinct possibility. Slowly, Angie sank back to her seat, uncharacteristically silent, her face clouded with confusion, her pretty mouth ruined by a troubled frown.

"Do you mean to say," Rae began, trying to form a coherent theory out of everything she'd just heard. "That as far as you believe, Typhon is coming back to rule the earth, and that we are due for a long period of chaos?"

"Yes, that is what I believe. In fact, there are others who take it a step further."

"In what way?"

"They believe the tenth planet—or the twelfth if you count the moon and sun as the ancients did—may be the home of those beings whom man once considered gods. Perhaps we will be visited again by beings far more advanced than we are."

"You mean aliens?" Angie wailed, tipping her head back to stare up at the sky. "Oh, God!"

Rae thought of Michael's remark when they had discussed Maren Lake, and his prediction that if her tarot theory didn't work out, she'd turn to alien intervention. Michael would be having a field day with the stuff Maren was talking about now. If he were here, he would be ripping holes in the Typhon theory—holes big enough for the twelfth planet to soar through as well as the comet and its big red tail. At the thought, Rae began to smile but stopped herself, knowing the conversation was far too serious to be undercut by her penchant for irony.

"But may I remind you both," Maren put in, drifting back to her bench. "That chaos is not necessarily bad. To have birth, we must have death. To have spring, we must have winter. Yin and yang. Remember that."

"But people could die!" Angie sputtered. "I mean, you know—the earth's water supply could be ruined and stuff!"

"Perhaps." Maren shrugged. "But isn't the world overcrowded, Angela? Isn't there war and conflict in practically every continent of our planet? How will the wars ever end unless a major cataclysm occurs to shake us up, to shock us out of our childish infighting?"

Rae could read the wildness in Angie's eyes and realized her sister was becoming overly distraught. She decided to guide the discussion back to reality.

"And you also think Thomas Gregory's death had something to do with all this?"

"Yes." Maren nodded. "He left me a voice mail on the night he was killed."

A chill coursed down Rae's spine. She'd been correct. Thomas *had* tried to contact Maren Lake before he died. "What did he say to you?" Rae asked, her voice barely above a whisper.

"Just two words: 'Set is—'" Maren's face paled as she recalled the last few minutes of Thomas Gregory's life. "Then the message broke off. I could hear a storm in the background, as if he were calling in the midst of a tornado. And then the message just broke off."

"Did you tell this to the police?"

"I have learned not to tell such things to the police." She blinked and her expression soured. "Let's just say they aren't interested in my observations."

"I was in the Gregory house after Thomas's death," Rae said, looking at her hands as she recalled the shock of stepping into the mess left by the supposed vandals. "The mess was unbelievable, like a cyclone had passed through it."

"A storm."

"Yes."

"A storm inside the house?" Angie countered. "Come on!"

Rae ignored her. "How were you and Thomas connected, if you don't mind telling me?"

"At one time he belonged to the same temple as your father and I."

"Rae, come on." Angie rose to her feet. "Let's go. I am totally creeped out by all of this."

Begrudgingly, Rae stood up. She would have preferred to stay and talk with Maren Lake, but knew her sister had reached her limit. She knew they had to go.

Maren stood up as well. "Before you leave, didn't you mention you had seen the Typhon tarot card somewhere too?"

Angie paled. "It was nothing," she replied. "Not that important. Just a reading."

"I see." Maren crossed her arms over her chest. She raised an eyebrow and turned her knowing gaze on Rae, as if seeking the truth.

To avoid Maren's penetrating stare, Rae reached down and grabbed her purse, knowing that to show the old deck of cards to the older woman would mean spending much more time in the garden. Angie, in her frightened closed-mindedness, would make any ensuing discussion a painful experience. Rae sighed, frustrated and far from satisfied. But she knew that showing the Forbidden Tarot to Maren would be better left for another time. She slung the straps of her bag over her left shoulder. "May I call you sometime?" she asked. "If I find out anything else about Dr. Gregory?"

"Of course. Any time at all, Rae."

"Thank you." She held out her hand.

Maren shook her hand. Her grasp was firm and warm, her smile genuine, and Rae knew she had found a soul mate in this woman.

"The more we can find out about your father's disappearance and Thomas Gregory's death, the better." Maren released her hand. Then she gestured toward the house. "Come inside. I'll get you my card."

# Chapter 14

During the half-hour drive back to Alameda, Rae and Angie discussed their father, now that they had received new information about him. They also argued about the merits of Maren Lake's theories. Angie was convinced the older woman was a nutcase, and criticized her clothing, her manners, and her unconventional interpretation of history. Rae played devil's advocate as usual, not fully believing what Maren had said either, at least not until she had time to research the subject on her own. But her previous experiences, both with Thomas's video and the photographs, prompted her to seriously consider the comet theory and the Egyptian connection before she discarded it.

"Do you think any of this has to do with the Forbidden Tarot?" Angie asked, her face still drawn with worry.

Rae guided her car toward the Posey Tube. "I thought you didn't believe anything Maren said back there."

"I don't. But what about Michael's dad? What about my sleepwalking?"

Angie failed to mention Michael's car accident, which could have been added to the list. But maybe it *had* been just an accident. Rae glanced at her sister and then back to the dark underwater tunnel they drove through.

"How could the cards have anything to do what's been happening? The man in Egypt said the tarot would affect whoever looked at them. Thomas Gregory never laid eyes on the cards."

"But you knew him."

"So that means everyone we know could be in jeopardy?"

Angie shrugged and crossed her arms. "God, Rae, I don't know!"

"Besides, I was the first one to look at the cards. And nothing has happened to me."

As soon as the words left Rae's mouth, she regretted them. To spout out such a pronouncement was to tempt fate to prove her wrong. All her life, the moment she had said something similar, such as, "I haven't been sick for weeks," Rae would come down with a horrible virus. Or if she said, "I have never failed an English test," she would get a terrible grade on a paper. She squeezed the steering wheel of her Jetta, suddenly wishing she had kept her mouth shut.

"I think we should get rid of the cards," Angie muttered, her lower lip pinched with worry.

"But what if they *are* cursed?"

"Let someone else deal with it. We have enough troubles."

"That wouldn't be very charitable of us, Angie."

"What about selling them, then? I bet we could get a good price for them. You could use the money for your resource center." Angie turned to her as the car sped out of the tunnel and up the rise toward home. "We could warn the buyer about what might happen, just to get it out in the open. But I bet someone would buy them anyway."

"Just like you opened them anyway?"

"Yes, well." Angie slumped in the seat. "I wish I hadn't. I should have listened to you."

Rae glanced at her in surprise. "That's a first!" she exclaimed, unable to remember the last time Angie had admitted to doing anything wrong.

"I just want to get rid of them. I want to work at Nordstrom, come home, have dinner, and chill. I just want to make some money and take it easy. No surprises, no Brent, no sleepwalking, and no Forbidden Tarot."

"Sounds like a plan, Angie," Rae replied, pulling up in front of the house.

LATE SUNDAY EVENING Michael grimaced as he walked toward the study, a wireless router in his hand.

Earlier that morning after his run, he'd felt okay. Not great, but okay. Now, however, the effects of the car accident permeated every bone in his body. He was so stiff he could barely force himself to keep moving. He saw light pouring out of the study doorway and guessed Rae must be in the windowless room, doing her incessant snooping around in his father's stuff. What would she find this time to shove under his nose as proof that his father had been in his right mind? She would have to find something really earth-shattering to convince him of that.

Just outside the doorway, Michael paused for a moment and breathed in, forcing his shoulders back and opening his eyes wide to try to dissipate the lines of pain he knew creased his face. He hadn't forgotten how Rae had found him lacking the other morning, and he wasn't about to go shuffling into the study looking like a beaten old man, even if he did feel like one.

When he judged himself suitably presentable, he stepped forward and through the door. Much to his surprise, he discovered not Rae at the desk but Angie sitting at the computer. He must have surprised her as well, because she gave a little gasp and put her left hand over something on the table. Then she gazed up at him, her expression blank and innocent, but the guileless look didn't fool him for an instant. After years of training under Vee's crafty tutelage, he could tell when a woman was truly innocent or just playing the part.

"What's up, Angie?" he asked, glancing down at the object she'd covered with her hand. But all he could see of it was the corner of what looked like a metal box. A small digital camera and a cable sat on the table next to the monitor.

"Just checking my mail," she replied, blinking too quickly to be believed.

Michael glanced at the computer screen, saw nothing that looked like an e-mail, and then surveyed her pretty face. What she was doing was none of his business. If she wanted to pretend she was checking her mail, he wasn't going to accuse her of lying.

"It's amazing how e-mail piles up," she added, reaching for the mouse.

"Then you'll like this." Michael held up the wireless hub.

"What is that?" She still didn't move her left hand.

"It's a wireless connection so we can all use the Net. Anywhere in the house. I need it for my laptop upstairs."

"That's cool."

"It'll be a lot more convenient. We can all be on the Net at the same time." He located the cable connection and glanced back at her. "Would you mind shutting down for a sec? I have to disconnect your cable."

"I was just finished anyway."

"Great." While he waited for her to shut off the computer, he pretended to be busy but kept an eye on her out of the corner of his vision. When she thought he wasn't watching her, she picked up the box and stood up. He caught a glimpse of a strange-looking container with a brown seal around its midsection. Why was Angie being so secretive about it? Maybe it was a female thing—a container for something better left un-inquired about.

Trying to keep from straining his bruised muscles, Michael dropped to one knee and loosened the cable connection from the computer and fastened it to the wireless hub he had purchased that afternoon. Then he put the hub up on a file cabinet and plugged it in.

"Would you mind turning on the computer now?" he asked, glancing at Angie over his shoulder. She held the box in her left hand and the camera in her right.

"No problem."

Michael watched as she put down the box so she could push the on button of the computer. The little carton didn't look like any feminine product holder he had ever seen, and Angie had tried to hide it, which made him doubly curious.

"What is that thing?" he asked.

She slid it off the table. "Just a box."

"What kind of box?"

"Oh." Angie shrugged and took a step for the door. "Just something Rae found."

He could tell she didn't want to discuss it. "Something she found here in the house?"

"No, not really." Angie walked to the door.

"Where, then?"

"Oh, I think on one of her trips."

"Angie, why are you being so weird about it?"

She turned in the doorway and faced him. "I'm not being weird."

"Yes you are. You look like a cat who just ate a mouse."

"I do not!" Angie rolled her eyes and propped the back of her right hand on her hip, as if to show him how relaxed and casual she was. "But if you must know, it's a deck of tarot cards."

"Tarot cards?"

"Yes." She tossed her head and glared at him, her blue eyes daring him to question her further.

"Rae has a deck of tarot cards?" Michael flipped on the toggle switch of the wireless hub. "That I find hard to believe."

"Well, believe it. She found them in the desert. She thinks they're antique."

"In the desert—you mean in Egypt?"

"Yeah."

"Tarot cards." He shook his head, still disbelieving that Rae owned them. "Maybe we can get her to read our fortunes tonight." He bent to the computer to work with the connection settings.

"I don't think so. She's out."

"With Avare?" Michael shot Angie a glance.

She nodded and shifted her weight. "Besides, Rae doesn't believe in fortune-telling."

"No, just that wacko on television who thinks my father was killed by lightning."

"You know about Maren Lake?"

"Yeah. Rae tried to convince me to have my father's body exhumed after we saw her on a TV program."

"Well, we went to see that woman today."

"What?" Shocked, Michael stood up straight and turned to face Angie.

"Yep. We went to visit her. Apparently she knew your dad and ours." Angie shook her head. "She thinks aliens are coming to visit Earth in a few years from a planet that hasn't been discovered yet."

"Oh, boy." It was Michael's turn to roll his eyes. "Then I'd better take the raygun in for a tune-up."

Angie laughed. "Yeah, like I believed her too!" But Angie gave a quick look over her shoulder that undercut her confident words.

"What did Rae think of her?" Michael asked.

"You know Rae." The laughter had faded from Angie's expression. "Most of the time it's hard to tell what she's thinking."

"But she does a lot of it—thinking, that is."

"She's always been like that." Angie propped one shoulder against the doorjamb. "Way too quiet. My friends thought she was the most boring person on earth."

"I wouldn't call her boring."

"Weird then."

"Weird maybe. Boring? Never." To tell the truth, he wouldn't call Rae weird either. She was simply an individual. And brilliant. A person like Rae would never fit in with the rest of the population. Plus the fact she went her own way without caring what others thought. He had to respect that. So few people he knew had the guts to lead such a life.

But why would such a levelheaded woman waste her time on a creep like Avare? That was one thing about Rae he didn't understand. What could she possibly see in the guy? Did she harbor feelings for him? Michael knew only too well how love and lust could cripple a person's judgment, but he just couldn't see Rae losing her common sense over a man.

"Uh, hello, Mike. Anybody home?"

Michael jerked out of his thoughts like a person coming up for air from a deep dive. He found Angie staring at him, her head tilted to one side, inspecting him for signs of life.

"Where did you just go?" she asked.

"I was just thinking—" he answered, shocked that he had

lapsed into thoughts of Rae again and unwilling to admit it to her sister. He rubbed the back of his neck.

"Thinking," Angie chided.

"About something else I need for the computer."

"Right." She smirked. "I'm going to go make a salad. Want something?"

"No, thanks. I'm good."

AS SIMEON LEFT to get a bottle of wine, Rae sighed contentedly and leaned back, idly surveying the vista of twinkling lights below the veranda. It was Sunday evening, and Simeon had invited her to his house for a private dinner, just the two of them for once. She didn't have to go to work in the morning, at least not to the university. Plenty of work waited for her at the Gregory house on Monday, including her much-delayed book, but even so, she refused to worry about how late she might linger this evening at Simeon's home in Piedmont.

For the last hour, they'd shared champagne and talked of Egypt while they watched the sun sink behind the city. Now, as the sky deepened from lilac to indigo, she could smell lamb being grilled by Simeon's cook, and the succulent aroma made her mouth water.

While she was still gazing over the rooftops of Oakland, she heard Simeon's light step behind her, and then felt his warm hands slip over the curves of her shoulders. Heat coursed through her body. She sighed and tipped her head back, feeling slightly buzzed on the champagne, as she hadn't eaten much all day and was now in a state of much-needed relaxation.

"You melt when I touch you," he murmured.

"Because your touch has an amazing quality to it," she replied.

Simeon's hands moved forward, down the slight curves of her breasts. Rae held her breath when his palms passed over her nipples as he lightly caressed her breasts. As an adult, she had never been touched this intimately by a man. She felt pinned to the chair, shocked by this new level of closeness between them, and not certain what to make of it.

"Do you like that?" he inquired, his breath fanning her neck.

"Yes," she said, but knew it wasn't the truth. She honestly didn't know what she was feeling at the moment. "You have such a warm touch."

"You need my touch." He leaned down, close enough so that his lips hovered just behind her left ear. "I know of your illness, Fay Rae."

She stiffened. "How?"

"I can sense such things."

She tried to twist around to look at him, but he chuckled and held her fast, pressing his cheek to hers. "It is all right, Fay Rae. Allow me to help you heal."

"But how can you?" she whispered, her moment of relaxation totally forgotten in the heat of his hands and what he was doing to her breasts.

"It is a matter of focus," he murmured into her ear. "I channel my energy into my hands, and I send my energy into your body. Like this."

His hands moved back up her breasts, and then he gently slipped his fingers beneath the edge of her pullover and into the cups of her brassiere. He sighed heavily when the firm orbs of her small breasts filled each of his palms. Rae closed her eyes as his energy soared through her chest and shot all the way down to her toes.

"That's marvelous," she gasped, her mouth agape with wonder.

"I can offer you a lifetime of such marvel." He kissed her ear. "You would never know pain again."

Rae swallowed, trying to make sense of what he was saying. Simeon could heal her? Could he actually free her from a disease whose prognosis was a life sentence of increasing pain and crippling joints? She couldn't believe it. To be free of pain would totally change her life, totally change her future.

"What are you saying?" she whispered, turning in his embrace, wishing to rid herself of the boundaries of the chair. His blessed hands released her breasts as he stepped around to the side of the chair, grasped her hands gently, and raised her to her feet. Then, as if enveloping her in a huge warm cloak, he pulled her against him and wrapped his arms around her, pressing her to his chest.

"I am saying," he murmured into her hair, "that we are good for each other. You for me and me for you. We should honor that and enjoy each other."

"But how am I good for you?" She pulled back and stared up at his face, not believing a man would ever choose her. She knew her limitations, and she had learned to live with them. To have the definition of her place in the world of men contradicted like this was difficult for her to comprehend.

"You share my interests. You are not frivolous. Your mind is a fascinating and ever-changing tableau that will be forever interesting."

"But I'm skinny and bookish. I'm not what most men want."

"I am not most men, Fay Rae." He hugged her. "Surely you know that by now."

"But I am so often ill—"

She broke off what she was going to say, not wanting to add that her illness would make her a lousy partner, especially in bed. Physically, her joints and bones would not withstand the rigors of sex well. And mentally, she wasn't certain if she would ever get over Albert's pawing enough to enjoy any amount of intimacy with Simeon.

"But that is what I am trying to tell you, my dear." He eased back to gaze down at her face. "With me, you will heal. I promise you. You will blossom and grow. Both physically and mentally." He lightly drew two fingers down the gaunt line of her cheek, and she wondered if he could read her mind. He had used the exact words she had been thinking about. Was he somehow aware of her reservations as well?

"The beauty you possess beneath the pain you mask will

burst out in a glorious awakening, Fay Rae. In fact, you have begun to change already, ever since the day we met."

Rae blushed and glanced down at his fingers, which slowly dragged across her lips.

"Have you not noticed?" he added, his voice husky. He raised her chin to tip her face upward.

"A bit," she answered, looking back up at him.

"And yet I see your full beauty even now as I look at you like this, because I know what you can become."

Rae saw his eyes begin to close and his mouth lowering to hers, and so she closed her own eyes and let him kiss her. His hands stroked her back and pressed her close to his lean body. She linked her arms around his neck and tried to return his kiss, but was still too shocked by his words to be able to feel any great swell of passion. She could tell that he was fully aroused by their embrace, but she was far too nervous to respond in kind. She had never been in a situation like this—man to woman—and had only witnessed embraces in movies.

Standing here with Simeon Avare was nothing like a movie. Far too many sensations and feelings buffeted her, making her feel light-headed and confused, and suddenly aware of the dryness of his mouth, the chasteness of their kiss.

She pulled back from his lips just as his butler appeared with the chilled bottle of white wine.

"Thank you, George," Simeon said, releasing Rae from his ardent embrace. They both watched George uncork the wine, carefully wrap the bottle in a crisp white linen cloth, and then pour two goblets.

George stepped back from the table.

"We are ready for our appetizers now," Simeon said.

"Very good, *neb*." The butler backed away as Simeon handed a goblet to Rae and held his up in a toast.

"Did he just call you *neb*?" Rae asked, remembering the strange name from Angie's sleepwalking escapade the other night.

"Yes. Why?"

"What does it mean?"

"Master. Or lord. Why?"

"Angie said it when she was sleepwalking the other night. We thought it was somebody's name."

"No, it is a common term of address," Simeon remarked. "At least in Egypt." He smiled. "But let us make a toast now."

"All right."

"To chance meetings," he said, "that are guided by Fate."

"Yes," Rae replied, still lost for words. "To Fate."

They drank to one another and then Simeon urged her to sit down.

He scooted his chair forward. "You seem nervous."

"I am." She played with the glass base of her goblet. "I haven't had much practice at this."

"That makes you even more precious to me."

She shot a quick glance at him. Was he looking for a virgin? A twenty-eight-year-old virgin? What kind of man was he?

"There is no need to be worried," he added as he studied her kindly over the rim of his glass. "I will never do anything that you do not wish me to do."

"You are a gentleman, Simeon. I'll give you that."

"Yes, but I am a gentleman who is not afraid to ask for what he wants." Simeon raised an eyebrow.

"I gathered that about you." Rae was finally beginning to feel her feet again, now that she was no longer standing in Simeon's arms and being distracted by his words and his hands.

He smiled again. "But I have found that my intensity can be frightening to some people."

"Maybe because you don't take no for an answer?"

"I rarely ever have to." He laughed softly and then put down his glass to study her seriously. "Does that mean you intend to play—how do you say it?—hard to get?"

"Not necessarily," Rae replied, feeling relaxed again. "I'm not the playful type."

"I bet that you are. Deep down." He leveled a knowing gaze upon her as he sat back, propping his wrist on the back of chair. "When you feel comfortable with someone. Sure of them."

"Perhaps." She caught sight of George returning to the veranda, carrying a tray, and straightened in her seat as he set their appetizers before them, both small dishes covered with domed lids of silver.

"Thank you," she said as he filled her wine goblet.

Soon they were alone again, and Simeon indicated for her to begin eating first. She lifted the small silver lid and gasped silently when she saw a black velvet box sitting on the plate in front of her. Rae glanced over at Simeon. His eyes gleamed, but he said nothing, and simply gestured with his hand for her to continue.

Rae looked down at the tiny box. The shape of the container could hold only one thing: a ring. She felt a cold sweat break out along her spine. Was she ready for this? Would she ever be ready for this? And yet, would she ever meet a man like Simeon, who could eliminate her pain with the mere touch of his hand, who loved Egypt as she did, who had money and taste and a good head on his shoulders? He was perfect for her. Even so, she felt a spiritual impropriety in the moment, something she could only attribute to the breakneck pace of their relationship.

"Go ahead," Simeon urged. "Please!"

She picked up the box, and her hands trembled as she opened it. The lid snapped upward, displaying a huge, incredibly light-filled diamond ring.

"It is but a trinket," he began, leaning his forearms on the table. The fingers of his right hand eased over her hand that held the box. "But I hope that it will show you how serious I am. To reflect how valuable you have become to me. And to let you know my intentions are to spend the rest of my life with you."

"With me?" Her voice cracked, betraying her unease.

"With you." He smiled at her, his silver eyes glinting, looking very much in control of the situation and his emotions. "As I said, I am a man who knows what he wants. And I want you."

"You barely know me!"

"On the contrary, my dear. We know each other very well."

Carefully, he pulled the ring from its white satin perch and held it up. The gem glittered in the candlelight, another celestial body in the night sky. "We knew it the moment we spoke on the plane. Tell me that I am wrong."

"Simeon, I don't know what to say!"

"Then say you will marry me."

# Chapter 15

Simeon slipped the ring upon Rae's frail finger, and it slid perfectly into place. He knew of her illness. Apparently he knew her ring size as well.

"Say you will be my bride and bear my child, and make a future with me."

She gaped at him, her heart pounding like thunder in her chest. Did he just say bear his child? She had never considered being a mother. Given her condition, carrying a child was beyond the realm of possibilities. And yet, if Simeon really could heal her—

"There is no rush." He grasped the fingertips of both her hands in his, interrupting her thoughts. "There is no rush, Fay Rae. Tell me you will consider my suit."

"Then, yes." Rae swallowed, still thunderstruck. "I will."

"Consider it?"

"Yes." She was suddenly so nervous, her mouth trembled, and she worried that her teeth would start to chatter. Was he so old-fashioned that he believed they had to be engaged in order for them to sleep together? Was that why he was doing this? Or had he truly fallen in love with her?

He raised her hands and kissed her fingertips, and she could see he made no effort to conceal his joy.

"You make me a very happy man!" he exclaimed. "Very happy indeed!"

She smiled to cloak her disquiet. She had to have time to think through all that had just occurred before she could form an opinion about it. Everything had happened so fast! But she did not want to offend Simeon with her reluctance to share his enthusiasm, for as men went, he was everything that she admired. Joy might come for her just as surely as it had come to him, but not until she had time to think things through, not until she was sure she was taking the right step.

To shift the focus from their engagement to their dinner, she pointed at his still-covered plate. "So what is the real appetizer this evening?"

He lifted the domed lid. "Ah, scallops in a truffle sauce. Delightful!" He shoved the dish to the middle of the table. "These are meant to be shared."

They ate in companionable silence and when they had finished, George brought out the entrée and then a salad for Rae.

"You don't eat any vegetables?" she asked as Simeon watched her poke her greens with a fork.

"I restrict my diet entirely to meat. And an occasional glass of alcohol."

"But that's unhealthy!"

"According to whom?"

"Well." Rae lifted a forkful of rocket. "All the dietary studies that have been done, for instance."

"Studies of lions? Of wolves? Of the Inuit?" He sipped his wine. "All powerful creatures. All carnivores."

"But where do you get your vitamins?"

"Apparently I get enough from the internal organs of animals. I can say in all honesty I do not suffer a lack of vitality."

She glanced at him, wondering if his words had a deeper meaning. She didn't doubt that he would be an ardent lover. His every movement was controlled, taut, and spare. Even his languid gestures were underlaid by the measured grace of an animal in its prime.

"In fact," he added, "I cannot remember the last time I was ill."

"Maybe I should try such a diet."

"Perhaps you should." He glanced at her nearly empty plate. "But it appears you enjoy your salad greens."

"That I do." She popped the last of them in her mouth. "And I don't think I would want to give them up, now that you mention it."

They spoke idly through dinner, and when coffee was served, Simeon's tone grew more serious.

"It is wonderful, sitting here with you like this," he said, draping his right hand over her left.

"Yes, it is. Thank you very much for dinner. For everything."

"Perhaps one day soon we won't have to part when dinner is done."

She nodded.

"I believe the sooner you buy out Michael Gregory, the better," he continued, giving her hand a slight squeeze. "So we may get on with our affairs."

"So do I, but Michael told me he would not sell to you."

"But it is you who are buying the house."

"Partly with your money."

"You told him I have agreed to help you?"

"Of course." Rae slipped her hand from his and lifted her coffee cup. "It wasn't a secret, was it?"

"No, not at all." Simeon's eyes clouded. "But he harbors ill feelings toward me. It would have been better not to have confided in him."

"I prefer to have things out in the open."

"With most people, I would agree with you. But with Michael Gregory? No." Simeon took a sip of his coffee. "Why do you not tell him that you have received a surprisingly large check from some deceased relative, that you have come into enough money to buy it on your own?"

"That would be lying—"

"But you would get what you want. You must manipulate this man, Fay Rae, or he will remain uncooperative. Do you not see this?"

"I see it," she answered, frowning, "But it isn't the way I usually operate."

"Then I will do it for you if you prefer."

"Right. Like he would even let you in the house."

"Michael Gregory cannot keep me from anything." Simeon's words were so chilled with hatred that Rae stared up at him, wondering for a moment if she had heard him correctly. But the hatred was reflected in Simeon's silver eyes and in the lines around his grim mouth, making him look suddenly much older than his thirty-some years.

Then, as soon as the anger had appeared, it vanished, and Simeon took on his usual charming demeanor. The lines smoothed and his eyes cleared.

"Let us speak no more of him, Fay Rae. I have no wish to sour such a wonderful evening."

"Me neither." Rae finished her coffee and carefully set the cup upon the fragile china saucer. "But I really should go. It's nearly midnight."

"So late?" He glanced at his watch. "Ah, how time flies with you." Then he stood up. "I will have my driver take you home, if that is all right with you."

"It's fine." Rae rose and placed her napkin beside her coffee cup. She was suddenly overwhelmed by fatigue. It had been quite a day, and she had much to consider. But though she was exhausted, she knew she would find it difficult to sleep.

THE LIGHTS ON the bottom floor of the Gregory house were dark as Rae carefully let herself in and closed the door behind her, not wanting to alert anyone to her midnight arrival. The last thing she wanted to do was talk to anyone else that evening. She was completely talked out. If Angie happened to be up and eager to hear how her dinner with Simeon had transpired, Rae knew she would have to beg for a rain check. Just in case anyone was still awake upstairs, Rae slipped the diamond ring off her finger and dropped it into her purse. If anyone caught sight of the huge diamond, she would be forced to explain what had happened, and she was just too tired.

As Rae reached the top of the stairs, she saw a movement in Angie's doorway. Rae prepared herself for the onslaught of her sister's curiosity, but was surprised to see Michael stroll out of the bedroom, his chest bare and his jeans unsnapped at the waist. Rae flushed, shocked that Michael had been with Angie. He must have heard her arrive, had jumped out of Angie's bed, and was now trying to appear all casual about it. Michael with Angie? The thought stopped Rae in her tracks and made her heart plummet to the floor.

When Michael caught sight of Rae, he paused and studied her face for an instant. "It's not what you think—" he began, holding up both hands as if to ward off the accusation to come.

"Michael?" Rae gasped, sick at heart. Of all the men in the world, she had thought Michael would be the last person to be seduced by her sister. On almost every level, Rae had always thought Michael was on her wavelength, was *her* friend, part of *her* world, not Angie's. Her mind went into a tailspin, and she staggered to the door.

"Rae, just a goddamn minute—"

Without waiting to hear his explanation, Rae plunged into her bedroom and shut the door. She leaned on it, gasping for breath, and trying very hard not to lose her dinner.

Michael did not let her retire gracefully. "Rae?" he questioned on the other side of the door.

"Leave me alone," she mumbled.

"No." He rattled the doorknob. "You never let me explain anything!"

"So?" Even in her distraught state, she realized how childish she sounded.

"Rae!" He knocked on the door. "Come on! Don't jump to conclusions!"

Maybe he did have an excuse. Maybe she *was* jumping to conclusions, the very thing she had accused him of doing.

"Rae!"

Rae sighed and peeled herself away from the door, unlatching it at the same time. Michael swung it open and stood in the doorway, his shoulder muscles backlit by the sconce in the hall, making his silhouette appear more powerful and masculine than ever.

"How could you?" she began, turning to face him, hot with angry disappointment.

"How could I what?" he replied, stepping forward.

Rae backed up, trying not to look at his bare chest. "Do *that* with my sister?"

"Do what?"

"Have sex with her!"

He took another step forward, forcing Rae to back into her room. "That would upset you?" he continued.

"Of course it would!"

"Why?" He tilted his head and stared down at her, studying her closely.

"Because!" She glared up at him and then away, her glance darting around, landing anywhere but on his naked torso. Her mouth had suddenly gone dry.

"Because why?" Michael pressed. "We're all adults here."

"Because she's vulnerable, that's why!"

"Is that it? Because she's vulnerable? It has nothing to do with you?"

Rae shot a second glare up at his serious face. His eyes were locked on hers. She swallowed, not knowing what to say or how to begin, or even if she should try to explain. Where did she expect her adult relationship with Michael to go, especially if he had started something with her sister?

"Why should it have anything to do with me?" she asked, her voice hoarse.

"Maybe because you're jealous?" He was throwing her own words back at her.

"Me? Jealous?" She gave a sharp laugh, and realized she was sounding just like him the other night, when she'd accused him of being jealous of Simeon. "You think I'd ever be jealous of Angie?"

"Yeah. Because of me."

"You?"

"Yeah." He threw his shoulders back as if he expected to have to defend himself.

Rae's stomach was pinched together in the aftermath of the streaking jealousy she'd just experienced, but would she admit it to Michael? He'd laughed the other night when she'd brought up the subject of jealousy and then had cut off her attempt at reconciliation. Why should she explain or admit anything to him now? He wasn't interested. He'd made that quite clear.

And yet, she longed to tell him everything, to clear the air, to go back to that simpler time when they were the best of friends with nothing to get in the way. She swallowed and hugged her chest with her arms.

"Michael—" she began, her voice far from steady.

"Rae, I swear." He stepped forward and grasped both of her shoulders in his hands. But this time his touch was light, just the barest of pressure, and she did not shrink from him. "I was just helping Angie to bed."

Rae looked up at him. "Why?"

"Because she had too much to drink. That's why."

"Oh." Chagrined, Rae sighed and dragged away her stare, down to the level of Michael's lean, bare chest. The fragrance of his clean body was like a drug she could not allow herself to savor. She forced herself not to take a deep, appreciative breath.

"Rae?" Michael bent down again to look directly into her eyes. "Just so you know, I am not the least interested in your sister. She's not my type."

"She's always been every man's type."

"Well, I'm not every man." He tipped up her chin, gently compelling her to look at him. "And you know that."

Her gaze poured into his, making that same connection of the other night.

"And whatever happened that day when we were kids," he continued, his expression deadly serious. "I have a feeling you jumped to a conclusion, just like you did a minute ago."

Rae's mouth went even drier. "That was what I wanted to talk to you about—"

"*You're* my type, Rae." Michael's voice changed to a softer tone as he dipped to her mouth. "You are."

Then, for the first time in their lives, he kissed her. Their lips met, their mouths touching as their hearts and minds had so often joined. But Michael's kiss was a deeper, more stirring connection than anything Rae had ever known. A surge of emotion burgeoned up, so strong that she grabbed Michael's elbows to keep from tumbling backward. But the kiss was brief, and Michael rose up from her mouth almost immediately, his breath coming hard and fast, as if he had been as overwhelmed as she had been.

Rae felt the kiss pull away from her lips, tugging at something buried deep inside that yearned to stay joined to Michael—to be part of this communion forever. Begrudgingly, she let the moment dissolve and gradually opened her eyes to find him gazing at her face.

"And that's all I wanted to do that day." Michael's voice was grave with emotion. "I swear."

Rae's tongue stuck to the roof of her mouth as Michael slowly slid out of her grasp, disconnecting from her.

"I would never force myself on a woman," he added. "And I would never come on to a woman, not unless she wanted me to."

"But that day," she stammered, glancing down at his unsnapped jeans and then back up to his face. "You had an erection. I could see it. And then you grabbed me!"

"I was a sixteen-year-old kid, Rae. Hell, I couldn't *help* but have an erection around you!"

"You shocked me! I had believed we were friends."

"We were!" Michael spread his long fingers in a gesture of frustration. "We *were!*"

"But that day I realized you wanted to have sex with me, that you thought about me in that way, that you must have looked at me and thought about it—"

"Jesus, Rae, what's wrong with that!" Michael cocked his head to one side. "Every red-blooded male thinks about sex. A lot!"

"But I thought you were different," she countered. "I thought you wanted my friendship, not all that other complicated stuff."

"I *did* want your friendship. But there can be more than friendship between a man and a woman, Rae. And it was becoming that for me. I wanted to go further with you."

"Why didn't you ask me, then?"

"I was trying to that day!" He ran his left hand over his black hair. "But I was young, I was clumsy, I got carried away—" He broke off and stared at the far wall.

"I wore that blue dress because I thought it was going to be a special day." Rae recalled the June afternoon when they were to pick up their report cards on the last day of school. Michael had asked her to meet him after class and had mentioned he had something to give her. She had worn a new dress that her mother had bought her as a reward for doing so well her sophomore year.

"It was *supposed* to have been special," he added, "Until you slapped my face and ran off."

"I felt so betrayed, Michael. You frightened me so much. I just ran."

"Because I had a hard-on?"

She nodded. "That and the way you grabbed me."

He sighed. "I was all worked up, thinking about going off for the whole summer to basketball camp, and you being left behind, not knowing how I was beginning to feel about you. I just had to tell you. I just had to kiss you. I just—" He sighed and shook his head. "I just scared the hell out of you, that's what I did."

She nodded. "And why didn't you ever call?"

"After the things you said to me?" He glanced at her. "I might have been clumsy back then, but I wasn't crazy!" He crossed his arms over his chest. "When a girl tells you she hates your guts, that she never thought of you in *that way* and never will, and that she never wants to see you again—hell, would you call her?"

Rae looked down at the floor. She'd allowed a knee-jerk reaction to destroy the best friendship of her life. She should have cleared the air long ago. How different their lives might have been. She raised her head.

"I'm sorry, Michael, for those things I said. I realize now how cruel they must have sounded."

"You didn't really mean them, then?"

"I did." She met his intense gaze. "Back then, yes, I did. There was a lot going on with me then. I was easily upset."

"And now?"

Rae blinked, knowing her reply might affect the remaining years of her life, but aware that a certain distance must be retained between them until she adjusted to the new information and decided where she wanted to go in regard to Michael. He was, after all, going through a divorce, and she had just been given an engagement ring.

What could she say that would not insult Michael again, give her time to think things through, and at the same time keep her personal business to herself? She had never been good with words, but tonight she felt more tongue-tied than ever.

"Right," Michael put in, his voice gruff, as he misinterpreted her silence. "Looks like it's always been one-sided. And it still is."

Rae opened her mouth to blurt out the overused phrase "It's me, not you," but the words died in her throat. If she said anything like that, Michael would demand to know what she meant and would insist she confide in him. She just wasn't ready to dump the load of dirty laundry from her childhood on Eagle Avenue—not on anyone, and certainly not on Michael.

He backed toward the door.

"Michael!" She reached for him, but he was already out of reach.

"I don't need to be told twice." He turned and strode into the hallway. Then he looked over his shoulder at her, his expression dark. "I'm not a complete idiot!"

His hot glance flared across her face for an instant, scorching her, and then he walked away.

THE NEXT MORNING as Rae poured cereal into a bowl for breakfast, she was surprised to see Angie appear in the doorway, her hair in a tangled mess on top of her head and dressed in a pair of jeans and T-shirt that looked as if she'd slept in them.

Rae glanced at her watch and then back at her sister. "Aren't you working today?"

"I'm going to call in sick."

"No you're not." Rae put her bowl down. "They'll fire you."

"But I can't go to work like this." Angie shuffled forward, rubbing her forehead. "I feel like hell."

"Angie, it's seven-thirty. You're going to be late."

"I told you, I'm sick!" Angie stumbled to the refrigerator and poured herself a huge glass of orange juice. Rae watched her gulp down the cold liquid as a dark suspicion took hold of her.

"Too much to drink last night?" she asked.

"Just some wine."

"How much?" Rae tugged open the cupboard door under the sink and looked in the trash bin. Sure enough, there were three empty wine bottles in the garbage.

"Just a little," Angie mumbled behind her.

Rae straightened as her anger escalated. She usually kept herself from getting upset at Angie for her drinking, because she knew it was a genetic propensity in their family and there were better ways than shouting to encourage her sister to stop her bingeing. But her temper was short this morning, after her discussion with Michael and the ensuing sleepless night that followed their strained parting words, and she lost her trademark self-control.

"A little?" Rae slammed the door shut and whirled around to face her. "A little? You got drunk, didn't you!"

"I couldn't help it," Angie wailed. "That Maren Lake creeped me out! All I could think about was—"

"Angie, you drank three bottles of wine!"

"Mike had some too."

"We're not talking about Michael. We're talking about you!"

"Rae!" Angie's pale features screwed up into a pout. "You're yelling at me!"

"You bet I'm yelling. I'm not going to allow you to mess up again and lose another job!" She pointed toward the doorway. "Now get your little butt upstairs and get ready for work!"

"But—"

"I'll bring up some coffee and some aspirins while you take a shower. Now go!"

Rae glowered at Angie until she obeyed. Then she turned to the stove to whip up a quick breakfast for her sister. Angie probably hadn't eaten much more than a salad the night before—far from enough food to counteract the effects of the alcohol she'd consumed. She shook her head as she stirred the eggs. What would she do with Angie if she decided to marry Simeon? Would Simeon agree to let Angie live with them until she got back on her feet? He would have to. She would make it an informal prenuptial requirement.

THE HOUSE WAS quiet for the rest of the morning, as Michael had obviously gone to work early, and Angie had left for work looking surprisingly presentable. Rae settled down in the study to work on her book and was making good progress on chapter ten when someone knocked on the front door. She glanced at her watch as she rose from her chair. One o'clock. Could Simeon be paying a surprise visit? She smoothed back her wispy hair and hurried to the door, and realized when she was halfway there that she had forgotten to put on her engagement ring. Simeon would surely notice. She'd just have to tell him the truth: that accepting the ring had been premature and that she would wear it when she felt truly in love with him.

She opened the door, only to find Michael's ex-wife standing on the porch.

"Hi, there," Vee greeted, taking off her sunglasses with a graceful sweep of her hand. "Rae, right?"

"Yes." Rae glanced beyond her, looking for signs of Michael, but found none.

Vee gestured toward the interior of the house. "May I come in?"

"Of course." Rae opened the door wider and stepped backward. "But Michael isn't here. He's at work."

"That's okay. I came to see you."

"Me?"

"I thought we might have a little chat."

Rae watched Vee march into the main hall and pivot, throwing one trim hip to the side, as if she'd had practice on a modeling runway. Vee surveyed the house, and Rae could tell she was pricing everything in sight.

"Come into the parlor," Rae suggested, wondering what value Vee had affixed to the hypostyle figures holding up the antique mantel, and whether the woman had any idea how ancient the pieces were.

"Thank you." Vee swept into the main room of the house and perched grandly in the center of the maroon sofa, her white Capri pants startlingly bright against the dense dark velvet.

"Would you like something to drink?" Rae asked. "Coffee? Tea?"

"Diet cola?" Vee answered as she carefully put away her sunglasses in an expensive-looking leather case.

Rae got her a tall glass of ice and soda, and grabbed a glass of water for herself. She carried the beverages in on a tray and set it on the coffee table, and then sat down, wondering what Michael's ex-wife had to say to her and hoping the woman wouldn't take too much of her time.

Vee reached for her drink. "When we were introduced the other day, I didn't know I was meeting someone famous."

Rae gave a little laugh. "I'm hardly famous."

"You're a professor at Berkeley already. I've been told you've published quite a few papers even. You've gone far for a girl from Alameda."

"I've worked for it." Rae sat back, still unable to tell where the conversation was headed, but not trusting Vee and her mercenary eyes.

"I'm surprised you haven't been on the local talk shows."

"I like to keep a low profile."

"I bet you do." Vee put her glass down, and her numerous gold bracelets jangled into place around her delicate wrist. "Knowing your family history."

"What do you mean?"

"Well, here you are, a very young professor at a prestigious university, volunteering at a shelter for the underprivileged, pretending to be everything they're not, when in reality you come from a family that's pure white trash."

Rae bristled, struck by the glaring truth. "I'm not ashamed of my family," she lied.

"You should be. Or maybe you don't know."

"Don't know what?"

"About your sister and your stepfather." Vee crossed her legs and draped her wrists over her knee. "I've had a little investigation done on you."

Rae stared at her, too shocked to say anything. What was Vee alluding to? What *about* her sister and Albert? How could there have been anything between her stepfather and her sister? She had protected Angie from Albert. He had promised to keep away from her. He had promised—

"If I were you," Vee droned on. "I wouldn't want my family history dragged into the open. Certainly not a history like yours."

"What do you mean? What are you talking about!"

"I was talking mostly about the abortion."

Rae jumped to her feet, her face draining of color. "I beg your pardon!"

"The abortion, Rae." Vee watched her, her ivory face beautifully cruel in its calmness. "When Angela was fifteen."

"There was no abortion!"

"Oh, yes there was. And guess who the father was?" Vee reached into her purse and pulled out a tiny leather notepad. She flipped through a few pages, as Rae stared at her manicured hands, caught in a horrible trance by this woman's damning information. "Albert. Then there were your mother's numerous DUIs, your stepfather's prison record, Angie's shoplifting—" Vee glanced up. "Need I go on?"

"How did you find all this out?"

"It was easy." Vee closed the notebook. "I know practically everyone in the city—anyone worth knowing, that is. I have lots of connections."

Shaken, Rae sank to her chair. All these years she thought she had made the ultimate sacrifice for her sister. She had allowed Albert to touch her body and had touched his in return, so he would never ruin her beautiful little sister. But all those years he had lied to her. He had probably told Angie the exact same thing—that if she did what he asked, he would leave the other sister alone. But he had gone farther with Angie, far enough to get her pregnant.

Why *had* he gone farther with Angie? Was it because she was so beautiful? Or because she was weaker? Did Angie blame herself for bringing on the sexual advances of a twisted adult, and that was why she could not sustain a normal relationship as a grown woman? Rae swallowed, a lump in her throat nearly choking her. How could she have been so blind as not to have seen what was going on? How could she have not known the pain and humiliation Angie must have suffered all those years? How could she not have known her own sister was pregnant?

"You really didn't know?" Vee asked, her voice breezy, bereft of sympathy.

Rae shook her head and stared down at the floor, totally distraught.

"Well, it doesn't have to come out." Vee took another sip of her cola and the ice cubes clinked, echoing in Rae's ears. "No one need ever know about any of this."

"It would kill Angie," Rae murmured. "To live through that again—and in print? Here in this town?"

"But it could remain our little secret, something only you and I know. Well, *and* the investigator."

Rae glanced up at her and narrowed her eyes. "What are you getting at, Vivian?"

Vee smiled and rose to her feet. "We both want something. And I'm willing to bargain."

"Go on."

"You want my silence." She propped one hand on her hip. "And I want this house." She waved her hand at the ceiling.

"Michael owns half of it, you know."

"I'll get that half in the divorce."

"You seem awfully sure of that."

"I am. Mike must keep me in the style to which I am accustomed to living, or make other compensations in kind."

"And my half?"

"You will sign it over to me, in return for my silence regarding your family history."

"Does Michael know about any of this?"

"Not yet." She curled her lip. "And he won't unless you don't cooperate."

"You're blackmailing me!"

She shrugged her left shoulder. "Call it what you like."

"Why? Why are you doing this? When you have so much!"

"Because." Vee leveled a flat stare upon her. "Michael Gregory owes me. I wasted the best years of my life on that bastard. And he's going to pay."

"But why do this to me? I've never done anything to you."

"You're in the way." Vee rose and brushed the wrinkles from her Capri pants. Then she reached into her purse and drew out a white envelope. "Here are the necessary papers." When Rae didn't reach for them, Vee set them on the coffee table.

"I haven't agreed to sign anything—"

"I'm sure you'll reconsider." Vee closed her purse with a snap. "If I don't hear from you by next Monday, I'll be back—with a reporter." She gave a cheerful wave, as if she and Rae had been having a light, pleasant conversation. "Bye now."

Thunderstruck, Rae watched Vee march out of the parlor and let herself out the front door. She left it wide open, but Rae made no move to follow her and close the door. She couldn't move. She felt so betrayed, so broken, so shell-shocked, that she just stood in the middle of the parlor, staring at the front doorway.

No wonder Angie had a drinking problem. No wonder she shacked up with lousy men. Beautiful Angela Lambers was undoubtedly full of confusion and sorrow, and must have spent years concealing the darkness inside her as thoroughly as Rae masked the outward signs of her disease. There was no way Rae would allow Angie's secret to be made public, even if it meant giving up the house she loved. She might not have protected Angie twelve years ago, but she sure as hell would now.

Slowly Rae turned, her eyes flooding with tears of heartbreak, as thoughts of what Angie must have endured seared through her mind. She sank onto the chair and dropped her head into her hands, weeping uncontrollably, and clutching her sides. She had never wept for herself. But tears spilled out for Angie, and then for their lost childhoods, their lost father, and their dirty little lives in the crummy little house on Eagle Avenue. She had been so strong for so long, only to have a vicious woman with a mercenary heart shatter her carefully constructed and zealously guarded security in a single afternoon. How could life be so unfair?

And whom could she turn to? Who would comfort her when she could not tell another living soul what was in her heart? Just as always, she would have to deal with this on her own. Not even Simeon Avare could be privy to this information.

Rae had never felt more alone. She was abysmally alone, so alone that when more sobs racked her frail body, she just let them come. She doubled over, moaning in sorrow.

She was still sobbing when a warm hand touched her on the shoulder.

"Rae?"

# Chapter 16

Rae jerked back, horrified that someone had come into the house and caught her crying. She glared upward, and through bleary vision made out the shimmering form of Michael Gregory dressed in a dark gray suit and silver tie. He withdrew his hand from her shoulder but remained standing just inches from her seat.

"Rae, what in the hell is wrong?"

She struggled to get up, but he blocked her exit from the chair.

"What's the matter?"

"Nothing!" Too distraught to look at him, she brushed away the tears still clinging to her chin and sniffed loudly.

"Like hell!"

"Please!" She scrambled to her feet, assuming he would move back enough to allow her to get by. "Leave me alone!"

Instead, he surprised her by grabbing her arms and setting her in front of him, with his hands still securely holding her.

"Let me go!" She pushed at him, but her puny efforts had no effect on the wide wall of his chest.

"Not until you tell me what's wrong."

"I'll tell you what's wrong," she retorted, swiping at her wet eyelashes. Her hands shook. "People are scum!"

Michael's eyes turned opaque as he studied her face. "What did he do to you, Rae?"

"Who?" She glanced up at him, the lids of her eyes burning, her mind clouded by her crying jag.

"Avare." He tilted his head as he bent to inspect her more closely. "If he hurt you, I'll beat the living daylights out of him. I swear!"

"Simeon?" Rae struggled for freedom again, and this time Michael released her. She brushed away the touch of his hands from her upper arms. "He didn't do anything."

Michael's brows drew together in confusion. "Then who?"

"Just leave me alone!" She stumbled toward the door.

"What's this all about?" he called after her. "Rae!"

Rae fled to the study with Michael close at her heels. Once again, she slammed a door in his face, shutting his looming presence out of her reality. But once again, he didn't take a closed door for an answer.

"Rae!" He pounded hard on the other side.

"Leave me alone!" She turned the lock, making sure he couldn't force his way in.

"What's got you so upset?" He paused, and when she didn't answer, he rattled the doorknob. "Rae, let me in!"

"No!" She marched to the desk and plopped down in the chair, knowing only one thing could make her get her mind off Angie and Michael: work.

"Rae, come on!"

"I'll call the cops, Michael," she warned. "If you don't leave me alone, I'll call nine-one-one!"

"Fine."

He fell silent, but he didn't leave. She could tell by the shadow cast on the floor underneath the door. Rae glared at the doorway, heartsick and spent, wondering if she had known the truth about anyone her whole life. From her father to Thomas Gregory, to Angie, all the people she should have been close to.

And she to them. When would the secrets stop? Ever? Was it possible to trust anyone? She couldn't even trust herself lately, the way she was running hot and cold whenever she spent time with Michael.

More tears threatened. Out in the hallway, she heard Michael's footsteps as he finally walked away. She swallowed and turned to the computer, leaning on her hand. For a long while she simply gazed at the screen, too numb to think anymore.

Then, just like all the times in her childhood, when life got too dark, she decided to shift her focus and set herself back on track. Sniffing, Rae sat up and reached for the mouse. She had a lawyer to locate regarding the house and facts to look up about the Hale-Bopp comet to verify what Maren Lake had told her—plenty to do to keep her busy.

WHEN SIMEON CALLED late that afternoon, Rae took the phone up to her room and closed the door, even though Michael had apparently left again. Rae sank onto her bed and chatted with Simeon, making sure to keep her tone light so he wouldn't guess what a terrible day she'd had.

"Has Michael agreed to sell the house to you?" Simeon asked.

"You know Michael," Rae replied, evading the question so she wouldn't have to divulge the truth to Simeon. She wasn't ready to tell him about Vee's blackmail and the reason she had to give in to it. "He can be stubborn."

"Such men try my patience." Simeon sighed. "It is time he realizes the house will be yours, no matter what he desires."

"I'm having second thoughts, though."

"What, about the house?"

"Maybe it *is* too rundown." Rae clutched the phone tightly, wishing she had never involved Simeon in her financial affairs. "Thomas didn't do much maintenance, you know."

"But the house belongs to you, Fay Rae," Simeon admonished. "You know that it does. You want it. And I shall see that you have it."

Rae nodded and looked down at the duvet cover as the maroon color swam before her red-rimmed eyes. She did want the house, more than anything she had ever wanted in her life. He must sense that in her and wish to fulfill her dream. How touching to be loved by such a man! How could she tell Simeon she had to give up the house and her dream, no matter how much he offered to help?

Later, Simeon made a date for the next evening, and told

her he would pick her up at seven. After he rang off, Rae lay back on the duvet and closed her puffy eyes.

The next thing she knew, she woke up to the smell of meat cooking on a grill outside and the gold light of evening slanting through the west-facing panes of the bay window.

Rae rose up on one elbow and blinked. She must have slept for three or four hours. Still feeling emotionally drained, she dragged herself to the bathroom and splashed cool water on her face, and then dared to look at her blotchy complexion in the mirror.

Sure enough, her eyes were still bloodshot and the flesh around her lids was pink and swelled. Rae held a cool cloth to her eyes and stood in front of the sink as she heard Angie and Michael talking in the yard outside. The sound carried easily on the summer air, wafting through the half-open window of her bathroom. She couldn't hear what they were saying, but she could tell by the tone of the conversation, Angie's occasional laugh, and the clinking of ice in a glass that no one was feeling any pain—especially her pain.

Michael must be cooking steaks on the barbecue. She knew Angie would never make such a substantial meal. Her sister was probably standing around in something sexy and slinky, drowning her sorrow in whisky or gin and making eyes at Michael. Rae shook her head, still not quite sure why Angie flirted so shamelessly with males, when she'd had such a shattering experience with a man during her childhood.

Rae glanced around the maroon-colored bedroom. She loved this refuge with its griffins and bay window, she loved the house with its huge rambling rooms, and all the artifacts Thomas had so carefully collected. It would break her heart to give it all up. She would also be turning her back on Thomas's request that she serve as a guardian.

But Rae had no choice. The house at 506 Chisholm Avenue would never belong to her. She would have to move back to her condo and soon. The fewer questions Michael had a chance to ask, the easier she would breathe.

Rae dragged her purse off the desk and grabbed a sweater

out of the closet. She'd buy a newspaper and find a quiet restaurant to pass the evening hours. Then she'd come back late, counting on Michael to be upstairs working as usual, and slip into the house without making her presence known. It should be easy. No one would even know she was gone, just as always. She'd been wandering through the world relatively unnoticed all her life.

THE SUMMER EVENING was languid and warm, but Rae barely took notice of it. She stopped in the little Chinese market on Lincoln and bought a paper. While she was waiting at the till for her debit charge to go through, she idly surveyed the bowl of goldfish sitting on the counter and suddenly thought of Maren Lake. This was the perfect evening for a quiet chat with the woman.

"Is there a phone nearby?" she asked the clerk.

"Right outside, miss."

"Thanks." She stuffed the receipt in her pocket, picked up the newspaper, and walked outside. One of these days she was going to invest in a cell phone. But until lately, she hadn't had much reason to call anyone.

Rae fished around in the outside pocket of her purse where she'd put Maren's business card. Then she dropped the required coins in the phone, dialed the number, and waited as the phone rang three times.

Maren picked up on the fourth ring. She would be delighted to have dinner with Rae. They agreed to meet in Rockridge, close to Maren's home, as she didn't own a car.

Rae's heart lightened considerably as she drove northward to the tube, and passed through the streets of Oakland. She easily remembered the route to Maren Lake's house, and rolled down the main street of the little district of Rockridge, looking for the restaurant Maren had mentioned.

A few minutes later, she was shaking hands with the older woman and sinking into a comfortable chair at a plant-filled eatery with low lighting that afforded a great deal of privacy. Rae felt her strain easing.

"I'm so glad you called," Maren remarked, arranging her

napkin in her lap. "I had the feeling we left some unfinished business the last time we spoke."

"We did." Rae picked up her napkin. "But it was difficult to talk with Angie there."

"You and your sister are so dissimilar." Maren smiled. "It's quite remarkable."

"Yes, I know. Only too well."

Rae looked up to discover Maren's intense eyes studying her again.

"You look pale, my dear," she said. "Are you all right?"

"Yes. I just had a rotten day."

"I'm sorry to hear it. Is there anything I can do? Anything you need to talk about?"

"It's a family matter." Rae frowned.

"I see." Maren opened her menu and surveyed the evening's offerings. "I recommend the catch of the day," she said after a moment. "It's always good."

"Sounds fine to me."

Maren put down her menu, her hands graceful, her every movement unhurried. "Tell me, is Michael Gregory anything like his father?"

"Not at all. He's emotional. He won't listen to reason most of the time."

"What do you mean?"

Rae spent most of the meal telling Maren about her numerous contentious confrontations with Michael, from their reintroduction to each other in the dark Gregory house when he'd thrown her out, to his run-ins with Simeon, to their last meeting when she'd caught him coming out of Angie's room. She left out the part about Michael arriving home unexpectedly that afternoon and catching her weeping inconsolably.

While complaining about Michael, she filled in bits and pieces about Angie and Simeon too, finding it cathartic to pour out her troubles to the older woman.

"But I didn't come here to talk about Michael," Rae said, finishing her last bite of halibut.

"It seems he has made quite an impression on you."

"We used to be friends." Rae gave a sad chuckle. "But now I can hardly talk to him without getting upset."

"You are quite passionate about him."

"Passionate? That's not what I'd call it!"

"You are much more passionate when speaking of Michael than you are when you talk about the Simeon Avare person."

"You're wrong there. I'm not that passionate about Michael. He just infuriates me."

"Really? I would say you seem more frightened than infuriated."

Rae looked up at Maren, momentarily taken aback by her words, and not able to make a logical reply. Michael frightened her? Why would Michael frighten her?

"And this other man. This Simeon?"

Rae nodded.

"A strange name, Avare," Maren murmured and frowned slightly. "I sense no passion in you whatsoever when you talk about him. And yet you say you are thinking of marrying the man?"

"I know. It sounds crazy, right?" Rae shoved her fork and knife together on the edge of her plate. "I am aware that I don't feel a huge romantic attraction to Simeon. But he's right for me. In every way."

"How can you say that?"

"He's kind, he's gentle, and his touch is soothing. It's hard to explain. His touch is unlike anything I've ever experienced."

"But you can't say that you love him."

"I'm not sure what love is."

"Yes you are, Rae." Maren slipped her warm hand over Rae's bony wrist and gave her a squeeze in warning. "Don't try to reason yourself into loving someone. It never works."

"But he's the logical choice for me."

"Love is blind, my dear. It doesn't involve logic."

"But logic is all I know. How else can I judge?"

"With this!" Maren touched the space just above the center of her eyebrows. "With your soul vision, Rae."

"Soul vision?" Rae scowled. "How do you know about soul vision?"

"I know many things. And so do you. You know how to see the truth and choose what is right for you, truly right. Right for your heart as well as your head."

Rae sat back, chastened and dismayed as another chunk of her world broke off and plummeted downward, sucked into her personal whirlpool of chaos, thanks to Maren Lake.

"Is Simeon Avare right for you, Rae? Yes or no? Answer only for yourself—not for the world, not for your sister, not for your career, and not because of some lack you think you have. That's the worst thing you can do—agree to marry someone because you think it will solve your problems or heal you in some way."

Rae paled. Simeon had offered to heal her, to bring her to fruition, to save her from a life of suffering. How could she not want that? The alternative was too grim to contemplate. Anything she might have to put up with in Simeon would be worth a lifetime free of pain. *Anything*.

"Remember, Rae, the key is self-sufficiency. Only when you are your own master can you be true to yourself and to others."

"I know," Rae muttered.

"Yes, you do. I know you do." Gently, Maren turned Rae's left hand over. "You don't even wear the ring he gave you—that's how I know you know." Maren withdrew her hand. "Your soul vision is right on target, my dear. Listen to it. Heed what it is telling you."

Rae shook her head and stared glumly at the table. What else could go down in flames today? What other rug could be pulled out from under her feet?

"I didn't mean to upset you, my dear." Maren's voice swept over her in a wave of kindness.

Rae glanced up. "I know. And I appreciate your listening to my problems. You don't even know me, and I just spent the last hour spilling my guts to you."

"I don't mind." Maren turned and ordered them two

more iced green teas. "I always enjoyed talking to your father."

"What was with him?" Rae asked. "What kind of religion did he follow?"

"Some call it the Left-Hand Path."

"As opposed to the Right-Hand Path?" Rae pushed her plate aside. "I don't even know what *that* is."

"One path is following a conventional religion—asking a higher being to guide you, to take care of you."

"And the other?"

"Believing that each one of us has the power within to become a higher being."

"You mean the power to become a god?"

Maren nodded. "Like I told you and your sister—it's aspiring to the ultimate in independence of intellectual consciousness. You aspire to become your own man, literally—in each and every way."

"That sounds kind of blasphemous!"

"I never liked that word, *blasphemy*." Maren thanked the waitress for their drinks. "And I don't believe it's a sin to work at perfecting oneself, or to push mental or physical boundaries. Our creator gave us minds, not because he wanted us to be like sheep in the fields, but to develop ourselves."

"So was my father pretty fanatic about this Left-Hand Path?"

"Yes. He was quite accomplished." Maren looked beyond Rae, as if sending her vision back to the past. "My theory is that your mother had intellectual differences with your father."

"I wouldn't use the word *intellectual* and the phrase *my mother* in the same sentence."

Maren laughed softly. "Is that who Angela takes after?"

Rae nodded.

"Anyway," Maren continued. "I doubt there was another woman involved. Your father just wasn't the type. I expect he left in frustration or she kicked him out. The Left-Hand Path can be a rigorous way of life that most people would find difficult to endure, especially a nonbeliever. Your mother probably got her fill of his unconventional thinking and told him to get lost."

"Well, he certainly was good at the vanishing act."

Maren sighed sadly. "It must have been difficult for you two girls."

"You don't know the half of it."

"She might have thought he was crazy and didn't want him around her children. There's that to consider, Rae."

"Well." Rae sighed. "It's in the past. Nothing we can do about it now. That's how I look at it." She reached for her purse. "But there's the question of Thomas Gregory's death still out there. And I think I may have had something to do with it."

"Really?" Maren paused for a moment, holding her glass in midair. "In what way?"

"I found something in Egypt." Rae fished through the two outside pockets of her purse and then the deeper interior section, and when she didn't find the deck of tarot cards, she unzipped the main compartment and looked there. She found the paper bag she'd wrapped them in stuffed under her checkbook and change purse. Odd, she'd thought she'd put the cards in the outside pocket. She must be losing her mind. She pulled out the bag and unfolded the brown paper as Maren watched, and then slipped out the plain golden box.

"What is it?"

"A container for a deck of tarot cards."

"May I?" Maren reached for them.

"You can open the box, but don't look at the cards."

"Of course." Maren gave her a hard glance, as if she'd just been insulted. "I wouldn't dream of contaminating someone else's tarot cards."

"Contaminating?"

"One's cards are one's own. Not to be touched by anyone else. Not if you wish their power to belong only to you."

"Well, this is one deck I don't wish to own."

"Now you have me really curious!"

"Go ahead." Rae pushed the box her way. "Take that seal off. It should fall off easily."

Carefully, Maren removed the sticky brown seal and then even more carefully took the lid off. Her eyes glowed as she studied the broken copper wire and the parchment covered with ancient writing.

"Aramaic?" She looked up for concurrence.

Rae nodded. "I found the box in a dried-up oasis outside of Luxor. It was half-buried in silt."

"It appears to be very old!"

"I think it is. That's real parchment."

"I know." She touched it gently with one fingertip. "And look at this old wire. Amazing!"

"The seal must have kept the cards from getting ruined by the water."

"And the parchment covers the cards?"

"Yes. Apparently, the writing is a warning not to look at the deck." Rae gazed at the small package, feeling the darkness of the cards as deeply as the night Angie had made her stare at Typhon, the Devil. Her heart thudded in her chest.

"Do you read Aramaic?" Maren inquired, bending closer to look at the writing in the dim light of the restaurant.

"No, we took it to an antiques dealer who read it for us. He told us to throw the cards in the Nile."

"In the Nile? Why?"

"He said they were cursed. That they were the—"

"Forbidden Tarot," Maren breathed, finishing her sentence.

Rae gaped at her. "You've heard of them?"

"Yes."

Rae studied her companion's face. It was Maren's turn to pale. Her turquoise eyes were like darts, as if trying to see through the old sheepskin to the cards underneath.

"What's wrong?" Rae asked. She clutched Maren's forearm. "What?"

"These cards. There are things my old temple had. Old documents, old records—some of them only the very learned could read, let alone understand." Her voice broke off as her stare raced over the cards.

"Yes?"

"These cards. I've read about them." Maren pushed them toward Rae. "Put them away, Rae. Don't show them in public again! Ever again!"

Rae scrambled to do as she was asked, convinced for certain now that the cards were everything she had suspected and more.

When the container was safely tucked away in her purse, Rae sat up and glanced at Maren, shocked to see the woman's face completely drained of color and her hands locked together on the tabletop, clasped so tightly that her knuckles were white. Her lips were pressed together into a grim terse line, but Rae knew Maren was going to say something. She waited.

"I never guessed the Forbidden Tarot still existed," she murmured at last.

"So you know of them?"

Maren nodded and swallowed. "I have read documents alluding to them. And of course, being a practitioner, I was very interested in such a subject."

"I never heard of them, in all my research," Rae countered.

"What do you know of the tarot?"

"Not much, really."

Maren leaned forward. "Did you know most experts believe the tarot originated in fourteenth-century Italy as a card game?"

"You mean like poker?"

"More like bridge." Maren gave a small laugh. "I find the idea so comical, so innocent. But then much of the Renaissance was simply that—a time for the children of the plague to rediscover lost knowledge. The Italians had no idea what they had stumbled upon. No idea. And after so much death and darkness they only wanted to have a bit of fun. You can't blame them for that. So they invented a card game using the tarot and adapted the images to suit their time." She laughed again, and then her turquoise eyes hardened and all traces of amusement vanished from her expression as she tapped the table with her right forefinger. "But I tell you, Rae, the tarot is much more than a deck of pretty pictures. Especially the deck you possess."

"If my deck is so important, why would there be no mention of it in Egyptian history?"

"You do know what the ancient Egyptians resorted to when someone or something became unpopular."

Rae thought of the famous heretic pharaoh, Akhenaton, husband of Nefertiti, who had stunned his priests by choosing to worship a single god—an unheard-of concept in the ancient world. "You mean like Akhenaton?"

"Exactly."

"They erased his name."

"Yes. Every instance of his name and likeness was chiseled off his statues, his temples, crossed out of the old scrolls. The city he built was razed to the ground. They literally turned their backs on him and refused to recognize he ever existed."

"So you're saying that records mentioning the Forbidden Tarot might have been altered?"

"Undoubtedly." She squeezed her hands. "The only records that would have survived would have been illegal, kept by someone who didn't fear death. And records like that sometimes get lost over the centuries. Put away and forgotten."

"But why would someone want to squelch information about a deck of fortune-telling cards?"

# Chapter 17

"**B**ecause, Rae, the Forbidden Tarot are no ordinary cards."

"What do you mean?"

"They were used by a very powerful oracle. An extremely powerful one."

"In Luxor?"

"No, in a place called Avaris."

"Avaris? I've never heard of it."

"It was in the north, in the east delta." Maren unclasped her hands and rubbed her forearms, more nervous than Rae would have expected. The older woman licked her lips, trying to moisten the sudden dryness of her mouth. Then she swallowed again.

"Avaris was the most important enclave of the worshippers of Set."

"Of Typhon?"

"Yes. And to have found the cards of the oracle—" She stared up at Rae. "I can't possibly tell you what this means!" She grabbed Rae's wrist. "You did heed the warning, didn't you? You didn't look at the cards or touch them?"

Rae gaped at her, swept by a wave of fear. Maren read her expression instantly.

"You looked?" She gasped.

"I had to. Angie opened them. She threw them on the floor."

"Oh, my lord!"

"Then she picked up a card and shoved it in my face. I couldn't help but look at it."

"And the card you saw was Typhon?"

Rae nodded. "Typhon, the Devil."

Maren looked up at the ceiling and then back at the table, her face taut with alarm.

"What will happen? What does it mean?"

"I'm not certain. I only know what I've read." Maren shook her head, seemingly reluctant to continue.

"And that was?"

Maren sighed. "The Forbidden Tarot was not just a local fortune-telling system, Rae, like you going to a neighborhood psychic and getting your palm read. The Forbidden Tarot are special cards of astounding power, held by the Temple of Set and translated by the Oracle of Avaris. Reputedly, these cards can affect the future of the entire world."

"That's what I was afraid of." Rae rubbed her forehead. "You know the tarot better than I do, and I only saw that card once. But what I remember was a crocodilelike creature carrying a sword and stomping across broken columns, with two people chained together beneath his feet."

"Did you say sword?"

"Yes." Rae glanced up. Could Maren know of the sword she suspected Thomas Gregory to have hidden?

"There is no sword on that particular card. Typhon carries a scepter, not a sword. And a torch in his left hand."

"I definitely remember a sword in his hand."

"That's strange." Maren narrowed her distinctive eyes. "And why do you connect the card to Thomas's death?"

"Because he died soon after I found the cards. And like you, I think he was murdered." She took a deep breath, deciding to trust Maren Lake with the heaviest secret of all. "I have reason to believe that quite a few years ago, Thomas found the sword of Set, the one depicted on the card. And that he concealed it in his house. And because of the sword, he was killed."

Maren stared at her, her mouth still grim and hard.

"I believe that Michael and I are the two people in the card, chained together by the legacy of Thomas Gregory."

"And the broken columns?"

"The house." Rae's voice drifted off as she lapsed into more possibilities regarding what had been depicted on the card.

Maren nodded quietly as her brow creased in concern. "The two people could be your sister and you as well."

"But what is the underlying meaning of the card, Maren?" Rae asked. "There is more to the tarot than just a physical description, isn't there?"

"Did you view it right side up or upside down?"

"Right side up."

Maren leaned back in her chair. "The card Typhon, or The Devil, is all about darkness. The dangers of the dark. Being trapped in darkness."

"Being trapped in darkness?"

Maren nodded. "Have you experienced that?"

"In a way. Metaphorically." She thought back to the darkness of her youth, before Albert had left. "And the fuses *did* burn out in the house. That was odd. And Michael had that car accident with the black plastic. Are there more meanings to the card?"

"The Typhon card can also herald the advent of an ominous, threatening power arising in the outside world or from the depths of your unconscious."

A chill passed over Rae, but she had no concrete evidence of an ominous power, other than whatever was drawing Angie out to the yard. But that could be attributed to simple bad dreams.

"Anything else?" Rae asked, her voice cracking.

"Yes. There's the sexual aspect."

"What do you mean?"

Maren sighed. "A person who draws this card may find their animal instincts can no longer be controlled. There is a danger of being enslaved by them. With Typhon comes some kind of an exaggerated or unhealthy sexuality. There may also be dependency or addiction."

Rae stared. Incredible as it seemed, the card described

both Angie and herself: Angie with her drinking problem and Rae with her awakening sexual desire.

"You might suffer from dark experiences like fear, a sense of doom, violence, oppression. There's a possibility of physical illness. Even Black Magic."

"So I could be bringing all of that into my life?" Rae's voice drifted off with worry. She had already experienced much of what Maren had just described.

"That and more. The card speaks of aspects surrounding the central theme, what has gone on before, what may come of it."

"It looks bad."

"For you *and* your sister, Rae. I would venture to say the card would affect both of you, as you both had a hand in its initial viewing. But it is affecting you in different ways, as you are two different people."

"Great. It frightens Angie. She's afraid to be left alone."

"It should frighten you too."

Rae frowned. "Whatever happens to me will be more psychological. I can see that now. It's a trend in our lives, Angie's and mine."

"Oh?"

"And she will be affected more physically."

"Perhaps that is why she is so afraid."

Rae nodded. "I should go. Michael knows nothing about this. He might take off and go to the gym in the middle of the night like he does."

"It might be best if she is not left alone." Maren reached for the bill, but Rae grabbed it.

"Oh, no. You are not paying." Rae took her wallet from her purse. "That was the best couple hours of therapy I've ever had."

Maren smiled sadly. "Thank you. But I hope this won't be the last I see of you. I'm worried about you and Angie."

"I'll keep in touch."

"I would like that." Maren leaned forward as Rae placed enough twenties on the tray to cover the bill and the tip. "But whatever you do, Rae, you should dispose of the cards."

"I thought you mentioned the Forbidden Tarot belonged to your organization."

"Not really. They belonged to an oracle who was held at a Temple of Set in Egypt—a precursor to the organization I belonged to."

"You said 'held'. Does that mean against her will?"

Maren glanced around, as if scanning the rest of the diners. And then she turned back to Rae, her face grim again. "From my research, I now suspect the oracle was a woman with special powers who was held prisoner in the temple."

"Oh."

"It is because of her that I no longer belong to the temple."

"Why?"

"It opened my eyes to the fact that members of the temple have been corrupt for centuries—in particular its leaders."

"Doesn't that happen in all organizations?"

"I suppose, but it really disappointed me to discover such corruption in my own group. After your father left, I left as well." Maren put her napkin beside her plate. "I could not be a party to the direction our organization was taking. And now, I'm pretty much a spiritual renegade."

"Well, you've certainly helped me, Maren. I truly appreciate it."

"Just be careful." Maren picked up her small bag and stood up, her long black top falling into place over her black leggings. "There are those who would kill you to get the cards. I would get rid of them. Or put them in a place no one would ever connect with you."

"I will." Rae retrieved her purse as well. "But is there any way to stop the course of the cards, once it's been started?"

"Another person would have to come into possession of the cards, I would imagine. Or at least another card would have to be consciously chosen."

"But I wouldn't wish that on anyone."

"That's because you are a decent human being," Maren replied, lightly patting her on the shoulder. "With a good heart." She lowered a hand. "I only wish there were more people like you in the world."

As they walked out to the street and into the soft warmth of the summer evening, Maren paused and reached for her purse.

"Oh, I almost forgot." She opened her worn leather bag and withdrew a folded piece of paper which she handed to Rae.

Rae took the paper and looked over at the older woman. "What is this?"

"A newspaper article I thought you might find interesting." Maren pointed at the black-and-white photo showing at the top of the story. "Read it when you get home. Let me know what you think."

"Okay."

Maren stepped away. "Thank you for dinner, Rae. Good night."

"Good night." Rae watched her walk away and then returned to her car. She didn't wait to reach home before she read the article. Instead, as soon as she sat down in her car, she immediately unfolded the paper and scanned the story, intrigued by the headline.

ANCIENT TEMPLE DISCOVERED
IN EASTERN EGYPTIAN DELTA

The photo depicted the tops of two huge pylons and a group of men standing nearby with baskets at their feet. The story went on to explain how a very unusual find had been discovered just last week, a temple built of Bekhen, a dark gray stone used in many Egyptian sculptures, and unlike that of any structure previously unearthed in Egypt. Scientists were baffled by the discovery and had yet to locate any items capable of being used for carbon-dating the structure, but they were guessing the temple might predate the Djoser

Step Pyramid, the oldest known pyramid in the land of the pharaohs.

Rae sat back, thinking about the photos of the strange black sarcophagus that Thomas had taped beneath the vanity in his bathroom. Was that plain black tomb connected to this recent find? She glanced up at the beginning of the story to see where the news had originated, and was shocked to see a familiar name staring back at her: Avaris. The temple had been discovered in Avaris.

RAE DROVE BACK to the Gregory house and arrived at eleven, to find Angie already asleep and Michael's bedroom door closed. Thankful to have been able to pass into the house unnoticed, Rae slipped into her bedroom and quietly latched the door. Then she got ready for bed, but her mind soared with so many thoughts about what she and Maren had talked about at the restaurant, that she could not get to sleep.

The night dragged on. She remembered looking at her alarm clock at midnight, then at one-thirty. When Angie tried to drift out of the house while sleepwalking, Rae heard her walk by her door, and returned her to her bed before she had the chance to get outside.

At two-thirty, Rae was still wide awake, half-listening to Angie stirring. At three, Rae got up and went to the bathroom, and then crawled back into bed, giving herself another half hour before she got dressed and did something productive, like working on her book. She shut her eyes and was just drifting off to sleep when she smelled something burning.

RAE SAT UP and sniffed the air. Something was definitely burning. It smelled odd, like the acrid smoke of electrical wire burning. The house was old. They'd already experienced a problem with blown fuses. Maybe the knob and tube wiring had finally burst into flames, overloaded by the demands of three people using all their modern conveniences in a not-so-modern house. Rae threw off the duvet, dashed to her door, and yanked it open.

Across the hall, she saw strange shafts of light dancing under the door of Michael's room. Was his bedroom on fire? She ran forward and threw herself at his door, turning the knob as she shoved it open with her shoulder. Rae hurled into the room, shocked at the sight before her.

THE TWO WALL sconces, in the shapes of ram's heads, had burst into flame, turning into torches on the wall. Michael's model of the living complex, on which he had spent hours of time, was totally engulfed by fire. The frame of his massive bed—an antique four-poster set on a pedestal and dressed in drapery—was alive with tongues of flame speeding toward the pillows, running down the drapery fabric instead of upward, defying the laws of physics, as if the fire had a will of its own.

"Michael!" Rae shouted, sprinting forward. In seconds, the flames would reach his hair. He would be burned—and probably disfigured—for the rest of his life if his thick black hair caught fire.

"Michael!" She lunged for the bed, but staggered back, repelled by a wall of heat far too intense for the flames before her. The sconces flared and sparked beside her, throwing fireballs at her. The model roared on the table behind her, sending black clouds of smoke into the air, choking her. She ducked and grabbed Michael's arm, pulling at him frantically. But his weight was far too much for her to drag off the bed. His eyes fluttered open.

"Wake up, Michael!" she screamed. She grabbed a pillow and flailed at the drapery at the head of the bed, trying to smother the flames, as Michael rolled away, his eyes white with alarm.

Heat singed her eyelashes and sucked the moisture from her face as she batted at the flames, frantic to give Michael time enough to escape. He vaulted from the bed, stumbling on his sleep-filled limbs, as the four flaming posts of the bed collapsed on the mattress, dragging the smoldering drapery with them.

"My God!" Michael cried, staring in horror as fire consumed his bed. He staggered backward.

Rae hovered at his side, staring at the carnage as well, amazed at the ferocity of the flames. Had she awakened him a moment later, he would have been trapped beneath the wreckage of his bed, unable to fight his way free.

Then with a thundering sound, a huge column of vermilion flared to the ceiling—like a mushroom cloud from a nuclear bomb—and swept downward in a sudden whoosh, as if sucked into a black hole, leaving his bed a charred shell.

"Call nine-one-one!" Michael shouted.

Rae pivoted, still holding Michael's scorched pillow, intending to run to the phone in her room, when to her amazement, she saw that all the flames had gone out.

"It's all out!" she gasped.

"What?" Michael jerked around to see for himself.

"Everything's out. All the fires."

He stumbled to the table where the remains of his architectural model still smoldered. Then he glanced at the wall sconces. Rae followed his line of sight, expecting to find the wall had been scorched by flames, but the wallpaper appeared untouched. She glanced around the room. Miraculously, not one fireball had hit the walls or the carpet. Michael dragged himself to the table where he had labored many hours over his project.

"My model," he muttered. "It's ruined." His voice trailed off in despair.

"But look." Rae pointed at the corner of the table where his laptop computer sat. "Your computer wasn't burned."

Michael glanced at his computer, and then lifted the board on which his model had been built. "The table wasn't burned either. Weird."

He glanced at his bed and then at the wall sconces again. "The wiring must have shorted out. But why? I didn't even have the sconces on."

"And how could flames shoot out of them?" Rae pointed at the sconces. "Especially if they weren't on?"

"I don't know." Michael drifted closer to inspect the faulty lights, and Rae followed him, watching him run his palm across the wallpaper. "The wall isn't even discolored or warm," he commented. "How could that be?"

"Strange." She watched him gingerly touch one of the sconces. The eyes of the ram stared down at her, as if warning her to keep her distance. Rae had never been this close to the old fixtures, and when she looked at the left one a third time, and far more closely than she'd ever done, she recognized the shape and remembered where she'd seen it before. There were two rams' heads with flames above them on the tarot card she'd found in Egypt.

A chill frizzled down her back. Had the Forbidden Tarot been responsible for this near-tragedy? Was Michael marked for death by the cards? The thought alarmed Rae that Michael might be taken out of her world before she'd had a chance to clear up the terrible misunderstanding they'd suffered so long ago.

While Rae pondered the tarot implications, she watched Michael stride to the bed and look down at the charred remains of the frame, his expression troubled. Rae walked up behind him, still in shock. Then he turned and gazed down at her, his regard sweeping across her face.

"You saved my life, Rae."

"I guess I did—" She broke off, unable to say anything more, for she suspected she was responsible for the entire episode, and could not accept his gratitude.

Still staring at her, Michael planted his fists on his hips. "Even though you would rather have seen me burn in hell, right?"

"Of course not." She glanced back at him, and for the first time realized his chest was bare, and that he wore his pajama bottoms tied dangerously low on his hips. His naked, hairless chest gleamed in the darkness, and she found it hard not to stare at his muscular physique. Surprised at how much the sight of him could distract her, she dragged her regard from his beautiful body.

"I would never want anything bad to happen to you, Michael." She touched his arm, trying to make up for the other night when her reluctance to share her thoughts had made him turn away in frustration. The fire had made her realize just how short their time together might be, and how precious their friendship had been and could be again.

At her touch, Michael paused and looked down at her as if surprised by the unusually forward gesture. The skin on his forearm was hard and sinewy, deeply muscled, unlike any flesh she'd ever touched, and the heat of him filled her arm and then her chest with a smothering, soaring feeling that compressed the breath in her lungs. Still, she did not withdraw her hand.

"It's not all one-sided," she said, her voice barely above a whisper as she finally put into words what her heart had always known. "It never was."

"Rae—" he murmured. Then, without saying another word, he clutched both her shoulders in his long, lean hands, pulling her upward against his body and sliding his hands down her back until he cradled her tightly against him. A long, beautiful sigh flowed out of him, echoing the sound she heard in her own soul, the song of release, telling her this was the place she belonged, in Michael Gregory's arms. For the longest time he just held her, his nose in her hair, his hands caressing her, seeking nothing more from her than the simple communion of their spirits, as if he finally realized how fragile she was in every way.

Rae held him in return, aching to be kissed again. She turned her head slightly, seeking his mouth. Their cheeks brushed, and every cell in her scalp and neck came alive with pleasure. Michael's mouth was warm and insistent, and she found herself tipping her head back to accept him, found her arms sweeping the smooth, rippled expanse of his back, found her body thudding for him in places she had never known existed.

His tongue pushed into her mouth and she moaned, struggling to reach up for his face. She slid her fingers over his cheekbones and into his thick dark hair, pulling him closer, aching to open herself up to this man in every way imaginable.

Under the smoky smell of his skin she caught the true

scent of him, clean and musky, and she dragged in a deep breath of appreciation. She wanted to breathe him in, taste every part of his body, touch every inch of him, and listen to his labored breathing, proof that he was overwhelmed by desire as fully as she was.

She forgot all the times her stepfather had pulled her into the shadows. She forgot the way Simeon had slipped his hands over her naked breasts and obliterated her pain. Here with Michael, she forgot everything but the way he was making her feel—gloriously fulfilled and starving for more all at the same time.

His breath came in quick bursts as he broke from her mouth and sank his nose into the small of her neck. Then, wanting more, he pushed her against the open door, his hips jamming into hers, trapping her. She cried out, as pain shot through the joints between her pelvis and thigh bones.

"Ow!" she wailed, unable to choke back the agony of having her legs splayed by Michael's powerful male body. In reaction to the sudden pain, she shoved him in the chest.

Instantly, Michael pulled back. His gaze darted up to hers. His cheeks were flushed and his eyes looked feverish, but she could see that under the flush, he had suddenly paled.

"Shit!" he gasped, misinterpreting her reaction.

"It's not you, Michael," she countered immediately, despising the frailty that had just splintered their moment of intimacy and despising the lame words she had resorted to using. "It's me!"

"Shit!" He looked down, avoiding her eyes and still breathing heavily, and set her upon her feet in front of the door. She knew it was over, and let her hands slide off him, but wanted nothing more than to have a second chance with him.

"It's not what you think!"

"Right." He stepped backward, rubbing the back of his neck. "Jesus!" He strode through the doorway and turned, still not looking into her eyes. "Sorry." Then he pivoted and hurried down the stairs.

She watched him go while the first real sexual desire

she'd ever felt for a man imploded inside her, leaving her shattered by disappointment. Would she and Michael never get it right?

She knew she could run after Michael and explain to him that she would have done anything with him, would have gone anywhere with him that night, if not for her arthritis. But the moment was gone.

Sick at heart, Rae limped back to her room. All she knew for certain any longer was that she was completely con- fused— regarding just about everything in her life.

THE NEXT MORNING Michael was not to be found, which didn't surprise Rae. She expected him to avoid her now as never before. It was probably for the best. Angie came down for juice and a bagel at seven, neatly attired in a tangerine-colored silk blouse and a pair of white trousers.

"What in the heck happened to Mike's room?" she asked, sweeping into the kitchen.

"There was a fire last night."

"Why didn't you wake me up?"

"It didn't last long. It was over before we knew it." Rae looked down at her coffee, glumly thinking to herself that her remark pertained to more than just the fire.

"Was Mike hurt?"

"Luckily, no." Rae sipped her coffee and shelved her thoughts of being in Michael's arms before a blush gave her away. "But we think the wiring is unsafe."

"It's probably really old."

"So I think we should move back to my condo, Angie."

"You mean in Berkeley?"

"Yes."

Angie chewed her bagel. "Isn't the condo kind of small?"

"Yes, but you can have the bedroom until we find some- thing else."

"Okay." Angie picked up her juice. "I don't sleep well in this place anyway."

"You were sleepwalking again last night."

"I know. I actually remember."

Because you didn't go to bed drunk, Rae wanted to say. But she held her tongue.

Angie took another bite of her bagel. "So when do you want to move out? Tonight?"

"I've got a date tonight. How about tomorrow night?"

"Or maybe just wait until the weekend?"

Rae shrugged. "I suppose we could. I'll get a couple of smoke alarms today, then, just in case."

# Chapter 18

That evening, after a busy day of running errands to the hardware store and the attorney, doing her volunteer work, and then editing a chapter of her book, Rae got ready for her date with Simeon. She dressed in the second "sexy and slinky" outfit she had bought for her first real date with him. This ensemble was a pair of navy-blue flared pants topped with the pink sleeveless pullover. Rae glanced at herself in the mirror, pivoting her hips to see her backside. With her slender lines, she was one of the few women who could wear such pants and get away with it. She also checked out the top, pleased to discover that the loose folds draping softly below her collarbones accentuated her breasts, however small they were.

As she clasped a necklace of lapis lazuli around her throat, she remembered Simeon telling her that she had already begun to blossom. She glanced up at her face and studied herself. Her reflection wasn't as drawn as usual, her eyes weren't so flat. Thinking the gauntness in her cheeks had filled out a fraction, she ran her fingers up one side of her face, only to be reminded of the moment she had run her hands over Michael's cheekbones and into his thick lustrous hair.

A flush coursed through her entire body, and Rae turned away from the mirror, forcing herself to shut off all memories of being held in Michael's arms. She concentrated on digging through the small bag of jewelry she had brought from her condo, and found the bracelet that matched the Egyptian necklace around her throat. She fastened the silver band around her left wrist, and then remembered she would be wearing the huge diamond on that hand. She switched the bracelet to her other arm.

As she slipped on the diamond ring Simeon had given her, she gazed at it, hearing Maren's words about passion once again. The ring felt foreign to her hand, far too large for her frail fingers, the symbol of a far too weighty decision for her to make right now. Why did she feel compelled to make a choice about marriage to Simeon? What was the rush? There was none. She would simply make it clear to him that she expected a long engagement so they could get to know one another before taking such an important step.

Satisfied that she looked presentable—in fact better than usual—Rae grabbed her purse and headed downstairs. As she reached the landing of the staircase, she heard the buzzer at the front door. Simeon was right on time.

A movement on the right caught her eye as she headed for the door, and she glanced over her shoulder to find Michael standing near the parlor doorway, a wallpaper steamer in one hand and a scraper in the other. As their eyes met, another flush washed over her. She felt like the emotional schoolgirl she was, and fought back the reaction at seeing Michael's tall figure and remembering how wonderful it had been to be pulled against his naked torso.

Then his gaze slanted downward to her left hand, and back up to her face, with questions hanging in his dark eyes. She knew he had noticed the ring.

They didn't say a word, and Rae reached for the door to pull it open.

"Good evening," Simeon greeted. stepping into the house. He bent down and gave Rae a quick peck on the lips and then straightened, his hands still cupping her shoulders while his back remained turned to the living room doorway.

"Going somewhere, Rae?" Michael inquired, his voice full of frost. Vapor from the steam plate floated in a cloud around his right hand.

At the sound of Michael's voice behind him, Simeon's hands dropped away from her and he turned to face the other man. Rae saw Simeon glance up the stairs and then back to

Michael. That single glance made her blood run cold. Why had he looked toward the second story of the house?

"Mr. Gregory," Simeon greeted. "What a pleasant surprise."

Michael ignored him. He nodded at Rae. "You won't be too late tonight, Rae?"

"No, we're just going out for dinner. Why?"

"I intend to go to the club tonight to work out—after I'm finished with this room."

"What would stop you from going?"

"Leaving Angie alone. She doesn't like it. That's why she got so drunk the other night."

As Michael spoke, Simeon draped his arm around Rae's shoulders. His arm felt heavy, more a burden than a pleasure this time, but Rae didn't want to insult him by ducking out from under him.

"Angela is afraid to be in the house alone?" Simeon asked.

"Yeah," Michael replied, bending down to turn off the steamer.

"Why would that be? Has anything happened besides the lights going out?"

"Nothing I can't handle." Michael rose up and faced him. "And nothing you need to worry about, Avare."

"Still a gentleman, I see," Simeon replied coldly.

"And you're still persona non grata."

"Fay Rae and I were just leaving anyway." He turned Rae toward the door.

"What's the ring for, Rae?" Michael called after them, his voice slicing through the tense air.

She glanced over her shoulder, uncomfortable with the entire situation, and more unsure than ever of the part she wished Simeon to play in her life. But before she could speak, Simeon slid his arm away from her shoulders and turned to confront Michael again.

"Didn't Rae tell you?" Simeon replied. "We're engaged."

Rae's hot stare met Michael's. She was shocked to see how hard his expression had turned. His eyes looked as cold and glittering as obsidian. She hadn't meant for the news to be announced this way, hurled as a challenge at him. She hadn't exactly decided how she was going to tell Michael and Angie about her plans, but it certainly wouldn't have been like this.

"Engaged?" Michael exclaimed. "You've got to be kidding!"

"Don't tell Angie," Rae put in. "I want to."

"Fine," Michael scowled. "Just fine!"

Rae put her hand on Simeon's forearm. "Come on, Simeon. Let's go."

SIMEON HAD PLANNED to take Rae into the city for dinner, but she asked if he wouldn't mind staying on the island and eating at a local restaurant, so she could get home before ten. He helped her into the limousine, saying her wish was his command. She suggested an old island landmark near the beach, and Simeon gave the address to his driver.

After their meal, during which Simeon repeatedly commented that Rae was off in her own little world, she asked that they take a walk. Her dinner had dropped into a lump in her stomach, her thoughts continually veered off in the direction of Michael, and she hoped that rigorous exercise might clear her mind and give her a new perspective.

She led Simeon down the sidewalk toward the trail that meandered through a grassy glen and onto the beach where wealthy San Franciscans once frequented a huge amusement park. All that was left of the park was the old bathhouse and the crumbling lines of the breakwater which had enclosed the swimming area. As they strolled, the limo slowly rolled behind them.

Rae glared over her shoulder. "Could he just park somewhere and wait?" she asked tersely.

"Assuredly." Simeon turned and held up his hand, gesturing for his driver to stop. Then he gently took Rae's hand and tucked it in the crook of his arm. "What is troubling you, my dear? I have never seen you like this."

"I have a lot on my mind."

"Does it have something to do with Michael Gregory?"

She glanced at his face, wondering again if Simeon could read her thoughts. "Why do you ask?" she replied.

"I sensed something tonight—something going on between the two of you."

Rae broke off her stare. Was she that transparent? She hoped not. "Like what?" she ventured, keeping her gaze locked on the ground ahead of them.

"A certain tension." Simeon stroked her forearm with his free hand. "Has he done something to offend you again?"

"No. He just has a way of getting under my skin." She slipped out of Simeon's light grasp to pass through the gate to the beach, and he followed her down the sandy path toward the water. Simeon caught up with her and reached for her hand again. Rae let herself be drawn close to his side once more.

"Michael should not be in the house with you," Simeon remarked. "He is not good for you."

She gave a dark laugh. "It's funny you should say that."

"Funny? In what way, funny?"

"There was a weird fire last night."

"Oh?"

"In Michael's room." She glanced at him in the dim evening light, intent upon reading his reaction to her words, but he stared straight ahead without a flicker of change in his bland expression. Then he noticed her regard and looked down at her.

"Really?" His voice held no concern for Michael, but that didn't surprise her.

"It was as if someone wanted to get to him, you know? Like hurt him and destroy something important to him."

"What do you mean?"

"Well, some things burned and some didn't, in a most peculiar way. And then, just like that"—she snapped her fingers—"the fire went out."

"And he was unhurt?"

"Yes, because I happened to be awake and smelled the smoke. I was able to get him out of bed in time."

"I wonder that you would make such an effort for the man."

"He may be hard to get along with, Simeon, but I wouldn't want to see him hurt!"

"It would make your life easier, though, wouldn't you think, if he were—how do you say it?—out of the picture?"

"Simeon!" She pulled to a stop. "What a thing to say!"

He shrugged. "I bear no love for the man. I won't deny it." His gaze studied hers. "And if you were honest with yourself, you would not pretend to care either."

"But that's so harsh!"

"As I said before, Fay Rae, I have amazing amounts of energy and have accomplished much in my life, but only because I have learned to focus myself. And that means not wasting time on people who don't have anything to contribute to my world. I include Michael Gregory in their number."

"Why wish him harm, though? He never did anything to you."

"He is obstructing your path, Fay Rae. And anything that blocks you is something that becomes my business. But"—he held up his right hand—"I never said he should be harmed. Do not fail to make that distinction."

"Sorry. I jumped to conclusions."

"And in what way, exactly?" He paused on the path and put a hand on his slender hip. "Are you assuming that since I bear no respect for Michael Gregory, I had something to do with the fire?"

"Of course not!" Disturbed by the turn in the conversation, Rae took off walking again, wishing they had never got onto the subject. She could not shake off a darkening suspicion about Simeon ever since she'd seen him glance toward the second story earlier that evening, a glance that made her believe he had known about the fire. Still, it could have been mere coincidence, that glance. She hoped and prayed it was.

They walked in silence for a few minutes until they reached the bathhouse and the long sandstone wall that swept out on either side of the old structure. Rae stepped up to the line of sandstone blocks and propped one foot on the edge of the wall, leaning on her knee as she gazed across the bay toward the twinkling lights of San Francisco. Simeon came up beside her and stood quietly, his hands clasped behind him, the breeze off the water ruffling his ash-brown hair, while he stood with his back to the water, obviously not the least interested in the magnificent view.

"I've decided to move," she said at last.

"Move?" He glanced over at her. "Where to?"

"Back to the condo in Berkeley. The fire made me realize just how dangerous living in the old house might be."

"But wasn't the fire restricted to Michael's bedroom?"

"This time, yes. But what about the next time?" She shook her head. "The wiring's probably shot."

"You don't know that for sure."

"But I'm not going to take any chances." She gazed back at the twinkling hills across the bay, still not willing to divulge to Simeon her real reason for leaving the house. "I'm moving Saturday, back to Berkeley."

"So you are going to give up your dream, just like that?"

She nodded.

"That doesn't sound like the Fay Rae I know."

"Simeon, like I said before—you don't know me." She straightened and stood on both feet. "That's why this all seems too rushed for me!"

"Are you referring to us?" He spread his right hand over his chest. "You and me?"

"Yes."

"You are having second thoughts?"

"I don't want to rush into anything, that's all. And I don't feel as if I should be wearing this beautiful ring just yet." She slipped it off her finger and held it out.

He stared at the ring and then back at her face. "What are you saying?"

"I would like you to take it back—for now anyway."

"Fay Rae, what has gotten into you today?"

"Things are too chaotic right now, Simeon. I appreciate your offer of marriage and this gorgeous ring, but I just don't believe it's right yet."

Slowly, Simeon plucked the ring from her outstretched hand and slipped it into the pocket of his trousers. He looked down at the ground. "I can't tell you how disappointed I am."

"I know. I'm sorry. I should have been more frank about the way I feel."

"And that is?"

She sighed and looked up at him. "To be honest, I'm not sure what I'm feeling. I'm just very confused. That's why I'm asking for time."

He gazed down at her, his eyes glittering, his expression bereft of warmth. "Perhaps time is not a commodity in this situation."

She blinked, momentarily confused by his words. Then she stepped back, drawing her hand away from his face. "Are you saying what I think you're saying?"

"I am only saying that I choose quickly and correctly. If you are not capable of doing the same, then perhaps you are not the woman I believed you to be."

"You're bullying me!"

"I speak only of personal preference."

"So it's your way or the highway?"

"If you must stoop to such a banality," he replied coldly, "then yes."

Rae stood a few paces away, staring at him, insulted by his haughty reply and suddenly seeing him in a new light. He professed to want everything for her, to look after her welfare, to help her dreams take shape—when in reality he wanted all of these things to come to pass according to his own agenda. And now that she had announced her plan to take a detour, he was withdrawing. She could sense it in his body language, hear it in his voice, see it in his glittering eyes.

But maybe his male pride had been stung for the first time in his life. Maybe a woman had never said no to him before. May this sudden frost was his way of protecting a sensitive heart. She would allow him that.

"I'm sorry, Simeon, but this is one thing we are going to differ about."

"I would carefully rethink your position if I were you." He took his hand out of his pocket and stood before her, a silhouette now against the inky sky. But though his features were lost in darkness, his voice was clear and cutting. "I can give you more than any man on this earth."

She made no reply. The wind blew her hair in her face but she made no move to push it back. Standing there in the twilight, she had the distinct feeling the words they were saying to each other were being chiseled into stone somewhere, never to be taken back. She knew she must be careful with her reply, and so she remained silent for a moment, weighing her response.

"You know that I can," he added, staring at her. She could see the glitter in his eyes and nothing else. The silvery glint unnerved her.

"Yes. I know."

"Without me you will suffer the rest of your life."

"Perhaps I will."

"And yet you think twice about it." He gave a mirthless chuckle. "How incredible."

"Because it doesn't feel right yet, Simeon."

"I grow weary of your doubts." He stretched out a hand toward her. "Come, I will take you home. I can tell you are overtired."

She glanced at his pale hand reaching for her and then up at his face. She backed away. "No, thanks. I'm going to walk for a while longer."

He withdrew his hand. "Alone?"

"Yes. Walking clears my mind."

"In the dark?"

"I am not afraid of the dark."

"Perhaps you should be." He brushed his hands together, as if ridding himself of the unpleasantness of their conversation. "But if you wish to be alone, such is your choice. Good evening, Fay Rae."

"Thank you for dinner—"

He made no answer. Instead, he turned on his heel and strode away. Rae watched him go, while the strange filtered light of evening played tricks on her vision. Simeon's silhouette seemed to change before her eyes, growing thin and then stooped, as his pace switched from a brisk stride to an uneven gait. She blinked away the effects of twilight, trying to see his rapidly diminishing figure more clearly, but soon he was gone, swallowed up by the shadowy vegetation of the park.

Rae felt a sinking sensation in her stomach, wondering if she would ever see him again. She hadn't expected such anger from him or such immediate rejection. It wasn't as if she'd totally spurned him—she'd only asked for more time! Had her doubts ruined her chances with Simeon? Only time would tell. And she wasn't about to be rushed by any man.

Rae hugged her arms as the breeze kicked up even harder, chilling her in her sleeveless shirt. Regardless of the cold, she felt a freeing sense of relief in having told Simeon the truth and finally taking control of her life and its current breakneck speed. Squaring her cold shoulders, she set off again, headed for the old mansion. As she walked, she rehearsed ways of approaching Angie, searching for a line that would encourage her sister to open up. It was time to get everything out in the open and clear the air between them after all the years they'd spent hiding secrets from each other.

She'd already ruined the evening. She might as well take it all the way.

"ANGIE?" RAE STOOD at the door to her sister's bedroom, holding two mugs of steaming tea. Angie sat in a chair near the fireplace, painting her nails in the light of a floor lamp. "Do you have a minute?"

Angie glanced up. "Sure."

"I made us some tea."

"Thanks." She turned back to finish the pinkie on her left foot. "I'm surprised you're home already. Didn't you have a date with Simeon tonight?"

"Yes." Rae placed the hot mug on a coaster near Angie's bottle of tangerine-colored nail polish. "But I cut it short."

"Why?"

"Things have been going too fast between us, and I told him I wanted to slow down." She shrugged. "I think I hurt his feelings."

"Men pretend to be big and strong, but they're really babies." Angie blew on her toes and surveyed her work. "The ones I've known anyway."

Rae watched her stuff foam spacers between the toes of her right foot. She'd never painted her nails before, and wouldn't even know how to go about it. But she hadn't come to her sister's room for a pedicure lesson. She'd come for answers.

She paced to the fireplace and turned at the hearth, raising her drink to her lips. The green tea was fragrant and warmed her after her brisk walk home. She took a quick sip to give her a moment to gather her thoughts, and then decided to just press onward—into the blackness of their past.

"Michael tells me you are afraid to stay in this house by yourself."

Surprised, Angie glanced up. Then she planted her cheek on her knee while she stroked color over her big toe. "Yeah, I am."

"Why didn't you tell me?"

"Because if you found out, you'd stay here with me. And I knew how important it was for you to spend time with Simeon. I didn't want to hold you back."

"So you just stayed here, frightened to death, while I went out on dates."

Angie nodded. "Kind of."

"Is that why you got so drunk the other night?"

The brush on the end of the polish applicator stopped stroking halfway down Angie's toenail. She glanced up at Rae, her bright blue eyes flat with shame. "Yeah. This house—it gives me the creeps, Rae. There's something about it. I can't sleep here. I don't like the statues and the stairs. I hate the urns and the old scrolls. It's like living in a creepy old temple."

"You should have told me!"

"But I know you like all of this stuff. And I'm grateful just to have a place to live for a while."

"I had no idea."

"Plus, I don't like being alone." Angie capped the bottle of polish. "I never have. I guess that's why I always shack up with guys."

Rae took another sip of tea, deciding to step into the abyss. "What about when you were a kid, Angie? Were you afraid to be alone then?"

Angie's glance darted up to Rae's face, but she quickly looked away and reached for the steaming mug beside her. "Sometimes," she whispered.

"Me too." Rae laced her fingers around her cup. "Because of Albert."

Angie nodded.

"I have something I need to tell you," Rae began, watching her sister closely for changes in her expression.

# Chapter 19

"I never told you before because I was too ashamed," Rae continued. "But now that I'm older, I have come to realize that what happened to me years ago was not my fault. And I think it's something you should know about."

Angie blinked rapidly and sipped her tea, intent on her mug.

"Albert used to touch me. And he would make me touch him. And I would do what he asked because he threatened to do the same to you if I didn't cooperate."

Angie glanced up, her brows drawn together. "He told you he wouldn't touch me?"

"Yes. I believed him. I did what he told me to. He made me feel so dirty, so disgusting. I would throw up just thinking about it. You and Mom thought I had the flu a lot. But it was all because of Albert."

Angie gazed at the wall beside the fireplace and drew both legs up in front of her chest, as if protecting herself from Albert even now. "God, Rae," she breathed, dropping her chin on her knees.

"I used to do anything to keep from going home after school because I knew Albert would be there, waiting for me. I got into a lot of trouble for being late, but it was nothing in comparison to what Albert made me do to him."

"Geez, Rae, I never knew." Angie hugged her calves.

"I should have told you. Or I should have told Mom. But I couldn't. I was too ashamed." Rae searched Angie's face. "It made me hold back from you, put a distance between us I could never seem to breach."

"I always assumed you didn't think I was smart enough to share things with."

"No. Never."

"Like we were sisters, but not really."

"Angie, I'm sorry you felt that way." Rae put her mug on the mantel. "And I hope that from now on, you'll let me know what's bothering you. I want to know. I want to be more of a sister to you."

Angie nodded and her mouth trembled. Rae could see tears welling up in her eyes. She swept forward and reached down to wrap her arms around her sister, something she could not remember ever doing.

"Oh, Angie!" she exclaimed.

Angie's slender limbs slowly unfolded in her embrace, and her arms wrapped around Rae's neck, squeezing her so tightly it caused pain to spike through Rae's shoulders. But Rae did not pull back.

"I'm sorry, Angie!" She hugged her tightly. "I'm sorry I wasn't there for you."

Angie wept against her, hiding her face in the soft folds of Rae's new blouse. Great sobs racked her body as she cried and shuddered in her arms.

"I'm sorry I believed Albert," Rae murmured, stroking her back. "That bastard!"

"I believed him too," Angie said, her lips thick with tears. She lifted her head and stared up at Rae's face, her beautiful eyes ruined from weeping. "I believed him too!"

"And what did he tell you?" Rae asked, cold with dread even though she knew the answer.

"He said he would leave you alone if I gave in to him."

"Well, he didn't." Rae hugged her. "The lying bastard!"

"I thought there was something wrong with me," Angie continued, clinging to Rae's shoulders. "Because he picked me and not you. Like I was some little slut or something."

"Oh, Angie!"

"I thought he left you alone because you were smarter or something, and maybe you'd found a way to get around him. But I didn't know how! And I thought if I ever told you, Rae, you would think I had asked for it. That's what

Albert told me. He said bad girls ask for it. That bad girls just ask for it and men can tell."

"Angie, he was scum."

She nodded. "I know that. But I still wonder what I did to make him come after me."

"You did nothing. He probably went after any nubile female he saw."

"But all this time I didn't think he went after you."

"Well, he did."

Gently, Rae stepped back until Angie's arms drew away from her. She gazed down at her younger sibling, wishing they had spoken years ago. If they had shared the threats that had entrapped them, they would have had the power to fight Albert. But they had been too young to know how devious an adult could be, and so had lived in their own private little hells, suffering unspeakable shame.

"That's why I hate being alone." Angie wiped her tear-stained face. "I know it sounds crazy, Rae, but when I'm alone I'm always afraid Albert will show up."

"He holds no power over you now, Angie."

"I know." She reached for her mug again. "But sometimes when it's dark and everyone is sleeping or gone, I just can't keep from thinking he's right there, Rae, right around the corner—like my bedroom door will open and he'll be standing there."

"Have you tried therapy, Angie?"

"No. I couldn't bring myself to talk about this stuff, especially with a stranger."

"Maybe you could try it now."

"Yeah, maybe. Now that we've got it out in the open." Angie sighed and slowly rose to her feet. "Thanks, Rae."

Rae nodded and touched her arm. "Are you going to be all right?"

"Yeah." Angie swallowed. She lifted her chin and smiled fleetingly. "Yeah."

Angie had not mentioned her pregnancy, but Rae was sure that particular secret would come out as well, in its own time. As for now, they had established a link they'd never known before, and Rae was sure it would strengthen and grow as time went on.

"I'm going to take the mugs downstairs and then turn in, Angie."

"Good night, sis."

"Good night."

She carried the mugs down the stairs, her mind full of memories of childhood, and was surprised to see the light on in the study. Always conscious of turning lights out in rooms not being used, Rae padded toward the small room at the end of the hall. She reached in to turn off the switch, but Michael's voice stopped her.

"Don't," he called out.

Startled, Rae glanced in the direction of his voice, surprised to find Michael in the study, standing near one of the floor-to-ceiling bookcases. He was dressed in jeans and a white shirt again, crisp and clean as ever.

"You might try to keep me in the dark," he remarked, closing the book he'd been looking at. "But I won't stay there willingly."

Rae lowered her hand, certain that Michael spoke of more things than the lights in the study. She watched while he carefully reshelved the book and turned to face her.

"So what gives, Rae?"

"What do you mean?"

"With Simeon."

"I don't believe that's any of your business."

His gaze darted to her bare left hand and then back to her face. "Where's the rock?"

"That's none of your concern either." She glared at him, holding the mugs in front of her like boxing gloves, a fitting visual for the way their conversations always transpired. Had he approached her in any fashion other than adversarial, she might have confided in him, might have told him what a draining day it had been, might have voiced her doubts about Simeon and asked for his advice on the matter. But his disdainful attitude put her off.

Michael took a step toward her. "A guy gives you a ring like that and you don't think I should care?"

"Listen, Michael," she retorted. "I'm not in the mood for Twenty Questions." She turned to leave, her cheeks hot.

He strode up behind her. "What do you know of the man, Rae?"

"That he's a gentleman, for starters."

"Is that all it takes to win you over?" he asked, his voice heavy with sarcasm. "An expensive suit and smarmy manners?"

"He is not smarmy!"

She swept out of the room and stomped down the hall to the kitchen, aware of a large shadow behind her. Perturbed, she slammed the mugs on the ceramic countertop. Michael came up behind her again, so close to her that she would have to brush past him if she wished to leave the room.

"You don't love him, do you?" His words were more an accusation than a question.

The time for secrets was over. "No. I don't." She stared at the countertop, speaking the truth at last. She felt purged but depressed, for abandoning Simeon came at a great personal cost to her physical health. She stood with her back to Michael, wondering how many other questions he would ask her, how personal he would get, and how she would form her answers. But she was determined to speak the truth, even if it frightened her.

"I don't get it." His eyes studied her. She could feel his gaze on the back of her head. "Why are you going to marry him then?"

"I'm not. I decided not to."

"Why?"

Rae swallowed. "Because of a lot of things."

She wasn't ready for this conversation, but then again, she might never be if she waited for her head to catch up with her heart. As Maren had told her, she could not use logic when it came to matters of the heart. No mathematical equation could tell her how to proceed or what was the best path for her to take.

Rae pivoted to face Michael, knowing it would be easier to retreat to the safety of her room but determined to stay and talk this time.

"But you *are* one of the reasons I changed my mind, Michael."

"Because of last night?"

"Yes." She flushed but did not break eye contact. "You've brought up a lot of issues for me, Michael, a lot of stuff to deal with."

"Like what?" He reached for her and gently held her shoulders. "That you might be attracted to me? That you might have feelings you can't rationalize?"

If it were only that simple. "Yes," she whispered, stepping closer and closer to the abyss of the unknown.

"Why does that bother you?"

"It scares me." She could feel her mouth going dry again. "I don't know what to make of it!"

"Well, you're making it harder than it has to be."

"What do you mean?"

"You're analyzing too much."

"How do you know?"

"I can see it in your eyes. You want to step back and make a list, don't you? Tally up what's good, what's bad, what's right, what's wrong, and come up with a total, don't you?"

The truth stung. She blushed and lifted her chin. "What's wrong with thinking things through?"

"Some things you just can't analyze, Rae. Some things are meant to be *felt*."

"I haven't had much experience with feelings."

"That's because you've forgotten how to trust, to let go." He leaned down and tilted his head to look directly into her eyes as he had done many times before. But this time his dark eyes were full of warmth and understanding. "It's time to loosen up, Rae. Go with the flow."

"What flow?"

"The one you're feeling right now."

She stared at him, her heart thudding in her chest, the alien ache rising up inside her. Ever since she'd come back from Egypt, she had sensed a change in herself, and ever since she'd met Michael again, she had felt a strange tide sweeping through her and a disturbing dissatisfaction with her current life.

His eyes skewered her. "It's like electricity, Rae. And no matter what you say, or how much you deny it, I know it's there."

Rae felt another flush wash over her at the mere thought of his mouth coming down on hers again, of his arms wrapping around her, of the electricity sparking the moment he touched her.

"You feel it," he continued. "I know you do. Trust it, Rae."

"I'm not used to trusting." She looked up at him, and found his mouth dangerously close to hers. "I don't know how!"

"Then let me show you." He leaned closer and kissed her, gradually gathering her into him, holding her in his strong embrace. "It's about this, Rae. About knowing there's someone who will hold you and never, ever hurt you intentionally." His warm voice was like a lullaby in her ear. She closed her eyes and let the words imprint her spirit.

"It's knowing there's a person in the world who will always listen to you, Rae, and care what you're feeling and care what you're afraid of. Someone to stand beside you."

Rae clung to Michael, her cheek pressed against the thump of his heart, against the rumble of his gentle voice, hearing from him what she had needed to hear as a child but had never received. She felt her reserve melting away, felt her doubts withering as her heart swelled with love for him. And the love she felt for him was so fathomless and so wide she thought it would burst out of her, breaking her in two, and flow outward in a huge hot wave.

"Oh, Michael!" she breathed.

"Rae," he said at her throat, pulling her off her feet. "It's like you never left. It's like you never left me."

"I know," she answered, her lips at the flare of his jaw. And then it became clear to her. Michael had been as wounded by abandonment as she had. Suddenly she understood him. His emotional nature had turned him hard and abrasive, just as her logical nature had sent her running from any emotional situation. He had turned to bitterness and sarcasm as she had turned to the world of numbers. Each of them had been hiding for years, hiding from the part of life that had deeply scarred them. It was time they both came out of hiding and started living a full and meaningful life.

"Michael, I—"

Just as Rae began her confession of love, she glimpsed Angie walking toward the kitchen. Rae pulled away, and Michael turned his head to see what had made her back off.

"Whoa!" Angie exclaimed, holding up both hands. "Have I interrupted something serious?"

"Michael and I were just—"

"Reminiscing," he put in, finishing Rae's sentence. He stepped away.

"I see." Angie glanced from Rae to Michael and then back to her sister. Then she grinned, put a hand on her hip, and wagged her finger at them. "I always thought there was something going on between you two."

"And you came downstairs because . . . ?" Rae asked, trying not to blush at her sister's knowing tone.

"I was thirsty." Angie padded to the refrigerator. "Is there any soda in the fridge?"

"I think so." Rae reached for the mugs to rinse them out, finally getting control of her galloping emotions. She turned on the faucet while Michael walked to the kitchen doorway behind her. There was still much unfinished business between them, but the moment had been lost for now.

"I'm off to bed," he said. "Good night."

Rae glanced at him over her shoulder. "Good night, Michael."

He turned and gave her a small smile and a wave, and then walked quietly into the shadows.

Soon afterward, Rae went upstairs as well. All the time she undressed and got ready for bed, she kept hearing Michael's words over and over again, that electricity flowed between them. It was true. She could feel the afterglow of it simmering just beneath her skin. But underneath the electricity was the glorious span of their abiding friendship, something she knew would never perish, never change.

Rae slipped under the duvet and pulled it to her chin, wondering how she would ever get to sleep with all that had gone on running through her thoughts. She ran her hand over the smooth mound of the pillow and closed her eyes, remembering how Michael's cheekbone and jaw had felt beneath her palm when she had stroked his face the night of the fire, how breathless and demanding his kiss had been, how muscular and vibrant his back had felt beneath her fingers, how his words had spoken directly to her heart. A stabbing sensation shot through her, setting her on fire, making her long for him.

She flopped over, trying to break free of the sensation, but she could not turn her back on the hunger she felt for Michael. It was there, wherever she turned, staring her in the face.

Then a thought came to her, like a beetle scuttling up a dimly lit hallway. Maybe what she and Michael were experiencing was just the effects of the tarot card. Maren had warned her about the sexual aspects of the card she'd drawn, and that she might become enslaved to lust.

Rae flung her arm over her eyes. Was Michael under the spell of the Typhon card too? And if he was, and should the curse be lifted, would he suddenly wonder what had gotten into him—to be attracted to professional loner Rae Lambers? It couldn't be possible. Theirs had been a special friendship as kids. Why couldn't such a friendship persist and grow, as they had grown into adults?

But doubt crept back in, fired by years of going it alone, of always being outside the world of human relationships, of never getting it quite right with men, of watching her beautiful sister always grab the limelight.

Beneath the crook of her elbow, Rae felt tears sting her eyes. For one brief moment, she had allowed herself to believe a man was falling in love with her, and she with him. How could she have been such a fool?

\* \* \*

DEEP INTO THE night, Michael stayed up working on the model for the new house he had designed for the classical pianist. He had set up a new workspace in the fourth bedroom across from Angie's room, a much smaller bedroom probably meant for a child. But it had a bed and was big enough for his worktable, which was all that mattered.

Worried about his livelihood as well as his life, he'd hired an electrician friend to check out the wiring in the house while Rae ran errands, and much to his surprise had been informed that everything was in order. The electrician couldn't explain the fire or the flames that had shot out of the wall sconces. In fact, he hadn't been able to find any evidence of a fire on the wall or in the fixtures, and had looked at Michael as if he were crazy to suggest his life had been threatened by the faulty wiring.

Michael turned his thoughts from the fire to thoughts of the project he was working on. He rotated the model so he could view the back of the structure. He had designed a house much like a crystal—multifaceted to display all four grand pianos. But not until he saw the design in three dimensions would he really get the physical impact of his original drawing.

Now, looking at the design take shape in his hands, he felt a rush of pride. This project was turning out better than he expected. He reached for a new piece of art board when he heard a shuffling noise out in the hall.

Wary from his previous experiences in the house, Michael sat up straight and craned his neck to see what was out in the hall. The shuffling grew louder, and he spotted Angie drifting toward the stairs, probably sleepwalking again.

Michael hurried out to the hall. "Angie?"

She actually turned and looked at him.

"Everything okay?" he asked.

She ran a hand through her golden hair. "I couldn't sleep. I'm going to get a glass of water."

He nodded, surveying her closely for signs of somnambulism, but she seemed lucid so he backed into his room and returned to his work. He got a fresh, razor-sharp blade out for his art knife and screwed it in as he gazed at the four-story town house, which spiraled around a central axis. Within seconds he had plunged deeply into his project again, hoping to finish the stair detail before he went to bed.

WHILE MICHAEL TOILED over his project, he felt the air change, as a cold front moved in. By three o'clock, his fingers were so chilled, they were too stiff to work. Michael got up and went downstairs to turn on the furnace, the first time they'd had to use heat since moving in. Just as he was switching on the thermostat in the hallway outside the sunroom, he heard the back door slam shut.

"What in the hell?" he muttered. The trees swayed outside, running shadows over the walls, and a glint in the sunroom caught his eye. A water glass sat half-full on the coffee table in the sunroom. It was then Michael realized he'd never heard Angie go back to her bedroom. She must have been watching television down here. And now where was she? Out in the yard again?

He rushed down the hall, through the kitchen, and out the back door—making sure it was unlocked. Wind flattened his pajama pants against his shins as he galloped down the steps. Guarding his eyes against the stiff wind, he scanned the back yard. No Angie.

Michael trotted down the narrow brick walkway, past the fountain, and into the overgrown side yard, shrouded by the tall black locust trees lining the drive, their shadows writhing on the lawn. There was Angie, on hands and knees, digging in the dirt.

"Angie!" he called, but the wind whipped away his words. He trotted closer and reached down for her arm, but she batted him off and snarled like an animal.

Michael gaped at her, shocked to see her long beautifully shaped nails black with soil, and her forearms dirty up to the elbows.

"Angie, wake up!" Michael shouted.

She turned her back on him and continued to dig furiously, her hair whipping across her face, and her tank top plastered to her rib cage.

"Angie!" Michael tried to grab her again, but this time she lunged for his arm and sank her teeth into the flesh on the inside of his elbow, biting him until he yelped in pain.

Shaking her off, he staggered backward, holding his arm, amazed at the force of her attack, and wondering what had come over her. By the looks of it, getting her back into the house was going to be tough.

She flung dirt on either side of herself, all the while talking in angry strings of gibberish.

Just then the back door slammed again and Rae soon appeared around the corner of the house.

"Michael!" she screamed, sprinting toward him.

He glanced back at her, alarmed by the fear he heard in her voice, and saw her point upward just as a loud crack rent the air.

Michael looked up in the direction she'd pointed, horrified to see a huge limb falling downward through the thorny branches of the giant locust tree behind him.

Before he had time to react, he felt Rae's hurtling body hit him with a thud, knocking him off balance. Together they tumbled to the ground as the limb crashed to the earth, lashing them with thorny foliage but landing mercifully short of their feet.

Michael rolled to a sitting position and reached for Rae. "You okay?"

"Yeah. That was close!" She backed away like a crab, staring at the huge limb, her eyes wide with fright, her blond hair swirling in the wind. Her arms were covered with long dark scratches.

Michael could feel stinging lacerations on his shoulders and arms where the smaller branches had slashed him. But it could have been worse, much worse. A limb that size falling from that height could have killed him.

"Come on." He scrambled to his feet and grabbed her hand. He saw her wince and was surprised by her reaction. Had she injured herself in the act of saving his life? He hoped not. But he didn't have time to dwell on minor injuries. He tugged Rae forward. "Let's get your sister out of here."

This time Michael used brute force to grab Angie from behind and carry her to the back of the house while she flailed her arms and legs and whipped her head back and forth. She was almost too strong for him to maintain a grip on her.

"Get the door!" he shouted, even though Rae had already scampered up the steps to grab the latch. She yanked it open, and Michael managed to get Angie into the kitchen. Her screams and strings of profanity were even louder in the quiet house, and Michael worried that if he let go of her, she would attack one of them and scratch them even more with her ragged nails. The wind swept the back door closed with a loud bang.

"Angie!" Rae cried, running around Michael to look at her sister's face.

Frantically, Angie waved her hands and kicked out at Rae.

"What do we do?" Rae asked.

"Take her upstairs. Maybe she'll cool off by then." He headed for the hallway.

"I'll start a bath. She's filthy."

"Okay."

"Can you make it to her bathroom?"

"I'll manage." He shifted her weight and doubled the pressure on Angie, struggling to keep her slender frame contained. She was much stronger than he had anticipated. "She's bound to get tired soon."

"Let's hope."

# *Chapter 20*

Rae hobbled up the stairs ahead of Michael, and limped into Angie's bathroom, where she turned on the taps and waited for Michael to catch up.

As soon as Michael staggered through the bedroom door, Angie began to wail. She wedged her long legs out in front of her, trying to impede Michael's progress.

"No!" Angie bellowed. It sounded as if her voice belonged to someone else, as if it came from the very bowels of her body, a dank and feral place.

Rae gaped at her sister, whose face was streaked with muck and whose extremities were black with dirt. Her hair hung in filthy strings, and saliva foamed at the corners of her mouth.

"Come on, you!" Michael turned to drag her into the bathroom. Angie grabbed the woodwork of the doorway, screaming at Michael to put her down. The water thundered into the tub, and Angie glared at it over her shoulder as if she believed it were acid, and they were going to drown her in it.

"No!" she cried. Her eyes rolled back. Her breath came in heaving gasps as she panted in terror.

Rae watched her, shaken to her core. She had never seen her sister like this. She looked like someone possessed by a demon—but that only happened in movies and in obscure villages, didn't it?

"Rae, drag off her pajama bottoms."

Rae managed to grasp one pant leg, but Angie kicked outward, throwing her violently against the wall. The impact knocked the wind out of Rae and sent shards of agony down her spine, but she lunged forward again, driven by adrenaline. This time she went for Angie's waist and dragged down the top of her pants. As the material bunched up, she could grip it more firmly, and it also bound Angie's thrashing legs. With a final tug, she ripped the pajama bottoms off.

Michael jerked forward, dragging Angie's hands from the woodwork. He staggered to the edge of the tub, holding her writhing, wiry body as she bellowed as never before.

Rae stood to the side, her knuckles held to her mouth, shattered by Angie's behavior, but not knowing what they could do to help her. Angie couldn't seem to snap out of whatever dream had sent her outside. Why couldn't she wake up? Why was she so afraid of the bathtub?

Rae watched in awe of Michael's strength as he leaned over and placed Angie in the tub without dropping her. As soon as she hit the hot water she screamed, and the wail echoed through the house. The cry burst out of her lungs, and went flying through the hallways and stairwells until it at last faded away, spent.

Suddenly all was quiet. Angie slumped in the tub, her head lolling to the side and her mouth slack.

"Jesus!" Michael gasped.

"I wish Jesus *were* here." Rae knelt down. "I'd feel a heck of lot better if He were."

Gently she reached out to touch Angie's shoulder, half-expecting her sister to lurch back to life and turn on her. But Angie didn't move when Rae's hand stroked her.

"She's ice-cold, Michael."

"I find that hard to believe." He bent closer. "She was writhing like a wild animal!"

"I've never seen her like this."

Angie moaned and her head rolled backward, revealing her slender throat, her larynx tipped toward the ceiling.

"Angie!" Rae called, patting her cheek. "Angie, wake up!"

"Can you hear us?" Michael put in.

Angie's eyelids fluttered and her arms trembled.

"Angie!" Rae repeated, intently surveying her for signs of consciousness.

Angie drew up her arms and hugged herself. "So cold," she murmured, her eyes still closed. "I'm so cold!"

"Move her legs, Rae." Michael reached for the hot water tap. "I'll warm up the water."

Rae swept Angie's slender legs out of harm's way and was shocked by the limpness of her sister's limbs. Whatever had possessed Angie had sapped all strength from her.

While the water heated up, Rae gently bathed her sister's face. A minute later Michael turned off the water and watched Angie for signs of life as Rae continued to wash Angie's arms and feet. While Rae worked, she could hear Angie's breathing becoming more regular, and gradually she opened her eyes. She regarded Rae and then glanced up at Michael standing over her.

"Rae?" she murmured, licking her pale lips. "Michael?"

"Angie!" Rae cried, happy to see her sister back to normal.

"What are you doing in my bathroom?"

"You had a bad sleepwalking spell," Michael explained, reaching for a large lavender towel. "A really bad one."

Angie's brows drew together, not understanding.

"You were sleepwalking," Rae put in.

"Oh." Angie glanced down. "Why am I in the tub?"

Rae sat back on her heels. "It was the only thing we could think of to wake you up."

"In my clothes?"

"We could barely get your pants off," Michael replied. "You were raving like a maniac."

"I was?"

"Yes." Rae studied her sister's face. "Do you remember anything, Angie? Anything at all about the last few minutes?"

"No." Angie looked up at Michael. "What happened to you?"

"A tree limb fell and scratched me. And"—he raised his left arm, rotating his elbow toward her—"you bit me."

"She what?" Rae stared at the oval mark, which was a deep crimson color.

"She bit me. She just about took a hunk of flesh out of my arm."

"Did she break the skin?" Rae asked, stepping closer.

"Not quite."

"Mike!" Angie gasped. "I didn't do that, did I?"

"I'm afraid you did."

"Sorry!" Visibly shocked, she ran her palms over her still filthy hair. "I can't believe I would bite you—or anyone!"

Rae touched her shoulder. "You weren't yourself, Angie. I'm not sure *who* you were, but you weren't yourself."

Michael draped the towel over the high side of the old claw-foot tub. "Why don't you shampoo your hair? I'll go make us all a nice hot drink."

"Thanks, Michael." Rae stood up. "I'll be right outside, Angie."

"Okay." Angie glanced up at them. "I'm sorry, you guys. I'm really sorry."

"It's all right." Rae followed Michael into the main bedroom, and then collapsed in the chair by the fireplace while Michael left for the kitchen. Outside the wind still blew, whistling around the gingerbread and scrabbling at the old windowpanes. Rae shivered, her clothes damp from leaning over the tub and washing her sister. She decided to start a fire.

THE BLAZE IN the grate had just taken hold when Angie drifted back into the room, wearing her robe and a towel wrapped around her head, reminding Rae of the time she'd taken a bath in Egypt and had walked out like this while Rae was investigating the tarot deck.

"I'm absolutely exhausted!" Angie sank onto the end of her big bed.

"You should be."

Angie shook her head. "And I bit Mike. Why would I do that?"

"You weren't in your right mind."

"And I wrecked my nails again." Glumly, she surveyed her hands. "I'm going to have to get up early tomorrow just to do my damn nails again."

"I think that's the least of your worries."

She nodded.

"The sooner we get you out of this place," Rae continued, "the better. I'm not waiting for Saturday."

"But I won't have time to pack."

"I'll do it for you in the morning."

"Okay." She yawned as Michael walked into the room with a tray holding three mugs. Rae could smell the sweet aroma of hot chocolate, and breathed in appreciatively as he handed her a cup.

"Thanks."

After giving Angie a mug, Michael returned to the fire and stood at the hearth sipping his drink. For a moment a heavy silence fell over the room as each of them lapsed into their private thoughts about what they'd just experienced.

After a minute, Rae broke into the stillness. "We're going to move out tomorrow," she said. "Angie's sleepwalking just keeps getting worse."

"It's probably a good idea."

"I think you should leave too, Michael."

He glanced at Rae. "Why?"

"Do you have a death wish?"

"Of course not!"

"Then I'd move."

Michael lowered his mug. "But what about the house?"

"At this point, the house is the least of our worries."

"I'm not following you, Rae. What's on your mind?"

"I think someone or something is trying to kill you, Michael."

"What?" Angie gasped, standing up.

"Do the math." Rae put her mug on the table near her elbow and faced Michael. "First you had that car wreck. Then that fire in your room. And tonight that tree limb almost hit you."

"Oh, come on!"

"And what about your baseball bat," Angie put in. "Remember that?"

"Okay, the bat thing was weird. I'll admit that." Michael finished his cocoa. "But the other stuff could be mere coincidences."

"Some coincidences. And why only you?"

Angie drifted to the fire and held her hands out to the warmth of the flames while Rae and Michael stared at each other.

"Why hasn't anything happened to me?" Rae went on as Angie sat down on the thick carpet at her feet. She watched her sister put her mug down on the hearth and draw up her knees, hugging her shins as she stared at the fire.

"Good question, Rae," Angie mumbled, propping her chin on her knees.

"Even if something strange *was* going on," Michael said, "I can't leave the house. What if it is vandalized again?"

"Vandalized schmandalized!" Rae fumed, frustrated by his lack of logic but even more by the blatant disregard for his own safety. "Who cares? What if the next time you aren't so lucky?"

"You mean, what if you aren't around to save me?"

"Me or someone else."

Michael sighed and threw a glance to the side as if his decision to listen to her went against his better judgment.

Angie rose, leaving her mug on the hearth. "I'm beat, you two. I've got to go to bed." She turned and looked at Rae. "Are you going to stay in here tonight?"

"If you don't mind me sleeping with you."

"I'd feel safer if you stayed."

"Then I will."

"Thanks, sis." Angie hugged Rae in an unexpected show of gratitude, and then ambled toward her bed. "Good night," she called over her shoulder.

"Good night," Rae called softly. Then she turned back to Michael.

She sighed, struggling to overcome her disquiet and to keep her voice low. "I wasn't ever going to tell you anything, because I didn't think you would believe me." She paused and was encouraged to continue by a flicker of interest in his eyes. "But now that I see you are considered a threat, I think you should know what's going on."

"Considered a threat by whom?"

"I'm not sure yet. But I think I know why." Rae reached

for her lukewarm cocoa and sat back down in the chair. She barely knew where to start, certain that if she went too fast and presented too much information, Michael would think she had gone completely crazy. Rae gathered her thoughts while she took a drink of her hot chocolate. Then she looked up.

"Do you remember those photos you found in your bathroom?"

"The old black-and-whites?"

"Yes. Did you look through all of them?"

"Yeah." He narrowed his eyes. "Why?"

"Did you see the photograph of that sword?"

One side of Michael's wide mouth quirked up as he thought back. "Yeah. I remember it. It was a color shot, wasn't it? And the sword was a weird color, as I remember it."

"It was red. Coppery."

Michael shrugged. "So?"

"I believe your father found that sword in Egypt."

Michael shrugged again, his expression bland. "It wouldn't surprise me. He found a lot of things."

"Nothing like the sword."

"What do you mean?"

"Your father believed it had a long history, that it was the object of a quest by groups of people for thousands of years."

"Why is that?"

"Because of its special powers."

"Which were?"

Rae sighed. "I'm not sure."

"I see. Well, that certainly explains a lot."

She hated the drag of sarcasm in Michael's voice, but she had expected such a reaction from him. She squeezed the mug between her palms, forcing herself to remain calm. If she lost her temper, she would forever lose this chance to convince Michael of the value of his father's work.

"Over the years your father did countless hours of research, hoping to find out just what he had discovered in Egypt. He eventually realized that the sword was powerful enough to change history if wielded by the right—or the wrong—person. But he didn't know whom to trust. He didn't know what to do. So he remained in this house for the rest of his life, guarding the sword from those who might use it for evil."

"Where's this so-called powerful sword now?"

"I don't know. He's hidden it somewhere."

"And he didn't tell you where?"

"He was afraid to, in case the information fell into the wrong hands."

"And you think somebody killed him to get the sword?"

"Yes."

"The killer probably has the sword then, and there's nothing more we can do."

Rae put her mug down on the end table. "I don't think the killer got the sword."

"Why not?"

"Because of the things that have been happening around here. I think somebody wants us out of the house—and you especially."

Michael gave a shrug of agreement. "I'm certainly the only one capable of brute violence."

Rae nodded. "And once we're all out, the killer can search for the sword unmolested."

"Why doesn't he or she just kill us all?"

"Maybe the person wants the sword but does not want to take human lives. Maybe that person didn't even mean to kill your father."

"Just accidentally set the Taser too high, huh?" Michael said. "And zapped him to death. Isn't that your theory?"

"It could have happened. Maybe the killer had been trying to induce him to give up the location of the sword."

Michael paced from one side of the fireplace to the other, his head tipped toward the ceiling, as if he were trying to take in her ideas and control his incredulity at the same time. At the end of his fourth pass, he pivoted.

"So what's it to you, Rae? Even if the sword is here somewhere, why bother yourself about it?"

"Because your father asked me to." She looked down at her hands. "He asked me to be the next guardian."

"And you believe all that crap he told you?"

She shot a hard glance at him. "Yes. Until I learn otherwise."

"But if he didn't know what to do with the sword, how do *you* expect to find out?"

"I don't know. But there's too much weird stuff going on in this house to just shrug it off. Something isn't right. And I think it all has to do with the sword. Look at Angie tonight. Was that normal?"

Michael looked at Angie's sleeping form on the bed. Slowly, he shook his head.

"I want to find that sword, Michael. I want to get it out of this house. And I want to find out just what it is and to whom it belongs."

"You want to find the sword."

"Yes!" She jumped to her feet. "Because if I don't and I leave, if I just leave this house and turn my back, it will be like everything your father did, all those years he spent protecting the world from evil—everything—would have been for nothing. I can't do that!"

Michael stared at her, his black eyes boring into her navy blue ones. "You really loved my dad, didn't you?" he asked, his voice softer than she'd ever heard.

"Yes," she answered, never breaking his stare.

He sighed and shook his head. "I don't know, Rae. It's so far-fetched. It's like something you'd see in a B movie."

"Maybe. But I have to find the sword. I just have to."

"And you've looked already, I take it?"

"From the attic to the cellar."

"And?"

"Nothing."

"What about the grounds?"

"I don't think he'd have hidden it where he couldn't be sure of its safety at all times."

"But it's going to be somewhere you don't expect. What about Angie's part in all this? Why does she dig in the side yard?"

"Maybe it's there somewhere?" Rae shrugged, stumped. "But why would your father have buried the sword in the dirt?"

"Maybe he didn't." Michael frowned. "There's an old cistern under that area of the yard."

"A cistern?" Rae gasped. From deep in her mind came the voice of the antiques dealer in Luxor, telling her to throw the Forbidden Tarot in the Nile, to throw the cards in water. Was Thomas's sword connected to the cards? A frisson of goose bumps burst out on her arms. She turned to look up at Michael. "That might explain his impersonation in the video!"

"What impersonation? What video?"

Briefly, Rae described the video Thomas Gregory had made at the end of his life, as if he expected evil to befall him. "Right at the end, your father impersonated Elvis," she added. "He said, 'Thank you, thank you very much.' But he was really saying '*tank*'!"

Michael narrowed his eyes. "All this is pretty far out there, Rae."

"But he was so serious about it!"

"I'm sure he was." Michael shook his head and bent to his hot chocolate.

Rae sighed. "But what if"—she pressed onward—"just for argument's sake, what if he *was* in his right mind? Put aside all your doubts and ask yourself, what if?"

"Rae." He lowered his cup to his waist. "The only reason I would ever do that is because you asked me to."

"Well, then, I'm asking, Michael."

He studied her face, his expression dark, his clean-shaven face lean and hard. His jaw flared as he clenched and unclenched his teeth. For a long moment he just stared at her, until the silence stretched into a thick long cord that hung between them, like a velvet rope at a theater. She couldn't tell what he was thinking or what he would do next. Then, he rubbed the back of his neck in his characteristic gesture of giving in.

"So you want to look for the sword."

"Yes!" She jumped to her feet. "Right now."

He smiled quietly at her serious eagerness and held up his hands. "Hold on there. What about Angie? I thought you weren't going to leave her alone."

Rae glanced at her sister and sighed. "You're right."

"Why don't you stay here with her, and we'll look for the sword first thing in the morning?"

"I won't be able to sleep!"

"Well, if everything you say is true, and Angie is involved, we can't leave her alone."

"That's true."

"Get some sleep, Rae." He touched her shoulder. "The sword has been hidden for years. A few more hours isn't going to make any difference."

# Chapter 21

The next morning, Rae led Michael down the cellar stairs into the low-ceilinged unfinished basement, tracking the dim path of the flashlight he held, her anxiety mounting with every downward step.

At the bottom of the stairs, Rae swept a glance around the dank shadows of the cellar. She'd found out from her previous search of the cellar that Thomas hadn't stored any valuables down here, probably because of water seepage in the walls. Shelves ran the width of the front of the house, and were filled with old paint cans and rusted, wooden-handled tools. A longer span of shelves ran the length of the side of the house, and was stacked with old jars of canned peaches and pickled beets, as well as old paper cartons and canisters from the turn of the century. Balloon-tired bikes, a rusted red wagon, and an ancient motorcycle sat near the unused bay of the narrow parking space. The small windows of the chained doors were so dirty that light barely filtered through the grime.

"So how do we get to the cistern?" she asked, her voice hushed.

"I'm not sure. Over there somewhere." He pointed toward a line of shelves. "I remember my father telling me the former owner of this house was a bootlegger during Prohibition."

"You mean he made his own booze?"

"Yes. In fact, he was the main supplier of liquor in town. Men can't live without their whisky!" He winked at Rae, his mouth quirking up at the corner.

Remembering how that expessive mouth of his had

branded her own, Rae felt a hot sweep of desire wash over her. She averted her gaze.

"My parents thought the bootlegger used the cistern for his operation." Michael reached for two dust-covered jars of canned peaches. He set them on the floor a few feet away. "Alameda is full of natural springs, Rae. And I remember my parents talking about the old cistern. How dangerous it was if the roof ever caved in. They had big equipment come in and tear up the yard when I was a kid."

Michael continued to unload canned goods while Rae helped.

"So if there's a cistern out there," Rae mused as she carried two more jars, "and the bootlegger used it, then you think there has to be a way of getting to it from down here?"

"Exactly." Michael lugged a carton across the dirt floor and set it on the ground. "I'll bet there's a door behind these shelves."

Rae nodded and scanned the dark wall behind the half-empty frame of the crudely built shelving unit. She couldn't see anything yet.

"Let's get all these shelves cleared," Michael said, standing close to her shoulder.

"Maybe we won't have to," Rae put in.

"What do you mean?"

"If your father moved these shelves in the last few years, he probably slid them along the dirt floor to get to the hidden door."

She picked up the flashlight and focused it upon the floor, walking along in front of the shelves, bent slightly to inspect the old dirt more closely. Sure enough, she discovered marks in the soil where the shelves had been dragged aside.

"Voilà!" Rae exclaimed, shining the beam on the skid marks while Michael strode up to look.

Michael shook his head as he gazed down at the trailing lines in the dirt. "You always were one step ahead of me, Rae." He glanced up at her and smiled.

Rae glowed with pride at the compliment.

"So it's this center portion." Michael nodded toward the wall. "The one with all the boxes."

"It should be easy to clear."

"Depends on what the boxes are filled with."

"True."

But to their relief, they discovered most of boxes contained canning supplies, old kettles and strainers. Swiftly, they stacked the fragile old cardboard boxes in a pile, and soon had emptied the shelves.

"Stand back," Michael warned as he reached for the wooden unit. He jiggled it outward until he could get a good grip, and then dragged the shelves away from the wall.

Rae directed the flashlight to the old brick wall. Sure enough, there was a door cut into the foundation, a small door painted the same color as the old brick.

"Bingo!" Michael crowed, dusting off his hands on his jeans.

"Let's go," Rae urged, anxious to find the sword, and certain now that they were on the right track. This hidden underground room was exactly the kind of place an archeologist would hide an artifact from the rest of the world. But she'd had no way of knowing the cistern existed. If it hadn't been for Michael's memory of the old house, she would never have found the sword, not in a million years.

"Give me the light." He reached back for the flashlight and Rae placed it in his hand, glad to let him go first.

The hinges screeched as Michael opened the old door and ducked into a cramped corridor lined with huge redwood timbers. A moldering smell, coupled with rotting redwood, blew past Rae as she followed Michael into the passage. Feathery tree roots hung from above and sprouted between the mildewing timbers, and she could hear echoing drips of water plinking in the distance.

Without thinking, she put her hand on his back, not wanting to be left behind in the dark in this hoary passageway. He reached back for her hand and she gratefully grasped his, and was struck by the warmth of his palm. His long fingers swallowed her frail ones.

After about twenty feet, the passage opened into a chamber, which Rae estimated to be about fifteen feet square. The walls were made of blocks of mildew-covered stone, the very same type she'd seen in the wall at the bathhouse in the park. And in the center of the room was a round hole, with a low wall built around it. The plinking sound Rae heard was condensation on the roof dripping down into the cistern.

"This is the creepiest place I have ever been in," Rae commented, walking closer to look at the black water in the hole. A drop from the ceiling fell, sending concentric ripples that fractured her dim reflection.

"I certainly wouldn't do much entertaining down here, that's for sure." Michael surveyed the ceiling. "My folks must have reinforced the top covering here. Looks like new concrete."

"I wonder they didn't fill the whole thing in."

"Maybe they couldn't. Maybe the water prevented them from doing so. It might have produced a big sinkhole."

Michael ambled to Rae's side and trained the beam of the flashlight upon the surface of the cistern.

"How deep do you think it is?" Rae asked, her voice hushed.

"I have no idea," he replied. "But it looks really deep to me."

"And how could the sword be in there?" Rae leaned over for a better look. "Thomas would never have just let it drop to the bottom."

"It must be suspended—if it's in there."

"It has to be, Michael!" She stared at him, realizing this was a definitive moment. If they didn't find the sword here, she had no idea where else to look, and she would be forced to abandon the Gregory house as well as Thomas's life work.

Michael looked down at her, shaking his head, as a quiet smile lightened his expression. "You are certainly the most driven woman I've ever met."

Rae didn't know if the comment was a criticism or a compliment. She held her hand out for the light, and he gave it to her without question.

Slowly she shot the beam around the periphery of the cistern, trying to see into the water, but the black pool sucked up the light as soon as it hit the surface.

"We need a tool," Michael said. "Give me the light, Rae, and I'll be right back."

She relinquished the flashlight and was about to run after him, when she realized how childish it would be. She was a big girl. She could endure total darkness for a few seconds.

As Michael hurried up the corridor behind her, the cistern room quickly plunged into its natural dank gloom. Rae hugged her arms and rubbed her shoulders, refusing to allow her mind to run away with notions of being trapped down here or having a subterranean creature rise out of the cistern and lunge at her. Even so, she glanced in the direction of the pool, surprised to see a pale glow beneath the surface.

"What in the—" She broke off her own words as she cautiously stepped closer, the hairs rising on the back of her neck and along her forearms. She craned her head to get a better view, still worried about denizens of the deep. There on the right-hand side of the cistern about a foot below the surface was a glowing object, and she could just make out a long narrow outline. It had to be the sword. It just had to!

Quickly, Rae felt her way around the edge of the cistern to get a closer look. Then she dropped to one knee on top of the musty wall and, with a grimace and a prayer, plunged her hand into the black water.

She ignored the cold water and refused to give in to her fears of something roaring up to bite her. Instead, she swept the side of the cistern with her hand until she felt the glowing object which had been wrapped in a plastic covering. She moved her hand upward. The object was suspended by a hook which had been screwed into one of the sandstone blocks. Carefully, so as not to knock the object into the depths of the well, Rae lifted it off the hook and raised it out of the water, just as Michael returned to the cistern room with the flashlight and a rake.

Triumphant, she held the object up, knowing by its size

and weight that she had found Thomas Gregory's rosy cross before she'd even seen it in the light.

"You found it!" Michael exclaimed, striding closer.

"It was glowing. When it got dark in here, I could see it glowing!"

"Get the plastic off."

"We'll need scissors. It looks like the plastic has been heat-sealed."

"Okay, then, let's go upstairs."

"Oh, Michael!" she cried, her heart soaring. "We found it!" She raised the heavy sword up and shook it in the air even though the effort caused a shard of pain to streak down her arm. "We found it!"

The excitement overwhelmed her and she opened her arms in joy, enough to allow Michael to swoop down and raise her up in a crushing embrace. He held her off her feet, against the warmth of his very broad chest as she focused on the thrill of the moment instead of the discomfort caused by his enthusiastic hug.

"Good for you, Rae," he said, a smile in his voice. "Good for you!"

"Your father wasn't a nutcase." She pulled back. "You'll see, Michael."

"Let's have a look at what you've got there before I decide about my dad."

He set her back down on the ground and gestured toward the door. He carried the rake and flashlight while she clutched the plastic-wrapped sword with both hands. Michael shut the door and pushed back the shelves, but they left the boxes and jars on the floor for another time.

"There are scissors in the study," Rae said, climbing the stairs ahead of Michael.

"Lead the way."

BY THE TIME Rae placed the sword on the desk, her heart had begun to thump in her chest. Michael found a pair of scissors in the top drawer of the desk, and he carefully cut away the top edge of the plastic. Rae could see the end of the sword hilt, an ornate knob covered in a basket-weave design. She reached for it but paused, her hand suspended inches above it.

"What's the matter?" Michael asked.

"I'm not certain we should touch it." Rae glanced up at him. "I have a feeling we shouldn't!"

"Well, I don't." Michael leaned forward and reached into the narrow sheath of plastic.

"No!" She grabbed his arm to yank his hand away before he touched the sword.

"What?" Michael retorted. "Do you think there's a curse on the thing? Something crazy like that?"

"I just have a feeling, Michael. One of your gut feelings. A really strong one." She slanted a hard glance at him and he immediately straightened.

"Okay, boss." He held up his palms and backed away.

Rae was surprised at his compliancy. "Let's just cut away the plastic and see what it looks like."

"All right." Gently, with the precision of hands accustomed to working with small objects and exacting measurements, Michael cut the length of the plastic as well as the lower end and then folded back the plastic to reveal the slender lines of the ancient weapon.

"It's not a ruby," Rae murmured, sidling closer for a better look.

Michael surveyed the large jewel set in the hilt.

"What is it, then?"

"It's a carnelian. Set in a dragon shape."

Michael bent closer. "That's what it looks like."

She reached out with her right index finger to trace the lines of the finely wrought creature, but once again caught herself and held back, certain this sword was not for her. Along with caution came another sensation, that of something she'd forgotten, something connected to this dragon-shaped setting. Something important.

"Some people believe dragons once existed in Egypt," she commented, still intently gazing at the sword. "There are representations of winged snakes in the old murals."

"That's news to me." Michael leaned down and tilted his head to inspect the edge of the blade. "Impressive," he observed. "That blade is still razor sharp."

"And the metal—what do you think it is?"

"I have no idea. I've never seen anything like it." Michael held up one side of the plastic to tip the sword toward the light. "Looks like there's a lot of copper in it. It's a weird color for a sword."

"That's why your father believed it was the rosy cross of the Rosicrucians. That it was something various sects secretly searched for throughout time."

"I have to admit, it doesn't seem like an ordinary sword. You can just feel it."

"So you feel it too?" She looked up at him.

He nodded, but then added, "Not that I'm buying into the whole thing, though."

"Oh, never," she retorted, her tone laced with wryness. "Not you. Not levelheaded Michael Gregory."

"There's nothing wrong with being levelheaded."

"Only when it borders on being bullheaded."

"Listen, Rae." Michael's dark eyes suddenly turned hard. "I did this for you. Not my father. Don't expect me to get all sentimental about it."

"You still don't believe your father—"

"He sacrificed a lot for this sword, Rae. A *lot*!"

"What you're saying is, your father sacrificed you."

Michael glared at her as the color rose in his face.

"It's still all about you, Michael, isn't it?" She felt her anger rising as quickly as his color. "Screw the world, screw history, screw the future—let's just concentrate on how your father let you down."

He stared at her as the edges of his lips turned white. She stood in front of him, seething with frustration that had built up over the last few days. Then, without another word, he swung around and stormed out of the study. She heard him stomp up the stairs.

Rae frowned and stared down at the sword as her vision blurred. Why did she and Michael always clash? Why couldn't she ever keep her big mouth shut? He had been an invaluable help to her this morning, and they had got along so well—like partners in fact. Yet Michael's sarcastic disdain of Thomas's theories triggered a smoldering anger in her that she could not contain. And that anger had just incinerated what little camaraderie she and Michael had enjoyed. Because of her, they were back to the same place they'd been when she'd first come to the house.

She sighed and drew the plastic over the sword. Logically she knew she could pack her clothes and drive away from the Gregory house without ever speaking to Michael again. But emotionally she knew she couldn't leave when their last words had been so harsh—at least hers had been. If she left without apologizing, she would never be able to live with herself.

Carefully, Rae carried the sword upstairs and into her bedroom, where she set it on her bed. Something told her not to leave it out in the open, so she gently slid it into the shadows next to the wall under the head of the bed. Then she rose, steeled her shoulders, and headed for the room down the hall where Michael had been bunking since the fire.

The door hung open and she stood at the threshold looking at him. He had his back to her and was gazing down at his newest model. After a moment, he must have felt her regard, for he slowly turned to glance at the doorway.

"Michael," Rae began, stepping into the room. "I want to apologize for how I acted downstairs just now."

"Apologize?" His eyes were still hard.

"I was out of line. There was no need for me to lash out like that."

He crossed his arms, his demeanor still unfriendly. "You seem to have meant what you said."

"But the way I said it was wrong."

"How do you say 'self-centered bastard' the right way?" He looked down his prominent nose at her. "You *did* mean to call me that, didn't you?"

She paused. She had come to apologize for her words, not whitewash the truth.

"Didn't you, Rae?" he repeated tersely.

"Yes. Yes, I did."

Michael's dark eyes glittered at her.

She raised her chin. "But if you won't accept my apology, there's nothing more to say."

She held his stare for a moment longer, and then broke it off and plunged back through the door. She hadn't expected the conversation to veer off to the left like it had. Yet she should have known better. Their "discussions" had always been unpredictable.

Even though she was accustomed to fractious exchanges with Michael, this last go-around made a lump balloon in her throat. Frustrated, she fled back to her room, choking on the hot ball of disappointment lodged in her neck. She was a master at stuffing emotions away to other parts of her being, always able to set them aside and look at them rationally at a later date, but not lately and not when those emotions concerned Michael.

As she returned to the bed, she heard the floor creak behind her.

"Rae?" Michael called from the doorway.

She didn't turn around. She was afraid she might break into tears if she faced him, and that was the last thing she wanted him to see again—Rae Lambers blubbering like a weakling.

His footsteps creaked closer until she was certain he stood only a few inches away from her.

"Please. Leave me alone," she said, her voice thick.

"I just wanted to know what you were going to do with the sword."

"Why should you care?"

"Rae!" He reached out for her arm, but she shook him off, still not turning to face him. She sniffed.

"Are you crying?" he asked.

"What if I am?" she retorted, her tongue sticking to the roof of her mouth.

He clutched her upper left arm firmly this time, not allowing her to break away, and then slowly urged her to face him while he reached for her right arm as well.

Rae glared at his chest, desperately trying to mask her feelings and stop the tears from burning in her eyes.

"Why are you so upset?" he asked, dipping down to get a look at her face.

She avoided him and glanced to the side.

"Because I'm a bastard?" he asked, his voice softened with gentleness.

"Because I didn't want to leave like this!" She raised her scalding eyes to his while the lump turned hard, threatening to burn a hole through her throat.

"Leave like what?"

"Angry with each other. When I might never see you again!"

He stared down at her, taken aback by her words. "Why wouldn't we see each other? You're part owner of this house."

"Not anymore." Rae heaved a huge sigh. Her shoulders slumped and the curves of Michael's hands slipped down and away from her.

"What do you mean?"

"I don't want to talk about it. It's just a fact, that's all. I will no longer be part owner after Monday."

"You sold your half?"

"No."

"No?" He took a step backward. "Then what?"

"Michael, I don't want to talk about it!" She backed away from him, but the backs of her thighs came up against the side of the bed. "It's over and done with, and we're leaving today, and that's that!"

"So you're just going to drop out of my life again?" Michael asked.

"Why not? We'd both be better off."

"Says who?"

She blinked in surprise and studied his face, trying to make sense of his last words as he stepped closer, trapping

her between his tall frame and the bed behind her. She felt
the old claustrophobia kicking in.

"Maybe I want to know what happens to that sword," he
continued, his eyes smoldering down at her. "Maybe I want
to know what happens to you."

"Why? So you can tell yourself that you were right all
along—that your father was nuts and so am I?"

"No." His mouth was set in a grim line. "So I don't picture you battling the world alone, all by yourself."

"I've done it my whole life, Michael."

"Maybe you have." He reached for her chin and tipped it
up as she stood unmoving, unable to retreat or advance,
forced to stay in the moment with this man in front of her.
"But maybe you didn't have to. I could have been there with
you, Rae. Right there with you all along."

She looked directly into his eyes to find him gazing down
at her, his black eyes full of tenderness. The expression
struck her to her core, but she knew she could not believe
that look or his words.

"You don't know what you're saying," she replied, her
voice cracking.

"I know exactly what I'm saying." He slipped his other
hand around her waist. "And what I'm feeling."

"You don't," she retorted as he bent for her mouth. He
silenced her protests with a hard deep kiss. In seconds, the
lump in her throat vanished, and she clung to him, surren-
dering to the wonderful sensation of his lips on hers. He
embraced her, pulling her off her feet, and sank his face into
the small of her shoulder, savoring the touch and taste of her.

Then he slipped a warm hand up under her tank top and
over her right breast, surrounding it with his palm and fingers, sighing as she sighed when the sensation sent spikes of
pleasure coursing through her. He kissed her neck and then
sank to his knees on the end of the bed, drawing her down
in a graceful arc as he lowered his head to her breast. He
tipped her nipple out of the cup of her brassiere and rever-
ently kissed it.

"Michael," she gasped, never having known such pleasure. She hung in midair, her breast offered to him like a tiny pagoda. He kissed her and nipped her while he unclasped her bra.

"We've waited so long for this," he said, his voice gravelly with passion. "Let me see you, Rae."

She didn't protest when he slipped her shirt and bra up her arms and away, and then paused to survey her slender torso. Rae closed her eyes as his hand lightly traveled the contours of her right breast and rib cage. This was not the harsh fumbling of the callused hand of an older man, but the appreciative caress of the man she loved. Beneath Michael's light but heartfelt touch she forgot about the scrawniness of her frame and the underfed buds of her breasts. Michael seemed to think she was beautiful and that made her feel beautiful.

Like two well-rehearsed dancers, they moved together, stroking each other as they sank onto the duvet. Nothing was forced between them, nothing was clumsy. It was as if they were meant to cling to each other in this way, as if this were a natural state between them, a natural extension of the special friendship they'd shared so long ago. Rae lay back, her eyelids half-closed as her body sang for Michael's. He knelt above her, pulling off his own shirt, tousling his thick black hair. Then his hands lowered to the opening of his jeans, and Rae was reminded of why they were really here.

She closed her eyes, wishing this moment could go on forever, but she knew it was wrong, knew it was fired by something much darker than love, and Michael would regret his actions one bright morning when they were free of this spell.

"Michael, no," she breathed, pushing at his chest as he sank back down to her.

He raised his head. "Why not?"

"It's not right."

"The hell!"

"You don't want this. Not really. You just think you do. It's all because of the cards."

"What cards?"

"Some tarot cards I found. We're just acting this way because of them. It's a curse. A spell."

"This is no spell, Rae." He pushed his fingers into the tops of her jeans, sending a hot wave of desire through her. "This is real."

"It's just lust."

"It's never been lust." Michael bent to her lips. For a long while she yielded to the kiss, taking in all she could of him even though she knew whatever she took, he would eventually want returned.

He pulled back at last and looked down at her, his face serious. "Does it feel right to you?" he asked.

## Chapter 22

"**Y**es," she whispered.

"It *is* right," he murmured. "And something we should have done long ago. Long ago, Rae."

Looking up at him, Rae suddenly realized they couldn't have done this long ago. She hadn't been ready for love when she was sixteen years old. She never would have been ready, either, if not for the shattering experiences of the past couple of weeks, when the secrets of their pasts had come to light and their wounds had been laid bare for each other to see. Finally exposed to the light of day, their old hurts were slowly beginning to heal. She could feel it in herself and see it in Michael's eyes. Not until this moment had Rae been ready to reach out for a real relationship and for love.

Here with Michael, Rae knew she would overcome her past. She would turn her back on Albert once and for all. Michael had fought his way through her childhood view of sex as sordid, hurtful, and emotionally ravaging. And now he was here with her, ready to change her opinion forever. Because of Michael, Rae felt nothing sordid—only love, completion, and a driving desire she could no longer deny.

Rae gazed up at him. "Yes," she said, her voice stronger.

Slowly, ever so slowly, Michael eased off her jeans, kissing her belly as he drew down the waistband, leaving her sprawling on the bed beneath him. She gazed at the top of his head, holding her breath, hardly able to believe she was about to lose her long-standing virginity to her old high school friend, but glad she had waited.

"You're so tiny," he murmured as he traced the curves of her hips with his palms.

"And you're so big." She reached up for him. "You'll have to take it easy, Michael."

"I will. I promise." He sank down upon her in stages, sighing with pleasure and rolling slightly to the side to take his weight off her. Then he enveloped her in his special brand of scent and heat, caressing her with his hands and entwining his long legs with hers. She gave herself up to him, to the strange combination of protection and violation, felt her flesh merging with his, and for the first time in her life knew what it meant to be one with another human being.

WITH UTMOST TENDERNESS, Michael made love to her again and again, until Rae was certain she knew every inch of his lean beautiful body, until her own body hummed with a sweet satisfied exhaustion that held her arthritis at bay. In the afterglow, she fell asleep in the small of his shoulder, her left arm slung across his chest and his palm splayed upon her left hip. She fell asleep to the rhythm of his breathing, to the thud of his heart against her cheek, and had never slept so unaware of the rest of the world.

After what seemed like hours, she heard Michael stir and then sit up suddenly.

"Shit!" He glanced at his watch and then down at her. "I'm going to be late for my meeting!"

Rae brushed the hair out of her eyes. "When is it?"

"In a half hour!" He leaned over and kissed her cheek. "Sorry, but I have to run." He bounded out of bed and Rae watched him gather up his clothes.

"That was wonderful," she said.

He paused, holding his rumpled shirt and jeans to his naked abdomen, gazing down at her. "It was," he replied.

Then he reached for his shoes and padded to the door, the mounds of his tight athletic ass rising and falling. He turned slightly before leaving.

"Don't leave before I get back, Rae." He tilted his head. "Promise?"

She nodded. "I promise."

Michael ducked out of sight. Rae sank back upon the pillow and sighed as she ran her hands over her breasts and belly. She had never dreamed making love could be so satisfying, so healing. His lovemaking had transformed her, leaving her with a feeling of hope, of new beginnings, and a sense of joy more glorious than she could ever remember. She could feel Michael on her thighs, could smell him on her skin, could still remember the way his smooth chest had heaved against hers. For a long while she just lay in the bed, wishing she could keep his brand upon her forever, wishing she would never have to shower off the remains of the exquisite last few hours. But she had to get up. She had to pack. And she had to do something with the sword.

AFTER TAKING A shower, Rae carried box after box down to the foyer, ready to be loaded in her Jetta for a trip to Berkeley. She had decided to take the sword with her and hide it in the hot tub on the patio of her condo. Just as she was carrying it downstairs, the front door burst open.

"Angie!" Rae exclaimed, unable to hide the object she carried in front of her. "What are you doing home?"

Angie closed the door and turned. "I took a few hours off. I'm beat, Rae!"

As she walked farther into the house, she glanced at the plastic-wrapped weapon in Rae's hands. "What's that?"

Rae frowned and looked down at the sword, realizing she could not conceal it from her sister, and perhaps shouldn't anyway. Angie was in this predicament as deeply as she and Michael. She stepped off the stairs to the main hall, level with her sister, and held out the sword.

"Pull back the plastic, but don't touch anything else," she instructed.

Angie did as she was told, and then stepped back, a hand over her mouth and her eyes wide. "It's the sword!" Angie's tired glance darted to Rae's.

"I'm going to take it to Berkeley."

"I thought you wanted to give it to Simeon."

"Not anymore." Rae gazed down at the weapon, certain she could detect a faint glow in the carnelian. "I think it's too valuable to give away to one person. It belongs in a museum."

"It does look really old."

"So I'll take a load up to Berkeley and be right back."

"And leave me here, alone?"

"You'll be fine." Rae gave her a reassuring smile. "I've noticed the bad stuff happens only at night."

"Okay. If you think so." Angie sighed. "I need to take a little nap anyway or I'm going to collapse."

"Okay, but not a long one. I want to be out of here tonight, Angie."

"Don't think I don't!"

Just then, Rae heard a light step on the porch and the buzzer rang. She glanced at the door. "Who could that be?"

Angie took a step toward the front entry, but Rae grabbed her arm. "No, Ange," she whispered. "Wait a minute."

Rae craned her neck to look through the dining room window to the street outside. Sure enough, she spotted a sleek black limo pulled up to the curb.

"It's Simeon," she mouthed. Then she handed the sword to Angie and pointed emphatically upstairs. Angie pointed to the sword and then to the second floor, making sure she knew what Rae had just indicated. Rae nodded. The buzzer rang again, longer this time.

Angie raced up the stairs, and Rae waited until she was out of sight before she reached for the doorknob.

Sure enough, Simeon stood on the porch, dressed in a crisp olive-colored shirt and sand-colored trousers. He held out a massive bouquet of purple irises.

"I would think the others I gave you have faded by now," he said with a smile.

Rae accepted the bouquet out of politeness, and suddenly thought of the first bouquet he'd given her at her long-abandoned apartment. She had forgotten all about the poor flowers. Surely they must be dead by now, their petals scattered upon her dining room table.

"How sweet of you," she murmured, sinking her nose into the cloud of fragrance and not wanting to look at Simeon.

She was reluctant to raise her glance, reluctant to have her mind read or to share a single moment of what had gone on with Michael earlier in the day.

Simeon gestured toward the doorway. "May I come in for a minute, or is your foul-natured roommate close at hand?"

"No, Michael's not here." She stepped back to allow him to enter the house. He looked around at the cardboard boxes stacked on either wall.

"What is all this?" he asked.

"Like I told you, Simeon, I'm moving back to my condo."

"Why didn't you call me? I would have helped."

"I thought you were angry with me."

Simeon tilted his head and looked at her much the way a parent looked at a child. "How could I be angry with you, Fay Rae?"

"The way you left at the park. I could tell you were upset."

"Only briefly. Upon reflection of our conversation, I was certain you didn't mean all that you said."

Rae threw a sharp glance at him. "But I did mean it."

His glittering eyes surveyed her closely, but Rae refused to allow him access to her thoughts. His perception of her had always been uncanny, and she wasn't about to let him pick up the difference in her. Instead of standing there beneath his intense scrutiny, she turned for the kitchen.

"I'll just put these in some water."

"We need to talk, Fay Rae."

"Now is not a good time, Simeon."

He followed her into the kitchen. She found a vase for the irises, settled the stalks in the glass container, and then carried it to the sink. She filled the vase with water, buying more time.

Finally she turned, wiping her palms on her jeans, conscious of his strong regard again, and unwilling to look at him. He stepped closer and cupped her chin with his hand, raising her face toward him, but still she did not meet his gaze.

"What is wrong?" he asked.

"Nothing." She ducked away and headed for the hall. "I just have a lot to do, Simeon. I want to be out of here by this evening."

"I will help you."

"Thanks." She waved him off. "But you would ruin your nice clothes."

"They can be replaced."

"I can manage, really, Simeon."

"No." He reached for her hand and pulled her to a stop. She turned and glanced at him. "I insist."

Their eyes met, and his gaze drilled into her, just as it had that first time they'd met each other on the plane in New York. She saw one corner of his sensitive mouth pull down, and his grip tightened on her.

"Something has happened," he murmured. "Something troubles you."

"I'm fine." She pulled to get away, but he did not release her.

"You've changed."

"Simeon, I never change." She gave a sharp laugh. "Ask anyone who knows me."

"You have closed yourself off to me."

"No I haven't," she lied. "You're being overly sensitive."

"I can feel it, Fay Rae."

She shrugged. "I don't know what you're feeling or why, Simeon. All I know is that I've got to load my car."

"Then load it." He let go of her hand, but in a way that felt as if he wished to fling it away from his. She backed off, wary of him for the first time since she'd known him.

She opened the door and then picked up a nearby box. Behind her, Simeon lifted a box as well, and followed her to her car. As she arranged them in her trunk, she saw Simeon gesture to his driver. The chauffeur lent his assistance, and soon her car was packed.

Rae returned to the house to see if they'd got everything, with Simeon close at her heels, insisting that he follow her to Berkeley and help her unload her car. She paused in the main hall and looked back at him, trying to think of a way to ditch him, so she could take the sword with her. But Simeon was not easily dissuaded once he'd made up his mind about a course of action, and she didn't want to raise his suspicions by arguing with him.

"I have to get my purse," she said.

"I'll wait here."

Just as Rae put her foot on the first stair, she spied Angie making the turn at the landing.

"I thought you might want your purse, Rae," she called, holding up her leather bag.

"Thanks, Ange."

Rae reached for her purse and noticed Angie staring at Simeon, too engrossed in looking at him to release Rae's bag.

"Angie?" Rae pulled at the purse strap.

Angie snapped back to reality. "Oh, sorry." She smiled and waved. "Hi, Simeon!"

"Good afternoon." He drifted close to the bottom of the stairs as Rae descended. "I hear you and Fay Rae are moving to Berkeley."

"Yeah. It's going to be like living in a dorm for a while."

"You are both welcome to stay with me."

"We couldn't impose like that," Rae answered. "Come on." She slung the strap of her purse over her shoulder. It felt lighter than normal but she was too busy to investigate the change in weight. "Let's go."

CRANKY AND STIFF, Rae walked to her car and got in as Simeon returned to his limo. She pulled out and away, and didn't make any effort to keep an eye on the sleek black car that trailed after her through the streets. How long would Simeon insist upon hanging around—the entire evening? She would have to use her health as an excuse to send him home.

As she drove, her thoughts shifted to Michael and the way he had looked at her that afternoon. Even though she was exhausted, she felt a surge swell up inside her at the thought of his lovemaking. He had showed her what sex was all about. It wasn't shameful or disgusting or degrading. It was wonderful. Fulfilling. More than she had ever dreamed. Rae tightened her grip on the wheel and tried to pay more attention to the road, but her thoughts continually slipped back to scenes from her bed.

When she guided her car into the parking lot of her condo, she looked in the mirror but couldn't see the limo. She parked and strolled down the sidewalk, looking for the car, but it did not appear on the side street. Rae returned to her car, got a box, and carried it to the lobby entry, and then to her condo unit. She could hear her phone ringing as she opened the door.

Rae grabbed the receiver and held it to her ear. "Hello?"

"Hello, Fay Rae."

"Simeon." She slipped her car keys in her pocket. "Where are you?"

"I'm afraid we lost you."

"Where are you?"

"We're somewhere in Oakland." He gave the cross streets.

"Simeon, you guys really took a wrong turn somewhere."

"I assumed that."

"By the time you get here, I'll be done unloading."

"I am sorry, Fay Rae."

"It's okay." She tried to hide the relief in her voice.

"We shall just return to the island then."

"Simeon, you really don't have to." She tucked her hair behind her ear. "In fact, I'm considering not moving any more stuff. I didn't know how tired I was."

"All the more reason to enlist my help."

"And Michael will probably be home from work soon. You know how he is."

"But I wished to take you to dinner. Talk with you."

"Maybe tomorrow, Simeon. I'm a little under the weather this afternoon. It's my arthritis."

"You need my touch, my dear."

She looked at the ceiling, well aware that with one caress from Simeon, her joint pain would melt in an instant. She would never get such relief from Michael.

"Fay Rae?" Simeon's voice brought her out of her thoughts.

"I'm here." She leaned against the wall next to the kitchen phone. "I'll see you tomorrow, then?"

"If that's what you want."

"It's what I want."

"Good-bye for now, then."

"Good-bye." She hung up the phone and peeled her aching body from the wall.

She carried the box of supplies into her bathroom and set them on the vanity counter, knocking something to the floor as she did so. Rae bent down, angling her head to get a sideways view of the floor between the toilet and the cabinet. She spotted a silver ring, one she usually wore on her right pinkie, and often left out on the counter.

She grabbed it and straightened. But just as she began to slip it down her finger, she had a burst of recall. The ring suddenly reminded her of another ring she'd seen on that day so long ago when Simeon had sat beside her on the plane, staring at her with his beautiful silvery eyes. He'd worn a ring. And that's what had been niggling at her ever since she'd found the sword.

Now she remembered. Simeon had worn a ring with a carnelian setting—a gem set in the shape of a dragon.

Rae froze, the silver band still halfway down her finger, as a terrible thought rose inside of her. Simeon wore a carnelian dragon. The sword had a carnelian dragon. Simeon had told her Dr. Gregory had something in the house that belonged to him. Could he have been referring to the sword? Why hadn't he told her about it? Did he not trust her? Did he not want anyone to know about it? Who was Simeon Avare? Could he have been the person who killed Thomas Gregory?

"No!" she breathed out loud as a huge feeling of betrayal swept over her.

She had been used. Simeon had used her to get to the sword. That was all she had been to him, all he had really wanted from her. She knew it was true as soon as the thought materialized.

Rae glanced at her reflection in the mirror, shocked at the white face she saw staring back at her, shattered by a truth that would never change. Men didn't want her. She should have known better. No man had ever made a fuss over her, no man had ever been even mildly attracted to her. Why hadn't she kept her head when Simeon had come on to her? Why hadn't she told Michael to keep his tarot-induced hands to himself? Neither man would look twice at her in real life once this was all over.

"You fool!" she cried at the woman in the mirror. "You stupid little fool!"

Then another thought struck her. Angie had spent many nights sleepwalking to the location of the sword. Had Simeon used her, too, in a more subtle way? Was she an instrument of his as well, leading him to the sword's hiding place? Rae had guessed he lacked the ability to see through water, and now realized that if that were the case, he would not have been able to find the sword by conventional means. Even if he had discovered the underground chamber, he would never have seen the sword hanging in the cistern, and Thomas Gregory had refused to tell him where it was.

So, unable to find the sword himself, Simeon had been using the two of them, befriending them to gain access to the house and its contents. Rae couldn't believe she had been so stupid.

Then an even darker realization loomed up, making her blood run cold. The ancient weapon was at the house now, out of water and completely accessible. Angie was at the house. And Rae was not.

Rae shoved the ring down her pinkie and tore out of the bathroom. She dashed to the phone, fished in her purse for the Gregory phone number, and dialed it. A mechanical voice came on the line.

"We're sorry. The number you have dialed has been disconnected or is no longer in service. Please check the number and dial again."

"Damn!" Rae looked at the number in her little address book and dialed again, her hand trembling.

"We're sorry. The number you have dialed has—"

Rae hung up the phone with a clatter and ran out of her condo, out to the parking lot, and flung herself into her car. The tires squealed as she careened out of the parking lot and sped toward the freeway.

"Lost, my ass," she mumbled angrily to herself, shifting hard as she merged into traffic. "That lying bastard. That lying murdering bastard!"

TWENTY MINUTES LATER, Rae sprinted up the steps of the Gregory house, her heart pounding, flung open the door, and raced into the main hall.

"Angie!" she yelled, pivoting in a circle to glance at the rooms on the first floor. "Angie!"

No answer. Rae galloped up the stairs and around the landing. She could hear a woman's voice making strange muffled whimpering noises in Angie's room. Rae raced to her sister's bedroom, shocked to see Simeon on top of Angie, his hands clamped upon her upraised wrists, and his lean body bucking between her legs. A piece of clothing was stuffed into Angie's mouth, preventing her from calling out. She turned her head toward Rae, and her eyes were bright with terror.

"No!" Rae shouted, just as Simeon reached his climax, snarling through his teeth, and glaring over his shoulder to see who had interrupted him.

At the sight of Simeon's face, Rae stared, frozen in the doorway. This was not Simeon raping her sister, but a very old man, whose wisps of hair hung off a nearly bald, liver-spotted skull, and whose sunken cheeks and emaciated features looked as if they belonged more to a mummy than a human being. As he snarled, she could see snags of teeth behind his thin wrinkled lips, and glaring eyes white with cataracts. This hoary old man was not Simeon, and yet she knew it was.

Rae snapped out of her state of shock. "No!" she yelled and lunged forward. She had no weapon to defend herself other than fury at seeing her sister violated.

Simeon jumped off Angie, amazingly spry for the old man she'd just seen, and landed on the floor on the other side of the bed. He grabbed something from the coverlet and held it up—the sword!

"Come no closer!" he warned. And when he raised his head, he appeared just like the familiar Simeon, young and virile, not a hair out of place. But unlike the man she had come to know, this Simeon's eyes flashed with hostility.

"You just raped my sister!" Rae cried, lunging forward again, ignoring her own safety.

"It had to be done." Simeon stepped back and held the sword in front of him, the tip toward the ceiling, the hilt near his mouth. "I've not the luxury of time." Then he kissed the carnelian.

Rae flung herself at him just as a cloud of red smoke billowed around Simeon. She stumbled through the smoke, clutching at air where Simeon should have been, and crashed against the wall. Simeon had vanished. All that remained was a choking spicy veil of smoke.

"Damn you!" Rae shouted to the cloud of vermilion as it whooshed toward the floor and disappeared, much like the fire had vanished in Michael's bedroom. "Damn you to hell!"

"Rae!" Angie called out. "Rae!"

Rae ran to her sister, and Angie grabbed her, crushing her with her arms.

"It was Albert!" she cried. Rae could feel Angie's entire body shaking. "Albert found me!"

"No, he didn't! That was Simeon!"

"I woke up," Angie continued, sobbing, "And I saw him standing there in the doorway. Albert was just standing there staring at me."

"Angie, calm down!" Rae stroked her back and her sweat-tangled hair. "It was not Albert."

"He was stroking himself. I could tell what he was going to do. But I couldn't move, Rae!" She clung even tighter to Rae's frail frame. "I couldn't move!"

"Angie, calm down. I'm here now. Just take it easy."

"Oh, Rae," Angie wept, her nose shoved into the small of

Rae's shoulder, her hands clawing at Rae's arms. "He's found me! Albert has found me!"

Rae hugged her and said nothing, knowing words were useless until Angie got over the initial shock of being attacked.

After a long while, Angie drew back, wiping her eyes. "I have to take a shower," she said, her lips puffy from crying.

"No, Angie. Not before you see a doctor and get this documented."

"No." Angie shook her head. "No doctors. No police."

"You were raped, Angie. And he's not going to get away with it."

"I can't, Rae." Angie backed away, hiding her nakedness. "I can't."

"Angie, it's the only way to get that bastard, to prove that he raped you."

"I don't want to, Rae." Angie swallowed. She stared off into space, her beautiful features haggard and smeared with ruined makeup. "You don't know what it's like," she whispered. "Everyone is so nice, and so gentle, but they just don't know what it's like. And the way they look at you—"

Rae slowly shook her head, her heart breaking for her sister, and not knowing what the best step would be. She couldn't force Angie to go to the doctor, and she certainly didn't want to traumatize her further.

"I wish you would get it documented." Rae rose from the bed. "But I can't make you go to the doctor."

Angie hugged herself and trembled, and looked as if she were going into a state of shock.

Rae put a hand on her shoulder. "Do you want a nice hot bath?"

Angie nodded.

"Okay. I'll start one and then I'm going to make you some tea." She turned for the bathroom, but Angie grabbed her arm.

"Don't leave me, Rae!"

"It's okay, Angie." Rae patted her hand. "That bastard got what he wanted. He won't be coming back."

"He'll always come back, now that he knows where I am."

"Angie, that was Simeon, not Albert."

Angie blinked and her eyes found Rae's. She looked genuinely puzzled. "What?"

"That was Simeon just now."

"Simeon?" Angie's brows drew together. "No it wasn't. It was Albert."

"I think you must have been in shock or dreaming, Ange." Rae studied her sister's face. "I know who I saw on that bed. And it was Simeon."

Angie shook her head, her expression clouded with confusion.

"Look, Angie." Rae sighed, furious with herself for not seeing through Simeon, for not putting two and two together until it was too late. Now that she knew more about the man, she recalled the times she'd caught Simeon staring intently at Angie, as if probing her mind. "I think Simeon has been able to read your mind."

"What?"

"And then, hypnotized you. Made you sleepwalk. He wanted you to help him find the sword."

"Why didn't he hypnotize you, then?"

Rae shrugged. "Some people aren't suggestible enough. That could be me." She smiled grimly. "Although he certainly had me fooled for a while. A good long while."

"I still can't believe it wasn't Albert."

"He made you think he was Albert. That's easy enough for a hypnotist to do. And he knew Albert had a certain power over you."

Angie sighed and glanced down at her naked thighs. "That bastard," she growled.

"Yes, that bastard."

Rae broke away, relieved to hear anger instead of fear in her sister's voice. She marched into the bathroom and turned on the water. Then she hurried down the stairs to brew them both a cup of strong hot tea.

But all the time she worked, she thought of only one thing: Simeon Avare had violated her sister and now had the sword in his possession. He was not the kind, caring gentleman she had thought he was. He was violent, manipulative, self-serving, and cruel. God help them all.

After making certain all doors to the house were locked, Rae carried two mugs up to the bedroom and sat on the bed with Angie, who had calmed down considerably after her bath. Rae told her about Simeon, how he'd used them both to get to the sword. Then she told Angie about the supposed power of the sword, and that there could be widespread ramifications if the weapon fell into the wrong hands. Angie took in all the information, and was uncharacteristically quiet, too traumatized to think or speak.

When Angie had finished her drink, Rae urged her to rest and assured her that she would not leave the room. Angie fell into a deep sleep while Rae sat in the chair by the fireplace, keeping guard, listening for Michael's step on the stair.

# Chapter 23

Not until six o'clock came and went did Michael arrive at the house. Rae watched him park his rental car in the drive and walk across the side yard. When she heard the front door close downstairs, she strode to the doorway of the bedroom, anxiously waiting for Michael to come up the stairs.

"Rae?" he called.

"Up here," she answered.

She heard his footsteps on the stairs and then saw his head appear as he turned at the landing and ascended the rest of the way. Surprisingly relieved to see him, she watched him materialize: his black hair, his dark blue suit, his blue shirt, and his blue tie hanging loose at his neck. He seemed so normal, so dependable, so strong. She had actually waited for him to come back before she decided what she was going to do, wanting to tell him everything and see what he thought of it all. She had never had a confidant and had never sought counsel from anyone but Thomas Gregory, and never for her personal problems. For Rae, waiting for Michael was wholly out of character.

"Traffic was a bitch on the bridge," he commented as he strode forward. Then he stopped and regarded Rae's face more closely. "Rae, what's wrong?"

"You were right about Simeon." She raised her eyes to meet his, expecting him to deride her for her faulty judgment of men. But Michael surprised her once again by showing only concern, which warmed his black eyes.

"What do you mean?" He stepped closer.

"He raped Angie this afternoon."

"What?" Michael threw a sharp glance past Rae's slight

figure into the bedroom behind her, as if he could see Angie in the bed around the corner, and then glanced back at her.

"When I was up at Berkeley taking a load of stuff, he came back here and attacked her."

"Attacked her? Why?"

"I don't know!" Rae hugged her arms and sank against the doorjamb. "He said it had to be done."

"What?" Michael made a move as if to take off in pursuit of Simeon, but then checked himself. "Where is the bastard?"

"I don't know."

"You just let him run off? Did you call the police?"

"I didn't have time! He had the sword, Michael. He held it out and—poof." She splayed the fingers of her right hand. "He was gone in a cloud of smoke."

"He just disappeared."

"Yes, in a cloud of smoke."

"What?" He lowered his brows. "People don't disappear in clouds of smoke."

"He did."

"And he has the sword."

"Yes. He must have induced Angie to tell him where it was."

"How did she know where it was?"

"I gave it to her to hide." Rae explained how she had carried the sword downstairs, intending to take it to Berkeley, and how she'd been interrupted by the arrival of Simeon.

"So he showed up to help, did he?" Michael growled.

"Yeah. To help himself." Rae sighed and looked down. "I see that now, and oh, so clearly."

"I tried to tell you, Rae."

"I know." She shook her head and rubbed the backs of her arms. "I wasn't accustomed to having a man attracted to me. I lost my head."

"Damn!" Michael ran a hand through his hair. "Is Angie okay?"

"Just shook up."

"Did you take her to a doctor?"

"She won't go."

"Why in the hell not?"

"It's a long story, Michael."

For a while, Michael looked deep into her eyes, as if probing for the dark secret she kept locked away from him, and then he sighed.

"Okay. I'm going to get out of this suit and make us something to eat. Do you think Angie will want a sandwich?"

"I'm not sure. But she'll drink something. No alcohol though."

"Okay. Think she'll get up?"

"I'll make sure she wakes up. If she keeps sleeping, she'll be up all night."

"Well, come downstairs then in a few minutes."

"All right." She watched him turn and head for his room. "Michael?" she called softly.

He stopped and looked over his shoulder.

"Thank you," she said, "for being here."

He gave a small, puzzled smile. "Sure," he answered.

RAE AND ANGIE ambled into the kitchen fifteen minutes later.

"How you doing, Angie?" Michael asked.

"I've been better." She collapsed onto a chair, propped her elbow on the tabletop and dropped her head onto her hand. Worried, Rae watched her.

"Hungry?" Michael asked, cheerfully whisking forward with two plates laden with ham and cheese sandwiches.

"I am," Rae answered, hoping Angie would take a few nibbles, enough to keep up her strength. She sat down across from her sister. "Thanks, Michael."

"Coffee? Soda?" Michael asked.

"How about some milk?" Rae tilted her head to get a better look at her sister's face. "Angie?"

"Whatever," she replied.

Michael brought over three milks and some napkins and sat down at the head of the table between Rae and Angie.

"So what's the plan?" he asked, picking up half his sandwich.

Rae took a long drink of milk and set down her glass. "Well, since the sword has been stolen, I don't know if there's much rush to move out tonight. I don't think we're in danger now."

"What about Simeon?"

"I doubt he'll be back. He obviously got what he came for."

Angie reached for her drink and pulled it closer. Her hand shook.

"Well, here's what I think." Michael swallowed. "It's almost eight o'clock. You haven't moved out entirely, and Angie's had a pretty tough day. I don't think it would be a good idea to go up to Berkeley tonight, alone. Or anytime for that matter."

"Neither do I," Angie put in, her voice a monotone.

"At least when you're here, I can lend some kind of protection. I can't be with you in Berkeley."

"I really don't think Simeon will be back." Rae put her sandwich down, suddenly losing her appetite at the thought of the betrayal she'd suffered.

"We don't know that for sure." Michael took a huge bite and chewed it. "And what about the sword?"

"What about it?"

"Are you just going to let the bastard have it?"

"No, but what can we do about it?"

"You know where he lives, don't you?"

Surprised, Rae glanced at Michael. "You would go after the sword?"

"The guy stole it! And he attacked Angie!" Michael waved his hand in front of Angie. "I'm not going to let him get away with that!"

Angie raised her head to gaze at Michael in awe. No man had ever stood up for her. No man had ever made an extra effort on her behalf.

"You would do that?" she whispered. "Go after him?"

"Damn right I would!" Michael grabbed his milk. "No

one comes into my home and violates it or anyone in it. I don't care who he is! The asshole!"

"But what if we're talking about someone with special powers?" Rae asked.

Michael tipped his glass toward her. "Don't go there, Rae," he warned. "He's just a guy."

"Maybe. But he's got that sword."

"One thing at a time," Michael replied. "That's the only way I can handle this. One thing at a time."

Angie stood up. "I don't feel so good," she announced and then dashed out of the kitchen.

Rae skidded back her chair and ran after her sister, only to find Angie in the first-floor bathroom, hanging over the toilet, puking.

As Angie retched, Rae got her a clean glass of water, and then held it out as Angie stood up.

"Thanks," she mumbled. She rinsed her mouth and stood at the sink, both hands propped on the sides of the counter.

"You okay?" Rae asked.

Angie nodded.

Rae regarded her sister's face in the mirror. She'd never seen Angie more pale or more bedraggled. Gently, she patted her thin shoulder.

"Why don't you come and lie down in the sunroom? I'll get you a blanket and a pillow. We can watch some TV, get our minds off everything."

"Okay." Angie trudged out of the bathroom and down the hall to the sunroom. Michael stood in the kitchen doorway, holding a beer. His eyebrows rose as Rae approached.

"Is she all right?"

"I don't know. I'm going to get her a blanket. Would you mind staying with her until I get back?"

"No problem."

BY TEN O'CLOCK, Angie was fast asleep again, her wan face finally relaxed in slumber, her uncombed hair hanging in clumped strings on the pillow, looking more like a lost little girl than a young woman.

Rae pulled up the blanket to cover her shoulders and then straightened.

"Turning in?" Michael asked from the nearby big leather chair.

"I'm beat. I'm going to go get a blanket and stretch out on the love seat."

"That won't be very comfortable."

"Maybe, but I'm not leaving Angie alone."

Michael stood up. "I'll carry her up to her room."

"She might not feel safe there, Michael, not after what happened."

"You might be right."

"I'll be back in a sec." Rae hurried upstairs, pulled the duvet off her bed, and grabbed a pillow. Then she paused and gazed down at the sheets where she and Michael had stolen their few precious hours. She could smell him on the pillow and sank her nose into the soft fragrant mound, closing her eyes.

This day had been special. She had known the touch of Michael Gregory. She had held that vibrant spirit in her arms, had felt his passionate kisses on her skin. Being with him, being part of him, had been everything she had ever imagined, even though a force outside themselves and not love may have thrown them together. But though Michael might be under a spell, Rae knew she was not. Her feelings for Michael had sprung to life long before she'd ever looked at the Forbidden Tarot. She loved Michael. She had since childhood.

Rae squeezed the pillow into her face as her heart ached. She could never let him know how she felt, especially not now when he was under the influence of the cards. It wouldn't be fair to him. He would someday stare at her and wonder what had possessed him—literally. And she had no intention of allowing that day to arrive. If Michael ever looked at her with disdain or repugnance in those intense black eyes of his, her heart would be scarred forever.

\* \* \*

HEARING RAE'S STEP at the doorway, Michael switched off the television and looked up, only to see a huge bundle of bedding walk into the sunroom. Rae was so slender and so small, she was dwarfed by the fluffy pillow and comforter. Michael stepped up behind her.

"Need some help?" he asked.

"I can manage." Rae spread the cover out on the couch and then folded it lengthwise like a sleeping bag.

Michael would have preferred that she spend the night with him. He'd been thinking about their lovemaking all day, and had looked forward to coming back to the house, back to Rae and the possibilities that lay before them. Now, however, Rae seemed to be pulling away from him, and he didn't know why. Would he ever understand females?

Michael threw a glance at Angie, who had turned her back to the television and was breathing slowly and regularly, sound asleep.

"Rae," he said, reaching out for her as she straightened from her task. She stepped away, out of his light grip.

"What's the matter?" Michael asked.

Rae turned, her face pale and serious. "It's been a long day, Michael."

"So long that you can't even look at me?"

Rae leveled her direct navy blue eyes at him and he suddenly felt foolish and childish. She'd been through a tremendous amount of emotional and physical trauma in the last few days, and here he was, pawing at her like a lovesick puppy, expecting her to shower him with attention.

"Michael," she said, her voice dry with fatigue. "We should go to bed."

"My thoughts exactly," he replied. "*We* should."

"Separately."

He knew his expression fell and that she saw it, and once again he felt selfish.

"Michael, we should forget what went on this morning."

"Why?"

"Because it wasn't real."

"It sure as hell was."

Rae sighed and turned away from him to fluff her pillow. Was she hiding her face from him? Something was wrong. She was worrying about something, but he had no idea what she was thinking.

He reached out and gently grasped her arm. "Rae, what's wrong?"

"Michael, please—"

He sighed and let his hand fall. "Is that why you're so bent on leaving?"

She glanced over her shoulder. "Because of you?"

"Because of this idea you have that you and I are not real together."

Rae turned to face him. "No."

"Then why?" He held out his hands, perplexed. "Why leave? Especially now?"

"I told you I didn't want to talk about it." Rae sank down upon the love seat and bent to untie her shoes.

"Don't I deserve to know?" Michael stepped closer. "I thought you were beginning to trust me."

She paused and then pulled off her shoe. After a long moment, she looked up at him, her expression a bit softer. "I trust you more than anyone in the world."

"Then *what*?" He stared at her, completely baffled. "Are you going to just move out of here tomorrow? Sayonara, Jack, nice knowing you, and that's it?"

"It's not like I'm going to Mars or anything."

"But it doesn't make sense!" He caught himself shouting and was suddenly worried he might awaken Angie. "It doesn't make sense, Rae," he repeated in a much quieter tone as he sat down on the edge of the walnut coffee table. He leaned forward. "Your condo has only one bedroom. You'll be living on top of each other."

"We'll manage." She peeled off her other shoe and put them both neatly together at the side of the love seat.

"What about your promise to my father?"

Rae shot a dark glance at him. "Don't think that isn't on my mind."

He watched her as his frustration level mounted. Why

were women so damned closed mouthed sometimes? He watched her take off her socks and stuff them into her shoes.

"Why this sudden cold shoulder?" he asked.

She straightened and looked at him, so close to him that he could have pulled her into his arms, melted her hardness with a kiss and caressed that damn steel from her spine. And yet he knew whatever was bothering Rae could not be treated with hands-on therapy.

"Because, Michael. One of us has to be logical."

"Why?"

"So nobody gets hurt."

"Who's going to get hurt?"

He saw her eyes darken and the set of her mouth falter, and he knew then that she was frightened, or in Rae's case— as he couldn't recall ever seeing her scared— deeply concerned.

"Listen, Michael." She propped her forearms on her thighs. The bones in her wrists stuck out like knobs. He hadn't noticed until now how truly thin she was. "We don't know each other that well anymore. I don't know very much about you or what you've been up to for the last twelve years. And you certainly don't know a lot of things about me."

"Such as?"

"Such as—just for starters—I have a disease."

"A what?" He straightened.

"Do you remember what I was like in high school, Michael, the last couple years of it anyway?"

He frowned and glanced at her, not sure where her so-called logic was going. He sure as hell didn't know. "I thought you looked tired back then. Like maybe you had a job after school that kept you up late."

"No, I just had a body that belonged to a seventy-year-old, not a seven*teen*-year-old."

He couldn't help but pass a swift check down her small frame. "What do you mean?"

"When I was young, I developed juvenile rheumatoid arthritis. I can't remember exactly when. It crept up on me in stages. But it began to hit me hard in high school. Now, as an adult, it makes my life painful at times. Really painful. It's chronic. It's like being old and rickety. The unrelenting pain can wear a person out. And it hurts to do things sometimes, like have sex."

"That hurt you?"

"A little. But mostly afterward."

"Jesus, Rae!" A hot wave of guilt scalded Michael. He would never have guessed Rae suffered from a chronic disease, maybe because he hadn't taken the time to really look at her or to notice. Rae had accused him of being self-centered. Was he?

For the first time in his life Michael felt ashamed of himself. His cheeks burned as he glared at the floor, not sure what to say, but he knew he had to say something.

"I'm sorry, Rae. I wouldn't have done anything—"

"No." She touched his arm, her fingers cool on his skin. "I could have stopped you, Michael. I could have said something."

"Why didn't you?" He craned his neck to look over at her.

Her dark blue eyes met his. "I didn't want to," she replied softly. "I wanted to know what it was like with you."

He stared at her, wanting nothing more than to pull her into his arms and kiss her pale lips. Another hot wave enveloped him, but this time it wasn't about guilt. It was about protecting this small woman, about caressing her with tenderness, about soothing away the pain and sadness hanging in her wise but tired eyes.

"Jesus, Rae," he murmured, shaking his head.

"And it was worth it." She squeezed his forearm and then sat back, lifting her hand from his skin. He wished she had continued to touch him.

"What about me in high school," he asked. "What did you think I was like?"

She glanced at him and then gave another shrug. "I thought you were like the other jocks."

"In what way?"

"In giving up on academics. Playing around."

"You thought I played around?"

"You had a lot of girlfriends."

"But that didn't mean I took any of them to bed. The last thing I wanted back then, Rae, was to get stuck in Alameda by an unplanned pregnancy. I had dreams. Goals. I didn't take any chances."

"That surprises me about you."

"Maybe you didn't know me either." He held her gaze, their glances hot and challenging. Finally she nodded and looked down.

"And believe it or not, I was never unfaithful to the Wicked Witch of the West, no matter how frigid she was."

"Vivian?"

"Yeah." He sighed and studied the side of Rae's face. "So don't go thinking what we did meant nothing to me. Don't try to tell me it was all about some tarot cards. And Rae." He reached for her left hand and enveloped it in his. "Don't leave."

"I have to." She stared down at the floor.

"Just tell me why, then. I'll lay off if you just tell me why!"

"I can't."

"I thought you said you trusted me!"

"I do."

"Then tell me. What do you think I'm going to do? Get up and walk away?"

"Probably."

"It can't be that bad. Why won't you tell me?"

"Because she's protecting me." Angie's weary voice interrupted them, startling Michael. Had she heard everything?

He whipped around. "What do you mean?"

Angie turned to face them and pulled the blankets up. "She won't tell because she doesn't want to hurt me."

"Then it's about you?"

"It's about both of us," Rae put in. She rose to her feet. "Angie, it's okay. You don't have to tell Michael anything."

"I want to." Angie struggled up on one elbow and brushed

the strands of her blond hair out of her eyes. "Mike deserves to know. You can't just leave him like this, not without telling him."

"Telling me what?" he asked, glancing back at Rae.

He saw her swallow and set her jaw. Good old stubborn Rae wasn't going to say a word. He could see it now.

"Our stepfather abused us. Not physically." Angie stared at the coffee table, her gaze dark. "Emotionally. And sexually."

"Shit," Michael gasped.

"I don't know what he did with Rae. I didn't even know he was doing anything with her. But he got me pregnant when I was fifteen years old."

Michael's heart twisted in his chest. He would never have guessed sexual abuse had been the reason for Rae's silence.

"Rae didn't know about me and Albert. Not until a few days ago when she made me talk about our childhood. She thought she had been protecting me all those years, because Albert said he wouldn't touch me if she gave in to him."

Without looking at Rae, Michael reached for her hand again, and this time he held it firmly. Her fingers were like icicles, and she did not respond to his touch.

"We could have kept it in the past," Rae went on, her voice toneless. "Except for the Wicked Witch of the West."

"Who's the Wicked Witch of the West?" Angie asked.

"My ex," Michael explained and then turned back to Rae. "What does Vee have to do with it?"

"Apparently she dug up information on Angie. Medical records, stuff like that. She threatened to go public with it if I didn't give over my share of the house to her."

"But you didn't." Michael stood up to face her. "Rae, you didn't!"

"What else could I do!" Rae yanked her hand away from his. "I couldn't do that to Angie! I couldn't have her name in the paper, let her be hurt by the scandal. You know what small towns are like—"

"You signed away your half of the house?"

"Not yet. But the papers are on my desk." Rae scowled. "I have until Monday."

"Shit!" Michael ran his hand over his hair and strode to the center of the room. "I can't believe Vee would do such a thing!"

"She seems to think she will get the other half when the divorce is final. Then she'll have the whole house."

"That witch!" Michael glared at the ceiling. "How much could she possibly need? She's got everything else!"

"Don't you see? She's looking for blood, Michael," Rae replied in her usual firm voice. "She won't stop until she sees you bleed."

*Chapter 24*

T hat night, Rae was awakened from a fitful sleep by the sound of glass breaking. She jerked awake, and realized in an instant that the entire house was shaking.

"Earthquake!" she cried, stumbling across the room to the mound of the comforter on the other sofa where Angie slept unperturbed.

"Angie, earthquake!" Rae reached for her sister, but her hand plunged through an empty pile of down. Her sister was gone.

Rae raced for the guest bathroom, wondering if her sister had become sick again. The house rumbled around her. She could hear dishes falling in the kitchen, shattering on the tile floor.

The door to the guest bath under the stairs was ajar, the room dark. Angie wasn't there.

"Angie!" Rae shouted.

She heard footsteps on the stairs above. "Rae!" Michael called, running down the steps. "You okay?"

"I can't find Angie!"

"Wait until this passes. Get in a doorway!"

Rae obeyed, darting to the doorway of the dining room off the main hall.

Michael squatted in the entrance to the living room, tying his athletic shoes. Rae glanced down at her own naked white toes. She would have to go back to the sunroom for her shoes. It would be madness to walk barefoot through the broken glass that littered the house by now.

"It's a doozy!" Michael shouted over the thundering noise.

The floor heaved under Rae's feet, and she yelped in alarm, grabbing the doorjamb to steady herself. She watched the eerie ripple roll toward Michael and then pass through the living room.

"Do you think the house can take it?" Rae shouted.

"It has before!"

Even though Rae had lived in the Bay Area most of her life, she had never experienced such a strong earthquake. She watched the walls sway and dance, thankful that the china in the dining room was securely locked behind the doors of a sturdy hutch. Even so, champagne glasses jiggled and tinkled into a pile of crystal, tiny cordial glasses rolled upon the vibrating shelves, and the ornate chandelier above the table swayed as if a miniature King Kong swung it back and forth.

After what seemed like hours, the heaving subsided and the rumbling quieted, only to be replaced by the whine of a powerful windstorm outside. Michael looked around as he stepped out from his doorway.

"Boy, that was something!" he exclaimed. "I bet that was at least a five."

Rae left her doorway as well, alarmed at how her legs shook, now that the danger had passed. She stumbled toward him, feeling like a rag doll with bandy legs.

"You okay, Rae?" Michael asked again.

"Just a bit shaken." She stood in the middle of the hall, too shocked to think straight.

"I need to go outside and turn off the gas, just in case there's been a break somewhere. Don't turn on any lights. The slightest spark could start something if there's a gas leak."

"Okay."

He glanced at her feet. "Where are your shoes?"

"In the sunroom."

Without saying another word, Michel turned and sprinted down the hall and came back with the pair of shoes she'd left by the couch the previous evening. He handed them to her.

"Thanks," she said.

He nodded. "See where Angie's got to. I'll be back."

"Okay."

Grateful for his levelheadedness, Rae jammed her feet into her shoes. She tied them quickly and then ran up the stairs, hoping Angie had got up in the night and mistakenly returned to her usual bedroom. While on the stairs, Rae felt an aftershock shudder through the house. The staircase tipped and swayed, and she hung tightly to the banister, the only thing keeping her on her feet. It was like being in a fun house at a carnival, except she wasn't having the slightest bit of fun. In fact, she was scared witless.

When the second quake abated, Rae plunged up the stairs, her knees buckling, her heart pounding. Her survival instincts told her to get outside, get away from the heavy beams and massive rooms of the mansion, but she had to find Angie first. She dashed to the green and lavender bedroom, only to find it empty as well.

Torrents of wind screamed through the gingerbread on the second floor, rattling the old windows. Rae's heart fluttered with alarm at the thought of a third quake hitting the house, but the heaving never came. Still jittery, she stumbled through the vacant bedroom searching for her sister.

Where was Angie? Had she walked in her sleep again? Rae couldn't believe it. She had been so certain the sleepwalking would end, now that Simeon had got what he wanted. Could Angie have wandered outside again, to the same old place in the yard?

Rae knew she could see the side yard from one of Angie's bedroom windows. In fact, now that she thought about it, she wondered if the placement of the window had given Simeon access to Angie, allowing telepathic messages to soar to the second floor and find her sleeping sister.

Trembling, Rae yanked up the blind and peered through the rippled glass of the old casement window. Sure enough, there was her sister, her hair glowing in the darkness, her nightclothes whipped by the wind, as she paused in the side yard and turned to look at something in the thrashing black locust trees.

Out of the gloom emerged the figure of a man, draped in a dark garment that billowed around his legs.

"Angie!" Rae yelled so hard her throat burned from the strain.

But Angie didn't hear her. She didn't look up.

Rae tore out of the bedroom and galloped down the stairs, as fast as her shaking legs would carry her. Then she burst out of the front door and careened around the corner of the house, keeping to the narrow cement walkway as best as she could. Leaves and branches flew through the air, striking her. She threw up one arm to shield her face and pressed on.

"Angie!" Rae yelled again, hoping to break the spell her sister was under, hoping the intruder would see her and run for cover.

But the man in black seemed unperturbed. He raised his hands, sweeping the fabric upward and outward, surrounding Angie in his arms, completely enveloping her in his voluminous cape.

"No!" Rae shouted over the howling wind.

The man glanced at her, but all she could see of his features was the glint of a glittering eye.

Unmindful of her own safety, Rae lunged for him, her hands ready to claw at him, to rip him to shreds, but she fell into nothingness again, landing on her hands and knees. Her palms took most of the fall, skidding not upon grass but onto something slimy and scuttling. Before she could move, something darted across the back of her hand. A lizard! The lawn teemed with them.

Crying out in disgust, Rae pulled back, just as hundreds of strange leathery flapping noises encircled her head. Rae scrambled to her feet, arms above her hair, as a mass of old wet leaves swirled around her, thick and putrid and dank. But then she heard one of the leaves squeak, and she realized with horror that she was not surrounded by a cloud of leaves, but by a cloud of bats.

"No!" she cried, trying to fight her way out of the mass of flapping wings. They followed her like a swarm of bees, funneling around her, holding her prisoner.

She could not see Angie, she could not see the house. She thought she was going to lose her mind. The bats were going to get in her hair! Under her clothes! She flailed her arms, mad with fear.

Then over the roar of the wind, she heard someone shout her name. Michael! He must have heard the noise in the side yard and had come running.

"Michael! Michael, help!" she cried, hunching into a ball, trying to cover her head with her bare arms. She could feel the brush of their wings, could smell their sickeningly sweet rodent odor, so strong it made her want to puke.

"Rae!"

She felt Michael grab her left wrist, saw the wide beam of his flashlight, felt the tendrils of her hair rising as the bats swirled upward and away from the light, squeaking and flapping through the branches of the black locust trees behind her and into the night sky.

"Rae!" Michael yelled.

She flung herself against him, clutching at him with every shred of strength she had left. She couldn't speak. She couldn't move. All she could do was burrow into Michael's wide chest, her eyelids pressed together, her face plastered into him, praying the creatures would not return.

"It's okay, Rae." Michael stroked her back. "It's okay. They're gone."

She pulled back, too worried about her sister to stay frightened for long. "So is Angie. A man took her!"

"Where?"

"I don't know!" Rae turned around and studied the side yard where shadows from the trees writhed across the overgrown lawn. "I couldn't see, because of all the bats."

"She was out here again?"

"Yes. And a guy came out of the trees and got her."

"Simeon?"

"Probably. But I didn't get a real good look at his face."

"They can't have gotten far." Michael broke away and loped out to the street, with Rae at his heels. He ran down the street in one direction while Rae ran down the other. She could see lights on in many of the houses, and people shuffling around, looking for damage from the quake. But no one was out in the road. She could hear a siren wailing down Webster Street, but couldn't discern any vehicles in the surrounding avenues or alleys.

A few minutes later she sprinted back to the house just as Michael jogged up to the front gate.

"Anything?" she asked, pushing back her wind-whipped hair.

"Nope."

"I'm going to call the police."

"Okay, but they don't do anything about a missing person until twenty-four hours have elapsed."

"She isn't missing. She was abducted. It's different."

"But why would Simeon want to kidnap her?"

"To cover up evidence of the rape?"

"Then he'd have to kidnap you too."

"That doesn't make sense, does it?" Rae crossed her arms. "If it was Simeon."

"Don't you think it was?"

She nodded.

Michael sighed and scowled at the empty lane littered with fallen branches and windblown trash. "What kind of weird ass is he anyway?"

"Probably weirder than we think. And where did the bats come from? Was that a coincidence? A freak occurrence because of the earthquake? I don't think so!"

"You think they're Simeon's special pets?"

"Something like that. There were lizards all over the ground too." Rae clutched a spike of the iron gate and pushed it open. "I'm going in and calling the police."

"Okay. I'm going to finish checking the house."

MICHAEL WAS RIGHT. The police couldn't do anything. In fact, the dispatcher told her they had been swamped by calls because of the quake. All three bridges to the island had been damaged, as well as the Posey Tube, cutting the islanders off from the rest of the world. Cars had plunged into the bay and some were even trapped in the flooding tube. A missing sister was the least of their problems right now.

Rae hung up the phone and sank to the chair in the study, suddenly overcome by a fit of shuddering she could not control. Her teeth chattered, her mouth went dry, and her hand shook as she brushed back the hair from her face, all the while thinking of her sister's disappearance. Where was Angie? When would the nightmare be over? How long would the Forbidden Tarot hold them in thrall? Until they were both dead?

She thought back to the card she'd seen. Typhon the Devil. The monstrous lizard, the broken columns, the flames, the chained people beneath the dragon's feet. Everything on that card had come to pass—even the earthquake, which had toppled the contents of the house. What kind of power were they dealing with?

She could hear Michael's steady tread as he slowly walked through the house, looking for signs of structural damage. Thank God he was here. If she had been alone in this house tonight, she would have lost her mind.

Rae hugged her chest, unable to keep warm, as her teeth continued to chatter from the chill and her bad case of nerves. What could she do to help Angie? Jump in her car and drive around? Was Angie's kidnapper trapped on the island as well, because of the bridge damage? Or was Simeon beyond such physical limitations? Could he possibly be a follower of the Left Hand Path, able to manifest himself in unconventional ways? He must have some kind of special power, to be able to disappear in a cloud of smoke.

Or was he simply a very talented magician?

She knew of only one person who might be able to answer her questions. Maren Lake.

Rae glanced at Thomas Gregory's Rolodex, still open to the strange black business card. Rae dragged the file closer and squinted at the card. She picked up the phone, and punched in the number. While she waited for the connection, she took a deep breath, trying to master her frazzled nerves.

"Hello?" Maren answered, her voice clear. She sounded alert and awake.

"It's Rae Lambers." Rae clutched the phone tightly to her ear, as if she could bring the woman physically closer to her. The strength of Maren's voice gave her a much-needed dose of security. "I'm sorry if I woke you."

"Nonsense, Rae. That quake woke me up a half hour ago."

"Good. I mean, I'm glad I didn't!"

"What's wrong?" Maren asked. "You don't sound like yourself. Are you okay?"

"It's Angie," Rae began. And then she told Maren everything that had transpired, including the hunt for the sword and the ensuing rape of her sister.

"Dear God," Maren murmured. "Dear God!"

"I don't know what to do!" Rae cried. "I don't know how to find her!"

"Wait there," Maren said firmly. "I'm coming over."

"But you can't!" Rae clutched the phone so tightly her fingers ached. "All the bridges are down and the tube's flooded."

"I'll find a way. You just sit tight, Rae, until I get there."

"But—"

Maren hung up.

Rae sat back, still holding the phone against her skull, as the dial tone buzzed in her ear. She sat there, shell-shocked, until Michael appeared in the doorway.

"Rae." He gave a half-laugh and strode forward. "Hang up the phone."

Gently, he pulled it from her grip and set it in its cradle. Rae stared at the wall, totally blank inside.

"You have to trust people sometimes," she said finally, hearing her voice as if she were outside her body. "Sometimes you just have to decide to trust people."

"What are you talking about?"

"The sword. Your father. About trusting." Rae swallowed. She glanced up at Michael's worried face. "I have decided to trust Maren Lake."

"What are you talking about?"

"She's on her way here. To help."

"She won't make it. I just heard on the news that Alameda has been cut off from the mainland by the quake."

"She said she's coming anyway."

"Well, we'll see her when we see her. If then. Come on. We need to make a plan." He urged her to stand up. "I've got coffee brewing in the kitchen. Not as good as yours, but at least it'll be hot. You look like you could use a cup."

"Cup?" She gave a wry laugh, her lips dry and numb. "I think it'll take a gallon to warm me up."

NEITHER OF THEM spoke as they sat hunched over the kitchen table, taking sips of the hot coffee. Rae felt as if she were suffering from a hangover, even though she'd never drunk enough to ever get sick. Exhaustion hung on her bones like a heavy coat, dragging her down. Her heart ached with fear and remorse, her head throbbed with lack of sleep, and her mind sat uncharacteristically still, numbed by helplessness. All she could do was sit there.

Michael seemed equally numb. When he finished his coffee, however, he pushed back his chair and stood up.

"Where are you going?" she asked.

"To look for Angie." He carried his cup to the sink. "I can't just sit here."

"I'll come with you."

"No, you need to wait here for your friend." He turned and swept a quick glance over her. "The bastard can't have got that far."

"He might have taken a boat."

"I thought you said he didn't like the water."

"I did. But who knows what he might do if he's desperate?"

"Let's hope he's trapped here on the island." Michael grabbed his car keys off the counter. "If there's one place I know every nook and cranny, it's Alameda. If he's here, I'll find him."

She walked with him to the back door. "Good luck," she said, longing to be pulled into his warm embrace again. At the door, he paused and looked down at her.

"Be careful, Rae," he said, reaching out to touch her cheek.

RAE SPENT THE next hour sweeping up broken glass in the kitchen and setting the house to rights. Fortunately, not too many dishes had shattered on the floor, and only a few books had fallen off the shelves in the library. She had just put the broom away in the closet off the kitchen when someone knocked on the front door.

Rae rushed to answer it, and felt an immense amount of relief to find Maren Lake standing on her doorstep.

"Come in!" she exclaimed, urging Maren forward with a sweep of her hand.

"My word," Maren remarked, looking around as she passed into the main hall. "Here I am in the Gregory house. After all these years!"

"How did you get across the water?"

"A friend with a boat." Maren peeked into the shadows of the living room. "Look at those statues," she murmured.

"It's like a museum," Rae put in. "Isn't it?"

"Impressive. Very impressive." Maren turned back to Rae. "But I'm not here for a tour."

"You can have one whenever you like though," Rae replied. "After we find Angie."

"As to that." Maren's eyes studied Rae's face, her expression deadly serious. "I'll need something that belongs to her."

"What are you going to do?"

"I'm a seer," Maren explained. "If I can pick up a strong enough vibration from something of Angie's, I might be able to see where she is."

"What can you use?"

"Something that's important to her."

"Like what?"

"A favorite article of clothing or a special piece of jewelry. Something like that."

"She doesn't have anything like that, that I know of."

Maren frowned slightly. "Well, then, may I see her room? Maybe I will pick up on something there."

"Of course." Rae gestured for her to follow her. "It's upstairs."

They hurried up the wide staircase, down the hall, and into Angie's room. Maren walked over to the bed and paused. She sucked in a deep breath, held it for a moment, and then slowly let it out.

"I smell death and decay," she said, turning her unusual turquoise eyes in Rae's direction. "Who has been in this bed?"

"Angie," Rae answered, her stomach tightening into a knot. "And Simeon."

Maren sniffed again. "Is this where he raped her?"

"Yes." Rae crossed her arms. "You said death and decay, though. What's that have to do with Angie?"

"It's what I sense." Maren turned to face her. "How old is Simeon?"

Rae shrugged. "Thirty-something." Then she glanced at the bed and frowned. "But—"

"But what?" Maren stepped closer, her eyes intent upon Rae.

Rae licked her lips, worried that what she was about to divulge would make her seem like a total lunatic. But she pressed on anyway.

"Well, I've had a couple of weird glimpses."

"Glimpses?"

"Of Simeon. As a really old guy."

"But not all the time?"

"No. His image shifts. That's the only way to describe it. Two times I've seen him as a really old man, but then when I looked again, he appeared normal."

"Hmm." Maren studied her face and then turned her gaze upon the bed again. "You see him as old, and I sense him as being very near death."

"Really?" Rae walked up beside her. "He made a comment that he didn't have a lot of time."

"And yet he raped your sister."

"Right." Rae scowled. "He had enough energy for that."

"Perhaps the sword *gave* him the energy."

"I hadn't thought of that."

Maren nodded, her expression as grim as Rae's voice. Then, without saying anything more, she drifted around the room, seemingly waiting for a vibration strong enough to reach her. Rae stood in the middle of the bedchamber, watching the older woman's peculiar search. After a few moments, Maren headed for the bathroom. She paused, her black thongs sinking into the plush violet rug, and then she reached out for Angie's metal cosmetic case. She picked up the little trunk and carried it to the bed.

Rae said nothing. Maren seemed to be in a trance, and Rae didn't want to do anything to impede the process. Silently she watched as Maren sat upon the bed, put the small box on her thighs, and flipped open the little latch.

The lid of the cosmetic case sprang open, revealing a jumble of eye shadows, liners, and lipsticks, and a glinting mirror housed in the lid.

"Ah." Maren sighed, running her fingertips along the perimeter of the lid. "Here we are."

Rae stepped closer. She could see nothing in the mirror, but it was obvious that Maren detected something much more than her own reflection in the glass.

Maren shut her eyes and framed the two sides of the lid with her fingers. For a long while she sat there unmoving, as if listening to something Rae could not hear.

"Rust," Maren murmured. "Cold. Hard. Dark."

Rae took another step closer. Was Angie being held prisoner in a cold, dark place?

"The letter S." Maren paused, frowning. "Chinese?"

Then she abruptly opened her eyes and looked over at Rae. "Do you have something to draw on?" she asked. "Paper? Quickly now!"

Rae glanced around but saw nothing available to write on. She dashed down the hall to Michael's room, grabbed a drawing tablet lying on his table, and ran back to Angie's bed.

Maren uncapped one of the lip liners and carefully drew an image of something she'd "seen" in the mirror of the cosmetic case.

After a few strokes, Rae recognized a shape. "A flower?" she asked.

"Yes." Maren looked up. "Or some kind of symbol. Very simplistic."

"That's all you got?" Rae asked, unable to connect anything Maren had said to a recognizable location on the island.

"That's it." Maren sighed and slowly closed the lid, snapping shut the latch. "Perhaps she couldn't see much. Could she have been blindfolded?"

"Not as far as I know." Rae shook her head. "But she was kind of enveloped in a cape."

"Enough to block her vision, perhaps."

"Great," a male voice remarked from the doorway. "Not much to go on."

Rae glanced over her shoulder, surprised to see Michael standing just inside the room. She hadn't heard him come up the stairs.

"You didn't find anything?" she asked.

"Nope." He strode forward.

"This is Michael Gregory," Rae said, turning to Maren, who slowly rose from the bed, her eyes sparkling with curiosity.

"Thomas's son." Maren held out her hand as her regard slowly took in every inch of his tall frame. "How very like your father you are."

"You must be Maren Lake."

"The same."

"May I see what you've drawn?" Michael asked.

Maren held out the tablet. He took it in his hands and studied the sketch, a simple design of a flower with five petals and no circle in the center.

"So you think Angie's in a place that has something to do with this flower."

"There's also rust involved," Maren added. "As well as the letter *S*, and something connected with Chinese."

"Hmm," Michael said, still looking at the sketch.

"You believe all this?" Rae asked, incredulous that Michael Gregory would take the words of a psychic at face value without a single sarcastic remark.

"Right now, Rae." Michael glanced down at her. "We've got to use anything we can."

She looked up at him, speechless at the change in him.

"Hanging around you has opened a whole new realm of possibilities." Michael arched a brow. "Not that I want to go there—"

He was interrupted by the soft ring of his cell phone.

*Chapter 25*

As soon as Michael answered his phone, he strode out of the bedroom. Rae could hear him in the hall speaking in punctuated tones with the person on the other end. Then, after a few seconds of silence, he stuck his head around the doorjamb while Maren Lake returned the cosmetic case to the bathroom.

"I've got to go," he said, holding up the phone. "The Wicked Witch of the West just called."

"She's here in Alameda?" Rae asked. "At the crack of dawn?"

"Her father has a boat. She's down at the marina."

"It must really *be* important."

"Not necessarily." Michael's expression clouded as bad memories swept over him. "But I intend to set her straight on a few things—the ownership of this house, for one."

"Don't tell her about Angie—"

"Leave it to me, Rae. I know how to deal with Vee." He stuck his phone in the pocket of his shirt. "I'll be back in a few minutes."

"What is your cell phone number?" Rae asked. "Just in case?"

He told her the number, and she committed the digits to memory while she walked with him to the top of the stairs. "I'm going out to look for Angie while you're gone," she said.

"Okay. Call me if you find anything." He waved without looking back.

Maren came up behind Rae. "I'm going with you," she said.

\* \* \*

RAE AND MAREN traversed every street of Alameda, crisscrossing the banana-shaped island, even going down Eagle Avenue and the tattered neighborhood of her childhood. Rae had healed enough wounds to openly stare at the old house, painted now in a friendly green color. But no amount of paint could disguise the unfriendliness of the black windows, especially the ones on the second floor.

"I sense this area is not a happy place for you, Rae," Maren remarked, glancing across the car toward her.

"No." Rae gripped the steering wheel more tightly, realizing that her shame had annealed to anger. "I'll tell you about it someday."

She drove two blocks in complete silence, and then forced herself to focus her mind on something else.

"Maren." She glanced at the older woman. "Do you get the feeling that Simeon is a human being or—" She broke off and swallowed, hoping she wasn't going to sound like a complete idiot. "Or something else?"

"What do you mean, something else?"

"You know—" Rae sighed. "Because of the card. Do you think he could be Typhon?"

"You mean a god?"

"Yes." Rae stared straight ahead, but her attention was focused entirely on the woman sitting in the car with her.

"If he is a god, then he's an awfully old and tired one."

"Gods get old?"

"In my belief system, Rae, there are no gods, not in the conventional sense. Only highly evolved beings striving for *kheffer*."

"So Simeon could be someone very close to *kheffer*?"

"Possibly, and maybe his age is making him do desperate things. Or maybe he is flawed as human beings so often are."

"But would a person that evolved have superpowers?"

"They may appear to. Certainly the power to deceive the average human eye and mind."

Rae squeezed the wheel. "Could one of these evolved beings have healing powers?"

"Very likely."

"Enough to cure my arthritis? In a real physical sense?" Rae glanced at the side of Maren's face. "Simeon claimed he could. Might that be possible?"

"That I could not say."

MICHAEL ROLLED INTO the parking lot of the marina behind the grocery store on the Oakland side of the island. He had agreed to meet Vee at the little deli at the marina where she'd moored earlier that morning. If he had his way—and he fully intended to—he'd listen to what she had to say and be out of there within minutes. The last thing he wanted to do was waste any time chatting with Vee when he should be searching for Angie.

Though the day had blossomed into a gorgeous windless morning, Michael hardly noticed the weather as he stormed down the sidewalk past the yacht dealer and the cruise place and then onward to the deli. He could see Vee sitting outside at one of the small tables, a black floppy hat shielding her from the sun, and a small man perched at her side. Probably her lawyer.

"Make it brief," Michael said without greeting her. "I don't have time for this."

"Why? Was the house damaged in the quake?" she asked.

"Why? Do you care?" Of course she did. He knew she did. She lusted after the house.

"Don't be like that, Michael." Vee tapped the seat of a chair. Her customary bracelets jangled. "Please, have a seat."

"I prefer to stand."

Vivian sniffed and then motioned toward her companion. "You've met my lawyer."

Michael scowled at him. "David."

"Michael. Nice to see you." The lawyer's lie was as crisp as his suit.

"Get on with this, will you?"

Vee sat back, her pretty face shadowed by the hat. "What's the matter, Michael? What's the rush?"

"Do you think I enjoy having my chain yanked?"

"I'm not yanking anyone's chain."

"Come off it, Vee." Michael squinted as the eastern sun poured full into his face, blinding him. "We just had a major earthquake. And you appear at an ungodly hour with something so pressing it can't wait. What's the deal?"

"It's this." Vee clasped her hands in her lap. "I have an opportunity to invest in a lucrative venture but the window is very narrow. I need you to sign over the house to me today."

"What?"

"You're going to sign it over sooner or later."

"Says who?"

"The State of California." The lawyer leaned back in his chair. "You make a good living, Michael. Your wife will suffer after the divorce. She has no means of support."

"And that's my problem?"

"According to family law statutes, yes, it is."

"Have her get a job at one of her charity places, then!"

"That isn't the point, Michael," the lawyer continued.

"Christ, her father is a millionaire! She'll be rich as Croesus someday!"

"That still isn't the point."

Michael glared at the lawyer and then looked over at his soon-to-be-ex-wife. What had he ever seen in such a woman? Sure, she was glamorous. Sure she was classy. Sure she had a killer smile. But that smile could turn deadly and cruel. She had a cold streak that had frostbitten their relationship soon after their wedding and had frequently stalled his amorous advances in the bedroom. No wonder he and Vee hadn't produced any children. He couldn't remember the last time they'd made love.

He had married a ruthless woman. And here she was, willing to do anything to get her hands on his father's house, uncaring whom she ruined in the process. How different she was from Rae, who had given up a dream and a valuable share in a piece of property to protect her sister from simple gossip. Vee would have no such qualms about sharing a confidence if it involved personal profit.

"Michael?" Vee pressed.

"Why should I do you any favors?" he growled. "I'm not signing anything until October."

"Then I'll have to go to the papers."

"The what?"

"The newspapers."

"And what, take out a classified?" Michael mocked her. "'Killer wanted for uncooperative husband'?"

"You think you're amusing, don't you?" Her icy voice shot back at him. "Always a smart remark. That's you. But I tell you what, Mike. I'm not laughing. And I never have."

He glared at her.

She plopped a manila envelope on the table.

"What's that?" he asked.

"A newspaper article I've had drafted."

"About what?"

"Your sick little friends and your sick twisted father."

"My what?"

"I've found out plenty about those little sluts living with you. What a stellar family background they come from."

"That's none of your business!"

"Isn't it?" Vee lounged back in her chair, her collagen-enhanced lips smirking. "It *is* when one of them was seduced by your father while she was underage."

"What?" Michael jumped to his feet.

"You can't tell me your father didn't lure Rae Lambers to that house when she was a kid."

"You've got to be joking!"

"He helped her get into graduate school. Did you know that? And then he fought to get her a job there at Berkeley."

"So?"

"Why would he bother?"

"Because she's brilliant?" Michael flung the words back at Vee. "Because they shared a deep and common interest? Because they cared about each other's work?"

He scowled at her. "I realize that must be a foreign concept for you—caring."

"Get serious, Mike! All she wanted him for was his money."

"The hell! She's not like that."

"And how would you know?"

"I've known Rae practically all my life."

"No you haven't!" Vee leaned forward. "You haven't seen her for years."

"Some people don't change, Vee. Rae is the most intelligent, steadfast person I know."

"Oh, really? As if you're a good judge of character!"

He couldn't argue with her there. He'd certainly misjudged the character of the woman he'd married.

They glared at each other again.

"Nevertheless," the lawyer put in, his voice calm and level. "Mrs. Gregory will be forced to publish this story if you don't sign the quit claim deed."

"That's coercion!"

"If you don't, your father's posthumous reputation will assuredly be ruined."

"Who is going to publish such trash?"

"Any paper in this city, Michael." The lawyer steadily regarded him, his expression bland, as if he made such threats on a daily basis. "People are still talking about the strange circumstances of your father's death. They will eat this story up, make no mistake."

Michael squinted, and looked back down at Vee, trying to see into her cold green eyes. "Don't try to blackmail me, Vivian."

"Why? What will you do about it?" Vee crossed a shapely leg over another. "You're in no position to threaten me, Mike, not with your father's reputation at stake."

"Oh, yeah? I know who my father was. Rae knows who he was. In fact, she *taught* me to see who he was. And that's all that matters."

"I would reconsider if I were you." The lawyer rose to his

feet and Michael glanced at him, half-blinded by the ascending ball of the sun rising over the Hayward Hills.

It was then, as he was trying to make out the attorney's face, that he saw the containers stacked on the old Del Monte dock in the distance, a place used solely for storage now. What stood out most in his sun-impaired vision was the flower design on the sides of some of the metal boxes— the very same design Maren Lake had sketched in his tablet.

"Michael?" Vee's voice came from far away.

Had that bastard Simeon Avare taken Angie to the old dock? Rarely anyone went there these days, except for a lone truck occasionally dumping off a container. It was a perfect location to hold someone for a few days. No one would hear cries for help on an abandoned wharf between two windswept marinas.

At the corner of his vision Michael saw Vee rise to her feet and plant her fists on both sides of her trim waist. "Michael! Are you going to answer me or not!"

Michael glanced over his shoulder at her. "Do what you want with that trash."

Then he turned and dashed through the maze of plastic chairs and tables.

"Michael!" Vee shouted after him.

Michael sprinted toward his car, his ex-wife's strident voice fading as quickly as his concern for her threats. As he dashed through the parking lot, he realized he was running away from his old life forever. Nothing of the past could touch him now or hurt him or ruin his newfound sense of balance. Regardless of what Vee did or how much money she tried to extract from him, it didn't matter. Money didn't matter. The shallow social life he'd known didn't matter. Building skyscrapers didn't even matter. His prime concern now was the frail little soldier he'd left behind in his father's house and all that she represented.

He didn't care if a strange deck of cards had brought them together again or not. His feelings for her were real, and always had been. Michael ran toward Rae, toward a life based on truth and values, toward a world that finally meant something.

WHEN MICHAEL GOT back to the house, however, he remembered Rae wasn't waiting for him there, but was out looking for Angie. He had no way of contacting her, as she didn't carry a cell phone. Anxious to get on with the hunt, Michael gathered the tools he thought he might need during the container search, and then paced the floor of the house, willing Rae to call him. He would give her thirty more minutes before he left for the docks on his own.

Thirty minutes dragged by like thirty hours. When the deadline passed, Michael carried the crowbar, screwdriver, and rope out the front door, just as a FedEx truck pulled up behind his car. Curious, Michael put the tools on the porch banister and waited for the driver to trot up the steps.

"FedEx is delivering today?" Michael asked, surprised any package had made it to the island after the quake.

"As many as we can," the deliveryman replied. "We had a boat bring over the shipment today." He held out the electronic clipboard. "Would you sign, please?"

Michael scrawled his signature and then accepted the flat package, wondering if Vivian had decided to hound him through the mail as well as in person. He scanned the mailing label. It was an overnight delivery, addressed to Angela Lambers, and the return address showed the package had been sent from Hollywood, California.

Assuming the packet must be important, Michael tucked it under his arm, picked up his tools, and headed for the car.

Just as he put the key in the ignition, he heard his cell phone ring. Michael grabbed it and pressed the call button.

"Rae!" he exclaimed when he heard her voice on the other end. "I think I know where Angie is!"

TEN MINUTES LATER, Rae pulled up to the buckled parking lot of the old Del Monte pier as Michael parked his rental car and jumped out. He opened the passenger door of the Jetta for Maren Lake while Rae scrambled out, her joints aching from the stress of the last few days. Together, they hurried to the chain-link fence and glanced up and down its length.

"The gate's locked," Maren observed.

"There's a hole down there to the left." Rae pointed to a gash in the fence near the edge of the dock, where pilings rose out of the deep olive-green water. "We can sneak through."

She led the way while Michael helped the older woman duck through the jagged hole in the fence. Strong morning sun beat down on Rae's head and back, freeing the fragrant smell of the tarred timbers under her feet and sending the odor wafting up like a heavy foreign perfume.

Maren glanced up at the rusting containers towering above her. "Michael, I believe you're right about this place." She pointed to the flower logo on the side of the third box from the bottom. "Sin Jin," she added, reading the name of the company next to the flower.

"Starts with an S," Michael put in. "And sounds like Chinese to me."

"But how do we get up there?" Rae asked. She tipped back her head to study the stack of boxes. Each container had to be at least eight feet tall.

"And how do we know which one Angie is in?" Maren shielded her eyes from the late morning sun with the edge of her hand. "Look at them. There are dozens bearing that logo, maybe even hundreds."

Rae scanned the stacks surrounding them. Standing there was like being in a small city made of huge metal building blocks. It could take them most of the day to check out each of the Sin Jin containers. She watched Michael inspect the end of one of the containers.

"I might be able to climb up, using the bars on the doors and the ridges of the sides." He lifted a foot toward the closest one.

Rae stopped him with a hand on his shoulder. "Wait a minute, Michael. Let's look at this logically."

"What do you mean?"

"Well, if Simeon is the one that took Angie, he would have had to force her to climb up there or would have had to carry her, right?"

"Maybe."

"And he's not a large man. So he probably would have trouble lifting her."

"True."

Maren crossed her arms. "Unless we aren't dealing with a man."

"What do you mean?" Michael turned to face her.

"I'm not certain Simeon Avare is your typical flesh-and-blood type."

"What are you saying?"

"He may have powers beyond your comprehension, Michael, especially if he is in possession of the sword."

Rae saw the darkening protest in Michael's eyes and stepped between the two. "Regardless of Simeon's physical prowess, let's limit ourselves to the lower-level containers. If we don't find Angie in any of the bottom ones, we can search the next level. And so on."

"Spoken like a true math professor," Michael remarked, but not unkindly.

"Let's start at the first one, there on the end."

"Okay."

"While you two do that, I'll go along and bang on the sides of each box," Maren put in. "In case Angie can hear us and respond."

"Good idea."

Rae walked alongside Michael, headed for the first Sin Jin container at the end of the dock, worried about Angie but hopeful they were on the right track.

Michael slipped his arm around her shoulders. "We'll find her, Rae," he said, giving her a light squeeze of encouragement. "Don't worry. We'll find her."

THE WORK PROVED more difficult than they thought. Most of the locking mechanisms on the ends of the containers were stiff with disuse, and Michael had to knock them loose with the end of the crowbar and then jiggle them until they slid away enough to let the vertical bars drop. Then they had to pry the doors ajar. Each time a door creaked open to reveal the cavity behind it, Rae's heart would pound with anticipation, as her vision adjusted to the dark interior, only to find just another long expanse of empty space.

Midafternoon burned down upon them as they continued their search on the second level. It would be difficult for a man to hoist another person up to the second tier of containers, but not impossible.

"We should have brought some water," Rae commented, wiping the sweat from her forehead with the swipe of an arm.

"I know." Michael glanced over his shoulder at her. "I never dreamed it would be such a job."

"And you're doing most of the work."

"That's because you're the brains of this outfit, and I'm the brawn." He winked at her and then turned back to the task of climbing up the ground-level container. She watched him scale the side, grateful for his help and thankful for his concern for Angie's safety, as a warm flush of love for him welled up inside her.

"I'll get some water for us," Maren suggested. "Seeing how I'm just standing by."

"Take my car." Rae handed her the Jetta keys.

THE SUN WAS already sinking behind the hills by the time they reached the last box of the second level, way out on the end of the pier where the old dock tipped behind them, half-collapsed into the murky water. Maren had left to make another water run, as well as to get them sandwiches.

Rae stood between the stacks of containers watching Michael climb up the last box, wondering if they would have to search the third tier as well, and wondering if there might be another dock somewhere on the island stacked with similar containers. Surely Angie couldn't have been stashed in the third tier.

"Hey," Michael called down. "This one's not latched."

Rae's heart did a weak but hopeful flip-flop. "What?"

"It's not latched." Michael wedged the crowbar into the crack of the door. Slowly the door opened, bawling in protest with a loud squeak. Rae put her right foot on the first ridge of the lower box and pulled herself upward.

"What do you see, Michael?"

"Nothing yet. It's too dark."

Rae struggled, dragging herself upward by clinging to the vertical poles while she copied the way Michael had walked up the side, using the ridges like ladder rungs. "Do you see anything yet?"

"Yeah. Looks like a person!" Michael reached for Rae as she struggled toward the open door above her. Michael made the climb look so easy. She could hardly get to his awaiting hand.

"One more step," he urged.

She called upon the last shreds of her strength to slide her right hand up the bar and then brace herself for the final step upward. At last, Michael grabbed her wrist and dragged her up the rest of the way. She stifled a cry of pain as he yanked her up to the open door. This was no time to give in to her physical limitations.

Michael left her in the doorway as he dashed to the end of the container, forty feet away. Rae's eyes adjusted enough for her to stumble after him, toward the heap of clothing in the far right corner. Michael knelt down as Rae ran up to his side. There lay her sister, sprawled on a dark garment, her slender limbs splayed carelessly and lifelessly, her head rolled to the side.

Michael placed two fingers upon her pale throat, just under her jaw. "She's alive," he said.

"Thank God!" Rae dropped to her knees and patted Angie's cheek. "Angie! Angie, wake up!"

Angie didn't stir, didn't even blink.

"She must be drugged," Rae exclaimed, looking up at Michael. It was then she noticed a dark figure hovering in the shadows at the corner of the container, opposite to where

Angie lay. Rae clutched Michael's arm, and he instantly followed her line of sight. What was over there?

The wind off the bay turned, swirling into the nooks and crannies between the stacks of containers and through the partially open door. The breeze wafted a sickening stench her way, the same odor she'd smelled when surrounded by bats in the side yard. Were bats clumped in the corner of the container, waiting to attack her again? She saw the shadow move slightly, as if shuddering to life.

While she stood there staring at the opaque mass in the far corner, she noticed the late afternoon sun waning just enough to shift the angle of light coming through the open door. Rae watched in alarm as the wedge of golden light narrowed and suddenly blinked off, leaving them in shadow.

Michael rose to his feet, taking Rae with him, as the dark clump in the corner undulated and straightened, raising its head from slumber and awakening to full and conscious alertness.

# Chapter 26

Spellbound, Rae watched as the dark mass stepped toward them, taking the shape of a human being, a very familiar human being.

"You found me," Simeon remarked, shimmering into full view. Rae was surprised to see him as immaculately dressed as ever, in khaki slacks and navy blazer, not a wrinkle in sight. "How amazing of you."

"Bastard! What have you done to Angie!" Rae lunged for him, but Michael grabbed her and held her back, saving her from the razor-sharp blade Simeon held in front of him, having produced the sword from out of nowhere.

"What's going on, Avare?" Michael demanded.

"I believe you Americans call it family planning."

"Family planning?" Rae wrestled for freedom, desperate to get at the man who had violated Angie. But she couldn't break loose. Michael gripped her too tightly.

"Don't let go of her, Michael. If she touches the sword, she's dead." Simeon tipped the weapon slightly, and in the dim light Rae could see a rosy glow surrounding it.

"I'm not afraid of that damn sword!" Rae lied. "I want to know what you've done to Angie!"

"Did you drug her?" Michael added.

"For her own good. She's the hysterical type."

"Who wouldn't be?" Rae retorted. "You raped her!"

"She has not been truly harmed." Simeon lowered the sword, holding it in both hands. "And I would not have been forced to stoop to such a level, had it not been for you, Fay Rae."

Rae's struggling broke off. She couldn't believe what she'd just heard. "Me?"

"Yes. Angie is here because of you." Simeon's silvery gaze swept over her. "Something happened this week. Something changed between us. And I realized you were wasting far too much of my valuable time."

"So you raped my sister"—Rae's voice narrowed to a shrill rasp—"because I put you off?"

"I have a pressing need to produce a child, Fay Rae. It is a long and complicated tale that we have no time for here. Simply put, however, I must father a son. Very soon. And until a few days ago, I had intended the child to be yours."

"Mine?" Rae paled.

"What?" Michael's grip tightened on her arms.

"A sexual union with me would have cured you, Fay Rae, would have released the pain in your bones. I tried to tell you that, but you wouldn't listen. A child given to you by me and carried in your body would have blessed you with such strength, such joy—"

"But why me?" Rae stared at him, unable to connect Simeon's parental plans with the violence he'd committed upon her sister.

"Because you are capable of infinite things, Fay Rae. More than you would ever dream. Your father was the most powerful human being I ever met, and you share that genetic heritage. I could feel it just by touching you, see it in your aura—as I do now."

Michael turned to glance at Rae, as if checking to see if he could detect her nimbus.

Rae ignored his inspection. "You knew my father?"

"Yes. Many years ago."

"What happened to him?"

"He became dangerously adept. Far too adventurous for his own good." Simeon tilted his head to one side. "And how do you say it? Curiosity kills the cat."

"You shithead!" Michael dropped his hold on Rae and lunged forward. "You bastard!"

"I warn you!" Simeon stepped backward and raised the sword higher. "Stay back, Michael. You Gregories have interfered with my affairs one too many times!"

"You killed my father, too, didn't you?" Michael demanded, his hands still raised in the air.

"It was an unfortunate accident."

"I'll bet!"

"He wouldn't cooperate. And because of it, I have lost valuable time. Much too much valuable time!"

"You killed my father?" Rae shook her head, wondering what else regarding her childhood was not what it seemed.

"But I never intended to hurt you, Fay Rae. Or your sister either."

"You just raped her, that's all!"

"I didn't want it to be rape. And if you hadn't barged in on me, her experience might have been most pleasant."

"Like hell," Michael spat.

Simeon didn't seem to register Michael's scathing comment. "Angela is the next best thing to you, Fay Rae. She has nearly the same genetic makeup. And she is much easier to manipulate mentally. I just need to keep her with me until I am sure she is pregnant. Then my task will be complete."

"You're insane!" Michael dove for Simeon's knees, knocking him backward. The sword clanked against the back of the container as Simeon hit the wall. Quickly recovering, he brought the sword down in a great sweeping arc. Fireballs flew from the tip of the sword, bouncing over the floor of the container, just missing Michael's feet. Rae screamed, knowing the blade could easily hack off Michael's head.

But Michael's many years of athletic training paid off, both in speed and agility. He rolled to the side, and the sword came down upon steel instead of human flesh. Simeon swore and raised the sword again, this time in both hands, while Michael scrambled to his feet. Michael eluded the second swipe as Rae dashed for the crowbar just inside the door. She grabbed it and ran screaming at Simeon, brandishing the heavy tool above her left shoulder.

He turned, his silver eyes blazing, and their weapons clashed in midair. The impact was so jarring, Rae felt the bones in her arms rattle as the crowbar glanced off the sword and flew from her hands. She paused, horrified at the expression of bloodlust in Simeon's eyes as he raised the sword again, this time to hack her in two.

For an instant, he stared deep into her eyes. "I am not all that I once was, Fay Rae," he hissed. "Beware of the next time we meet."

His hesitation gave Michael just enough time to run at him from behind, knocking him to the floor as Rae jumped out of the way. Simeon fell forward, and the impact jarred the weapon from his grip. The sword skidded across the floor of the container and sailed through the opening. Rae heard it clatter as it ricocheted between the metal boxes and then landed upon the wooden pier with a soft clank. She stood for a moment, paralyzed by her close brush with death, unable to move or think.

Simeon and Michael wrestled upon the floor of the container, and for a moment Rae was sure Michael would overpower the slighter man. But Simeon managed to roll away and leap out of the opening in pursuit of his weapon. Michael followed, hurtling his athletic body to the opposite container, grabbing the metal rods, and sliding down to the dock. Rae grabbed the crowbar again and followed the men, hoping she could do something—anything—to prevent Simeon from regaining control of the powerful weapon that had affected all their lives for so many years.

She dropped to the ground just as Michael dove for the sword, which had come to rest at the corner of a container.

"Michael, don't touch it!" Rae yelled. She had always had a premonition about the weapon, that to touch it would be hazardous, maybe even deadly. Michael checked himself, his hand outstretched, his fingers only inches from the hilt.

At Michael's hesitation, Simeon raced forward and stomped on the back of his hand, crushing his fingers, and then viciously kicked him in the rib cage with his other foot. Michael writhed in pain, rolling precariously close to the edge of the dock.

Simeon hoisted the sword. "Time to die!" he shouted. He swung.

Wincing, Michael rolled aside, and the force of the missed swing sent Simeon reeling off balance, which gave Michael enough time to scramble to his feet. Simeon swung the sword again, but once more Michael dodged the blow. Rae watched, terrifed, and wondered how long Michael's luck would hold. She had to do something to help.

"Here, Michael!" Rae tossed the crowbar through the air, praying he could catch it without being broadsided by Simeon's sword.

It was then Maren appeared at Rae's elbow.

"Oh, my God!" Maren gasped, taking stock of the situation as Michael barely succeeded in warding off the blows of the sword with his much shorter crowbar.

Little by little the two men backed toward the ruined edge of the dock as their weapons clanged together. All around them parts of the pier had collapsed in upon itself, leaving gaping holes a man could easily fall through. Rae watched anxiously, worried that Michael might accidentally back into one of the holes, or put his foot down on a rotten section and break through.

Rae stepped closer to the men, frantic to help Michael. Maren's voice followed her.

"That may be no mere man Michael is fighting!"

"What do you mean?"

"Use your soul vision, Rae. You alone will see who Michael is *really* fighting."

Rae glanced at Maren just as Michael cried out in pain. Rae pivoted, horrified to see Michael falling to one knee, his left leg buried in a hole in the rotting pier. The crowbar flew across the dock, coming to rest near Rae's left foot.

She could see Simeon lifting the sword above his head. She could see the wild look of triumph in the man's face. It couldn't end like this. Michael couldn't die like this.

"No!" Rae wailed.

"Use your soul vision, Rae!" Maren shouted behind her. Rae stared at Simeon, summoning every ounce of her spirit, focusing every shred of fear and outrage she felt, recalling every word of the teachings she had read during her research. She had learned that humans possessed three strengths: intelligence, heart, and that special knowing sense, the thing she called soul vision, the thing Michael called a gut feeling, the sense that revealed pure truth to those who had the strength to see it and deal with it.

"Use it!" Maren repeated.

Rae would use anything to save Michael's life, even something as far-fetched as the soul vision Maren claimed she possessed. She would make the leap from safe, predictable mathematics into the world of the unknown, just as she had made the leap toward trust—all because of Michael. If she had a long-suppressed gift, it was time to use it now.

She drew on her third sense, tunneling it into a beam that streamed from somewhere between and just above her eyes, never guessing she possessed such power. Maybe this was her father's legacy, a genetic inheritance she'd never fully tapped until now. She thought of her father, drawing upon his strength as well, certain at last that she had been loved by him, that her father had not abandoned his little family but had been killed because of his unusual talents.

For a brief moment Simeon paused and glanced her way, and his image shifted, just as it had shifted the day Rae had found him on top of her sister.

"He's not what he seems," Maren continued. "It takes most of his energy to make you see him as he wants to be seen! Look at him, Rae! Take from him all that you can! Take his energy! Strip him of his lies! Of his façade!"

Rae stared, and before her eyes she glimpsed the Simeon Avare she'd seen before—the ancient man with the wisps of hair and the dried, shrunken skin, the frail arms, the watery eyes, the slathering mouth.

"Look at him, Rae!" Maren urged, pointing at the figure still poised above Michael, ready to wield a death blow to the man trapped at his feet. "Strip him of everything!"

Rae stared, her forehead on fire. Simeon's figure shifted again, shimmering, changing color, changing shape, into a dark green roiling cloud. Only his eyes remained visible, staring back at her in astounded amazement that a mere mortal possessed the power to see him as he really was, to rob him of his ability to mesmerize.

Then, around the glittering silver eyes, Rae detected a new form taking shape. Was this a version of Simeon she'd never seen? Something even older, more hideous? Her mouth went dry, her palms sweated, but she continued to concentrate every bit of her mind on the creature, willing it to completely materialize.

The frail old man disappeared. In his place a monster now stood, a beast with the body of a lizard, the head of a crocodile, the wings of a bat, and a great protruding, very humanlike penis. From his navel waved a black serpent, its red forked tongue flicking in and out, smelling for death on the air.

She'd seen this beast before. She knew him well. He was Typhon the Devil—the image she'd seen on the tarot card.

"No!" Rae gasped. She'd never been more terrified in her life.

The monster threw back his head and bellowed, his eyes blazing at her. One stomp of his cloven hoof would split Michael's skull as easily as puncturing a ripe melon. Rae dared not look down to see what Michael was doing or if he had freed his leg, fearful that a single glance away might release the beast from the thrall of her eyes.

Typhon backed up, bellowing again, flapping his black, leathery wings. Suddenly the dock came alive with lizards. Over the timbers the creatures slithered, scrambling for Rae and Maren, their little legs pumping like slimy pistons. Typhon bellowed again, and this time a cloud of bats spewed out of his mouth, between the gaping rows of his jagged teeth, circling around his head before churning toward Rae, in a squeaking, disgusting horde.

Rae knew he was using his powers to distract her. She could feel the lizards on her feet, crawling up her legs, the bats darting for her head, but she refused to break her concentration. She refused to be frightened. They couldn't be real. They must be illusion—even if they didn't feel like illusion. She couldn't give in. She had to save Michael. She had to give him time to free his leg and get away.

Then suddenly the ground heaved beneath her feet. She blinked, unable to maintain a grip on her concentration as she lost her balance. Behind her, a terrible rumbling thundered, like a huge train going by, and the dock tipped sickeningly. Rae staggered, trying to keep on her feet, as she saw Michael rising up on his haunches, compressing himself like a coiled spring. In the mere instant she had lost her concentration, Typhon had disappeared like a bad dream, leaving the image of Simeon in his place once more.

"Earthquake!" Maren yelled.

The dock shuddered. Simeon's hands came down, and the sword flashed in the dying light of late afternoon. At just that instant, Michael sprang into action, jumping to the side and rising up on one leg as Simeon sliced thin air, just missing Michael's shoulder. Michael spun, sending a pummeling blow into Simeon's gut. Simeon lumbered backward but maintained his grip on the sword. He swung again, and this time caught Michael's right arm, slicing through the muscle of his bicep.

"No!" Rae cried. She picked up the crowbar and ran forward, forgetting about her own safety. Simeon turned, his eyes cruel and hard, and warded off her blow, his sword clashing into the bar she'd raised above her head.

The ground heaved again, hoisting them upward, as if creating a statue of the two of them, locked in combat. She could feel Simeon's labored breath on her face as she strained against the sword he held, her crowbar wedged against his blade, her forearms trembling with the effort.

"Who are you?" she gasped.

His eyes glittered down at her, and for the third time, his handsome face looked not only haggard but slightly indistinct, as if the edges of his figure were turning transparent.

"The world's worst nightmare," he replied.

Then suddenly, Rae felt a sharp prick on her side, like something biting her. She hesitated, the crowbar sliding down his sharp blade, as a stinging sensation spread through her torso. Her arms felt strangely heavy, her thoughts dragged. She couldn't even make herself move. What had he done to her? She had a strong suspicion this scalding feeling was no illusion.

Then the quake rocked the wharf again and Simeon fell backward. Rae watched, her vision sparkling, while her adversary fell backward and downward, as his part of the dock collapsed into the water. Someone grabbed her from behind and pulled her backward, out of danger, but she couldn't tear her gaze away from Simeon. One moment she saw him falling, the sword glowing in his right hand, his arms and legs extended as if he were skydiving from a plane, as if the distance behind him were miles instead of feet—and the next moment he was gone. She never saw him hit the water. She never heard a splash. And then the remaining part of the dock listed forward and fell into the void where he'd just disappeared, burying whatever was left of him in timber, twisted metal, and rubble—trapping him in a watery grave.

"Rae!" she heard Michael shout.

Rae tried to look for Michael, but her vision had turned to quicksilver. She couldn't see anything through the swirling metallic liquid in her eyes. She tried to speak, tried to turn around to see if Michael was all right, but she couldn't move her arms or legs. Her forehead burned as if a hole had been branded between her eyes.

"Michael!" she screamed. His name filled her throat, but she couldn't get the sound past her numb lips. Was he all right? Or was he bleeding to death on the dock? Where was Maren? Had Angie survived the earthquake, trapped inside the container, or had her metal prison cell slid into the bay? Was Simeon really dead?

A hundred questions swirled in the clogging miasma of her mind as the silvery light slowly faded to gray and then went out.

\* \* \*

RAE DREAMED OF *Egypt, of trudging across the desert sand—walking, walking, walking—lost in the Sahara, all alone. The sun was a boiling furnace and she was so hot, so parched, so exhausted, she couldn't take another step. She paused, swaying, and then fell, rolling down a long sand dune, coming to rest on her back, her lips coated with coarse granules of sand, her face tipped backward, fully exposed to the sun. She was too tired to get up again, too tired to keep walking. But the glaring light was so unbearable, she moaned.*

"RAE!" SOMEONE GENTLY touched her shoulder.

"No!" she murmured, too weak from thirst to say anything more. Was it Simeon talking to her? Typhon? Wait a moment, didn't she recognize that voice?

"Rae!"

What man spoke her name like that? Whose deep, dry voice was so familiar, so compelling? Why did that voice make her forget how thirsty she was and how willing she was to just lie on the sand and die?

"Rae! Can you hear me?"

*Michael*? She mouthed his name. She could feel her lips moving, felt how swollen and dry they were.

With a huge effort she forced her eyelids to open just a crack. Blinding light as sharp as spear points seared into her eyeballs. She clamped her lids shut again. Then she felt a moist sponge on her mouth, dripping beads of blessed water upon her lips. She lapped the drops greedily, desperately. Michael was there! He'd found her in the desert. He had come with water. She was saved!

WHEN NEXT RAE awoke, she found herself in a dark room, lying in a hospital bed with a tube stuck in her arm and a crisp white sheet tucked around her. She tried to sit up but discovered she was so weak, she could only manage to lift her head, and that for just a few seconds. Someone sat slumped in a chair near the window. She turned her head to get a better look. It was Michael. He'd survived the blow from the sword. And looked none the worse for wear, thank goodness. Or had the incident at the old wharf merely been an installment in the series of terrible dreams she'd been having?

On the tray near the bed, she spotted a glass of water. All her dreams had featured unbearable heat and thirst. Her throat was parched even yet. She reached for the glass, but her arm shook so badly, she bumped the tray, jiggling the glass against an empty pop can. Michael stirred and came instantly awake.

"Rae!" he exclaimed. He jumped to his feet, grinning like a kid, obviously overjoyed to see her awake.

"Michael?" She lay back, overcome by the effort of just lifting her arm.

"Let me get that for you." Michael picked up the glass and tipped the plastic straw to her lips. She drank greedily, just as she had in her dream. When she was finished, she released the straw from between her lips. "Thanks."

He drew away the glass and stood near the bed gazing down at her, smiling. "Man, am I glad to see you with your eyes open."

"What happened? Why am I here?" She glanced at the window and back to his face. "Am I in the hospital?"

"Yes. You nearly died, Rae."

"I what?"

"You almost died."

"How?"

"Believe it or not." Michael put the glass on the tray. "From snakebite."

"A snake bit me?"

"There must have been one on the dock. I didn't see it but you've got the marks to prove it. It bit you, right in the gut."

Rae glanced down at herself but was too exhausted to throw off the sheet to look for evidence of Michael's claim. She vaguely remembered the stinging sensation she'd felt moments before Simeon had fallen into the bay.

"There was a snake on Simeon," she explained.

"On Simeon?"

"Well, on the real Simeon that is."

"What are you talking about?"

"You know, on the creature."

"What creature?"

"The one on the dock!"

Michael frowned and studied her face. "There was no creature on the dock. Just Simeon."

"But Simeon *was* the creature! He turned into Typhon! I saw it! He became a big crocodile thing with a snake coming out of his navel!" She struggled to sit up, but Michael held up a hand.

"I saw only Simeon, Rae."

"You didn't see him as a crocodile?"

"No." He stroked her again. "Try not to get all worked up, Rae. For the past two days you've been dreaming a lot. You probably *dreamed* you saw a creature."

"Michael, it was no dream!"

"It could have been. The venom made you delirious, you know."

She sank back, too tired to argue any further. "So I've been here for two days?"

"Yeah. Apparently there was a bucketful of venom in you. The doctors said it's a miracle you even survived the trip to the hospital."

She stared up at him, incredulous at the turn of events, unable to make sense of everything. He looked down at her and gently cupped her face.

"You may look frail, Miss Fay Rae Lambers, but you've got a will of iron."

Michael leaned closer and slowly kissed her chapped lips. Rae closed her eyes, savoring the touch of him and the coolness of his hand on her face. When he rose up, however, her thoughts turned swiftly from delirium to reality.

"But what about Angie? Where is she?"

"She's fine." Michael's hand slipped from her face and traveled down the sheet to her hand. He gave it a light squeeze. "She's perfectly all right. Don't you worry about her."

"Where is she?"

"She's staying with Maren."

"Is she okay, though? I mean, is she handling everything okay?"

"She seems to be."

"And you? How is your arm?"

"It's healing. I will have to do physical therapy, and I may never play basketball again. But luckily it's my right one."

"And Simeon?"

"That bastard?" Michael looked away and scowled. "He's at the bottom of the bay. Where he belongs. Along with that sword."

"I'm not so sure, Michael. I never saw him hit the water."

"He couldn't have survived the cave-in."

"I won't believe he's really gone until we get rid of the Forbidden Tarot, once and for all."

"Angie's already done that."

"What do you mean?"

"She sold the deck on eBay."

"What?" Rae gaped at Michael in disbelief.

"Some person in Hollywood bought the deck for half a million dollars," he went on. "Sent the check to her and everything."

"Half a million? When did this all happen?"

"The check was delivered the day we found Angie in the container. It came FedEx. Angie must have been plotting and planning for a while, to get that kind of money for a deck of cards."

"They are no ordinary cards." Rae tipped her head into the pillows, and gazed at the ceiling, her mind racing. Angie must have slipped the cards from her purse the day she'd handed her the bag on the stairs. That was why her purse had felt lighter. But she'd had no time to worry about her purse because of Simeon's attack and Angie's kidnapping. As the events of the past few days fell into place, Rae's thoughts then turned to the strange and sudden way Simeon had vanished before her eyes, as if he were falling into a black hole in space, not just San Francisco Bay.

"You don't suppose," she mused, slanting a glance at

Michael's handsome face. "That the curse has been lifted then, that someone might have looked at another card and closed the Typhon chapter for us."

"Anything's possible." Michael gave her hand another soft squeeze. "Even miracles. Like seeing you wake up." He bent to kiss her again, but she put a hand up to stop him.

"Michael, we've got to warn them—"

"If they've looked at the cards, Rae, and broken your so-called spell, then it's too damn late. There's nothing we can do."

She sighed and frowned. "Still, we must contact them."

Michael sat back, aware that she was in no mood for romantic advances. He sighed. "There's one more thing, Rae, but I'm not sure I should tell you."

"What is it?" She felt a sudden chill and pulled away her hand. She stared up at him, not knowing what to expect, but anticipating the worst.

"That second quake? The one that wrecked the dock?"

"Yes?" Her voice quavered.

"It did something to the house."

"Your house?"

"Our house." He swallowed and looked down at his hands. "It burned to the ground, Rae. We lost everything. Everything."

She stared at him, at the fringe of coal-black hair hanging over his forehead, at his beautiful lean hands spread upon his thighs, at the wide shoulders that had protected her from demons, imagined or real. She had never loved him more than at this moment.

"Oh, Michael," she murmured, her voice full of sadness.

He turned and slanted his dark glance at her. "So that means we've got to find a new place to live."

"Angie and I can stay in Berkeley."

He blinked for a moment and studied her face. "I was thinking." He paused and rubbed the back of his neck in his trademark gesture of doubt. "I was hoping, Rae, that you and Angie might find a place with me—a place where we could all live together—just like at the house."

She stared at him, trying hard not to believe his words, trying very hard to keep her heart from bursting in her chest. Michael wanted to live with her? Even after the spell had been broken, he still wanted to live with her? Could she trust this version of Michael yet?

"I got used to having you two around," he added when she didn't make a reply. "Especially you." He reached for her hand again, and this time raised it to his lips. He kissed the back of her hand in a tender gesture that brought tears to her eyes. "I love you, Rae. I can't imagine living without you. I don't want to."

"Michael," she breathed softly, gazing into his serious eyes. She could have sat there and looked at him forever, but she knew in her heart she had no such option, not until she was sure of his love.

Rae was certain what she had to do. True love was never easy. It wasn't something two people fell into without careful thought. And she had to be sure. She wanted no regrets when it came to Michael Gregory. "Living with you sounds wonderful, Michael, but—"

"But what?" His head rose. "You're saying no?"

She nodded. "I need time to think this all through. To make sure we're not just experiencing aftereffects."

"You mean of the cards?" He lowered her hand. "That's crap, Rae! What I feel has nothing to do with them!"

"Are you sure?" She reached for his cheek, mustering the strength to caress him. "Are you sure, Michael?"

"Hell, yes!"

"I'm not going to be easy to love, Michael. I won't always be able to participate as fully as a healthy person would."

"I don't care about that. I care about you!"

She let her hand slide from his face. "And look at my family, my past. Do you want to take on a woman with such baggage? No one survives that kind of situation without a few scars."

"Do you think I'm worried about that?" He stared down at her, his eyes blazing. "Have you ever really looked at yourself, Rae?"

She pulled back, startled at the question. "What do you mean?"

"Did it ever occur to you that all the crap you went through might have been a good thing?"

"Good?" She felt her cheeks grow hot with affront at his insensitive evaluation of her past. "How can you say such a thing!"

He ignored her anger. "Look at it this way. Do you think just anyone could have done what you did?"

"Survive a snake bite?"

"No! Befriend my dad, find that sword, fight off the man who murdered both our fathers, and then save your sister." Michael grabbed her hands again. "How many average American women do you think could have accomplished such a task?"

Rae stared at him, speechless. She hadn't stopped to look back on all they'd been through, all they'd done.

"Did it ever occur to you that all the pain you've suffered, all the shit that's happened to you, made you strong? Maybe even indomitable?" He squeezed her hands. "You've got a will of iron, Rae. Where did that come from?" He raised an eyebrow. "Not from a goddamn mall, that's for sure."

Rae gazed at him, struck by this new view of herself which he held up for her to see. She'd never thought of herself as strong. She'd never imagined the pain and darkness she'd endured might have transformed her into a better person, a stronger human being.

"I never thought of it that way," she murmured.

"That's what we do for each other, Rae. We bring out the real stuff inside of us. No games."

She nodded.

He stroked the top of her left hand with his thumb. "In fact, before I met you, I didn't realize what a bastard I was."

"You're not so bad." She smiled kindly at him, her heart brimming with love for him.

"Maybe not now. Not after what you taught me."

She sat back against the pillows again. "And what was that?"

"That you can't stuff the past. That you have to deal with it." He smiled ruefully and leaned closer. "That you have to deal with it so you are free to really live. To really love."

She nodded. "We should have talked long ago, Michael. I'm so sorry I never reached out to you. Our lives could have been so different."

"Our lives *can* be different, starting today, starting now." He squeezed her hand. "I love you, Rae. I want to spend the rest of my life with you."

Rae gazed up at him, and then reached for his wrist. She stroked the side of his arm. "But not immediately, Michael. You need to get your divorce. If this is what we think it is, we'll still feel the same way come October first."

"Are you saying what I think you're saying?"

She nodded. "No living together, not just yet."

"But Rae!"

"We both have a lot to do, Michael. I have a book to finish. And you're going to have to start over on that house for the pianist."

"But—"

"And when October first comes along, we can see if we still feel the same. And if we do, we'll be free to make a rational decision about the future."

"Jesus, Rae!" Michael jumped to his feet. "Just dating? That's it?"

"Yes." She stared up at him, her strength quickly fading. "Do for it me, Michael?" She held his gaze, knowing if he truly loved her, he would accept her terms with grace.

# Chapter 27

Rae parked her Jetta in the lot behind the math building and walked across the pavement toward her office. The morning was absolutely stunning, the sky as blue as a robin's egg and not a breeze in the air. She tipped her head back and let the golden sunshine wash over her as she strode up the sidewalk.

She'd always loved early fall when the students came back to campus, and the freshmen arrived with their brand-new backpacks and their hopeful smiles. Life seemed bursting with possibilities in the fall, as new beginnings and new friendships were forged—many of them for a lifetime.

Rae smiled. She felt as if she were on top of the world. She'd finished her book just last night, and the manuscript was tucked safely in her briefcase, ready to be mailed. Angie had become the most diligent Nordstrom employee in the history of the company, and had actually made arrangements to buy a little house in Concord, using half of the money they'd got for the Forbidden Tarot as a down payment. Angie's newfound sense of responsibility amazed and pleased Rae. But most of all, Rae had not suffered a single bout of rheumatism since her discharge from Alameda Hospital.

Every morning since July she had been waking, expecting the old familiar stiffness to hobble her steps, but every morning since that fateful day on the dock, she had leaped out of bed like a teenager, full of vigor and blissfully unaware of her joints.

"Good morning!" she greeted as she walked by a dour-faced coed, her eyes puffy from sleep. The young woman gaped at her, shocked that a faculty member had made eye contact, let alone spoken to her.

"Hi," she mumbled.

Rae grinned. She couldn't have suppressed her buoyant heart even if she'd wanted to. She was well aware of the date. It was October 1—the day she'd told Michael they could take their relationship to a new level, if they both still wanted to. Since they'd parted at the hospital he had honored her request for restraint. He'd taken her to dinner and a few movies, with nothing more intimate than a kiss passing between them. It had been difficult to break away sometimes, to say good-bye to him, but she had willed herself to maintain her trademark rationality.

Struggling with the little tray of coffee and her briefcase, Rae managed to get into the building and then walked down the hall toward the suite of offices of her department. Her pumps clicked smartly on the linoleum floor. She could wear such shoes now and not suffer all night as a consequence, and had taken to dressing with much more flair.

Angie had been thrilled to help her select a more feminine wardrobe, and Rae had discovered she approved of the image in the mirror for a change. Over the past two months, she had begun to look more and more like her younger sister, as her figure filled out and her hair and skin took on a healthy sheen. It was amazing how her body had surged to life once released from constant pain.

Rae shoved open the office door with her shoulder and glanced down at Connie sitting at her computer.

"Good morning, stranger!" Rae called, setting the coffee on the high counter between them. Connie had taken leave for the entire month of September, and this was her first day back on the job.

"Dr. Lambers!" Connie pivoted in her chair. "My gosh!" Slowly she rose to her feet. "Is that you?"

"The same." Rae popped a coffee cup from the cardboard holder and held it out. "Here's a welcome-back latte!"

"Thanks!" Connie reached for the cup, all the while staring at her boss. "What did you do to yourself when I was gone?" she asked, coming around the end of the counter.

Rae sipped her Americano. "You wouldn't believe it if I told you."

"You're in love!"

Rae blushed. "That could be part of it."

"Don't play games with me." Connie winked. "I'm in on your little secret."

"What secret?"

"I know who it is and what you've been up to. You and that Mr. Right!"

"What do you mean?" Rae's sunny day took a small cloudy dip.

"Have a look at this!" Connie crossed the floor to the door of Rae's office and threw it open.

"Oh, my God!" Rae breathed, her coffee cup forgotten in her sinking hand as she took in the sight before her.

Her office was completely filled with vases of purple irises.

"What a guy!" Connie remarked. "He's a keeper, Dr. Lambers. Take it from me, he's a keeper!"

"Oh, my God," Rae repeated, stepping backward, her hand at her throat. The sun completely sank on her horizon as her worst fears materialized. Purple irises could mean only one thing: Simeon had not perished in the bay.

"What's the matter?" Connie asked. "You look as if you've just seen a ghost!"

"Who put these here?"

"I don't know." Connie shrugged. "They were here when I came in to work. I just assumed—"

"There's no card?" Rae stumbled forward, her mouth dry. She dropped her briefcase on the floor and searched the nearest bouquets for the customary white envelope. "No note?"

"Aren't they from your friend Mr. Avare? I just assumed they were!"

"He's not the one I want flowers from." Rae's hand shook

as she checked the arrangements on her desk. If Simeon Avare had come back to interfere with her life again, she didn't know what she would do. She had assumed the dark part of her life was completely over and that she could start a brand-new life with the man she loved, with the man who had filled her thoughts and heart for the last two months.

"There's somebody else?" Connie asked, helping her search. "Another guy?"

"Yes." Rae straightened. Over the tops of the hundreds of purple blossoms, she glanced out the window as a vision of Michael's face rose before her eyes. *Michael.* Her heart twisted in her chest. Why had she thought it would be easy now? Or simple? Her life had never been easy.

"Take them out, Connie," she declared, her glorious mood in shambles. "Take them out of here! Every last one of them!"

"Okay, but—"

"I don't care what you do with them, just get them out!"

Rae plopped down in her chair and pushed away the nearest vase, not wishing to take a single breath of the fragrance of her favorite flower. Irises had a different meaning to her now. She would never look at them the same way again.

Before she could gather her senses and recover from the effect of seeing all the flowers, she heard a commotion in the outer office.

"Wait just a damn minute," she heard a man exclaim in the hall outside Connie's cubicle. "Where are you going with those?"

Rae's heart skipped a beat. She felt her blood rush downward as she stood up, leaving her light-headed. Who had just spoken? Who was out there? She couldn't hear the voice distinctly enough to tell.

"Dr. Lambers doesn't want them in her office!" Connie replied.

"Why the hell not?"

That had to be Michael. Two swear words in two sentences? It had to be Michael! Trembling, she stepped around the corner of her desk, faint with relief.

"Michael?" she called from her office door.

At the sound of her voice, he turned his head in her direction. He was dressed in a charcoal-gray suit with a light blue shirt and dark blue tie that set off his almost black eyes. He looked fit and tan and even more attractive than usual.

"Rae!" he greeted. "Why are you throwing my flowers away?"

Rae stepped back, her hands dragging down the sleeves of Michael's suit. "You sent the flowers?"

"Yeah. Who'd you think?"

"They're purple irises!"

"Yeah." He rubbed the back of his neck. "Jesus, Rae, I thought you liked irises. I thought they were your favorite!"

Rae looked at the ceiling, amazed by the flood of relief that washed over her. The relief made her giddy. She started to giggle, holding her hand over her mouth, shocked at the noise coming up her throat. She hadn't giggled for as long as she could remember. And then the giggle turned to a laugh—joyful, bubbling laughter that poured out of her, cleansing the last dark corner remaining inside her.

"You sent the flowers!" she gasped, holding her sides. "Oh, Michael, *you* did!"

"Of course!" He grabbed her by the waist and pulled her close again. "And there's more to come. Each and every year we have together. I'm going to shower you with flowers, Fay Rae."

She gazed up at him, all laughter dying but the smile still on her lips. "So you're an available bachelor now, I take it?"

"Not for long, I hope."

"Got someone in mind then?"

"Maybe."

Rae blushed as he kissed her again. Then he brushed her lower lip with his left thumb and gazed down at her, his eyes sparkling.

"I've got plans for you," he said. "Both architectural and matrimonial."

"Architectural?"

"Yeah. I've been working on a design for the lot, where the old house was."

"What kind of design? Your apartment house?"

"No, your resource center."

"Are you serious?" She backed up a step, holding his arms at the elbows.

"As serious as I get, Rae."

"Michael!" She squealed and hugged him.

When he finally managed to peel her away, he looked down at her, laughing. "But there are strings attached."

"What kind of strings?"

"Marriage to the architect for one."

She cocked her head and smiled at him. "I might be convinced to consider it."

"In that case, I have something for you." He reached into the left pocket of his suit jacket and pulled out a small box. "This is something I've wanted to give you for twelve years."

He held out the box and opened it. Inside was a small silver band with a line of tiny diamonds arcing across its surface.

Rae glanced up at his face. "You've had this for twelve years?"

He nodded. "It's what I was going to give you that day. A promise ring."

Rae felt tears scalding her eyes. She raised a hand to her lips, entirely overcome by emotion, unable to do anything but stare at Michael. He had planned to give her a promise ring on the Day of the Dark Blue Dress?

"You kept it all these years?" she gasped.

He nodded. "Getting rid of it would have been like getting rid of your memory. I just couldn't do it."

"Oh, Michael!"

He held the box closer. "Go ahead! Try it on."

Gently, she drew the tiny band out of its velvet nest and slowly slipped it on the ring finger of her right hand. Then she held it up to the light. "It's beautiful," she whispered. "Thank you!"

This time the ring felt right. The man felt right. And her heart felt extremely right.

Smiling and crying at the same time, she flung her arms around his neck and hugged him with all her strength.

"I'll follow that up with an engagement ring," Michael said in her ear. "But first we're going to have a nice long courtship. Just so you will be sure of my intentions."

"Is this some sort of payback for my October first deadline?" She pulled back and arched an eyebrow at him.

"Just want you to be sure." He grinned. "Besides, I quite enjoy wooing a calculus professor."

"Oh, Michael!" she exclaimed, rising up to kiss him once more. "Me too!"

# *Epilogue*

Claire Coulter tucked her travel hair dryer into her suit-case, did a final pass through her mental checklist, was satisfied she hadn't forgotten anything for her trip, and then pulled over the flap of her suitcase.

Just as she reached for the zipper, she heard her doorbell ring. Claire frowned. It was eight o'clock at night. Who would be at her door at this hour?

Always careful, she quietly padded down the hallway of her apartment to the front door and looked through the peep hole. The face of her friend, Maria, stared back up at her, wildly distorted by the fisheye lens. But even beyond that distortion, Maria's face looked contorted. What was wrong? Claire pulled open the door.

"Hey, Maria," she greeted, surprised when her smaller fiery friend swept past her without so much as a hello, and stormed into her living room.

"Hello to you, too," Claire remarked, closing the door.

"Claire!" Maria tossed back her mane of long black hair and pivoted as she flung her purse on the couch. "I am so upset! I could just scream!"

"What is it this time?" Claire asked, indicating for her guest to sit down on the couch. Maria glanced at the cotton upholstery but stomped across the floor and back again, her high heels clattering on the wood.

"Ah, no, Maria," Claire chided kindly. "It can't be that Jonathan again."

Maria spouted a string of Spanish against the wall, as if a god lived above Claire's fireplace, and Maria were chewing him out for deserting her in her time of need. She crossed her arms over her chest.

Claire sighed and sat down on the couch. "Okay. What has he done this time?"

Maria whirled. "Bought *La Puta* this!"

Maria never referred to Jonathan's wife by name. She called her *The Bitch* instead, as if never speaking her name would keep her out of her reality.

Maria flung a metal box onto the coffee table. The container flew across the glass surface and would have fallen to the ground if Claire hadn't reacted quickly enough to catch it. She picked up the box, which was not quite as large as a paperback novel but was much heavier.

Claire turned the plain golden box to view it from the bottom and back around to the top again. It looked old, but not valuable enough to whip up such a frenzy of jealousy. Still, Maria would be offended by anything Jonathan bought for his wife. She placed the box safely in the center of the table. "So what is it?" she asked.

"A deck of tarot cards!" Maria spit. "Really old ones. Gold leaf and everything!"

"How do you know?"

"Jonathan told me all about it. He was so excited. '*La Puta* loves tarot decks this,' he says, and '*La Puta* loves antique tarot decks that!' He spent a fortune on them. Half a million dollars! But that's not what gets to me, Claire." Maria flung both hands in the air. "He expects me to gift wrap them for her birthday. For *her*, Claire! He expects me to wrap a present for *her*!"

Claire didn't say anything. It was obvious Maria wasn't in the mood to listen to words of caution about affairs with married men.

"He should have given *me* those cards," Maria continued, her color high as she jabbed a finger in the direction of the box on the coffee table. "I know the tarot like nobody else, especially her! I am the tarot expert. Me!" She thumped her chest.

Claire nodded.

"You know what *La Puta* can do with that tarot deck?"

Claire raised her dark eyebrows.

"She can stick it up her big white *culo*, that's what!" Maria whirled and stomped to the fireplace and then back to the coffee table. "Wrap her birthday present. Wrap her present!" She tossed her hair again, planting a hand on her hip like a toreador. "He promised me he was going to leave her, and now he asks me to wrap a present for her. Me!"

Claire tilted her head. "You are their maid, Maria."

Maria stamped her foot and glared at Claire, but she could not find words to refute the truth.

Claire leaned forward. "When he told you he would leave his wife, you didn't believe him, did you?"

Maria's nostrils flared and the whites around her irises showed like those of an enraged bull. She lifted her chin in an effort to fend off the truth behind Claire's question, and stood there, breathing heavily.

"They always say they're going to leave, Maria—that they're so unhappy, so bored. That their life with the wife is so pedestrian. But they never leave their wives. You know that."

"But I am like a flower!" she sputtered. "And she's but a thistle! Wrinkled and prickly!" She crossed her arms again, her eyes blazing. "How could he choose her over me? Impossible!"

"Because, Maria. You are a maid." Claire rose and put her arm around Maria, squeezing her shoulders gently. "Not that being a maid is bad. And you are the best maid in Silicon Valley." Claire felt the flare of Maria's anger subside somewhat.

Maria sniffed. "I care about my work."

"I know you do, Maria. You care about your work more than anyone I know."

"There is a lot of dust in the hills. But not in my house. Never." She sliced the air with the edge of her delicate hand. "Not one speck of dust!"

"But it is not your house, Maria. And it never will be. No matter what that bastard Jonathan promises you."

For a moment Maria was still, as if Claire were finally getting through to her. And in that moment, her fiery outrage broke. Maria sagged against her friend and put her hands to her pretty face as she slowly rotated into Claire's embrace and hung there, sobbing.

"How could he do this to me, Claire, how? How could he break my heart like this?" Her shoulders shook.

"Ah, Maria." Claire hugged her friend and quietly swept her hand across Maria's slender back and over her glossy black hair. No one had comforted her then, not when she had needed it the most. No one had spoken words of support to her when her world had collapsed and spun out of control at the age of twenty. She had been too ashamed to tell anyone of her affair, not even Maria. But the shame of being spurned still burned her like a brand.

When at last Maria's sobs subsided, Claire urged her to sit down on the couch, and then she slipped into the kitchen to get them both a glass of red wine. Though she knew Maria would have preferred a shot of tequila, Claire never kept tequila in the house. In fact, she never kept anything remotely connected to her heritage in the house, as if purging the past from her environment could purge it from her heart. She'd even legally changed her last name to *Coulter* to distance herself from her roots. She'd never known the name of her father—which her people customarily added as a third name—so she had made one up, something that didn't sound at all Spanish.

Maria took the goblet of wine in both hands. "*Gracias,*" she murmured, her tongue thick from crying.

"You're welcome," Claire replied. She sat down beside her friend and reached for the cards in an effort to change the subject and clear the air.

Maria sniffed beside her. "You are a good friend, Clarita Francisco. I don't know what I'd do without you."

"Hush now." Claire patted her arm. "What about giving me a reading before I go off on my big adventure?"

"You want a tarot reading?"

"Yes. Just the short one. You know, where you have me pick a card and then you tell me the future?" She offered the box to Maria. "I don't think you're in the right mood for an extensive reading, are you?"

Maria shook her head and set down her goblet. Claire watched her, relieved to see the anger and sadness already ebbing from the large dark eyes of her childhood friend. She knew Maria well, knew how easily she could be distracted, even by the smallest of gestures. It was both her biggest downfall and her most endearing quality.

Taking a deep, purging breath, Maria reached for the golden box and slowly opened it. She set aside the top section, glanced down, and then swore under her breath.

"Oh my God—" she murmured, her voice lowering to an unusually subdued tone for her. "Look at this writing, Claire."

Claire leaned closer as she took a sip of her wine and looked down at the deck. Strange writing paraded across yellow parchment that had been wrapped around the cards. She guessed it was some form of Aramaic. Unfortunately she couldn't make out any of the words, as she'd never studied any of the Middle Eastern languages.

"I don't think we should touch these." Claire whispered, wondering even as she whispered why they had both lowered their voices, and why she suddenly wished to hold the cards in her hands, even though she'd been taught by her years at CommOptima never to subject an archeological object to the destructive oils of human flesh.

"Why not?" Maria shrugged. "*La Puta* will touch them."

"I think that's real parchment." Claire leaned closer to stare at the writing. "These cards really *are* old, Maria."

"So why give them to *La Puta*? She would not appreciate such a thing."

"Probably not." Claire agreed, simply to appease her friend, even though she knew differently.

*La Puta*, known to the non-Maria world as Diana Allman, was a huge collector of antiques, but Claire wouldn't press the point and risk having Maria whip herself into a frenzy again. Instead she added, "She probably doesn't even know how to do a reading."

Maria blew air through her teeth in agreement as she carefully opened the parchment to reveal the deck of cards.

"Wow," Claire gasped as she caught sight of the top card.

Though she knew she was only looking at the back of the cards, the design was magnificent enough to take her breath away. And though she'd never studied much Egyptian history, she'd taken enough general knowledge classes in college to recognize the Eye of Horus staring back at her, exquisitely fashioned with gold leaf.

"Man oh man!" Maria exclaimed.

"You shouldn't have taken these, Maria."

"Pah!" Maria waved her off. "What is Jonathan going to do? Accuse me of stealing?"

"Someone might." Claire shook her head. "Those cards look very valuable. I wouldn't be carrying them around!"

"Why?" Maria's lip curled. "No one knows. The Allmans have left for Paris and won't be back for a month." She dropped the deck into her left hand. "Besides, Jonathan could buy a hundred decks like this. Easy."

"Only if another like it existed." Claire took another sip of wine. "And I doubt one does!"

"Hmph!" Maria shrugged a pert shoulder and fanned out the cards, turning toward her friend. "Okay, think about your big adventure and pick a card, Claire."

Closing her eyes, Claire concentrated on the morning to come, when she would be whisked away to Lake Tahoe by her boss, Tobias Benton, and then continue into the wilderness of the Sierra Nevada.

"Okay. I'm ready." Claire reached out, slipped a card from the fanned deck, and carefully placed it upon the table.

Maria squinted at it. "What?" she murmured, staring at the card, perplexed.

"What is it?" Claire wasn't accustomed to Maria pausing at anything put before her. "Is it bad?"

"The Two Urns?" Maria scowled prettily. "I don't know. I've never heard of The Two Urns!"

"You don't recognize the card?"

"This deck must be a lot different than mine. Hold on." Maria set the golden cards on the couch beside her and reached for her purse. She pawed through the contents of her huge bag until she brought out a velvet pouch that Claire recognized as the container of Maria's usual set of tarot. "What number is on that card?" she asked over her shoulder.

Claire looked at the roman numeral in the lower left corner. "Fourteen." She glanced over the strange card, which showed a man standing on bare ground, a huge burst of light behind his head, and wings on his back as well as at his ankles. He was young, dark haired, with a flame coming out of the top of his head, and was naked except for a striped sheath of cloth slung over his left shoulder. In his hands he held two urns, and he was pouring the contents of the upper urn into that of the lower one while he looked intently at something in the distance. In the top right corner was the astrological sign for Scorpio, and in the top left was a symbol comprised of three concentric circles, which she surmised was the glyph for the sun. The card made no sense to Claire whatsoever.

She surrendered the card to Maria who absently added it to the pile beside her, and then opened the velvet bag.

Maria expertly shuffled through the top section of her cards. "Fourteen," she repeated. "Just what I thought. Temperance."

"Temperance? What does that mean?"

"Opposites attract, Claire." Maria wiggled her eyebrows at her friend, much more cheerful than she had been a few minutes before. "Maybe you and this Tobias Benton guy are going to click?"

Claire took a thoughtful drink of her wine. She was fairly certain she was opposite in every way to Tobias Benton, at least from what she'd seen of her boss. But she was dead certain she would never pursue a romantic relationship with the man, no matter how much money and power he possessed. Not even if she had to leave the Nimian Project.

"The forces of purification and transformation are in the air." Maria added. "A very fruitful union can be the result."

Claire stared at the card thoughtfully. The Two Urns depicted a positive outcome. Was this tarot card her window to the future? Was this the sign she'd asked for?

# If you enjoyed this book, you won't want to miss...

*NEW YORK TIMES* BESTSELLING AUTHOR

## CONSTANCE O'DAY-FLANNERY

Shifting Love

0-765-34889-6 • $6.99/$9.99 Can.

**SHIFTING LOVE**
CONSTANCE O'DAY-FLANNERY
**IN PAPERBACK NOVEMBER 2004**

Tor is proud to launch its Paranormal Romance line with a passionate tale of magic and love from *New York Times* bestselling author Contstance O'Day-Flannery.

**"An author of incredible talent and imagination. She has the magic."**
—*Romantic Times Bookclub*

www.tor.com